W9-BDY-615

THE CRIVELLI CONUNDRUM

A NOVEL

MARCIA MUELDER EATON

ISBN-13: 978-1481157704

ISBN-10: 148115701

ACKNOWLEDGEMENTS

This is a work of fiction. All of the characters are fictional. There is no true story upon which my tale is based, although, of course, there really are wars, espionage, and fraud. Most of the art works mentioned are real, and readers can find images of them on various websites and books. I have "created" a few that appear in the story that do not exist. Carlo Crivelli did, of course, exist and this book would not have been possible without Ronald Lightbrown's definitive study, *Carlo Crivelli,* published by Yale University Press in 2004. I also benefited from several scholarly articles dealing with events during World War II. I have footnoted sources where appropriate. But, again, this is a work of fiction, and I have also benefited from poetic license. Neither Lightbrown nor any of the other authors I cite should be held in any way accountable for historical inaccuracies.

I taught philosophy for nearly forty-five years. There are far too many colleagues and students and friends who have encouraged and taught me along the way to thank them individually. You know who you are, I hope. Special thanks must go, however, to Susan Muelder, Debbie Mackenzie, Claire Bettag, and Charles Randall who provided detailed corrections of typos and other mistakes in the first versions of my book.

Finally, nothing I do would mean much without Dennis, Christine, Isabel, Emma, and Joe. Joe and I did have dinner in a restaurant in Padua where a scene much like the one depicted in Chapter 1 did take place. We still wonder what was happening. If by some incredible coincidence the couple we watched should read this book, I would be very grateful if they could tell me what was actually going on.

THE CRIVELLI CONUNDRUM

Chapter One

Padua and Amsterdam, August, 1990

It was luck and our Fodor's that led us that early August evening to the restaurant in Padua where the puzzle emerged. A few weeks later it was luck and our Frommer's that led us to the restaurant in Amsterdam where the solution, I now believe, finally began to unfold.

We were near the end of a sabbatical year in Europe, and had a few days between sojourns in Perugia and Amsterdam.   Roger had never been to Venice, but the dollar was weak that year and our budget precluded spending many nights in that city. So we opted to stay in the nearby and much less expensive Padua and make day trips by rail to Venice. An added attraction was the chance to visit the Arena Chapel in Padua, with the glorious Giotto frescoes that I had long wanted to see for myself since my first art history course.

Fodor's recommended that tourists with more than a day in Padua should visit the Museo Crivelli. Carlo Crivelli is not a major artist, but his strange and complex works have earned him space in most of the world's major museums. I had always been intrigued by his work. So on the way back from the Arena Chapel to our hotel on the Piazza della Frutta we took the guidebook's recommendation and stopped in at a small, rather dark museum just inside the Porta Altinate. Some scholars believe that Crivelli received some of his early training in Padua, so it was not surprising that one would find a collection of his works there. Still, I found the case for his tenure in their town rather overstated in the brochure we were given and on the wall placards describing his life and work. Most of the paintings were copies of works from other locations, primarily The Marches where Crivelli spent most of his career. One room was devoted to the school of Mantenga, another painter who spent time in Padua and had a major influence on Crivelli. Another room boasted works that were asserted to be Crivelli originals. They were works I had never seen reproduced nor even referred to, but this was not surprising since Crivelli usually gets at most one or two images in art histories and often only a few paragraphs when he is mentioned at all.

I had only gotten to the third or fourth of a warren of small rooms before I began to feel a mixture of oppression and impatience. It was impossible to deny that Crivelli had great skill, but there was something grating about his work that day. In part I attributed this to the inevitable comparisons I was making with the Giottos we had just seen. Giotto's works were simpler, certainly, and always struck me as honest and straightforward, traits I seek in both art and people. His colors were brighter, his depictions less cluttered. Crivelli favored strongly linear representations, and his elongated figures were often surrounded, some may say crowded, with elaborate garlands of flowers and fruits and even vegetables. His scenes were by no means without psychological impact, but though he painted more than a hundred years earlier, Giotto, at least for me, spoke more emphatically. I found myself musing that I would much rather share an espresso or vino with Giotto than with Crivelli.

I was standing in front of a large St. Catherine when Roger, who typically got ahead of me in museums, returned from his perusal and asked, "What's with the cucumbers?"

"They are odd, aren't they? Flowers and fruits often were used as symbols---the rose for Christ or grapes for his blood and so on. But I have no idea what all the vegetables are doing. Maybe he just liked painting them."

"Well, you can stay here and enjoy them. I'm feeling Madonna and Child overload. I'm going to get a coffee and then go back to the hotel for a shower before dinner."

"I was just thinking that I would rather have coffee with Giotto than Crivelli," I laughed. "But I'm happy to settle for coffee with you. Let's get some fresh air."

I thought I might get back to that little gallery, but our day trips to Venice took priority. Given what has happened since that visit, it will be some time, I think, before I know for certain whether I shall ever re-enter it. In fact, it might be safer to stay away from Padua completely.

Still, I chose our restaurant that evening mainly because of its name, The Crivelli. Our Fodor's gave the place high marks. It represented it as a moderately priced place offering the classic Paduan cuisine of "courtyard meals"—fowl, to us.

Also recommended were a Ristorante Michelangelo, a da Vinci Terraza, and a Trattoria Caravaggio. We almost chose the last since our well-thumbed Michelin Guide gave it two stars and I had always considered that painter's chiaroscuro a high point in the history of art, but budget considerations gave the edge to the unstarred but honorably mentioned Crivelli.

We had tickets to a cello recital in a church across the old center of town and we wanted to allow sufficient time for a postprandial stroll. Thus we arrived at the restaurant unfashionably early even for Americans, let alone Italians, and we were the sole diners in the, to my taste, over-mirrored space. We were surprised when, soon after the antipasta had been cleared and our second glass of wine poured, an Italian couple entered and were shown to a table across the room.

They were a striking pair. The man was young, in his early thirties, I guessed. He was tall for his nationality and rather lighter haired and skinned than most. But his costume was unexceptional for the well-heeled of his tribe: expertly fitted suit, tie and shirt in harmonious hues, superior shoes. He held the elbow of his companion and smoothly led her to their table. She, too, was paradigmatically attired. A pale rose- colored suit was accented with a floral scarf in mauves and pinks and taupes, one shade of which was matched by shoes that easily cost more than several nights at our hotel.

She was clearly older than the man, but it was hard to assign an age. Fashionably highlighted hair was pulled back in an elaborate twist. She looked familiar, but I could not for the life of me remember who she looked like. Her face was somewhat lined but exquisitely applied make-up made it impossible accurately to determine her age in the dim soft light. I initially assumed she was his mother, but would shortly question this assumption.

The couple became the focus of our attention, and that of the entire wait staff, as soon as they entered the restaurant. It was not just their beauty but a presence that made this inevitable. They did not act as if they owned the place--they were far too comfortable with themselves to need to do this. But they were supremely self-assured and a bright laughter and chatter, particularly on the woman's part, drew attention almost as if the curtains had opened on an eagerly anticipated drawing room comedy. I read Italian well, but my listening skills were too meager to allow me to understand what was being said. Still it was clear from body language and gesture that the head waiter was eager to please them. Even before they were seated it was obvious that this woman was happy to be who she was, where she was, and with this adored companion. I quickly reassessed my hypothesis that this was a mother and son. Revision went in the direction of lovers.

Roger is a mathematician, a set of individuals who neither give much attention to nor care much about nuances of fashion. Both of us had spent our childhoods in small American towns, his in northwestern forests, mine in Midwestern corn and soybean fields. Sartorial elegance was not a priority in either region. Indeed, concern with the latest styles was deemed a character flaw. My father had frequently said, "You should never wear a hat that has more character than you do." Furthermore my aesthetic training was theory, not practice. I could recognize the skill and practice in the way the woman's scarf was tied and draped, just I as could appreciate the unique brush strokes of a Vermeer or a Crivelli. But I could emulate neither. I lacked the talent to become a painter and the patience to master nuances of style and grooming; there were too many other projects I wanted to get to, a puzzle to solve or some aesthetic itch to scratch. Roger and I could have purchased the exact outfits this couple wore, but would never have carried them off with the same aplomb. Even an Eagle Scout badge in knot tying would not have made it possible for me to achieve the same scarf arrangement and my ankles would have looked silly above those winsome shoes. Roger retained a lumberman's swagger, imitated since his toddler years from his father and grandfather that would have precluded the easy yet flawless fit and flow of the man's suit.

Nonetheless, the elegant tableau the couple created was undeniable.

"They are from the beautiful set, aren't they?" I remarked.

Roger agreed. However, a few minutes later he noted, as if offering up some compensation, "But look, they've ordered the same Fruili that we're having." The pride he took in his knowledge of wines--as in his expertise in number theory-- sufficed to remove any feelings of inferiority on his part. But I couldn't help but lament my own lack of style.

We both watched as the waiter carefully poured their wine and placed a plate of antipasti on their table. He said something to which the pair both responded with a shake of the head, slight movement of hands, and quick remark that resulted in the waiter's bow and departure from their immediate space. He and his colleagues, however, remained close enough to respond immediately if beckoned. Like all well-trained waiters , they had mastered the fine line between hovering and ignoring.

Fodor's had recommended either the *fagiano* or *anatra*. Roger ordered the duck and I the pheasant. They arrived just as our co-diners raised their glasses, made short, seemingly intimate remarks, laughed, and, leaning toward one another, engaged in comfortable, cheery conversation. For several minutes we concentrated on our food and on trying to sample each other's dishes without creating too great a mess on the starched pink linen tablecloths. We also chatted about our plans for the next day and our upcoming trip to Holland. I don't know how long it was before we looked back at the pair; it could not have been more than ten minutes. But the alteration that had taken place was incredible.

Not much had changed with the young man. He still looked calm—just slightly more erect in the high-backed chair than he had been moments earlier. His hands rested lightly on the edge of the table, his head was slightly tilted forward. However, there was something about the way he perched that made it clear that he was carefully watching his companion, indeed he seemed to scrutinize her with a view to preparing to react with dispatch should she strike out.

But what accounted for the scene's radical transformation was precisely allied with a sense that there was no possibility of such action, at least not immediately. The woman seemed to have aged a decade or more in the short time that our attention had been diverted. Her whole body seemed to have deflated. Her shoulders slumped over the table and her head had fallen into her hands. Even the scarf, with the arrangement that I had so envied, seem to droop.

Roger and I did not speak to one another, nor take a bite or sip. We just watched as the woman slowly raised her head but still relied on her hands to support it. I could see that she was pale—her make-up seemed strangely to have been wiped off, contributing to the impression that she had aged.

I suddenly felt that I was looking at a Vermeer painting. That artist had a way of appearing to have captured the totality of a particular moment---every hair or brick or thread, every facet of the psychology of the people depicted. But it was precisely his version of reality that enthralled and made one feel almost duped. Here is a woman handing a letter to her servant---- or is the servant handing the letter to her mistress? Here is a young girl turning toward the viewer---or is she turning away? Everything is given to you except that which you most want to know: What is actually happening here? And when you realize this, you recognize that you are confronting a conundrum---even a paradox. The characters are completely revealed to us and completely hidden.

That's how I felt now. I could see everything---and nothing.

"What the hell do you think happened over there?" Roger asked.

"God only knows. Whatever it was, it was really something."

We then speculated on the possible causes of the total change in aspect. Had this young man been her lover and was he trying to break off their relationship? Was he her son and had he just told her something she found completely unacceptable? Was he gay? Was he going to marry someone of whom she disapproved? Was he moving away? Had she simply had too much to drink before she came to The Crivelli?

"Could he have some disease he's just telling her about," I wondered.

"No," Roger rejected this suggestion completely. "No son would bring his mother to a restaurant to tell her something like that."

And, indeed, this was a big, if not the biggest, part of the mystery. Why would anyone say something in a public space that was bound to have such an adverse reaction? Surely the man must have known that he was about to drop a bombshell. Maybe he wanted the news to be presented in public, where the response would have to be contained, at least to some degree. He must have known that a sense of decorum would prevent this woman, whoever she was, from losing all control. He must have needed to insure that the woman would recover from the initial blow in circumstances where decorum demanded that she restrain any hysterical responses or reactions.

The waiters obviously had seen what we had seen and looked questioningly at one another. Should one of them approach the pair? After a few moments, the waiter who seemed to be in charge, hesitantly moved in the direction of their table. He had to have realized that only an idiot would have asked if they were ready to order. But he did say something. The reaction was dramatic. The woman waved him away as if he were an annoying insect.

Roger and I returned to our meal, but periodically looked into the mirrors, whose abundance I had now come to appreciate, to see what change might have taken place. None, except that the pair did occasionally exchange a few words. From time to time, one of the waiters---apparently they had decided to take turns braving the scene---would move uncertainly toward them, but the response was always the same---a dismissive wave. When the young man filled his own wine glass and offered to pour more into that of his companion, she flicked her wrist at him contemptuously. It was not until our dessert was served that there was change in body language. The woman straightened her back and sat rigidly against the back of her chair, her hands now placed firmly on the edge of the table as if ready to engage fully with the situation that had been presented to her. The pace of the exchange of words quickened, but as our espresso was served, they again became silent.

How we both wished we could have heard and understood their conversation. The waiters, too, seemed as a group to edge toward the table in an effort to eavesdrop. But then a large group entered The Crivelli and they were forced to direct their attention to the new patrons. Roger and I had to leave in order to get to our concert on time. As we stood up and walked to the door, both of us cast last looks across the room in hopes of gleaning some bit of information that would provide a clue to what had and was happening. But we garnered nothing.

As we walked across several busy piazzas and down narrow streets to Padua's oldest church, Santa Sophia, we repeated our speculations about what had occurred, as if mere repetition would make one of the options we considered the most likely explanation. During the concert my thoughts kept drifting back to the scene. A lovely polychrome Pieta over the altar provided a stark contrast to my mental image of the pair in The Crivelli.

For the next several days Roger or I would comment on the mystery. But we eventually reconciled ourselves to the fact that we would never know. We had had a glimpse into the lives of two characters whose story, except for one brief and, to us, inexplicable episode, would remain undisclosed. Even now, I am not absolutely certain that they are characters in the dangerous drama in which we would come to play a role—and would explain my reluctance to return to the Museo Crivelli.

***

Roger and I had spent a year in the early eighties doing research in The Netherlands and we knew Amsterdam well. We always tried to arrange to spend at least a few days there going to or coming from other European destinations. We felt lucky that there was a conference for Roger to attend that gave us a good excuse to spend time in our favorite city before we had to return to our regular duties at the University of Minnesota. Although our Dutch was not up to eavesdropping on conversations, we certainly felt more at home in Holland than in Italy. One of our Danish friends once observed: "In Italy everything is beautiful and almost works;, in Holland everything works and is almost beautiful." Things do work there, I believe, and I have found much that is, in fact, truly beautiful.

In any case, we did not need a guidebook for dining recommendations, but we did consult our Frommer's for the phone number of our favorite restaurant. We were delighted to be able to book a table on short notice our first night. Located on a short street between the Rijksmuseum and the Concertgebouw in a building that had once been an apothecary shop, it is simply called "Het Drugstore." It has become one of Amsterdam's most popular restaurants.

Roger and I were trying to decide whether we should go with that night's "Verbassings Menu" (Dutch love being offered a "surprise menu") when someone behind my chair said, "I should have known Roger Conger would be eating at the place with the best wine list in Holland."

I turned around and saw, with great pleasure, a good friend from Minneapolis, Howard Pletcher. He was, as usual, dressed impeccably--- this evening in a light grey silk suit, apricot shirt, and bold floral tie. Every white hair on his head contributed to gentle waves that framed his handsome, indeed beautiful, face. He leaned ever so slightly on a long paisley umbrella that he held in his left hand.

We stood to greet him, I with a hug and a kiss, Roger with a warm handshake.

"Actually I'm here for the best crème brulee in Northern Europe---though the wine list is definitely a bonus," Roger laughed.

Pletcher was the curator of European paintings at the Minneapolis Institute of Arts, so it wasn't strange that he should be in Amsterdam. Still, it is always a surprise to run into someone so far from home.

"Can you join us?" I asked.

"No, thank you. I have tickets for a concert. I've just finished my meal, and I definitely recommend the turbot."

"Are you here for a meeting?"

"No, I'm just passing through. On my way back from Italy, a funeral of a friend in Padua."

"What a coincidence! We were just there a few weeks ago ourselves."

"Really?"

"Not someone close, I hope," Roger said.

"The son of one of William's best friends, a young main named Marco Zollino. His father was Enrico Zollino, the Director of Museo Crivelli. Did you know him?"

"My God, we also went to that museum, but no, I didn't know Zollino," I replied. " I did hear William speak of him, of course. But I'd forgotten that was his gallery. Mostly William talked about their work together on committees that wanted to get art back in the right hands." William had been Howard's lover and my colleague until his death.

Pletcher looked at his watch. "I do have to run, but I wonder." He looked sharply at me, hesitated briefly, and went on. "I'm flying to London tomorrow afternoon. But is there a chance we might meet tomorrow morning?"

"Of course. Roger has a meeting at the Free University, but I'm free. I was planning to be at the Rijksmuseum when it opens at ten."

"Excellent. Let's meet front of The Nightwatch---say eleven—and then go for a coffee in the café."

"Wonderful."

Again we embraced. He took Roger's hand and said, "Call when you get back to Minneapolis and I'll cook us dinner if you bring me something perfect to drink with it."

"You've got a deal."

The Rijksmuseum was featuring a special exhibit on still life paintings. Though not my favorite genre, I found more than enough to fill the hour thinking about how artists managed to capture the distinctive textures of lemons and peaches before I made my way to the large gallery where the museum's crown jewel hangs. As usual, scores of visitors crowded into the space in front of Rembrandt's ingenious "team picture," as a friend had described it, quite aptly, I thought. Howard Pletcher was standing off to the side looking at one of the more pedestrian examples of the genre that flanks *The Nightwatch* and gives it such a comparative edge.

"Look at the way the man in the plumed hat is reflected in that andiron," he remarked, after we embraced.

"Yes, wonderful, isn't it?"

We strolled back through a long gallery. "That's it," I said with great relief, when I spied a Renaissance portrait. "I've been trying to think of who a woman I saw in a restaurant in Padua reminded me of. It's her. I've always loved that picture." But Howard had gotten ahead of me and didn't hear my comment. I decided to share our restaurant conundrum with Howard as soon as I got a chance. But I never did. We made our way through the gift shop—always the most crowded space in that museum, in almost any museum, for that matter, and walked down the elegant staircase to the cafeteria.

"How long are you and Roger in town?"

"We've been here about three weeks. We have only two more days. We were in Italy for three months and Brussels seven months before that. Now the sabbatical is coming to its dreaded end."

We sat at a small table, cups of dark Douwe Egberts in front of us.

"Was it productive?"

"I finished revising my volume on Jan Steen. Roger worked with the people in Italy and Belgium who seem to be the only other people in Europe who really understand what he's doing, so he's been happy as a clam. Now I've had enough time here to arrange for reproduction rights for some of the pictures I want to include in my book, so I'm feeling pretty good about things, too."

"Congratulations."

"Sorry about Zollini's son's death. You said it was an accident."

"Yes. He fell, apparently in the middle of the night, a couple of weeks ago. Quite a freak accident—hit a cabinet in his study at just the right, or rather wrong, angle. Broke his neck and evidently died instantly."

"God, that's awful. How old was he?"

"Thirty-five."

"Did he have a family?"

"He was engaged---supposed to get married in November. But he lived alone---in a small house down a hill from this Mother's villa. She's distraught, of course. I stayed a few extra days to try to help out. She's the one who discovered his body, unfortunately."

"That's really terrible."

"Yes." He looked at his watch and around the room and then pulled his chair closer to the table and leaned toward me.

"Did you by any chance read that article by George Steiner in *The New Yorker* maybe ten years ago—about Anthony Blount and his combining art history with spying?"

"No, I don't think so," I replied, surprised at the quick change of topic.

"Steiner couldn't understand how someone who cared so much about art could get himself involved in treason. I've never forgotten how he put the question. I don't remember the exact words, of course, but the question that really perplexed him was something like this." He hesitated and swallowed as if trying to control his emotions. And again I was surprised—how could an old *New Yorker* article cause someone to choke up?

" How could a man who spent his days trying to teach students why it matters so much whether they're looking at a real or fake Watteau, spend his nights passing intelligence secrets to Soviet agents?"

"The question that perplexes me is how anyone could spend a whole day on Watteau," I replied.

Howard smiled, but remained serious. "Yes, yes, but don't you think the issue is intriguing?"

"Of course I do. I've often wondered how people who loved Kant and Bach could become

Nazi's. It's the same basic question, don't you think?"

He nodded. Then he looked around the cafeteria again and lowered his voice. "I have something that I think answers Steiner. Not about Blount, but about someone else who cared deeply about art and..." He paused.

"Still lacked a moral compass?"

"Not exactly. More a case of losing a moral compass."

"Sounds intriguing."

"It's more than that. It may even be a little dangerous." His voice had become almost a whisper. "I have a manuscript. I found it while I was helping Senora Zollino sort through some papers. It was in a large envelope addressed to William. Since I'm his heir, I put it in my bag." He looked around again. "I just remembered it on the flight here---and read it."

"Can I read it?"

"Perhaps one day. But first I have a great favor to ask of you."

"Okay."

"The manuscript is in the cloak room. I've already made one copy and sent it to my office at the museum. After I saw you last night I made another copy in the business center at my hotel. I'd like to take it to the Post Office next door and, with your permission, mail it to you at your home address."

22

"Why not to my office at the University?"

"I think it's safer to send it to your house. I've become afraid that someone might try to take it from me. I know it sounds crazy, but I think I'm being followed. I could send it to your department address, but it's too easy to lift things from department mailrooms."

I began to think he was suffering from some sort of paranoia. Academics are certainly political animals and maneuvering behind doors about an agenda item for an upcoming department meeting can be intense. But the issues we fight about are never really dangerous. He read my mind.

"All right, maybe I'm being paranoid, but I would just feel better doing it this way. Is someone living in your house?"

"A Norweigian couple has been living there, but they've gone back to Oslo. A neighbor is looking after things 'til we get back. She's putting all the mail that looks like it matters in a box in my study."

"I'll just mark the envelope 'personal' then." He sighed. "I'm undoubtedly imagining all of this. But I think when---if---you read it, you'll understand why someone might want to get rid of the manuscript. At the very least, it could ruin some reputations."

"Look, Howard, you certainly have my permission to send me a copy ---wherever you think is best, or safest. But there's one condition. You have to let me read it when I get home. After this conversation you can't expect me to just destroy it, or give it back to you unread."

"That's fair. And after you've read it we'll have dinner one night and talk about it."

"Another condition----you have to do the cooking."

"Right, and we agreed last night that Roger will bring the wine." We stood up and kissed in the European style. "You sit back down and finish your coffee. I'm going to retrieve my things and go to the Post Office. Then I'm catching a cab to the airport. I'll be in my hotel in Mayfair before dinner, if all goes well."

"And when will you be back in Minneapolis?"

"Ten days or so."

"Good. I'll be back at my desk, worse luck, before that."

Howard walked out of the cafeteria and crossed the entry hall to the cloak room. I sat back down and started to take a sip of my coffee, but put the cup down when I saw two large men get up from their table near the cafeteria entrance, stand briefly outside in the hall and then go in the direction of the museum's entrance. For a fleeting moment I could have sworn that both men looked at me and said something to each other before they left. Now I thought, *I'm* the one imagining things. Had I read the manuscript before my meeting with Howard, however, I would have been even more suspicious.

Chapter 2

Chicago, March, 1987

Dearest Marco,

The idea for writing this came to me during a conversation I had with Steven Brenner last week in Chicago. We ran into each other at O'Hare airport on the closing day of the annual meeting of the International Association for Renaissance Art. I spotted Brenner in a noisy doughnut shop. He was pensively staring at a closed portfolio-sized notebook of some sort next to a coffee mug and greasy plate on the small table at which he sat. I hailed him as I approached, and he quickly placed his hands on the volume as if in an attempt to hide it. Nonetheless, I could see that it was not the sort of thing one would expect Brenner to possess. In a profession marked by sophistication and self-conscious attention to style and elegance, Brenner was even more meticulous than most. The volume exposed in spite of his attempts to conceal it, could only be described as tacky. It was covered in the sort of vinyl that only the least observant would confuse with genuine leather and was decorated with crude, gaudy botanticals.

Brenner and I had been convention friends for several years. Two days earlier we had shared a drink at the hotel bar and had bemoaned a singularly dull session on management strategies for small galleries, a presentation memorable solely for having attained new levels of slick, vapid overhead slides.

He was clearly embarrassed at having been discovered with the volume in front of him and, after we had exchanged pleasantries, began to explain himself.

"My daughter gave me this with the assignment that I am to complete it before the end of the month when my oldest grandson turns eighteen. You've undoubtedly been spared this sort of thing in Europe. It's called an Ethical Will."

I shook my head.

"My daughter belongs to some women's group, and one of her friends introduced her to the idea. Evidently it's all the rage. She, in any case, has become obsessed with the idea. You are supposed to write an essay for your children and/or grandchildren where you express your moral views---explain how they developed, what your life's lessons were, that sort of thing. The idea is that they will benefit from it. I can only imagine that they'll find it laughable."

"Perhaps when they are older they will appreciate it," I said, trying to alleviate his embarrassment. "It's an ancient idea, really. Remember in Genesis when Jacob, in his last days, calls his family together to pass on his legacy of values? Doesn't Rembrandt or someone have a painting with that subject?"

"Well, this ugly scrapbook certainly doesn't quite come up to Biblical standards. Worse, you're even supposed to include snapshots or other memorabilia along with the essay. And there are tips for what to include---not just names and birthdates of one's parents and grandparents, but your favorite song when you were a teenager, where you were on special days like the assassination of Kennedy, that sort of thing."

"Your favorite song is supposed to have shaped your moral outlook?"

"Maybe it did. But as I recall, it just made me hornier."

We laughed.

"Still," I suggested, "these things may matter. It's rather like being known by the company we keep, perhaps--the company including music, books, and of course the art we're drawn to."

Brenner smiled rather maliciously. "Do you really believe that a love of Renaissance Art, has resulted in a homogeneously admirable moral character in the group we've just spent four days with?"

I laughed. "A life spent looking at paintings of the Holy Family and associated saints has certainly not turned us all into Ghandi's has it?"

"God, no. Quite the opposite. I should think the level of back-biting, political intrigue, and mean-spiritedness is as high among art scholars as it is among any other profession---maybe higher!"

Brenner followed this with some cases in point---gossip that kept us both entertained until we had to leave to make our separate flights.

"Why not start your ethical will on the long flight to Venice," he chuckled as he waved his farewell.

On the flight back the idea kept coming back to me. Try as I might I could not remember any actual paintings of Jacob surrounded by his family as he must have provided them with what amounted to a sermon. It could be a powerful scene. What did his sons think of it? Were they moved or embarrassed, enlightened or confused? How would a Rubens or a Rembrandt express their reactions? How much did Jacob share with them? Did he confess his sins along with the platitudes he must inevitably have resorted to? Would his sons have loved him more or less if he was totally honest? Did Jacob himself reach any kind of final self-knowledge or self-acceptance?

By the time the plane landed I knew that I had to try to write this for you, Marco. Now that we have learned about my illness, writing all of this down has become more important to me. Perhaps you will benefit from learning my story. Or perhaps the only benefactor will be me, myself.

Your loving father,

Enrico Zollino

P.S. Each section of my manuscript has affixed to it a postcard reproduction of a work by Crivelli. Why I've done this will become clear in due course. There are copies of some of the originals are in our museum. Others you'll be able to look up for yourself.

Front of Postcard: Carlo Crivelli, Crucifixion, 1487, acquired by Chicago Art Institute in 1929

Back

Dear Professor Moore,   *October 5*

The Crivelli Crucifixion you mentioned is indeed puzzling. The town in his background is so obviously not Jerusalem. I count about six trees—why are they all bare? And why only two people? Where's the Virgin? Does the sailboat mean something?

I hope you can help,

Nancy

Chapter Three

Chicago, 1934

    As a small boy I found the pictures that hung on the walls of our villa far more interesting than those in my collection of picture books. Stories seemed to lurk in them--puzzles that I thought might be solved if I only looked long and hard enough at them. Some of them were frightening---dark and distorted and full of landscapes that bespoke monsters. Although I would often avert my eyes as I passed these, I could not help going back to them time and time again. It was a little like tonguing a loose tooth even when it hurt.

This passion itself was probably odd enough in a child, but even odder was the time I spent imagining how to re-arrange the paintings. I spent hours walking around the spacious rooms wishing that I could move some saint or other to what struck me as a much more appropriate location. St. Peter should have been closer to St. Paul, or the blue-draped virgin in the sitting room should have been allowed to greet visitors in the front hall. A reproduction of Rembrandt's *Man in the Golden Helmet* (attribution now contested, of course) really needed to be facing a Titian self-portrait in the library. My parents dismissed my suggestions, of course, but amused their friends with tales of them. Occasionally I did manage, for instance, to exchange a vase and small sculpture—with a great sense of relieved satisfaction.

I spent hours drawing floor plans of the villa that indicated how I would rearrange the artworks. And I spent an equal amount of time sketching copies of the works themselves. My parents provided me with colored pencils and watercolors and, as I progressed, even occasionally with a canvas and oils. I took delight in scrupulously attempting to duplicate Renaissance methods of preparing surfaces and paints---mixing and grinding and applying grounds. I was never really interested in expressing my own ideas or emotions. I found it far more satisfying, and I confess safer, to copy originals. As I acquired the skills needed to re-create those works that had frightened me, I felt increased power over them. Originality, I believed then and continue to believe, is over-rated.

An academic friend of my Father at last insisted that I must be allowed to study art history and restoration. Even before I went to Rome to study I had sold a dozen or so reproductions to my parents' friends. I meticulously identified them as having been copied by Enrico Zollino in homage to

Rembrandt, Mantegna or, most often, Crivelli, since my parents owned more of his works than those of any other artist. The income mattered less to my parents and me than the way the activity fit with our vision of a cultured aristocrat. They were quite content for me to become a gentleman scholar, which is, I suppose, what I have become—as long as the term 'gentleman' is interpreted liberally. But the path has not been any more ordinary than my childhood.

I completed my studies in the Early Renaissance in Rome and those works continued to enchant me with their dark mysteries just as they had before I learned to read. However, I felt myself wanting what I can only describe as a breath of fresh aesthetic air. My closest friend at the time felt a similar need and we spent hours over coffee and wine debating where we could best refresh ourselves, He decided to spend a year in Shanghai---and would die of influenza there a month after his arrival. He was my closest friend, and his death hit me very hard. Thus I not only looked to the New World, as we still thought of it, as an adventure to distract me from my sorrow as well as a place to loosen my Renaissance laces, as it were.

It was just at this time that my father decided to establish a small museum in town. Leaving a kind of cultural legacy was, after all, in the family blood. A distant ancestor of my father was Enrico Scrovegni, the man who hired Giotto to decorate a chapel on the grounds of their family estate by way of atoning for the sins of his usurious father. Art lovers had already discovered that a trip to Padova---so easy via the train from Venice---was well repaid by the Arena Chapel whose walls glittered and gleamed with the frescos of this Florentine genius. A small museum devoted primarily to the works of Crivelli (who had studied in Padova and would certainly have admired Giotto's genius) would be a natural addition to the culture of our community. Crivelli was considered only a minor early Renaissance artist, but we hoped to enhance his reputation, and thereby our own. Our family could supplement the Crivelli works we already owned by selling and trading others.

My parents were not happy at the thought of my leaving Italy in what were becoming increasingly unstable political and economic circumstances. My father had expected that I would become an enthusiastic partner in his project. And indeed I promised to be just that. But I wore them down with my insistence that I had always been a good son and deserved a reward---one that would, in fact, only enhance what we all expected would be a distinguished scholarly and curatorial life when I returned to Padova.

For reasons that always remained enticingly mysterious to me, my grandmother's youngest brother had immigrated to America in the late 1800's. He made his way from New York to Cleveland to Indianapolis before settling and, apparently settling down, in Chicago. He made a small fortune importing Italian leather goods and eventually opened a stylish shop on Wabash Street. He died young but a large number of more or less distant cousins continued to prosper in the area. So instead of finding myself in some elite eastern university, after spending a few weeks in New York City and Boston, I took a train from Grand Central Station to Union Depot. I was greeted by my cousin, Albert (who, like most of my American relatives, dropped the vowel on their first names except when corresponding with family in Italy). For several days he and his family did their best to convince me to take an apartment near them in Lake Forest. But I longed to live in the city whose architecture—really at its prime, then, I think---had seduced me after only a few short visits from the suburbs. The University of Chicago was also experiencing a Golden Age and I at once decided that my mother had been correct to insist that I study there so that I could be close to family. I chose to live within walking distance of its great library, the recently built but already renowned Rockefeller Chapel, a flourishing art studio, and Gothic classrooms. Some of my cousins had real estate connections and they helped me to find a large flat on Hyde Park Boulevard with a view of Lake Michigan, a newly opened Museum of Science and Industry, and the Midway greenway that ran from one end of the campus to the other and had already become a moat, albeit drained, isolating the university conclave from the city to the south. My flat was large enough for me to devote one room to a studio, for I could not imagine not spending some time reproducing some of the very art that had lured me the States. Ultimately, however, although I appreciated the American artists I studied, I quickly stopped trying to copy them and returned to my old Italian friends.

Classes began in late September and I soon learned what the phrase "cooler near the Lake" meant. The stiff breeze was itself a metaphor for the freshness and exhilaration that I felt. I had enrolled in a master's degree program and was at first surprised to discover that students regularly attended class and did "homework"---rather than sporadically visiting a lecture and cramming late in term for exams as we had done in Rome. But I quickly fell into the new rhythm.

I was something of a novelty---there were relatively few foreign students, even fewer than usual that fall as clouds of war thickened both in Europe and Asia, further darkening the skies of an already economically depressed world. Still the circle of graduate students I fell in with represented a fairly wide range of European immigrants. At first I found the characteristic American urge to take respectable strangers under their wing a bit smothering, but I soon adjusted to that, too. Studying and socializing were taken equally seriously by these students, almost as if they considered them two sides of the same coin. A new exhibit at the Art Institute could generate both debate and debacle; critical positions gelled as wine and beer flowed. One never knew in advance exactly who would show up for a meal or a party. There was a core group, of course, but each member felt free to bring guests, particularly if that guest had the wherewithal to contribute to the supply of alcohol.

It was at one of these gatherings in late October at the apartment of my fellow student and new friend Billy

Beauchamp when I first saw Judith. She was standing next to a gramophone on which a recent Gershwin tune was playing, looking through a pile of records. She squinted as she studied the label of each, frowning as none seemed to be *the* or *a* right one. Although the university recruited and attracted students from all over the country, most tended be from the Midwest in those depression years. Judith looked different from most of them. Her coloring was striking; indeed her complexion, features, and mass of dark hair made me think that she might even be Italian. She was shorter than most of the other women in the room and not as slender. She wore a black sweater and a vermillion skirt made of a fabric that draped softly over buttocks that suggested, if they did not quite invite, love-making. She had removed her shoes and the soles of her silk stockings—just slightly darker than those of the legs---were visible from moment to moment as her feet moved up and down in place causing her bright skirt to waft gently from side to side as her hips swayed to the beat of the music.   I was already well on my way to enchantment, when she looked over at me, smiled, and tilted her head, clearly inviting me to join her.

"Who *are* you?" she asked.

"Allow me to introduce myself. I am Enrico Zollino. I come from Padova, Italy. I think you say Padua here in The States. I am here studying American Art." My English was good, but its sound and structure belied years of British tutors and this seemed to amuse her.

"I knew you weren't from around her."

"And are you?"

"Close enough. I come from Galesburg—I'm sure no one in Padua has ever heard of it. It's a town, little city really, about two hundred miles southwest of here."

"In Illinois, then?"

"Oh, yes, it is definitely in Illinois----just closer to the Mississippi than to the Lake."

"Is that significant?"

She paused very briefly. "There's probably a bigger difference between Chicago and Galesburg than there is between Florence and Venice," she laughed.

"And how is it that you know about differences between Italian cities?"

"I'm studying European history. That's why I was invited to this party. I'm taking a course in Renaissance culture and Billy is the teaching assistant. He thinks I'm very promising."

Up until this moment, I had found American flirtation somewhat alien. But as I chatted with Judith, I felt that the enterprise was almost native to me.

"I'm sure he's not alone in that."

She arched her eyebrows and looked back down at the records she was holding.

"Are you looking for something special?" I asked.

"Something special----yes. But not for anything in particular. What I really need is another beer."

I followed her to a small kitchen crowded with others looking for drinks and snacks. It was loud and smoky and I suggested we find a quiet corner.

"May I ask your name?" I said when we found ourselves in a quieter spot in a hallway that ran from the kitchen to the living room.

"I'm Judith. Please don't call me Judy. I left that name in Galesburg."

"Judith."

"Enrico." To my surprise, she offered her hand to be shaken. "I suppose there will be times when I call you 'Rick', maybe even 'Ricky.' But tonight we'll stick with Enrico."

The thought that there would other times, more times, did not strike either of us as at all surprising. It was a given from the outset.

"Are you a nobleman, Enrico?"

I laughed. "Why is that one of the first things that people who pride themselves on living in a democracy always want to know? No, I am not. There is one Visconte and a Barone and Baronessa on the family tree, but several branches up from mine. My only real claim to fame is that I have two ancestors that Dante put in his Inferno."

"Oh my, God. That's wonderful. In which circle?"

"Do you know *The Inferno*?"

"Of, course. I told you I'm majoring in European history. And I'm very smart and very well read. I spent a whole quarter on the Comedy---and I remember lots of details."

One of Judith's greatest charms was her ability to say things about herself that from others would sound immodest when positive, or self-demeaning when negative. From her lips they sounded like simple statements of fact that did not evoke inferences as to her psychological or moral make-up.

"Both are in the seventh circle. My father's family name, Zollino comes from ties to Ezzolino de Romano, Count of Onora."

"Remind of his dates."

"First half of the 13th century."

"A Guelph or a Ghibelline?"

"Exactly the right question. How wonderful that you know about this. He was a Ghibelline Vicar in Padova and he slaughtered huge numbers of people."

"I remember now, he was a monster."

"Yes, he was. The family has nothing to be proud of in that regard."

"And he's in the Seventh Circle because he did violence against his neighbors!" She actually clapped her hands, as if applauding herself for winning prizes on a radio quiz show. "And the other one? Did he or she also kill lots of people?"

"No. Remember that Dante also puts those who do violence against art in the Seventh Circle."

"I do remember that. How appropriate that you are studying art, then. Is this some kind of Italian form of absolution."

"No, like everywhere else, we favor the sort that results in financial gain."

"So what did he do?"

"He was a usurer."

"Not the one whose son built the Arena Chapel?"

"The very one. And again may I say that I am very impressed with your knowledge. He's also on my father's side of the tree."

"This is amazing. I literally just this week in my art class have been hearing about Enrico Schrovegni. We had a heated discussion about why usury is fraud against art. Are you named for him?"

"Hard to say. There are plenty of Enrico's on the tree."

"But that Enrico did try to expiate the sin of his usurious father by doing more than buying his way out. He built a beautiful building and got the best artist around to decorate it. My God, I'll bet you've seen those Giotto frescoes hundreds of times."

"Probably."

"And if your ancestors had left money-lending to my ancestors as they were supposed to have done, Giotto would have had to paint somewhere else!"

And now it struck me. This beautiful, black haired creature with her Mediterranean features was not Italian. She was Jewish.

"Yep, Rick, I'm a Jew. Don't be too shocked. There are actually quite a few of us at U of C. Fewer at Northwestern, but even there you might come across a handful."

"I hope I didn't look shocked."

I really did hope that. But in all honesty, and that's what I'm trying to provide in writing this document, Marco, I was certainly taken aback. There were Jews in Padova; a few were acquaintances of my parents. I had Jewish teachers there, I think, and certainly there were Jewish scholars in Rome. But I really believe that I had not had a conversation with one until the evening I met Judith. Was I anti-Semitic? Not actively, certainly, for nothing in my life thus far had called for relevant action one way or another. I think I was passively prejudiced against Jews in the vague way that many, maybe most

Europeans were then. But with a few exceptions, Jews and Christians had gotten along well in Italy, I thought. Mostly, being Jewish seemed rather exotic. Looking back, I realize now how ignorant, in fact, I was about the history of Jews in my homeland. Still I think that even then I sensed that religion would not be irrelevant and that more was at stake than there would have been if she had, for example, just been a Baptist or Methodist. Others would later ask why I didn't walk away right then and there, that, hard as it might have been, it would have saved us both. Something along these lines did, in fact, cross my mind then.

And Judith read my thoughts, or, more likely, my face, for she said, not without some contempt, "The door's only ten feet away. You can make your escape right now."

"I'm sorry. I am surprised. I thought you looked Italian. I definitely do not want to escape. It just doesn't matter."

She shook her head. "Poor, Enrico. In this case I think the girl from Galesburg is way ahead of the Count of Padua. It's going to matter a lot, I'm afraid."

"Look, can we go somewhere and talk more?" I pleaded.

"Sorry, no. I live in the dorm and I have to check in by midnight. I'm the one that's going to have to make a beeline for the door if I don't want black marks."

"When can I see you?"

She laughed. "I won't be going to church. Will you?"

"No, I don't usually go to Mass. Could you come to my apartment for breakfast?"

She shook her head again, not to indicate refusal but as if she were reconciling herself to the situation. "Give me your address. I'll be there by nine. And by the way, my full name is Judith Rachel Goldenshane. The customs officers at Ellis Island had a bit of trouble with umlauts. I'm one of the golden and beautiful ones." Laughing, she grabbed a jacket from a coat hook and walked out the door.

There has to be something to the phrase, "Love at first sight," for so many people claim to experience it. Probably insisting that "I knew from the minute I saw him (or her) that he (or she) was the one" is grossly over-stated. Like most coincidences, the favorable cases are reported and repeated so often that the far more frequent negative outcomes get overlooked. It must be far more common for someone to think they've met The One but to find out in a few days or weeks or months that The One must be somewhere else. But for Judith and me it was clear at the outset that we were going to be the loves of each other's lives.

Golden and beautiful, she was at my door at two minutes before nine the next morning. My apartment had been furnished by my Chicago cousins and I was well aware that my surroundings were far more stylish and elegant than the tattered cast-offs and bricks and boards that served in the rooms of most of my student friends, though not in Billy Beauchamp's, of course. I took her jacket and for a moment we stood awkwardly but then, as on the previous night, she offered her hand to be shaken. There was an enticing combination of independent forthrightness and composure bordering on aloofness in Judith.

She looked around the living room slowly and then issued her judgment. "You're rich, Enrico. I never even see furniture like this." But then totally without guile, she ran to my couch, stroked the smooth dark leather, and cried with delight, "Or felt such wonderful---I don't know, ah, skin."

"That one came from Milan via my Uncle Giovanni's den."

She jumped up and sat with a bounce on the matching chair.

I would learn that Judith took less time that most women "preparing herself for the public," as she described it. For one thing, her hair was so thick that it defied much organization. That morning she had pulled it back off her face and had tried to contain it with a variety of small jeweled combs. Her outfit, like that of the evening before, did not emphasize, but nonetheless did not disguise a complete awareness and comfort with her body. She wore soft dark wool slacks and an ecru silk blouse. Both more than hinted at the body beneath, without being in the least bit tawdry.

"I don't have too much in the kitchen for an elaborate breakfast. But I have coffee and toast and oranges. And I can offer you some eggs"

"No, thanks. Fruit and toast will be fine." She pulled herself up from her sprawled position in the chair and followed me along the hall toward the dining room and kitchen, past the bedroom and my studio. She stopped at the studio door. "You paint, too. I thought people became art historians because they couldn't do that," she joked.

"I'm not sure most people would consider what I do to be real painting-- not in this time and culture. But I'll show you that later. Let's get some food." The kitchen was unimpressive as a room, but I had again benefited from the largesse of my Chicago family.

"Oh, my God, is that a real Italian coffee maker?"

"Yes, and real Italian coffee, courtesy of my Cousin Tomaso, and authentic Italian cups and saucers courtesy of my Aunt Maria."

41

"Just how much family do you have here?"

"Quite a lot. A great uncle immigrated here and married a woman with lots of brothers and sisters. Tomaso and Giovanni—or Tommy and Johnny as they preferred to be called---aren't immediate family, but they are family nonetheless. And family is important to Italians."

"To us, too, you know." More or less oblique references like this to our respective cultures cropped up often in our conversations.

I remember making coffee that morning with the conscious intention of trying to make my own style match the splendor of the pot that so enchanted Judith, and I was rewarded with her attention and enjoyment. She took such pleasure in the simple meal I prepared that my heart ached.

"Okay, now I want to see your painting," she announced as we finished.

I removed the cloth that was covering my current project.

"Oh, my God, I've seen that painting. It's in the Art Institute."

"Yes, the real one is. I'm making a copy."

"Why?"

Oh, Judith, why, indeed. I'm not certain that she ever really understood in spite of how often I tried to explain. Without explicitly saying so, I know she thought that I had enough talent to do what would have pleased her most--- something original. How had she put it the night before when I asked her if she was looking for special music? Something special, if not something in particular. She admired my skill and even took pleasure in my re-creations. She definitely appreciated the ways I would apply my skills later, at least the activities she knew about. However, I suspect that making copies never quite measured up to her ideals of specialness. Not much in the world did. Fortunately, I seemed to be special enough in other ways in her eyes to make up for this lack.

"It's something I'm good at. Really good at, I think. It's the only way I know to truly see what's there. And I love doing it. I love trying to duplicate the old methods and trying to put myself into the place of these geniuses from four or five centuries ago, to see with their eyes, so to speak. I've been doing it since I was a young boy. "

"Okay, to each his own. But how do you do it? Don't you have to sit in front of the real one?"

"Yes, especially in the beginning of the process. But then I also have a photograph," I gestured at the table next to the easel where a colored photograph was propped up against a stand. "And I go to the museum and sit and look really hard for a couple of hours every week. Sometimes they let me set up my easel there."

"I suppose there's another cousin who has some influence there."

"Uncle Giovanni, again. He's actually on the Board of Directors. He's a benefactor"

"Of course, he is."she jibed.

"His Paduan connections made him a strong advocate when the museum considered purchasing this work five years ago. He also made sure that it was included in the Century of Progress Exhibition at the Institute this year."

" But I thought that exhibit was supposed to celebrate American Art. This is clearly not an American painting. And the artist can't be one of the famous ones. I can't even remember who it is."

"You're right, he's not all that famous. But the exhibit is also honoring American collectors. Anyway, the artist is Carlo Crivelli."

"Some second-rate Renaissance guy?"

"I prefer the term 'minor' to 'second-rate.'"

"Okay, minor. But, still, why do you want to copy this one when there are so many more beautiful works? Crucifixions are so brutal. And this Christ is sort of grotesque."

"Many people do find Crivelli's figures a bit ugly or misshapen or eerie. But I really like them. I didn't always. My family has several of his works and when I was a little child I was really frightened by them. But I kept looking at them and suddenly they became my friends."

"Do you only do Crivelli's?"

"No, in fact I'm going to make a copy of a Raphael for Billy Beauchamp's father. He has a Madonna in his mansion in Minneapolis, but he wants a copy for his hunting lodge."

"Why? Wouldn't a still life with stag carcass be more fitting?"

The vivid mental picture we simultaneously formed made us both laugh at the thought of what a Crivelli or Raphael might have done with a dead deer.

"Who knows? Maybe he really likes his Madonna and misses her when he's away from home. Or maybe he thinks it will give the place some sort of cachet. I haven't seen the painting yet, only photographs. But I don't think I'll enjoy copying it as much as I do Crivelli. I really love all the details he puts in---the fruits and vegetables and birds."

The painting in front of us was certainly a Crucifixion—no one could mistake that, naturally. But instead of the more typical version with the two Mary's flanking the Cross, the Virgin is absent and Mary Magdalene on the left is balanced by St. John on the right---the latter with flowing golden hair. Christ's pallor indicates that he is close to death, if not already dead.

Judith and I would in our time together spend hours looking at pictures and speculating about the meaning of details. She told me about a children's magazine she had gotten in the mail every month as a child where there was a game of finding hidden pictures. She had loved it and had, as a result, developed a wonderful eye for minutiae.

"Who's skull is that?" she asked pointing to a detail.

"It could be just a generic momento mori. Often in this period a skull placed like this near the cross was a symbol of Adam---of the flowing of biblical time."

"And the towers in the background. They certainly don't look like they would have been found in Jerusalem."

"No. In many of his Crucifixions, Crivelli did depict what was obviously supposed to be the temple in Jerusalem and the road leading in through the city gate. But here there is no road through the gate and the towers are clearly Italian. He probably wanted to honor the city where he was commissioned to paint the altarpiece this came from. Some scholars think it's Ascoli."

"The landscape is so barren. All these jagged rocks and the bare trees. Not very springlike, is it?"

"Another momento mori, perhaps. Or an emotional expression of this particular tragedy."

She snorted. "Or Catholic propaganda that's supposed to remind the viewer of the wicked religion of the people who put Jesus to death."

"I don't think so. Crivelli often represents Jews in his works, and with respect. I think he appreciated the traditions that flowed from the Old to the New Testament."

"Well, in any case the only happy thing here is that little sailboat in the background. What's it supposed to mean?"

"I have no idea. Maybe just another reference to Ascoli. I like it because it was so easy to paint."

"Will you paint a portrait of me?"

"No."

A mixture of anger and hurt darkened her face. "Why the hell not?"

"I already told you. I have no talent for originals. And you, my dear, are definitely an original."

This placated her somewhat.

"Am I an original that you would like to kiss?"

The suddenness of this question startled me, of course. I had been told that American girls steadfastly adhered to a rule that disallowed kissing on a first date. But perhaps this was a second date?

"I have wanted to do nothing more since I saw you across the room last night."

The first kiss was a bit tentative. The second was not.

Judith pulled away. "I have to tell you that I'm a virgin."

I broke into a hearty laugh.

"Why is that funny," she pouted.

"Oh, my dear, that isn't. What's funny is having this conversation in front of this painting."

She smiled. "Okay, let's have it in the bedroom."

She left the studio and entered the bedroom determinedly. She walked to the side of the bed and turned as she began to unbutton her blouse. "I assume you are not a virgin," she said matter-of-factly, "but do you know what to do with real virgins, or only with the ones you want to copy?"

I had paused in the doorway. "Are you certain about this? "

"I'm twenty-one years old, I am not drunk---in fact all the caffeine in that coffee has made me more clear-headed than usual. I've done heavy petting, but I have always stopped at the crucial moment because I wanted to wait for the right one. You are the right one. I'm sure of that. I was sure from the instant you asked me to allow you to introduce yourself. I think you are a gentleman."

I crossed the room and took her in my arms. "I hope I am a gentleman. I am not a virgin, but I don't think I've made love to one before. I will use protection and try to be careful."

"I know that."

I finished unbuttoning her blouse and then let her unbutton and remove my shirt. She took off her blouse and turned to place it neatly on a chair. With her back to me, she removed the rest of her clothes and then turned and stood naked, except for red jeweled earrings and a golden chain around her neck, three or four feet from me.

"My body is not an Early Renaissance one. Much later. Actually I think of myself more along the lines of a Rubens or a Rembrandt's." Indeed her hair, breasts and hips at that moment reminded me of nothing so much as a painting of the

47

Dutchman's--one that I had seen in the Louvre on a trip with my parents to Paris. It's the painting of Bathsheba reading David's letter inviting her to his bed. She is naked, except for a wispy cloth covering her pubic area. A servant is bathing her feet. Judith was certainly smaller than that Bathsheba, but like her offered an ample, genuine body that promised to be warm and soft, but firm. Bathsheba is looking down, as if contemplating how to respond to David's request, indeed as if trying to figure out how she herself feels about it.

There was no hesitation in Judith's stance, and no hesitation from me now as I finished undressing and put on a condom I retrieved from a drawer next to the bed. Judith watched this process with curiosity and some impatience. She lifted both arms and removed the combs from her hair---a gesture that I found more seductive than any I had heretofore encountered. For as long as she lived all she would have to do to arouse me was to put her hands on her head.

"Your body is perfect," I murmured before pulling her gently onto the bed.

I realize now as I write this that these are details you probably can do without, Marco. Young people are always embarrassed, if not actually disgusted, at the thought of their elders making love. So I will only say that cymbals did not clang and the earth did not shake, but our lovemaking then and from then on was of a piece with the rest of our relationship--- passionate, exciting, questioning, exploring, challenging, but never tense.

When we had finished making love that morning, Judith turned to me and said, "I am so glad my first time was with an Italian. Especially with this one. I promise you that I fully intend the last time and all the times in between will be with this very special Italian."

I am confident that she kept that promise.

Front of Postcard : Carlo Crivelli, Le Christ mort soutenu par deux anges, 1485? Louvre

Dear Professor Beauchamp,   *March 22*

Thank you again for serving as outside examiner on my honors paper committee. I particularly appreciated your introducing me to Crivelli---as you can see I have sought him out on my three month tour of Europe. This one raises so many questions—e.g. why are the frescos on the railing in the front of this X & A fading? Is this a Momento Mori? And why so Small (only 5 x 7)? I return to my home in Kansas City on 9/18 and will write a proper thank you then. All the best, Richard

Chapter 4

Galesburg, November, 1934

    Judith wanted me to spend the two week winter break at her home, but I had already promised Billy Beauchamp that I would go with him to Minnesota and make the copy his father wanted. So we decided that we would go to Galesburg for Thanksgiving. Judith had had lunch and dinner with her parents together and separately when they made trips to Chicago, but she had not yet introduced me to them. She had not even told them how serious we had become in the few short weeks since our meeting. She simply told them that she had an Italian friend who was far from home and needed a friendly host to show him what this American holiday was all about. I

50

suspected that any parent would guess more was afoot when their daughter brought a young man home, but if Judith shared my hunch she kept it to herself.

Friends asked me what my expectations for Galesburg were. But I did not really have any. My knowledge about Midwestern towns was strictly limited to what I had gleaned from regional paintings---particularly those of Grant Wood, who happened to have been granted an exhibit that fall at the Art Institute. Galesburg was a railroad hub, boasting service on both the Chicago, Burlington and Quincy and the Santa Fe lines, so there were several trains running there from Chicago each day. We decided to leave on Tuesday night---in spite of the professors urging students not to skip class the day before the holiday. It was dark when we left Union Station so I was not able to see whether the landscape between Lake Michigan and the Mississippi Valley was in reality like that represented by Wood.

I was surprised as we stepped down from the train onto a broad brick-paved platform to see that we had arrived at a station nearly as large as the one in Venice. We had to cross two other platforms before we entered a cavernous waiting room. Rows of dark wooden benches filled a space canopied by a shallow dome. A café with a semicircular counter and several tables covered with red-checkered cloths lay to the left of three sets of handsome glass doors that led outside. Edward Hoppers famous painting, "Nighthawks," would not be painted for a few years, but every time I see it reproduced now I am reminded of customers in the Galesburg depot drinking coffee that night from clunky white mugs, seemingly unaware of anyone else.

We had been met on the platform by Judith's brother, Aaron, two years younger than Judith and a student at the local Knox College. The well-lit station allowed me to see the siblings' resemblance. Aaron shared Judith's thick, curly hair, dark complexion, and sharp Mediterranean features. He was taller than she, however, and thinner. He walked with the easy gait of an athlete, but I learned soon that his interests went less in direction of sports and more toward science and mathematics. He put our luggage into the trunk of one of the largest cars I had ever seen.

Aaron saw me looking it over. "It's a 1933 Cadillac," he said proudly. "Do you like it?'

"It's amazing," I replied honestly.

A few blocks from the station we came to what was actually named Main Street. By coincidence, we were reading Sinclair Lewis's novel by that name in one of my seminars on American culture, so I shouldn't have been surprised that the main thoroughfare in Galesburg had that eponymous designation, but somehow I was. It contributed to a kind of sense of unreality to my initial impressions of the town. We waited briefly at a red light, turned left, and followed Main Street for three or four blocks to a roundabout---or as they incongruously called it, the City Square. The first of four spokes leading from the plaza was Judith's street, aptly named Broad Street. Streetlights with granite bases and lantern tops lit the wide elm-lined street. In a few minutes Aaron turned left into a driveway consisting of two concrete strips set off to the right of a substantial brick house on the northwest corner of an intersection Broad made with what, had nomenclature in Galesburg been consistent, should, I thought, have been named Narrow Street. (I later learned it was, equally aptly, dubbed "Elm Street.") Before Aaron and I could retrieve the bags, a couple appeared on a porch that ran across the façade and stood with welcoming gestures under a porchlight globe.

Judith ran up the steps and succeeded in embracing both of her parents simultaneously.

"Get up, here, Enrico, it's time."

I wasn't sure exactly what it was time for, but I feared that Judith might precipitously reveal the nature of our relationship. In late October, only a few short but heady weeks after we had met, I had asked her to marry me and we were secretly engaged. The reason for the secrecy was our awareness of so many problems that would confront us. Both parents probably would frown on a marriage between a Jew and a Roman Catholic. My parents would undoubtedly have some misgivings about my marrying an American----European aristocracy then, and probably to a great extent still, snobbishly looked on Americans as crass and essentially uncivilized inhabitants of a *zona arretrato.* Judith herself referred, not unlovingly, to her home in "the backwoods." I would not be able to convince them that a Hebrew jeweler counted as an artist. Judith's parents would, we knew, be appalled at the thought of her returning with me to Italy. The distance would have been distressing in the best of times, and 1934 Europe hardly counted as the best of times. On the train, we had decided to wait a day or two before we broke the news.

Judith's father held the door open for all of us and as I passed through I saw on the right side, about two-thirds of the way up, a small piece of metal attached at an angle on the frame. The two older people and Judith ignored it, but Aaron paused to kiss his fingers and then touch it lightly.

"Dad, Mom, Aaron I want to introduce you to..." Judith looked in my directions and saw me shake my head slightly. She had already introduced me to Aaron at the station, of course, and the fact that she included him now indicated that something more than "my friend" was about to come out of her mouth. Fortunately, this time, she suppressed her impetuousness and finished, "my good friend, Enrico Zollino. Enrico, I'd like you to meet my parents, Fred and Ruth Goldenshane."

We all shook hands; even Aaron shook my hand again, looking sharply at me and then Judith. She had told me how close they were, and now I realized that he perceived

53

something in the situation that might not auger well for an easy, uneventful Thanksgiving.

"Aaron, take the bags upstairs, please," Judith's mother said. "I'll show you your room, Enrico." Judith and I had reconciled ourselves to the fact that not only would we be in separate rooms but that there would be no mid-night encounters for us here. She had held out some hope that, weather permitting, we might have an opportunity for intimacy one afternoon in a secluded rural spot favored by young lovers.

At the top of the stairs was a large rectangular hallway, carpeted in thick dark blue wool. Five doors led from it, one to a bathroom, the others to bedrooms and one to a small library or study. I was assigned the guest room just to the right of the stair top.

Mrs. Goldenshane opened the door to this room and indicated to Aaron that he was to place my bag in there. She led the way into it and, without speaking, first opened a closet door and then a door to a small bathroom reserved for the guests. A four-poster bed covered with an ivory chenille spread stood dead center against one wall. Above it were two floral still-lifes---not to my taste, but certainly not jarring. The windows of the corner room were draped with rich, precisely pleated deep green velvet. The walls were covered with a jacquard patterned paper in a paler green and the floor boasted what I was sure, even without closer sunlit inspection, was an expensive Oriental rug. A small round table of equal quality sat next to one window, flanked by two small chairs upholstered in the green velvet of the drapes. A dresser with three large drawers and a central mirror flanked by smaller drawers topped with rectangles of marble stood against the other wall. A comb, brush and hand mirror sat on one of these slabs at a distance from one another that could only have been achieved with a ruler. On the other a small crystal vase of marigolds had been placed precisely in the middle. The woodwork and doors were of a hardwood slightly lighter than the wood of the floor. One knew without looking that bathroom accessories would have been displayed with the same exacting care.

Absurd as it was, I felt as if Illinois had been transported to Flanders and that I was looking at an interior genre painting, where the objects represented had been arranged to achieve a stable, balanced composition. But more than anything, what made me feel as if I were looking at a tableau was the presence in it of Ruth Goldenshane. She was about Judith's height and weight and had the same mass of dark, curly hair. But whereas Judith most often allowed hers to find its own course, Ruth had restrained hers in a black net snood. I never saw her without one of these accessories and, to me, it became a metaphor for the way she managed, or attempted to manage, her world. Everything and everyone was to be in its place. That first night she wore a dark brown suit and green blouse tied with a perfect bow at her neck. How, I wondered, had she managed to find a green the exact the shade of the drapes and upholstery? It was as if a painter had mixed these colors in order to reinforce the rhythm of his composition.

"I hope you will find this room comfortable, Enrico," Ruth said.

"I'm sure I shall, thank you."

"We'll meet downstairs in fifteen minutes for a light supper, unless you'd rather retire now."

"A supper would be very nice. Thank you, Mrs. Goldenshane."

"Judith will fetch you." She turned toward her daughter who was standing just outside in the hall with Aaron next to her, and there was a palpable softening of her face and stance as she wrapped her two children with her glance. She closed the door of my room behind her and I began the task of putting my own things in places that would not disturb the setting or its composition. I resisted an urge to move the vase of marigolds slightly off-center.

Judith rapped softly on my door a few minutes later and stepped inside. We kissed briefly, but warmly.

"Are all of the rooms like this?" I asked.

"Do you mean is everything always in its place? Oh, yes. Aaron and I learned very early not to mess up her world too much. But she adores us, and we have never had to doubt that for one second. It'll be easier with Daddy. You'll see."

I followed my beloved down the stairs, through the entry way and into the room Americans call the living room. It would easily have served as a small salon in my own home. Another Persian rug lay on gleaming hardwood floors. Like the room to which I had been assigned, all the furniture and adornments harmonized. A fire burned in a large brick fireplace on either side of which stood bookcases that went three-fourths of the way up the wall to windows consisting of leaded and stained glass panels. Reproductions of European classics adorned the wall, but the controlled atmosphere here stimulated none of my habitual desires to rearrange things.

"Welcome, again, Enrico," said Fred Goldenshane and he offered me his hand to shake again.

"Thank you, sir. You and Mrs. Goldenshane have a very beautiful home."

"We have been very fortunate," he said. "Now let's have some food." He crossed the room to a pair of heavy, carved wooden sliding doors that, when opened, revealed a richly furnished dining room. Had photography of food and its presentation been in the 1930's what it has become today, the display of edibles on the table could have come from or inspired a photograph in a magazine for gourmets. The table was not overfull, but its organization was of a piece with everything else

I had up to now experienced in this home. Once more I felt as though I were being inserted into a still life representation.

"What can I get you to drink, Enrico?"

A multi-bulbed crystal chandelier permitted me to observe Fred Goldenshane more closely than the more dimly lit living room had allowed. He was a tall man, probably close to two meters, with almost black, deeply set eyes, a sharp hooked nose and narrow oval face. He was balding and retained only a narrow semi-circle of black, slightly graying hair. He shared Aaron's slender physique and, like him, moved gracefully. He wore a blue serge suit and a red tie with narrow blue stripes. His costume was as conscientious as his wife's, but his demeanor was more relaxed. An ease with himself communicated itself to others. I could sense that he would be a canny salesman.

I paused, not knowing what beverage choice would be most suitable.

"Tell him what the choices are," Judith helpfully suggested. "I'll have a beer."

Ruth looked slightly askance at her daughter, but remained silent.

"I have beer---only American, I'm afraid, but I can also offer you some wine. Am I right in thinking that I don't have to list the available soft drinks?"

All of us, including Ruth, welcomed a chance to laugh together.

"My husband," Ruth said, "has the finest wine cellar in Galesburg."

"Probably the only one," said Aaron. "This is pretty much a coke and beer town."

"My cellar was greatly depleted during our failed American experiment with prohitibiton. Forunately my work takes me often to Holland and Belgium and I always try to bring back a few bottles of wine with me," Fred explained. "In your honor I put a bottle of Pinot Grigio in the icebox-- in case you would like to try it with me."

"That sounds wonderful, sir."

My family in Chicago served a lot of Italian wine, but even they referred to it as "Dago red." This was the best wine I had drunk since leaving Padova, served in a perfectly shaped crystal glass. With our University friends, Judith always insisted on drinking her beer from a bottle, but here both she and Aaron drank from steins that had obviously been brought from Europe.

"Again, welcome to our home," Fred said. All of us raised our glasses, Ruth a crystal goblet that I assumed, wrongly it turned out, held only ice water. She turned and went to sit in a one of two velvet upholstered chairs that flanked the brick fireplace. The rest of us filled our plates, but she had chosen to eat nothing.

As soon as we had all arranged ourselves around the living room, Judith and I sat as close as respectfully possible on a large grey damask sofa, Ruth said, "Tell, us about your family, Enrico." It is not easy to describe Ruth's way of uttering seemingly inconsequential words. She was far too decorous to blatantly issue commands, but neither was her use of the imperative case here merely a request. Had she said, for example, "Have some more potato salad," declining would not have seemed possible, even for an instant.

"Mother, give him a chance to catch his breath. We have the whole week-end for this inquisition."

Ruth merely smiled at her daughter and then looked back at me, waiting for my compliance.

"It's all right, Judith. I'm happy to talk about my family. My father's family has lived in or near Padova, or Padua, as you call it, for centuries."

"A couple of them are even in Dante's *Inferno,*"Judith half-joked, half boasted. She clearly thought better, however, of giving the details of their crimes.

I limited myself to briefly mentioning my paternal family's ownership of farms and vineyards in the area. "My Mother's family is from Venice. They have been in the shipping trade for generations. Most recently they have been coffee importers. They import coffee from all over the world, but they are most proud of the beans that come from their own plantation in Ethiopia. They somehow managed to hold onto it even during the war in 1896. My grandfather insists that his beans are among the most sought after by the major coffee companies in Europe."

Fred's face darkened. "I would guess that your family is very interested in Mr. Mussolini's intentions for Ethiopia." He was the first American I had met, outside of my Italian family in Chicago, who seemed to have any idea about relations between my country and Africa. I was about to respond, but Ruth lifted her hand.

"Political discussion can wait, Fred. It's late and I'm sure we all want to get a good night's sleep."

Again there was clearly no room for debate. In unison, we stood and carried our plates to the kitchen.

"I'll see you in the morning, Enrico," Judith said as she helped her mother scrape plates. "I'll help Mother in here."

"Don't worry. Breakfast is not a formal affair," Aaron quipped.

"No," Ruth said. "Fred and Aaron are often off before I get up. And I'm sure Judith will help you to find whatever you need." She left the kitchen and went into the dining room where I could hear her freshening the ice in her glass.

"I'll knock on your door when I'm up." Judith surprised me by walking across the kitchen and kissing me on the cheek. The eyebrows of Fred and Aaron rose as they glanced at each other, and I sensed that they were relieved that this scene had not been played out in the presence of Ruth.

Her father had in fact left the house when Judith and I went downstairs shortly after eight the next morning, but Aaron was sitting at a small round oak table in one corner of the large kitchen, reading a magazine opened to an article illustrated by a collection of mechanical designs that would have gladdened the heart of daVinci.

"The coffee is hot. Judy wrote to us about your great coffee and it won't be that good, I'm afraid. But Ruby did bake some of her famous apple muffins yesterday. And somehow Mother managed to squeeze some orange juice last night. I hope she at least let you cut the oranges, Judy."

Judith glared at Aaron. I thought, incorrectly, that it was because his use of the diminutive form of her name. But she said nothing and quickly regained her usual cheerfulness. She poured juice into small crystal glasses—the same pattern as the wine glasses of the previous evening---and set two small fine china plates and with matching cups and saucers on the table. The muffins, in a covered basket in the center of the table, were covered with a starched pink linen napkin, whose color matched the tiny roses that circled the dishes. Next to it was a silver butter dish and silver tray on which three small bowls of jam, each with its own delicate spoon, had been placed. Once again I had the distinct impression that I had entered an interior painting, this time "Still Life With Muffins and Jam." Breakfast may not be a formal affair, but neither had it been left to chance.

We heard the back door open and a large Negro woman carrying a large floral cloth purse and an even larger satchel climbed up the short flight of steps that led from it into the kitchen..

"Mornin'," she sang, as she entered the room. Judith jumped up and grabbed her in a hug before she even had a chance to make much headway.

"Lordie, child, let me at least put my bags down so I can give you a proper hug!" She set the bags on the floor and gave Judith what can only be onomatopoetically described as a smooch. This accomplished, while still hugging my darling, she looked over her shoulder at me. "And this must be the Italian boyfriend." My nationality was pronounced as I had heard many Americans pronounce it, with a heavily stressed long "I."

"Now Ruby," Aaron said, "No one has said that this is a boyfriend."

Ruby humphed. "No one needs to say much in the house."

Judith turned. "Ruby, this is Enrico."

"Pleased." She took the hand I had offered. I was tempted to kiss her hand, but decided it might be misconstrued. "I spose Her Majesty is still in bed."

Aaron and Judith giggled. "Believe it or not, Enrico," Aaron said, "She even calls Mother Your Majesty to her face. She's the only person in the world who could get away with that. But Mother knows, as do we all, that if it weren't for Ruby this house would fall apart."

"Darn tootin," Ruby chortled as she hung her coat and hat on one of a line of pegs that lined the stairwell wall and proceeded to take a large apron from another. "I'll have a cup of that coffee while I start tomorrow's jello."

I listened as the three of them made small talk of the sort that children, no matter how old, make with servants they have known forever.

As we were finishing our coffee---indeed, it was not Italian, nor even Dutch---Judith's head suddenly snapped to attention.

"Do I hear Nochie?"

Aaron nodded. "Yep. He's out shooting a few before we leave for our ten o'clock math class."

"Shooting a few?" I queried.

"Baskets, you Italian ignoramus," Judith laughed, mimicking Ruby's pronunciation of my country. "Nochie was a star basketball player for Galesburg High School."

"And now for Knox," Aaron added.

"Come on." Judith ran to the closet and grabbed our coats.

"You'd better run if you want to see him. His mother has to work tomorrow so he's going to Peoria to spend Thanksgiving with his grandmother. Won't be back 'til Sunday night."

"Ruby, you know everything," Judith called as we went down the stairs and out the door.

"Uh-huh," she replied, nodding her large black head.

I had not seen the back of the house the night before, but nonetheless knew it would be of a piece with the inside. It was, indeed, a formal landscape; even the leaves that had fallen since the last raking seemed to have been arranged to harmonize spatially and chromatically with the objects in the foreground and background. To the right of the house the driveway we had entered led to a large garage---a building that must certainly have served as a carriage house in earlier times. The back garden, or yard as they called it, was smaller than the front, but still quite spacious. November is the bleakest month in the Midwest, I think. Whatever snow they might have had had disappeared, but the ground was hard. The trees and bushes were nearly bare, but still one could see that this area was as well tended as the home's interior. A gracefully curving hedge, fronted by a broad flower bed, separated the yard from what I had, the previous evening, thought of as Narrow Street, and provided the border of the Goldenshane's property and one that lay behind it. Judith ducked through a narrow opening in the bushes. I, of course, followed her.

A wooden house, neat but much, much smaller than the Goldenshane's stood on a small lot. There was no carriage house here, nor even a garage. But a shed not far from the back door and directly behind the Goldenshane's garage, provided enough height for a metal ring that served as the hoop for the beautiful young man who darted from side to side and then turned to arch the ball in its direction. It would undoubtedly have gone through the ring had he not, at the last moment, been distracted by Judith's gleefully shouting at him.

"Nochie!" She ran and embraced him with the same exuberance that had greeted Ruby.

"Enrico, this is Raymond Thomas--Nochie to all his friends because of his nightly complexion."

I would have described him, particularly in comparison to the dark brown of Ruby's skin, more as of *crepuscolo* as we describe that dusky time of evening. I knew he was a Negro, because Judith had often spoken of him, but he was certainly light enough to have counted as Mediterranean. Indeed he was only slightly darker than Judith herself.

Nochie stuck his basketball under his arm and moved toward me with an extended hand. "So this is the Italian boyfriend. Welcome to Galesburg." There was no trace of the long, over-emphasized "I" that I had heard in Ruby's speech nor, for that matter, of any of the accents I had come to associate with Negroes in Chicago.

"I'm very happy to meet you. Judith often speaks of you." Indeed, she had. Nochie had been Judith's neighbor since she was three or four and he and Aaron were the same age. The three had been inseparable. Nochie was the only Negro in their elementary schools, since the rest of Galesburg's black population lived "on the other sides of the tracks," as Judith put it, and went to other schools. And Nochie was further distinguished from most other schoolmates in having a single parent. There had never been a Mr.Thomas to anyone's knowledge, but Mrs. Thomas managed to support herself and her son in a comfortable, if modest, style.

"I'll bet." Nochie smiled at her warmly. "She and Aaron and I think of ourselves as The Three Musketeers."

"When we're not acting like The Three Stooges," she laughed. "Ruby says you're off to Peoria tonight."

"Yes. I'll be back tomorrow night, but early Friday I have to leave with the team for Iowa. We have games there this weekend at Coe and Grinnell. I'm afraid we'll have to wait until the Christmas vacation to find some trouble to get into."

Aaron made his way through the hedge. "Come on, Nochie. We have to get going if we're going to make it to class on time."

Judith hugged her friend again. "Why can't you just have Thanksgiving dinner with us?"

"Actually your mother did invite me. But my Mom wanted me to go to Grandma's. She's been sick, you know. I have a feeling that dinner at your house this year will be very interesting with this guy here. I'm sorry I'll miss it. Good luck, Enrico. I hope you find some things to be thankful for."

I looked at Judith. "I already have."

Chuckling, Aaron followed Nochie into his house, and Judith and I returned through the hedge.

"You didn't even try to deny the fact that I'm your paramour."

Judith stopped in the middle of the frozen lawn. "No point. When Ruby and Nochie put two and two together they are happy to announce that the result is four. I have never brought a young man home with me before. Aaron and Mommy and Daddy must have added things up, too."

"But we're still going to wait until Friday to say anything?"

"Yes. Mother---and, Ruby, of course----will have created too beautiful a feast to disrupt things tomorrow. And I know you well enough to know that you can play your role to perfection. The perfect, sophisticated gentleman."

"All right, my love." We kissed quickly.

A raw November gust of wind disturbed a few dead leaves, arranging them into a small tornadic spiral. Judith momentarily looked serious.

"I hope that's not a sign of a coming storm." But then, as her face cleared, she grabbed my arm and pulled me toward the house.

65

"Come on, Daddy has left me his car so that I can give you the grand tour of the buckle on the corn belt," she laughed gaily.

Judith drove her father's large car with the enthusiasm and joyfulness that attended almost everything she did. She showed me where she had attended school, homes large and small of her friends (accompanied with tales of their adventures and misadventures), some of the farm fields on the outskirts of town, Knox College, with its building that Judith boasted had hosted one of the famous Lincoln-Douglas Debates. Then we drove to and parked on Main Street and strolled by small shops and two or three larger department stores. We visited her father's jewelry store, a space crowded with a range of goods, from trinkets to expensive watches and jewels set both elegantly and gaudily. Her father apologized that he did not have time to spend with us that day as he and his employees were busy preparing for the opening of the Christmas shopping season the day after Thanksgiving----a tradition that, to my mind, has unfortunately given way to earlier and earlier seasonal marketing with no clear opening boundaries. The Depression had closed several shops and many stores that were still open were on the seedy side, but Goldenshane's had evidently not been so affected. When I mentioned this to Judith, she nodded and simply said that people always needed to buy presents and engagement rings.

We walked North a few blocks from Main Street to large yellow brick building in the middle of a large green space. A small sign identified it simply as "The Galesburg Club."

"This is where we'll have lunch," Judith explained as we walked through heavy glass doors into a reception area richly but rather unharmoniously decorated with a mix of Louis XV and Prairie School.

66

"Oh, Judy, there you are. Your Mother said you and a friend were coming home last night---and Nochie called to tell me he'd managed to see you."

The receptionist, a tall, strikingly beautiful Negro woman, whose demeanor demanded that one think of her as a lady, came from behind a dark walnut counter and embraced Judith warmly, but with more reserve than either Ruby or Nochie had displayed.

"Enrico, this is our neighbor, Nochie's Mother, Violet Thomas." We shook hands and I remarked to myself on the disparity in skin color between Nochie and his mother. Clearly Mr. Thomas, whoever and wherever he was, had been much lighter complected than Violet. This explained why Judith had once said that people speculated that Nochie's nickname was due to the fact that his father may have been one of the itinerant Mexicans who spent some time working on the railroad in Galesburg.

"I think your family is planning to be here for dinner on Friday. But I hope we have a chance to have a really good chat while you're here."

Judith did spend some time Friday with her, but I only saw Violet that noon and briefly when she seated us at dinner on Friday evening. I think I would have retained a clear picture of her in my memory even if events did not unfold as they did. The rhythmic smoothness of her motion made it clear where Nochie had gotten his athleticism. Similarly his height and slender build, as well as deportment and manner of speech, had come from her. Her way of expressing herself was soft, precise, and refined. She was neatly, fashionably dressed in a black suit. A single pearl that hung from a narrow golden chain stood in lovely contrast to her clothes and skin. Smaller pearls hung from pierced ears. Comfortable formality was exactly what this private club must have prided itself on, for this was what their receptionist communicated. Yet, as she led us across the dining room with its starched white linen tablecloths and crystal vases each with a single red rose, I picked up distinct hints of not so latent sensuality. Her movements and attitude hinted at dark mysteries that any man would have wanted to delve into, and accordingly several of the men already seated followed her with their eyes.

"Are you wondering why Jews are welcome at this club?" Judith asked.

"Actually I was thinking what an incredibly sexy woman Violet is."

"You'll make me jealous."

"I doubt that."

After we had ordered, we returned to her question.

"So why are Jews welcome at this club? Or is membership limited to them."

"God, no. There are barely enough of us in Galesburg to have a reasonable game of majong. No, the fact is that for some reason there is essentially no anti-Semitism here, or at least none that's open. I never felt the slightest bit of prejudice here. Negroes and Mexicans are kept in their place---that's why having Nochie and his Mom live next to us is so strange----but no one even seems to notice that we're Jewish. Maybe it's because there are so few of us, or because almost all of us are rich. Or maybe it's because we don't have a synagogue so they don't think of us as a group."

"Or maybe it's because you just don't act Jewish. Are all of the Jews in Galesburg as non-religious as you are? We Italians don't act all that Catholic, either, but we do mention God occasionally, and go to mass from time to time, and give up meat on Fridays, and have Crucifixes and pictures of Christ in our homes. I haven't seen any Jewish artifacts in your house."

"It's true. Almost all of us are non-practicing, maybe because the nearest synagogue is fifty miles away. We do have a special meal sometimes and we know some of the stories, but we think of being Jewish mostly in ethnic and ethical terms---the Ten Commandments and all that. Only Aaron does a bit more. He's the one who put that Mezuzah up."

"That what?"

"You know, that little piece of metal by our front door. Aaron touches it when he enters the house."

"Oh, yes. I did see him he do that last night. What's that all about?"

" 'Mezuzah' means 'doorpost' in Hebrew. We don't just have ten commandments, you know, we have hundreds---at least one for every day of the year, probably more. One of them says that a little piece of parchment with writings from the Torah has to be attached to our threshold."

"What do the writings say?"

"I forget. Something about loving God and teaching godly things in your home."

"Sounds pretty innocuous to me. It's at least more sophisticated than hanging a chain of garlic over your door to keep away the evil spirits. Some of the people in Padua do that."

She laughed. "If Aaron had just said one day, 'Let's put up a Mezuzah,' everyone would have been fine about it. But he gets these periodic enthusiasms---like now, he's on this airplane and Army thing. He's scaring the dickens out of Mommy and Daddy with talk about joining up and trying to fly fighter planes or bombers or something. Anyway, about a year ago he got into this Jewish thing and we were all supposed to get excited about observing a few rules. We all just laughed, so he got into a snit and put up the Mezuzah all by himself and makes a big show of genuflecting to it."

We laughed at the mixed metaphor.

"Anyway, I was really surprised when I went to Chicago and heard someone call me a Kike for the first time. I have a Jewish friend who went to Northwestern and she couldn't believe how many places in Evanston were closed to her. Another friend applied to Princeton and someone on the East Coast told him that he'd never heard of anything so completely futile. So he went to Columbia. And of course at UC, most of the faculty is Jewish, so Hyde Park is almost as insulated as Galesburg. I'll probably have a really rude awakening in Europe. Who knows what they'll call me or prevent me from doing there."

"I really don't think there will be any problem in Padua. Italians have gotten along with Jews pretty well. Mussolini's even had a Jewish mistress."

"Really?"

"Well, that's the gossip, at least. People notice it and talk about it, of course, but I think they find it exotic rather than disgusting."

"It's funny, Enrico. I really don't know whether my parents will be upset because you're not Jewish. They won't like the thought of my moving to Italy, that's for sure."

"Well, we'll find out on Friday."

Over lunch we decided to wait until we returned home from our dinner at this club Friday night to break the news of our engagement. And then we decided to stop speculating in favor of a continued tour of Galesburg.

We only stopped at two places that afternoon, but after what came to pass they have both become the stuff of my dreams—and nightmares. Judith first wanted to show me one of her favorite spots----the local railroad switch yard, supposedly the largest of its kind in the world. We parked the car and walked to the middle of a long high bridge that spanned an enormous network of tracks. The bridge was high enough to allow us to watch scores of freight cars moving back and forth, switching from one track to another.

"It's the largest humping switch yard. It works because cars move by gravity down those humps just fast enough to connect to the car it runs into without damaging it." She pointed to gentle inclinations in the tracks. "Isn't it amazing? In high school my best friend's father would bring Mary and me here and explain what was happening. It was like watching a ballet with the dance master. I think it's just about the most beautiful spot in Galesburg."

"I don't know that I think it's beautiful, but I agree that it's amazing."

"It's way more important economically to the town than the college or any of the factories, let alone Main Street. People say that if there's a war, it will be the third most important bombing target in the United States."

I found this hard to believe, but did not say anything to curb Judith's pride and pleasure. I certainly did not want to spend time discussing wars or bombs. We stood for a long time watching----Judith focused on the tangos and foxtrots below us, I concentrated on her wonderful head as it, too, seemed to sway to some rhythm that was hidden from me. Finally the sharp November wind forced us back to the car. We drove across the bridge and down a small street where Judith pointed out the birthplace of Galesburg's most famous son, the poet Carl Sandburg. As we drove north she recited some of his poems, explaining that learning them had been a high school

71

literature class requirement. I did not know this American poet and my English was not up to appreciating nuances of the poetic language, but again Judith's delight was contagious.

We drove around the city's square, up Broad Street, past the terminus of the streetcar at the north end of town, and through two brick pillars, one of which informed us that we had come to Lincoln Park. A flower garden, bandstand, playground and small lake greeted us before Judith pulled off the road to a spot next to the lake. Her face darkened.

"Over there, behind the hill where the swings are, there's a bear cage. Some idiot alderman somehow got the idea that kids who come to play here should be able to see some bears. I hate it. The bears are kept behind bars and have almost no room to move. Still they keep them on a leg chain. Some kids torment them. I can't stand it. Imagine how awful it must be to be imprisoned!"

"We won't go look at it then."

"Absolutely not."

I reached over and pulled her to me and we allowed ourselves a few moments to relieve that build-up of physical yearning that had accumulated since we left Chicago. Suddenly we were startled by a darkening of the sky that turned out to be a huge flock of geese that landed on the lake, apparently a stop on their way south—and ultimately into my nocturnal images. Now, in sharp contrast to the darkness that had covered Judith's face when she described the bears, I watched as total glee lit her whole aspect.

"This has to be especially for you, my love," she said. "It's very late for geese to be here---usually they land in droves like this in late October." She literally clapped her hands at the cacophony of honking and splashing.

I love the word 'cacophony',Marco. You'll see why later.

"It's an omen. Remember, a goose is the symbol of marriage and childbirth. And look how many there are. All will be well. I just know it."

I would remember that train yard and those geese later when real bombing targets changed everything for us. But for now we allowed ourselves to believe that the future would bring a cacophony only of delight and ardor.

***

That evening and the next day all did seem to be going well. After dinner on Wednesday, Judith's friend Mary called and asked us to join her and two other high school friends, Anne and Barbara, at a downtown bar. So Judith, Aaron and I drove to the town's biggest hotel and went into The Crown Room, a warmly furnished, well-appointed room with several small tables, a few booths, and a long sweeping bar with high-backed leather stools. The three friends made room for Judith in a booth and Aaron and I pulled over two chairs as introductions were made.

Illinois had a very strange law at that time---I had encountered it already several times in Chicago. Women were allowed to purchase liquor at the age of eighteen, men had to wait until twenty-one. Thus Aaron technically should not have been served alcohol, but the bartender did not object when I asked for six glasses to take back to the table with the pitcher of beer I bought at the bar.

"If I can join the Army, I should certainly be able to have a beer."

"Aaron," Judith said, shaking her head, "let's have no Army talk tonight. Let's drink to something cheerful. "Happy Thanksgiving, everyone."

73

Aaron, Mary, Anne, and Barbara all were Knox students so the conversation naturally covered college gossip for several minutes. Then Mary asked me to "tell us all about yourself."

Judith spoke quickly. "He's Italian, he's descended from nobility, he's rich, he's smart, he's gorgeous, and he's mine. What more is there to tell?"

Barbara raised her mug. "To being Italian, noble, rich, smart, gorgeous, and Judith's, then." Conversation drifted then from one topic to the next, from politics (all were devoted supporters of Roosevelt, convinced that he could lead the country out of the depression and sway the world in the direction of peace), movies, a proposed WPA project for the town's post office, mutual friends---and enemies. I did not have much to contribute, but I felt completely comfortable with these forthright, intelligent but unassuming people. In those days, in such places it was so easy to suppose that somehow all would go well.

Thanksgiving Day and dinner were a happy surprise. I had expected things to be pleasant, but I had not anticipated that we would actually have fun. Ruby arrived early and helped with preparations before leaving to join her own family for the holiday. She left behind a young woman, Velma, who would handle final preparations and serving. Ruth was relaxed and gay and even playful at times. She and Judith puttered in the kitchen until early afternoon when we all went to our rooms to dress for the main attraction of the day. I had brought my tuxedo since Judith had told me that Thanksgiving dinner would be a formal affair. In nature, it is the male of the species whose colors and markings dazzle, but I have always approved of our human custom of requiring men to wear black when it is the women who should dazzle. And this is what Judith and mother did. Ruth wore a long-sleeved gown of dark green silk overlaid with a fine chiffon embroidered with tiny magenta roses. A scooped neck and the colors perfectly framed the ruby necklace and earrings that she had chosen. Like her home, everything in her costume was perfectly composed. Small jewels dotted her snood. Judith wore blue brocade the color of which matched sapphire necklace and earrings. The fabric draped in a cape that flounced just above her shoulders. I doubt that any other house in Galesburg boasted such a stylish pair that day.

Like Hopper's night scene, Norman Rockwell's famous (most of my friends would say "infamous," of course) depiction of a bountiful American Thanksgiving would not be painted for several years, but he could easily have used Ruth's table as the setting. A molded cranberry salad, for example, sparkled nearly as much as the perfect china and crystal. Two heavy leaded glass decanters allowed us to choose red wine or white wine, or both, to accompany an incredible variety of side dishes that complimented the turkey and ham. Clearly this was a household in which there was no observance of the Jewish dietary laws, though I did notice that Aaron did not serve himself any ham. Ruth glowed under praise of everything from spiced peaches (a totally new taste to me) to scalloped oysters. Fred entertained us with stories he had heard about petty arguments that had arisen between merchants whose stores were to be represented in the parade that would be held on Main Street the next day —one that would usher Santa Claus into Galesburg for what everyone hoped would be the best shopping season for several years. Aaron described a new airplane that he had read about in one of his mechanical magazines, but he cooperated by not connecting his remarks to any military topics. I even managed to tell some humorous stories about growing up in Padua, while Judith repeated some of the news she had gotten from her friends the previous evening.

The happy mood continued after the meal. Velma cleared and cleaned up while the rest of us changed clothes and went for a long walk in the chill evening. The large neo-Victorian homes and more modest bungalows glowed in the dark. We encountered several others out walking and I was introduced to more people than I could possibly remember. We returned home and Ruth served Port while we seemed to be settling into an evening of classical recordings and reading. Aaron suggested that perhaps I would like to join him in a game of chess, but Fred interrupted him.

"I wonder, Enrico, if you'd like to join me in my study for a brandy."

Like the "wonderings" of Ruth, this particular utterance of Fred's left no doubt that he was not really making a request. I had no choice but to rise and follow him. I looked at Judith, who had been curled comfortably with a book in one of the chairs next to the glowing fireplace. She straightened, closed the book, and gave me a small but firm nod of encouragement. As I followed Fred up the stairs to his study, I sensed that our plans for waiting until the next day for our announcement had been, to say the least, altered.

Front: Carlo Crivelli, The Annunciation from Ascoli, 1486, London, National Gallery of Art

Back:

Dear Dr. Wilson,   *Nov. 21*

Doesn't this Mary look like she might be studying in Seymour Library? Of course the street doesn't look much like G-burg's Main St---or even Peoria's for that matter.

We love being stationed only 12 miles from London. Hope you and your family have a lovely holiday.

Best, Robert and Marion

Chapter 5

Galesburg, Thanksgiving, 1934

Fred led me upstairs to his study, a room furnished in dark woods and leathers. There were two chairs, one behind his large desk and one in a corner next to a reading lamp that was already lit.

"Please sit down," he said, pointing to the corner chair. He pushed the desk chair around the edge of the desk, as if wanting to indicate to me that he did not want any more barriers between us than potentially existed already. But before he sat down himself, he went to a small table that held several bottles and decanters. He poured us each a brandy.

"I think we may need this." He offered me a cigarette and we both sat smoking for a few moments. Finally he began our conversation.

"This week-end will be very busy for me and I'm afraid there won't be time for much serious talk before you have to go back on Sunday. I think we have some things to discuss, don't you?"

"Yes, sir. Judith and I had intended to have a discussion with both you and Mrs. Goldenshane. But perhaps it is better for you and me to speak first."

"Judith's Mother and I sense that you're a more than just one of Judith's university friends."

"I want to ask for her hand in marriage."

His head jerked back and for a moment he seemed to coil. Then he relaxed a bit. "I like it that you do not beat around the bush. Are you familiar with that phrase?"

I nodded. "Judith does not like such beating either, I've found."

He smiled. "And if I, that is we, give you her hand, as you so politely put it, do you plan to stay here or go back to Italy?"

"I promised my parents that I would return after one year. My Father is establishing a museum in Padua and I promised him I would be his partner. My promise would be reason enough to return, but I also feel it is my life's calling--- and Judith is as excited about this work as I am."

"Perhaps we'll discuss that later. But first there are several other issues we must face."

Since he had expressed a preference for not "beating around bushes" I dived immediately into what I had thought would be the primary concern.

"Do you object to my religion, Mr. Goldenshane?"

Fred paused for a minute, turning his head toward crowded bookcases that lined the south wall of his study. He slowly turned his head back toward me. "You know, I've asked myself that over and over—ever since Judith wrote that she wanted to invite you for Thanksgiving. It would undoubtedly be easier if you were Jewish. Ruth and Aaron would certainly prefer that. But I honestly think I don't care. I know I believe that, ah, passion, is not confined within religious boundaries."

He paused, sipped his brandy, and drew deeply on his cigarette. He took another drink and continued.

"No, what I care most about is that my children be loved, cherished, and protected. And that's the real issue isn't it-------protection?"

"You must know that I love and cherish Judith."

"Yes, yes." He gestured with his hand as if that topic need not be broached—or had already been covered sufficiently.

"Money will not be a problem, sir," I said.

"Yes, I've gathered that."

"I intend to earn some on my own by restoring and reproducing Renaissance masters. And the new museum might eventually provide a modest income. Mostly, however, we shall live off income from my grandfather's business. I already own a substantial interest in the trade and coffee companies. I shall inherit more. I do realize Americans worry about the Puritan work ethic."

79

His chuckle was more of a chortle. "We Jews have never conceded that a work ethic is the sole property of the pilgrims and their descendants. I won't even grant them that on Thanksgiving Day."

"No, of course not. I just want you to know that although I have never really had to work, I am a hard worker. I shall always take care of Judith."

Ah, Marco. I so meant what I said that evening. If I hadn't believed it, would I, could I have returned to Italy without Judith? Would she have allowed it? It's been years, and I still ask myself these questions nearly every day.

"But, my dear young man, it's not just care that I worry about. It is, as I said, protection. I fear that all the love and money in the world may not be able to protect my precious daughter if you insist on taking her with you to Europe next summer."

"I do understand your concern, Mr. Goldenshane. Since I first met Judith I have been thinking about what it will be like in Italy for her. I was never very interested in politics, I confess. But for the last two months I have been doing everything I can from this distance to follow what is going on, not just in my own country, but in the countries surrounding it. Please believe me---I would not have asked Judith to go to Padua with me if I did not think she would be safe."

Fred looked piercingly at me now. He shook his head, stood, picked up the decanter and walked over to fill my glass, then his, before returning to his chair. He lit another cigarette and offered me one, but I declined.

"Your family is rooted in Italy," he said. "Mine---and Ruth's---are essentially rootless. Both of our paternal grandfathers arrived in New York, but had no clear memories of where they started from, or when. One ancestor is said to have been carried as an infant from a village somewhere in Russia; another came from a town in Pomerania. We know little else. Most of our family was chased and hounded across Europe for years----centuries probably."

"With all due respect, sir, you seem to be doing very well now. I must say that I have been surprised at how well, given that unemployment in your country is well over fifty percent."

"As my wife said the other night, we have been very fortunate. Things are hard for most people in your country, too. But some professions and businesses----the coffee business, I presume----always seem to manage. Ruth's father became a successful surgeon in New York City. Mine turned his father's junk business into a group of jewelry stores. He sent me West to set up more. And I have, one here and one in Peoria. I'm also a partner with a cousin in a small loan company in Chicago."

"I too have cousins in business in Chicago."

"And you have been there long enough to know that Galesburg is much safer---precisely my reason for settling here. I thought that at last we could establish our roots and stay out of harm's way. Now Aaron wants to join the army and Judith wants to go away with you. Both of them will desert the haven I've created and end up in the very parts of the world that caused my ancestors such suffering and heartache."

I knew, Marco, how troubled he was. But it was only after I had become a father myself that I fully appreciated the depth of his feelings. I also know now, of course, that his fears for his children were mixed, not without guilt, and tempered

with some excitement about what their leaving might mean for
his own personal desires.

"But, sir. Italy is not Russia or Pomerania or, one has to say of course, Germany. This history of Jews in my country is quite different."

"You know all about it, I suppose?"

"No, of course not. But I have put some effort into learning more about it---for obvious reasons, I think."

"Well, I confess that I don't know much about Jews in Italy. I do know that I don't trust this Mussolini fellow."

"But sir, he has done a great deal to support Jewish projects; and as I've told Judith, he's had a Jewish mistress. There are Jewish professors, doctors, lawyers. There are even many Jews who are members of the Fascist party.

"There are fools in every religious group," Fred spit out. "But go on---tell me more about what you've learned."

I sensed that there was even more than Judith's and my future at stake in how successfully I laid this out. So I took a large swallow of brandy and a deep breath, and continued. I surprised myself at my readiness to give what amounted to a well-prepared class report.[1]

"There have been Jews in Italy since at least the time of the Diaspora when Titus forced them to leave Jerusalem. In

---

[1] Vera Auretto,"The Holocaust in Italy—A Curriculum Meeting the Challenge of Holocaust and Genocide"
1999, web source.
Susan Zuccotti, *The Italians and the Holocaust: Persecution, Rescue, and Survival,* New York: Basic Books, 1987.

fact, there have been Jews in Rome longer than in any other city outside the Holy Land."

"But you are not going to claim that they weren't persecuted there."

"No—only that it was somewhat better for them in Italy than in, say, Russia or Pomerania. Jews in the south of Italy did suffer exactly the sorts of harassment and expulsion under Ferdinand and Isabella as they did in other areas under Spanish domination. But they were allowed to flee to the north---and that, of course, is my part of the country.

"But wait a minute. I do know something about the history of the term "ghetto." I know that the first of these was in Venice---not far from Padua, if my geography is correct?" he said with some bitterness.

"I grant you that. In the 16th century the Pope did order Jews into their own neighborhoods where they were locked in from sunrise to sunset.

"And happy times did not exactly follow."

"I grant you that as well. Jews could not consort with Christians and they had to wear special hats and badges and they were falsely accused of all sorts of crimes. This went on more or less for three hundred years. But what's important for us is that it's been so much better for nearly a century now."

He looked almost eager to hear some good news, so I continued with a sense of something approaching excitement and optimism.

"In Savoy----and we're in the north now---there were enlightened leaders, ones whose efforts eventually led to Italian unification---admittedly with some reluctance on the part of the Venetian republic. Still, after unification, we did away with ghettos and Jews became full citizens. How else could Marconi have done the work that got him the Nobel Prize? Prominent Jews are found in every university and hospital and...."

"And vilified in the press. What about the Ponte Tresa affair? Weren't all Jews blamed for that?

"You mean those radicals who were arrested last spring for smuggling in anti-Fascist pamphlets? They were just stupid. I really don't think that activity is very significant. Those troublemakers weren't even all Jewish---and only a handful of newspapers reacted so irrationally. Most Italians dismissed the whole thing almost immediately----if they heard about it at all."

Fred stood and paced for a while. I thought it best to keep quiet. He stopped at a window that gazed out over the backyard toward the Thomas house. I could heard the faint sound of rubber tires passing over Galesburg's brick streets. Undoubtedly my memory of what happened next has been affected by what happened the following summer. But I do think my recollection is fairly accurate. Still looking out of the window, he pulled his shoulders back, and then raised and lowered his fists in front of him---as if to emphasize a point or decision. He turned back to me quickly, nodded and said, "All right, Enrico. I shall not stand in your way."

I leaped to my feet. "Oh, thank you, thank you, Mr. Goldenshane."

"But, I warn you," he held up one hand and cautioned, "It will not be pleasant---and that's putting it mildly---to break the news to Ruth. And Aaron will certain not be happy to have his sister marry a gentile."

He offered me his hand to shake and then actually, if tentatively and awkwardly, embraced me. Together we moved toward the door of his study.

"One more thing," Fred stopped me by gently putting his arm on my elbow. "I do have a request. I would like you and Judith to come to the store tomorrow so that I can let her choose her engagement ring from my special stock."

I knew that there was undoubtedly at least one of my Chicago cousins who would be offended because I had not allowed him to let a friend of a friend of a friend give me a bargain on a ring. But it was so easy now to honor this request.

"Of course. It will be our pleasure."

Then he led me out of the room and back down to the living room where the scene was as I had left it---except that all of the players were slightly more rigid. I simply nodded at Judith, hoping to sustain the composition. But she jumped to her feet and hugged first me, then her father.

"No," Ruth whispered. Then, more and more loudly, "No, No, No."

"This will be a disaster," Aaron said sadly.

"Perhaps," said Fred. "But I have given Enrico permission to marry Judith if that is what she wants."

"Oh, Daddy, you know it is. I have never wanted anything this much."

If I had expected histrionics, I was wrong. Ruth simply stood up and went to the dining room where I heard first the sound of ice then liquid being added to her glass. Without a word, she passed us and slowly mounted the steps.

"Surely you won't let them go to Europe, Dad?" Aaron pleaded.

"That is not up to me. Judith will make that decision with her husband."

"But that's insane." He turned to me. "Stay here a few years at least and see what happens. You might be able to get a job at Knox. At least stay in Chicago."

"We are going to Padua," Judith said vigorously. "I am going to be his Jewish bride. If things go badly, we can always come back."

"You won't be free to move about. Those people are monsters. They...."

"That's enough, Aaron," Fred said. "It's late. Enrico has convinced me that he has thought these things through. There will be time tomorrow for you to discuss it with him---and Judith, of course. I think you and I should let the couple have some time alone now."

Aaron surprisingly did not continue his tirade. But, as he went to the stairs he did turn to me. "I want you to promise me that you will talk to me about this tomorrow."

"Of course. I know I owe you that," I responded.

Judith and I sat on the couch and watched the fire die down and talked about a June wedding in Galesburg and a July steamship honeymoon. We kept our exuberance and passion sufficiently quiet so as not to disturb those upstairs any more than we had already disturbed them that evening. Only a master painter could have captured this couple in that setting in such a way that their happiness would be tinted with concern.

Later that night, I had trouble sleeping, and at one point rose to look out my bedroom window---one that looked on the same scene that Fred had seen earlier from his study. A light had been left burning on one corner of the garage, and to my considerable surprise I saw Fred walk from the house into the garage. I stood watching for a while, but did not see him come out. I felt no little guilt at the fact that I had disturbed his sleep and wondered whether anyone in that home had found rest.

86

I was surprised again when I went down to the kitchen the next morning and found Ruth already up and, with Ruby's help, putting things away. Ruby smiled at me encouragingly; it was clear that she had heard something of what had happened the previous evening.

"I wonder if I could have a word in private, Mrs. Goldenshane," I said.

She put down the silver platter she was buffing and walked into the living room without saying anything. I followed her into the room and waited for her to turn toward me. But she continued to stand facing away from me.

I cleared me throat and said, "Mrs. Goldenshane, I am sorry that we have upset you. I want you to know how deeply I wish that that had not been necessary. I also realize that it will be difficult for you to have me in your home now. If it will make things easier, I can return to Chicago on the train today."

Now she turned and looked at me with a combination of scorn and condescension. "You were invited to be a guest in my home until Sunday. That arrangement will stand."

I did not know whether I should thank her or not, but was saved from having to make that choice by Aaron's coming downstairs and into the room.

"Enrico has just offered to return to Chicago today, Aaron. I have told him that he will stay until Sunday as planned. I do hope you will have the power to talk some sense into him and your sister. Your Father seems to have failed in that respect." And without further ado, she returned to the kitchen.

"There's doughnut shop a couple of blocks from here. Why don't we go there for our breakfast and leave Mother and Ruby to their work. Judith is upstairs---she asked me to tell you that she's already eaten and is going over to visit with Violet. She should be back when we return."

I was glad to be able to get out of the house and away from Ruth for a while and so agreed, even though I was not eager to confront what I knew would be Aaron's hard line.

Snow flurries were beginning to fall and the wind was sharp. "We could take the car," Aaron said, "but the shop is close and I think we could both use some fresh air." I agreed and we walked briskly toward Main Street. In an effort to forestall the inevitable conversation, I apologized to Aaron, as I had to Ruth, for causing discomfort in their lives.

"Your Father did try to dissuade me. And I know I have caused him distress as well. I happened to look out my window, and I saw him walk to the garage in the middle of the night. Clearly he was not sleeping well."

Aaron's head turned with a jerk in my direction. "What time?"

"I'm afraid I'm not sure. Does he have a workshop out there?"

"Yes, yes. And he often takes walks late at night. He worries about us and the business and Mother, of course."

I looked questioningly at him.

"Surely you've noticed that Mother's a......" He paused and started his sentence again. "Surely you've noticed that Mother drinks."

"Well, all of us do," I responded.

"Not like she does. She has a serious problem. Often she falls asleep on the couch and Ruby has to take her upstairs when she arrives in the morning. It's one of the reasons I can't understand why Father has agreed to let this wedding take place. It will only make things worse for Mom."

"Then I'm even sorrier. Judith had not said anything to me about this."

"Well, she doesn't like to think about it-----I guess she just hopes if she doesn't talk about it, it will go away. But it won't. Not without a lot of help. Mother compensates by trying to keep everything in her environment under the strictest control when she's sober. But it's all a fake."

Aaron's tone was one of profound bitterness.

We walked in silence the rest of the short distance to a corner where a low white building with parking spaces on two sides housed a drugstore and soda fountain. Condensation on the windows made it impossible to see out from our table, but we had not come for the view. The one other customer sat at a long counter made of marble that matched the tops of the tables. An aging waitress brought us coffee in large white mugs and two plates of sugared doughnuts. A strange looking machine stood against the wall not far from our table; it seemed to be some sort of peanut roasting device. It gave off an earthy odor that mingled with the smell of weak coffee and sugary dough. The chairs on which we sat where made of wrought iron painted an unpleasant shade of pink and their appearance was not made up for by comfort. All in all, this was not a breakfast that I would like to repeat.

"Perhaps I could begin by repeating some of what I said to your Father last night."

Aaron nodded and I gave essentially the same speech concerning my optimism about Judith's future in Italy as I had delivered Thanksgiving evening.

"I do know there are hard times ahead, but I would not take Judith to Italy if I did not believe we will be all right," I concluded.

"There is going to be a war and that ass Mussolini will not keep Italy out of it and if you think otherwise, you're a fool."

"You can't be sure there will be a war."

"I'm sure enough that I have already decided to join the Army Air Force. I'd do it today, but I've promised Dad that I'll wait until I graduate. That's another reason I was hoping Judith would come back to Galesburg---she could help Mom and Dad when I leave."

"Isn't that rather selfish of you?"

Aaron looked at the peanut machine. His head rotated ever so slightly as he watched a large tray in the middle piled with assorted nuts turn round and round under a heating lamp. "Yes. But I said 'hoping'. In my heart I knew she probably wouldn't come back here after she finishes at the U of C. But she doesn't have to leave the country."

"She wants to. Or rather, she wants to be with me, which comes down to the same thing. And if you join the Army you'll probably be leaving the country as well. What's the difference?"

"I'll be trying to protect the safety and freedom that my Father and men like him have worked so hard for in this country." Then his voice became less pompous. "You'll be taking my sister back to the very places where it's been taken away from us."

"But I've told you that Italy is different."

"Even if it is, and I don't really buy that, Italy is a peninsula, not an island. There's no way it won't be caught up.

And you two with it. I like you, Enrico, I really do. But you are naïve and so blinded by your love that you aren't facing reality. And, as much as I adore my sister, she is so much in love with living that she has never really faced reality---even when it's in her own backyard."

It seemed to me that Aaron thought he had gone too far. He shook his head, spread his fingers out on the cool marble, and took a deep breath.

"But I know I am not going to convince either one of you to give up this folly. So I will try to look on the bright side---wherever that is---and help us all get through this without creating too much havoc."

"You mean you'll even help us with your Mother's misgivings?"

He laughed. "Misgivings, missteps, mis-everything. I'll pretend I think all will be well---and pray that I don't live to say, 'I told you so.'"

I wish his prayers had been answered, Marco.

When we returned to the Goldenshane house, Ruth and Judith were sitting next to each other on the couch. Both had been crying, but now they sat holding hands. Someone, Ruby probably, had lit the fire but, in spite of the darkness of the day outside, no one had turned on any of the lights. The crackling and hissing of the logs provided a quiet percussive accompaniment to the lights and shadows that danced across the carpet and the women's bodies. A chiascuro concentrated attention on their beautiful faces. I found it almost impossible to keep from crying myself. Some sort of understanding, the kind that only mothers and daughters, I think, can attain had been reached between them. I, however, was never to be part of that particular circle. While Judith looked lovingly at me,

Ruth's expression was one of anger and hatred. But even this she carried off with her controlled civility. She stroked Judith's unruly hair in a motion that conveyed unhappy recognition of the fact that neither these tresses nor this situation was one that she could dominate. She stood up and with both hands made sure that her own snood was in place.

"The parade begins at 2. I think we should see to lunch if we are going to get to the store on time."

"Enrico and I are going to The Coffee Corner for lunch. I've been promising him their blue plate special for weeks. Why don't you both come too?"

Aaron shook his head. "Sorry, that would be fun. But I promised Dad I'd see to the store while he and his clerks ride down Main Street urging people to forget their troubles and buy as many baubles as possible between now and the end of December."

"Oh, God, Aaron, just say the word---it's Christmas."

"Now, children," Ruth managed to smile. "Thank you for asking me to join you, but I'm want to bathe before the parade. I probably won't have time before we leave for dinner."

Instead of going upstairs, she went into the kitchen and we heard what I now realized was the all too familiar sound of ice being dropped into a glass. Aaron looked at Judith and shrugged. Judith just looked down briefly and then grabbed my arm.

"Come on, let's go have the thirty-three cent hamburger, French fries, and coke. The best you'll ever taste."

"At least for the price," Aaron added.

I would like to attend a Santa Claus parade in Galesburg now that times are prosperous. The insulation that the University of Chicago and Goldenshane's way of living had provided me along with the success of my Italian family both in the US and Italy, had not prepared me for this event. It was pitiable. The local merchants had made a valiant attempt to display some optimism. The color guard carried their flags with evident pride. But there were no floats. A few cars with signs advertising everything from jewelry to hardware moved slowly down Main Street, interspersed with a few straggly bands, some troops of Scouts, a clown or two, two groups of men from local lodges, a quartet of riders on horseback, and three or four tractors. The culmination was a seedily dressed Santa riding on a flatbed pulled by Belgian work horse decorated with two ribbons and a few bells. I could not help comparing this scene with one of the Renaissance processions painted by Gozzoli or Bellini. Where were the banners? Where were the fifes and drums? When would we hear the cymbals?

But the bleakest thing about the parade was the crowd. The snow flurries had stopped and a weak sun was trying to make an appearance, but the wind had not diminished and the temperature had fallen since my walk with Aaron. Judith and her Mother, who had joined us in front of the family store, were dressed warmly in fur coats, but this was in sharp contrast to most of the spectators. Men, women, and children shivered under worn, thin coats inadequate for the cold. Even reddened cheeks could not conceal an unhealthy pallor. How, I wondered did they have the energy to cheer the musicians and animals and shopkeepers? Surely, no matter what hard times faced Judith and me in Italy, it would be better than this. And I vowed we would never be poor.

Thoughts of poverty were quickly dispelled when, after the parade, Judith's Father led us into the backroom of his store. He closed the door, signaling to Ruth and Aaron that this was to be a private affair between us. He opened a safe and, on a purple velvet cloth, displayed a score of rings set with a variety of large stones---mostly solitary diamonds, but some diamonds accompanied by rubies or emeralds or sapphires.

"I've never seen these, Daddy," Judith exclaimed.

"No, I don't even show them to my wealthiest customers. I've collected them from several countries. I think of them as a kind of ultimate insurance policy."

He touched several---fondled them really---and gazed upon them much as I would gaze at my favorite paintings.

"Do you see one that you like?" he asked his daughter.

"I want you to choose---or at least tell me which one you think I should want."

Her father laughed. "I have never known you to let someone else tell you what to want." He took several moments and then pointed to a large diamond flanked on its sides by two small emeralds. "This is not the most expensive, but it has always been my favorite. I got it in Antwerp from one of my favorite dealers."

"It is truly beautiful, sir," I said.

"You think it's okay?" Judith asked me. Like her father, I was surprised that she was giving over this decision to another.

"I think it is wonderful. And I think we will always appreciate that it is your Father's favorite."

Fred looked at me with gratitude, and thanked me with slight nod and eyes that brimmed with tears. He and Judith put their arms around each other, and once again I recognized a deep bond different from my own with Judith, but nonetheless profound. When they released one another, Fred gestured toward the ring and I picked it up.

"I'll leave you alone," he said as he returned the remaining jewels to his safe.

I placed the ring on Judith's finger. It was a perfect fit, as I somehow knew it would be. I expected her to make some joke, about the ring's size, or ways it would keep the wolf from our door. But she simply took my hand in her ring hand and held the gems up to my mouth.

"Let's both kiss the ring and promise that we shall always be this happy."

"A very easy promise for me to make, my darling."

The rest of the weekend was, to my great relief, fairly uneventful. We ate Friday evening, as planned, at the Galesburg Club where the beautiful and elegant Violet cordially led us to our table. Judith showed her the new ring. Violet smiled. "It is lovely. I confess that Ruby already told me something like this was afoot." She shook hands with Fred and Ruth and kissed Aaron and Judith and, to my surprise, kissed me as well, before walking off to seat more diners.

Conversation was forced, but not unpleasant. We stuck to topics that were safe. My own thoughts shifted frequently to comparisons between the diners here and the people I had seen on the sidewalks of Main Street that afternoon, but I did not speak these thoughts. I was more attentive than I had been to Ruth's steady drinking. Aaron was tense, but Fred strangely relaxed. From time to time I saw Violet watching our table, but this did not seem unusual, given that she must be aware of the turmoil that was so close to the surface both at this table in her dining room and in the house just across a lawn from her home.

Saturday Judith and I spent most of the day in the Knox College's Seymour Library studying for exams that would begin a week after we returned to our own campus. Most of the students at Knox could not afford to travel home for Thanksgiving---indeed this college had decided to have classes on Friday since everyone was around. Thus Seymour Library was crowded. We sat in a large reading room furnished with heavy oaken chairs and tables where green shaded lamps shed soft light on our texts. Life-sized, competently executed but uninterestingly painted portraits of bearded men alternated with glass-fronted bookcases along the walls. A kind of clerestory was created by windows that consisted of small diamonds of leaded glass.

The college, Aaron had told me as we had walked to campus that morning, had been founded by abolitionists from New York and although there was no longer any direct connection to a particular Protestant sect, it retained a strong moral core. I sensed this in the silence that embraced the students seriously bent over books and carefully making entries into their notebooks. What would it be like to be a part of this, I wondered. Was Aaron right---should I try to get a job teaching art in this community? In spite of the harshness I had witnessed in yesterday's parade crowd, wouldn't it be safer to stay here with Judith?

But then, as I reached into my briefcase for another notebook, a photograph fell out on the table. It was a picture of the Raphael *Mother and Child* that I had been hired to reproduce for Billy Beauchamp's father. No matter how safe, did I really want to live in this town where I would not be in touch with Raphael and Crivelli and Mantegna and da Vinci? In Italy Judith's spirit would flourish. Here wouldn't she wither— worse yet become like her Mother? In Padova we could match our passion to that of great masters, delight in ravioli and risotto instead of hamburgers and French fries. Aaron was right, they had been very good-----but for the price. Surely, I decided, the price of living here would be too high. How was I to know how great the price would be for taking Judith away?

Front. Attributed to Carlo Crivelli, 1477? St. George and the Dragon, Hermitage Museum,Leningrad

Back: *June 16*

Dear Dr. Starr, Should St. George really be in a landscape with mountains---and snow-covered ones at that? This dragon also looks strangely meek. I don't believe for a moment that CC did it. Certainly not in '77. Surely you agree.

I saw BB in Lisbon. We both send our warmest regards,

Kathy

Chapter 6

Minnesota, December, 1934

Judith was tempted to tell her parents that she was not coming to Galesburg for the winter break. She knew how tense it would be and, of course, preferred the prospect of spending the weeks with me. But I would be busy; and we hoped that she could improve relations with Ruth somewhat by perhaps infecting her Mother with some of Judith's enthusiasm for planning our June wedding. We compensated by arranging for her to come North for the New Year holidays. We arranged that Judith would come by train to Minneapolis and that an old Minneapolis friend of Billy's would drive her join us for a small party on New Year's Eve.

Billy Beauchamp had explained to me that his father had sent the Raphael he wanted copied to his retreat on a lake seventy or so kilometers north of Minneapolis so that I could do my work *in situ*, as it were. We would spend two nights in the city and then drive to the lake. He regretted that he would have to leave me there alone for a few days while he celebrated the actual Christmas days with his family, but I insisted that I would be too busy to require company. Besides, I was to be paid my biggest fee yet, and that was sufficient solace.

Examinations finished on December 15 and from Union Station Judith went southwest and Billy and I northwest. I knew that Billy's family was wealthy. His father and uncle owned department stores in Minneapolis and St. Paul, and from mutual friends I had heard that "Beauchamp's" was something of a household word in The Twin Cities, as they were called. Many people had taken to just calling the stores "Bo's"—exhibiting that American propensity to subtract rather than add syllables to oft used words, a habit I never really became accustomed to.

I had never been to the Scandinavian countries, but accepted the theory that immigrants from that part of Europe had found in the northern Midwestern landscape a familiarity that seemed to welcome them--abundant lakes, hardy trees, and soil that responded to hard work. Most years by December the ground was already covered with several inches of snow, and this year was no exception. The Beauchamp mansion sat on one of the city's lakes (now frozen, of course) not too far from the city center---or as Americans say, the "downtown." This home was even larger than the Goldenshane's and even more lavishly furnished and appointed---though with less of the controlled and tight composition that characterized Ruth's domain.

Theodore and Margaret Beauchamp were avid travelers, and treasures from around the world abundantly graced walls, shelves, and niches. I was immediately sorry that I would have so little time to spend in this home scrutinizing the

99

beautiful objects. Of course, I instantly began imagining how I would rearrange things. I had, in Italy, visited some very fine estates, and our own villa was not lacking in fine adornments, but never had I seen such a large collection of original European masters---and the Beauchamps mixed them unselfconciously with more contemporary European works, paintings by American artists (most of whom I was not familiar with), and a varied assortment of Asian silk screens, ceramics, and statues that represented several cultures and dynasties.

Our train---The Empire Builder, as the railroad magnates dubbed it with characteristic American "modesty"---did not arrive in Minneapolis until almost midnight, and as Billy and I were away from the house touring the cities the next day, I did not meet his parents and siblings, Teddy and Sally, until cocktails were served before dinner the next evening. Billy had told me to bring evening clothes, as his parents would dress for a guest (and we intended to dress on New Year's Eve).The group assembled in the large living room (not to be confused with the enormous formal drawing room adjoining it) was as stylish as that which had gathered for the Goldenshane's Thanksgiving. And as impressive as the gowns Judith and her Mother had been, the Beauchamp's business gave them direct access to the later and more elegant fashions. These women would have fitted into any drawing room that I had seen in Rome or Venice. Margaret wore a brown velvet evening dress with a fitted top and a skirt than did not flair sufficiently to conceal widening hips. Rows of braided bands crossed at her neckline and made an inverted v-shape across her bosom. At the top of this upside-down vee was a large diamond brooch. Both women had elaborate, tightly curled coiffures---one in black streaked with gray, the other in light brown. Sally was in a shade of cyan that would have matched the mineral I was taking with me to the cabin in order to prepare the paint for the Virgin's tunic. Most Renaissance painters chose to depict Mary in the garb of their day, and Sally's dress would certainly have been appropriate to the Queen of Heaven. Long crepe sleeves billowed from a vee necked bodice (clearly this was the neckline in fashion) and a large flower made from velvet of a slightly darker blue marked the area between her ample breasts, attention to which was further drawn by a large diamond surrounded by pearls that hung from a blue velvet ribbon. Her hips would probably broaden as she approached her Mother's age, but for now her skirt flowed elegantly in soft drapes to the floor.

As I shook hands with Mr. Beauchamp he said softly to me, "Let's wait until after dinner to discuss our project, okay?" Then, more loudly, "I hope everyone is ready for one of my special Manhattans." He poured the dark amber liquid from an engraved silver shaker (engraved with rather too convoluted calligraphy, I thought) into matching stemware that had already been provided with two bright red cherries. Billy distributed the drinks and I had the distinct feeling that I was a member of a party in one of the John Singer Sargent family groups that Billy and I had seen in the Minneapolis Institute of Arts that afternoon.

As if she had peered into my mind and seen the image for herself, Mrs. Beauchamp said, "What did your think of our little museum, Enrico?"

"If I may say so, Mrs. Beauchamp, I was nearly as impressed with its collection as I have been with your own."

I had said exactly the right thing. Both Mother and Father beamed with pride and pleasure.

"Thank you," she said. "But I'm afraid that some of our best pieces have been temporarily put away to make room for our holiday decorations. I particularly would have like you to see our Raphael."

Billy was about to speak, but Mr. Beauchamp forestalled him by quickly saying, "Another time, I hope."

Sensing that his father did not want to discuss the Raphael project, Billy instead joked, "But Enrico finds both our collection and the MIA's lacking, Mother. There are no Crivelli's in either."

"Don't think I know that one. Should we get one?" Theodore asked.

This allowed me to say a bit about my old friend and as drinks were refreshed the conversation moved easily across aesthetic genres and milieus. Teddy and Sally politely contributed from time to time, but clearly hoped that the conversation would veer eventually to other topics. It did; particularly when, after we had taken our places at the large dining room table, Teddy informed me with pride that all of the china and glassware we were using could be purchased at "Bo's." I was able to make appropriately complimentary remarks about the patterns and delicacy and hence made a friend of Teddy for life. Sally was more reserved and seemed satisfied simply to respond when it was called for. Mostly she appeared intent on checking from time to time in one of the many reflective surfaces offered up by the table and mirrored room that her hair and dress duly complimented her skin in the candlelight.

After the meal, Theodore Beauchamp suggested that he and I retire to the library for port and cigars. Teddy and Sally left to attend holiday parties on their own, and Billy accompanied his mother back to the living room. If Margaret was surprised that her husband had taken me off on my own, she did not show it. Mostly she looked pleased to have her son to herself for a while.

What Theodore had referred to as "the library" was precisely that. A large rectangle, it was lined on all four walls with floor to ceiling bookcases. French doors led to a porch on the west side and provided the only natural light---though of course now there was only northern winter darkness coming through them. There were an enormous number of books on the shelves, but the spaces were also laden with objets d'art. Again I felt a strong urge to rearrange things. The room was furnished with several pieces of what I had come to recognize as American Craftsman work—chairs and tables and desks and two sideboards fit into niches in the shelves. Floor lamps and chandeliers with stained glass panels provided warm illumination. I had only recently been introduced to the style by one of my professors at the U of C who was an enthusiast. I felt a bit reluctant to appear to be more of an expert about it than I actually was. Still, I took the risk.

"Are some of these pieces genuine Stickley's?" I asked.

"By Jove, you are good!" Theodore exclaimed, as he poured us each a glass of port from a Waterford decanter on one of the sideboards. "Billy said you knew everything about art. Yes, Gustave Stickley actually came here himself to decorate the room. Some of the things, of course, were also done by his brothers. Do you like it?" He lit a cigar, but I opted for one of my own cigarettes.

"May I be completely honest, sir?"

"I never want you to be anything else."

What a lie this turned out to be, Marco!

"I find the strong vertical and horizontal lines a little too harsh. I do like the materials---the oaks and leathers and metals—especially the brass and copper hinges and handles on the sideboards. And of course I admire the workmanship. But my eyes have always favored the Renaissance and it's all a little heavy and, well, too simple, I suppose for my taste."

103

"Good God, you aren't going to like the cabin, then. Stickley did that whole thing for me."

"Oh, please, Mr. Beauchamp, don't misunderstand me. I certainly don't dislike this style. I do appreciate originality and genius when I see it. Who knows, in a few weeks, I may actually come to admire it as you obviously do."

"Well, luckily it's popular with my customers---though mostly, of course, I have to sell cheaper imitations. I can't tell you how many of these library tables we sold last year. I'm sure Teddy could give you the figures."

"Yes, I'm sure he could, sir. He is obviously an accomplished businessman."

"Thank God we have one in the family. Not that I don't respect what Billy is doing. He'll be a real asset, too. He'll be able to organize our collections and help me with some of my other, ah, enterprises."

"I feel very fortunate to have met your son, sir."

"Good. But now, let's get to our own business. My Raphael is at the cabin. You've seen the photograph of it."

I nodded.

"So you know its round and fairly small. I've arranged for there to be several cartons of eggs in the refrigerator. That's for the tempura paint you'll be mixing, I gather?"

"Yes, sir. I've brought the pigments with me, but of course I was afraid eggs would break or freeze if I tried to bring those from Chicago. I know my expenses are to be taken out of the fee you're paying me, so be sure to keep track of what the eggs cost."

"Not a big deal," he replied. "Billy also had me order the wooden panel you requested." He chuckled. "I had a little fun with the lumberman about that. I had a long work table put up, and I've had an easel-like thing put up in a room facing north, as you told him. Why is that, by the way?"

"Northern light doesn't play the kinds of tricks that the brighter light from the south can. That probably wouldn't be much of a problem in Minnesota winters anyway, but it's always a good idea to be as careful as possible."

"I agree with you there. Okay, so I've also had plenty of floor lamps brought in and feel free to move any of the furniture in the room around as you need to. It's in a small bedroom on the second floor. If you want the bed or anything else big moved out of the way, just asked Olaf to take care of it."

"Who is Olaf, sir?"

"He and his wife, Christina, are the caretakers who live down the road from our place. They'll come by every day to stoke the furnace and clean and bring you whatever you need in the way of groceries. They've worked for us for years---Billy's known them since he was a child. They know you're going to be there painting---I'd rather you didn't discuss the exact nature of the project with them, however. Or with anybody else for that matter."

I looked inquiringly at him.

"Oh, it's a bit of a secret---even Margaret doesn't know. Billy knows what you're doing, of course, but he's the only one." He looked a bit concerned. "Have you told anyone about it?"

"Why, my fiancé---and her parents know that I am up here doing a reproduction, though I don't think they know what it's of."

He seemed relieved, but I saw no reason for this, so thought I might be misinterpreting his expression, particularly as he continued.

"Nothing to worry about. I'm having this copy made for my sister. She lives in Boston and always raves about it when she visits. I want it to give it to her for her birthday in the spring. I don't want Margaret to know about it because I'm afraid she'll let the cat out of the bag before then. She thinks you and Billy are going to work on a class project."

"I must have misunderstood Billy. I thought the reproduction was to remain at your lodge. However, I hope it will turn out to be a lovely gift, Mr. Beauchamp."

"Yes, yes. Will you have time to complete the work? Billy said you have to be back in Chicago in just three weeks?"

"Oh, yes, I think so, especially if I decline your kind invitation to come back here on Christmas day. It will take a few days to prepare the wood panel---but I've brought the materials for sanding and making the gesso. Billy will help me mix the paints. I think he's actually looking forward to that."

"Excellent, a little manual labor will be good for him."

"And we're lucky that Raphael was still using an egg-based paint rather than oils when he painted this Madonna. It will dry faster. I assume I'm to leave the reproduction at the cabin? Will you be able to come to see if you approve it before I return to Chicago."

"I'll try. You got the advance I sent to Billy?"

"Yes."

"And I'll give you the rest of the payment when I come up to the cabin---eggs and panel deducted," he smiled. "Or if I don't make it, I'll have Billy pay you. Cash will be all right? And the amount we agreed on is satisfactory?"

"More than generous. And cash is fine."

We stood and shook hands.

"But one more thing, sir. I just can't resist. I hope you won't be offended if I make a suggestion."

Theodore's head moved up and to the right. "What is it, young man?" He clearly had thought this conversation was over.

"That small Italian miniature---15th century, I think---next to the dictionary. I think it would better on the shelf below."

Beauchamp laughed heartily. "Suit yourself----feel free to move anything else about. Not the furniture, of course. Stickley would have a fit. We'll see you in the living room."

I busied myself placing and re-placing several objects and was deep in concentration when Billy came into the library.

"Oh, God, what are you doing? Don't you ever get tired of arranging other people's spaces?" I had, of course, been given full license to arrange and rearrange Billy's Chicago apartment. "Give it a rest, and see who's come to pay his respects."

I turned and beheld the most handsome man I had ever seen standing close to Billy in the doorway. The light from the hall curiously had sketched what can only be described as a halo around his head. But from his stance—one hand resting against the door frame, the opposite hip thrust out in contrapposto-- and the angle of that beautiful head, I knew at once that this was no saint.

107

"Enrico, I would like to introduce you to the person who has been my closest friend since third grade---Jimmy Albright."

Jimmy walked across the room to the area where I had just moved a small Chinese Bodhisattva so that it could be closer to a slightly larger bronze statue of Siddhartha. Jimmy was nearly two meters tall and walked with his feet slightly turned out. The event that he had come from, or was going to, had, like our dinner, required formal dress. But that he had a sense of flair was immediately apparent from the bright paisley cummerbund that was visible under his open tuxedo jacket. His complexion was nearly as dark as mine, but his eyes were deep aquamarine. His face was narrow, his features nearly sharp, with just the touch of the asymmetry that true beauty requires. His dark black hair was longish, but perfectly combed and his eyebrows full and faintly peaked. He was clean-shaven, but a hint of beard shadowed the line of his delicately pointed chin.

"Billy has told me all about you," he said, shaking my hand firmly, and holding it just a moment longer than one normally expects. "But I understand he has kept me as a complete surprise for you. One of his secrets, I expect."

"It's a pleasure to meet you," I replied. "I hadn't realized Billy was secretive."

"Oh, I would guess you have a lot to learn up here on the tundra."

"For God's sake, behave yourself, Jimmy. Otherwise Enrico won't trust you to drive Judith up for our New Year's Eve gala."

Jimmy smiled and reached for a peach from a bowl of fruit on one of the nearby library tables. Holding it in both hands, he smelled it and sighed, "Perfect---as always at Chez Bo. Wherever does he find peaches at this time of year?" He picked up a small knife and began to peel it.

And then I realized what he reminded me of—Carravagio's painting of a young man peeling fruit. It was not so much that Jimmy looked like that young man. Jimmy had ten years on the boy and his face was less full and more leathery. Furthermore, the young man's shirt is open, exposing a breathtakingly lovely, smooth chest. He gives full attention, loving attention really, to his task. One doesn't see him actually eat the fruit, of course, but one knows that he will taste it and concentrate fully on the aroma, the sweetness, the texture. The mere fact that he is peeling this fruit rather than just chomping on it the way most teen age boys would gives the viewer an entry into his life and character. The upshot is that, as with so many of Carravagio's works, one is presented with pure and intense sensuality. And that is what Jimmy was providing us in this room devoted to learning and reflection. It was as if reason and sensuality were in a vivid, but certainly not wholly unhappy, debate.

"Anyone want some of this?" Jimmy asked.

"No, thank you. And get on with it if you're actually going to eat it. We're are terribly late already," Billy said. "Jimmy and I are going to a party, Enrico. You're welcome to come along if you'd like. Though perhaps you'd rather stay here and continue restaging things."

The fact that he gave me this option without previously mentioning the party, suggested to me that Billy wanted me to decline his invitation.

"Thank you, I'm sure it will be a splendid affair, but since we plan to leave early in the morning I'd probably better see to some preparations here."

That was a lie---I could do no preparations before we got to the cabin that I had not already done. And Billy knew that it was a lie and that I knew he would know that it was a lie. But he smiled with gratitude and appreciation for my perceptiveness. For Billy also knew that I had just discovered about him something that he wasn't certain, until that moment, he wanted to share. I understood now why Billy, a very good looking man in his right, had not found his own Judith. His apartment in Chicago was often full of friends, but there was no steady girl friend. Now I realized that if he had not found his Judith, he had found his Jimmy.

"A wise choice, old man," Jimmy also smiled at me. "It will undoubtedly turn out to be just some boring cacophony."

"A cacophony?" I asked. "I'm afraid that I don't know that word. You must remember that I am not a native speaker of your tongue." I managed to emphasize the word tongue sufficiently to allow for the possibility of ambiguous reference.

"Jimmy likes to use words that no one knows the meaning of. I think he spends hours each day looking them up so that he can impress people or make fools of us."

"Not at all. I do it so that I can keep the language alive, though I confess that it does help to have an adequate vocabulary when one competes with other egos in the laboratory." He gave this last word its English pronunciation. "It makes everyone there think that I'm not just better than they are at the microscope but everywhere else as well."

"The laboratory?" I imitated his pronunciation.

"Jimmy is finishing medical school at Yale."

"Lots of classes in human anatomy, naturally," Jimmy added with a grin.

"Now he'll never let you drive Judith to the cabin," Billy warned.

"No, no, I think she'll be quite safe. But you still have not told me what a cacophony is."

"Ah, good---you persevere. A cacophony is a harsh, discordant noise. Tonight's is to be provided by a counter-tenor doing Christmas carols. I have already decided that I will have to take a piss during Silent Night."

We all laughed.

"But I promise you that we shall not do anything cacophonous on New Year's Eve. All will be harmoniously scintillating. Need help with either of those words?"

Billy walked to the table and grabbed Jimmy's arm. "Okay, that's enough. Let's go before you've completely alienated Enrico. I assure you that Jimmy is not as difficult as he likes to appear. I'll make sure he's better behaved at the cabin."

"Not at all. I look forward to our *scintillante* time together." I felt it was necessary to show Jimmy that I, too, knew words over two syllables long and that there were Italian matches for his extravagant English.

Jimmy walked over to me and patted my arm. His manner became warm and charming. "You are a good guy. Billy was right about you. I look forward to seeing in the New Year with you and your lady."

He put his arm around Billy's shoulders and they walked to the door of the library. He dropped his arm and turned around, his manner returning to the lascivious posturing that I learned he could turn on and off like a water faucet.

"Don't be too hysterical about getting an early start in the morning. I expect Billy Bo will need his beauty sleep after our soiree."

I myself slept fitfully. As I had in Galesburg, at one point I got out of bed and went to the window of my room. The guest

111

room Billy had given me faced out onto the frozen lake across the street from their home. A single street light in front of the house next door shed enough light for me to see across a shallow, snow-covered expanse to the ice. Through scattered evergreens and bare deciduous trees (Jimmy's focus on language made me rather uncomfortably aware of the fact that I did not know the English name of a single one of these trees.) I could see that someone had shoveled a large area to create a skating rink and farther down the shore I could just make out what must have been some sort of warming hut. I wondered how an artist might solve the problem of depicting this wintry landscape. He could not have used white, for a pale moon and the yellowish streetlamp produced an uncanny mix of grays and browns and ecrus and ocher's and even deep olives. I was trying to locate even more colors in the scene when a black car pulled up in front of Chez Bo, as Jimmy had called it. I could not identify the make of the car, but I could, again thanks to the street lamp, see two men in the front. A cigarette lighter flashed, and I saw that it was, as I had already guessed, Billy and Jimmy returning from their evening out. After several minutes, Billy got out of the car and started up the sidewalk. About halfway to the house, he turned and blew a kiss toward the car. I could not see his face, but I knew from his walk that this was a happy man.

In spite of Billy's late return home and my restless night, we did manage to get an early start after a hearty breakfast. "There no place really to stop along the way so eat up," Theodore urged us. Two uniformed servants placed steaming dishes on a buffet under a striking Canaletto of Venice that made me a bit homesick---especially as this was my first time away from home at Christmas time. Freshly squeezed orange juice was served in crystal tumblers and hot, but, as usual inferior, American coffee in Chinese porcelain mugs. Theodore---he was the only other family member dining with us---put down the newspaper that he had been reading.

"I have to get to the store. Busy, busy days these----
Thank God. We're doing better this year than we have since
The Crash. I hope you boys enjoy yourselves---I don't expect all
work and no play for you young ones. And I'll definitely try to
come up before you leave. I hear Jimmy Albright will be with
you and Enrico's girl friend for New Year's. His father and I may
go up there ourselves after the January White Sales."

He walked around the table to my chair and I rose to
shake his hand. "Thank you for this opportunity, Mr.
Beauchamp."

"You are very welcome, Enrico. But I'm sure I'll be the
big winner here. Me and my sister, that is."

*And that, Marco, was the last time I ever saw the man that
turned out to be the one who got me started on the path that
has led me to this place in my life, to this occasion of trying to
explain to you what happened. Of course, I really had no way of
knowing, as I sat eating those scrambled eggs and drinking that
insipid coffee, that I was on any particular path at all.*

"Charles thinks we should take the Ford," Billy said as
we walked to the large carriage house that had been turned
into a garage at the back of the house, just as had the smaller
one at the Goldenshane's. I assumed that Charles was one of
the many servants who magically appeared and reappeared as
occasions demanded—the chauffeur probably. "It has a better
heater and is more likely to start if the weather should turn
really cold."

I, naturally, felt that that was where the weather had
already turned. Though not cold in the same way as Chicago,
where wind had a way of transforming walks on even merely
cool days into painful experiences for me, Minnesota's

113

temperatures were, as everyone knows, among the lowest in the nation during the winter months. This year everyone spoke about what a mild winter it had been, but I, not being familiar with the norms, would not have made such an observation. As we hurried down the driveway, I pulled my woolen scarf more tightly around my neck and pulled on a pair of supple leather gloves that Mother had sent in my Christmas package. Billy, on the other hand, had not even bothered to button his coat, and his head and hands were bare.

"You should be glad that we're not having a real Minnesota winter. We can't be more than a few degrees below freezing this morning. If we're lucky you'll get a taste of the real thing before we're finished. Last year it was two below zero on Christmas Eve—Fahrenheit, of course."

"That's not my idea of luck," I laughed.

But the heater did work pretty well and the trip across the snowy miles was very pleasant. The roads were fairly clear and we were able to talk as we drove through the countryside outside Minneapolis. The day was overcast and the landscape reminded me of a photogravure by Alfred Stieglitz that I had seen at the Art Institute. The barren branches and sharply angled rooftops stood starkly against puffy gray clouds. In spite of the absence of colors, the contrasts were remarkable and offered up their special bleak beauty.

"I hope Jimmy didn't offend you last night. He really is one of the sweetest people I know. But he loves to strike different poses. Last night he was in one of his, I don't know, take-me-or-leave-me humors. I think he may have been a little jealous of you---worried that you and I might have become too close. I've never brought a friend home from school before. He was hoping we'd have more time together. He resents it that I'll be spending so much of the vacation at the cabin."

"I can probably manage without an assistant."

"No, no. I really want to do it. And Jimmy knows that he can drive up whenever he wants."

"I think I'll really enjoy getting to know him better."

There was a pause and then Billy asked bluntly, "Does it shock you that I'm a homosexual?"

I waited before answering. "I'm not sure. I have to admit that it had never crossed my mind before, but somehow when I realized it last night it didn't even surprise me really. And, no, I'm not shocked. How can people studying art history be shocked by such a thing?"

We both laughed and our mirth served to let us relax completely and accept from then on the way things were. We were often to joke darkly about how unfortunate we both were in love—I with a Jew and he with another man.

"We have friends in Minneapolis who know, of course--- others like us who manage from time to time to have their own parties---like the one last night. Jimmy and I both appreciated your uncanny ability to know that you should turn down the invitation to join us. How did you know, by the way?"

"I have no idea, really. Partly it was that Jimmy reminded me of that young boy in the Carravagio of the youth peeling a piece of fruit. But mostly it was just the way you two, well, just were with each other."

"But I don't think anyone else has even suspected. Maybe it's because up here I've always done the required amount of dating. I even went steady once---just for the sake of appearances. Jimmy and I have been together---in the shadows, of course---since we were juniors in high school Even though our families begged us to go to Ivy League schools, we both went to the University of Minnesota as undergraduates just so that we could be together longer. We were afraid we wouldn't both get into the same school. Do you know what Oscar Wilde called it?"

"No. My English isn't good enough to catch his wit."

"He called it the love that cannot speak its name. It's a tragedy, isn't it---that there is a kind of love that cannot even be named?"

We drove on for several minutes without speaking.

"I'm surprised that Jimmy is studying medicine," I finally broke the silence. "I would have guessed that he would study literature or history or philosophy or something more...."

"More girly?" We laughed again. "No---he's great at science. When we took biology in high school we were given these horrible frogs to dissect. I have to say I was pretty girly myself when the teacher put them down on the lab tables. But you should have seen Jimmy. He picked up his scalpel and had it cut up in minutes. It was as if he had been born doing it. And I think from that day on he knew he wanted to be a surgeon. He's the best in his class, of course. He could have been an intern anywhere, but he's chosen Mayo's. That's a great place-- the best hospital in the world, we Minnesotans like to think."

"Do you suppose it's high on the top of places to be bombed?" I asked---and then had to explain the joke to Billy.

"Well, Jimmy chose it so that he can be close to me when I get home on vacations. And I'll probably settle down back here anyway, and so will he. We love this." He gestured with his right hand toward the landscape. "It's amazing how many Minnesotans come back here after they've gone somewhere else for a while. You'd think we'd all want to get away from the cold, but we keep coming back for more."

"Italians tend to stay put, too. I'm lucky that Judith is willing to leave America."

116

"You are lucky. She's an incredible woman. We are going to have one helluva New Year's eve."

The roads became narrower and snowier as we drove farther North. Fewer and fewer houses gave way to more and more farms separated from one another by considerable distances. We drove silently, but comfortably from then until we reached our destination. I reflected on how much had happened since I had left Padova only a few months before. And I watched the terrain that provided the backdrop for our journey. How can such bleakness be so beautiful, I wondered to myself. It occurred to me that the reason Minnesotans kept coming back must be tied to their knowing the answer to that question, even if they could not put the answer into words. Not even Jimmy.

The last few kilometers were slow ones, but at last we drove up a long driveway . Someone had cleared it of snow, but it was covered with a sheen of ice and we had to move at a snail's pace. Thus I had time to study the so-called cabin as it came into view. It was an enormous three story log house that actually was more the size of a small hotel. Smoke was coming out of three of eight chimneys. A deep porch stretched across the front and wide steps led up to the middle of it toward heavily carved front doors----rather incongruous in a log cabin, I thought to myself.

"Dio mio, Billy" I exclaimed. It's enormous."

"Yes, it is rather. Most of the rooms won't be heated, of course, but we'll manage. We own the land on this side of the lake. There aren't any other houses, except our guest house and the house a mile or so down the road where our caretakers live. Did Dad mention to you that a couple will come in from time to time to help? They come in regularly----the house has to be kept moderately warm even when no one is in residence. Dad would kill someone if his wine froze."

"Olaf and Christina---yes, he did mention them." I started to open the door on my side of the Ford.

"Wait, Enrico."

I turned toward Billy. He placed his hand on my arm.

"I'm not a bad man," he said.

I started back. "Of course you aren't. I've never thought so for a moment."

"I just hope you'll always remember that you once felt that way."

"I have no doubt that I shall always feel that way. And I hope I shall never do anything to disappoint you---or anyone else, for that matter."

Billy stared out into the forest surrounding the house. "Your friendship means a lot to me."

"And yours to me. Right now," I said, trying to lighten what had become a foreboding atmosphere, "it means that we need to unpack and start work on the panel. You can't hurry gesso."

He laughed, and the emotional clouds passed. "May I quote you?"

Front: Carlo Crivelli, The Delivery of the Keys to St. Peter, from
Altarpiece of San Pietro de Muralto, Camerino, 1488 191x196
cm. Berlin, Gemaldgalerie

Back: *Dec. 21*

Dear Rico, There it is again---the infamous cucumber; but in such
a prominent position. Is it cancelled by the pieces of good fruit?
Symbol of lust, isn't it? Or was it redemption? Always the
puzzle. Here's to more good times in Munich. Billy

Chapter 7

Minnesota, December, 1934

    Needless to say, I could hardly wait to see the Raphael
that I was to copy. I had studied and re-studied the photo I had
been sent, but there was no way that image could adequately
prepare me for the impact of the real thing. Billy had offered to
unpack the car, so I went alone to the room that Olaf had
prepared for my work. My Madonna, as I came to think of the
painting, was hanging on the north wall—the wall that I faced
when I entered the room. Several lamps had been placed near
her and as I turned them on one by one the colors became
more and more astonishing. I don't need to tell you, Marco,
what it is like to see a painting in real life that you have only
seen in photographs. Some paintings are more successfully
photographed than others; some defy it completely. There is
no way, for instance, that anyone can understand Van Gogh
without seeing in person the ways in which he builds up paint.
It has been my own experience that not nearly as much is lost

119

with, say, a Vermeer; so much of the power of his works is due to the perspective and subtle psychology. But with Raphael's it is the colors that matter and as I stared at this lady and her son for the first time I found it almost difficult to breathe.

The psychology of the moment Raphael chose to depict matters, of course. The infant Jesus sits on Mary's lap, one leg bent in front of her right knee, the other hangs over her thigh. With his right hand he is playing with the Virgin's hair, his left rests on his knee, palm up as if offering the promise of salvation. He looks directly and lovingly out to the viewer, a smile on his tiny mouth. In a classic Renaissance pose, Mary's head is tilted down toward her child but she is not watching him. Nor does she direct her eyes at the viewer. Instead she looks slightly to the right, over her beloved child's head into the distance--pondering things in her heart, as Luke says of her. Is this the expression of any Mother contemplating the future of her child, or does Mary have special insights into the suffering that awaits him and her? Any reflective viewer cannot help but ask this question. But for me, particularly with the task before me, it was the colors that demanded most attention.

A tunic, a luscious, almost unearthly color of blue covers an under-dress whose long white sleeves can be seen---- but they are not pure white, of course. It would be a challenge to mix the right paints to capture the ethereality. The only nod in the direction of the Renaissance practice of presenting Mary in the garb of a Queen, is gold braid that trims the neck and sleeves of the tunic, and a gold veil that covers her brownish hair. The baby is naked, but a diaphanous blanket covers his legs. He sits on a lap draped in a skirt a shade of red so pale as to be almost pink. The back of a cream-colored throne frames the pair. A simple scene, but to me it glimmered and gleamed and for some time I felt that I was not up to reproducing it. The contours would not present too much of an obstacle, but these colors.....

My thoughts and doubts were interrupted by Billy's entering the room.

"They make a lovely couple, don't they?"

"How long has your family had this painting?" I asked.

"No idea. It's been in the living room for as long as I remember. It's one of the reasons I decided to study art history. It must have been the same for you."

"It was. And I also grew up with some fabulous pieces. But this.....I can't believe it's just been sitting here waiting for us. Isn't your father afraid of theft?"

"It's probably safer here than it is in Minneapolis. Olaf and Christina make wonderful watchdogs. They had it in their house until today. It was safer there than in a bank vault."

"I'm not sure that I can do justice to it."

"Only one way to find out. Where do you want this valise with all the supplies?"

And with that we got to work. We laid the supplies out on the work table and I placed the wooden panel, a circle slightly less than a meter in diameter, next to them. Billy was a great assistant. Although he had no experience in manipulating the mediums, he knew the theories behind Renaissance painting from his classes, and he was a careful and attentive student. The gesso to which the egg-based paint would be applied was built up of several layers of gypsum and glue, each of which had to be delicately sanded to a smooth finish. That process took us most of three or four days, for we had to allow time for drying. As the glue dried, we began the business of grinding the minerals and preparing the pigment. Renaissance painters had a fairly limited repertoire of minerals available to them, and I limited myself to these---cyan, vermillion, malachite, all the usual sorts, even some of the more expensive,

121

like lapis lazuli. The gold leaf for Mary's veil and the braid on her tunic would be prepared last.

The days flew by. Each morning Olaf and Christina arrived early to do their chores. Olaf made sure the rooms we were using were kept warm and that water in the other rooms did not freeze in the pipes. He moved around the house quietly----and surprisingly gracefully for his height and bulk. He had very little to say, but was never unpleasant. Christina, who was more prone to chat but never intrusive, was a reasonably good cook, though our menus were limited. I was introduced to a variety of the Norwegian dishes that kept her and her husband plump. We ate breakfast and dinner in the large but cozy kitchen and had sandwiches and milk for lunch in the studio. After dinner we lit the fire that Olaf had laid in an enormous stone fireplace at one end of the living room and drank fine wines and whiskeys and brandies from a constantly replenished cart in one corner of the room. Often we would play some of the phonograph records from a large collection in one of the cupboards----a rather strange motley of the sort that accumulates more or less accidently in second homes. Mostly we just chatted before retiring early, tired from the day's concentrated efforts.

By midday on December 23, when Billy left to drive back to Minneapolis, the panel was ready for the real challenge confronting me. I slowly began with a charcoal pencil ---rather more modern than anything Raphael had had at his disposal, but I allowed myself this small bit of "cheating"—to sketch in the main contours. I was totally absorbed in this and Christina had probably been standing in the doorway for some time before I sensed her presence.

"I'm very sorry to bother you, sir." It is difficult for non-native speakers of a language readily to hear accents in another tongue, even one in which they are as proficient as I had become in English. But Christina's lilting Scandinavian speech was unmistakable even to me. "I brought your sandwiches and milk earlier, but you didn't hear me come in. It's already after two."

I set the pencil down. "Thank you, Christina. I didn't realize it was lunchtime. When I get busy here I often lose track of the time."

She remained in the doorway "Olaf and me wonder if you'd like to join us for Christmas dinner. I hate to see you up here all alone this way."

I was ready to decline, but re-considered. This could be one more of those American memories I would be able to share with my grandchildren. "I hate to intrude on your holiday, Christina."

"It would be an honor, sir. All our family's up in Duluth, and they can't get here and we can't get there, so it will be very quiet, and not fancy."

"The honor will be mine, madam." I bowed.

A broad grin lit up her plump face. "I know you like to work 'til dark, sir, so I'll come over Christmas morning and make breakfast and lunch then Olaf will fetch you about four, if that's all right."

"Perfect. I look forward to it. Thank you very much, Christina. And please thank Olaf for me, too."

"You betcha." She turned to go, but then turned back.

"If you don't mind, sir, could I ask what you're doing?"

It surprised me that Theodore had not explained to Olaf and Christina what I had come to do. I did not quite know how to respond, so I kept my answer as short and direct as possible.

"I am attempting to make a copy of this painting," I pointed to the Madonna and Child, "and I am trying to use the methods that would have been used in the early 16th century when Raphael painted it." I thought about adding that it was a hobby of mine, but decided that Christina would find it much too strange to spend time alone over the holidays in this frozen locale only to indulge a hobby. I was afraid she would press me for more in the way of explanation. But she was too good a servant to do that, or perhaps too good a Norwegian.

She looked at the original and at the panel on which I had started to make my marks. She smiled thoughtfully. "You've picked the right subject for this time of year, haven't you, sir?"

We both gazed at the Raphael for a few moments.

"Do you think she knew he was going to be crucified, sir?"

I turned and looked into her eyes. "I've been asking myself that for a week now, Christina. I think she knows that her son's life is going to be difficult, but I hope that she does not know the whole story yet."

"That's just what I was thinking," reinforcing my strong belief in the power of art to draw people together. "Well, I'll see you later this evening then, sir."

"Please call me Enrico. If I'm to be a guest in your home I think we can drop all this formality."

I turned back to my barely marked panel and realized with no little surprise that my simple, uncomplicated conversation with Christina had provided me with exactly the entry into this stage of the work that I had been waiting for. It was the right subject for this time of year; but even at this time of celebration one knows how the story will end---in the later tragic event also depicted by so many artists. Raphael had the genius to somehow convey this through the very colors he uses.

The task of reproducing and re-presenting them seemed now more manageable.

     I have not said much about the Beauchamp's retreat, Marco. I think you've gotten some idea of its size. It was located in a heavily treed area and, like the home in Minneapolis, faced across an expanse now snow covered, of course, that sloped down to a lake---one much larger than the one in the city. A smaller, but nonetheless substantial, log cabin was set off about fifty meters to the left of the main house---the guest house, I presumed. A boat house and dock were located between them. A large porch, even deeper than the one in front, spanned the back of the house. We had not spent much time out of doors, though we had stepped outside for a breath of air occasionally and where we did a clear, cloudless, sky greeted us. Not even Titian would have dared to attempt so blue a sky. I have to this day never seen landscapes sparkle as those did. The house faced west, and one evening we were treated to a sunset that no tempuras, or oils, or even modern acrylics would have been adequate to capture.

    The main floor of the house consisted of only a few rooms, but they were all spacious. There was the kitchen, of course, the large living room with the stone fireplace, a dining room with a smaller fireplace, and a huge sunroom, fitted with alcoves where one could sit with some privacy to read or just look out over the porch to the lake. The two floors above were, as far as I could tell, all given over to sleeping rooms and porches, though one imagined that the owner must have a den somewhere.

    As Theodore Beauchamp had mentioned, the entire first floor had been decorated by Gustave Stickley in the craftsman style. Growing familiarity with this style did not breed my contempt---quite the opposite. I had come quite to like it. The chairs and sofas were very comfortable and the wide

125

wooden arms that had at first looked too heavy to me now looked stable and balanced----and provided a wonderful space on which to rest one's drinks! The sunroom was furnished not in wood and leather, but in the wicker and chintz that many of the craft style designers also favored. The rooms were appointed with several pieces of pottery, again rather heavy and darkly colored for my taste, but which, I am sure, came from several of the American ceramic factories that would become so famous. The paintings on the walls were mostly landscapes depicting scenes from all seasons of areas of the sort we had driven through on our way from Minneapolis. I had not learned enough about American art to recognize the artists, but I could appreciate their abilities. I enjoyed prowling through the rooms and even occasionally gave in to my compulsion to change the positioning of one or two objects.

The house was very quiet without Billy and although I had no trouble enjoying a quiet Christmas Eve (a scratchy but lengthy telephone call to Judith helped) I was glad that I had accepted Christina's invitation for Christmas day. I missed my family, of course, and especially longed for some of the calamari and scungilli that we always ate on Christmas Eve. But I was too busy and excited to feel very homesick.

Fortunately the mild temperatures everyone had commented on held. Nonetheless, when Olaf came to fetch me Christmas afternoon, he pointed to a closet where a supply of boots of all sizes was available. "You'll be wanting to wear a pair of these, I'd guess."

We went in silence the kilometer or so to a modest house surrounded by trees, set on a lot between the road and the lake. The inside, like the outside, was neat but welcoming. The smell of freshly baked bread and other aromas that I could not quite identify greeted us as we took off boots and outer layers of clothes. A living room, dining room and kitchen constituted the main level, with the bedrooms, I assumed on the floor above. The furniture was simple and not everything matched, but this was clearly a home that was cared for with pride and affection. In both the living and dining room scores of candles in a variety of candleholders in bright primary colors had been placed. A small Christmas tree stood near the front window and on its branches were small white candles. In the dining room a round table covered with an intricately embroidered scarlet tablecloth was laden with dishes most of whose contents were unfamiliar to me. Christina proudly explained each one, pointing out the ones that were special to the season. We filled our plates and Olaf poured us each a small glass of aquavit and large tankards of beer.

Earlier in the day I had taken the time quickly to sketch with colored pencils a Madonna and child drawing. It could not compare to the Raphael, naturally, but Christina was obviously moved.

Her empty hand flew to her mouth. "Whenever did you do this?"

"I could not be so rude as to come empty handed," I said. "It was done hastily, but I hope it conveys my appreciation at being included in your Christmas celebration."

She passed the picture to Olaf. He nodded several times, thanked me simply, and returned it to Christina.

"I could not have asked for anything more thoughtful. We shall treasure it," and she placed it on the mantle where, I have no doubt, it took pride of place for many Christmases to follow.

From a small radio in one corner of the living room carols were playing softly. A fire was crackling in a small brick fireplace. Our conversation was meager but not forced or uncomfortable. After dessert----a special Christmas cake that had obviously taken hours to prepare---Christina walked to the radio and turned it off. "Olaf will play now," she quietly announced.

127

I watched with some curiosity as Olaf opened a violin case that had been sitting on a shelf behind the chair he'd been sitting in. Out of it he lifted the most elaborately adorned instrument I had ever seen. I had seen some beautiful stringed instruments in Italy, particularly when my family took me as a child to the violin museum in Cremona, but their beauty depended on the shaping of warm woods and one's imagining how they would sound. Olaf's instrument was actually adorned with intricate designs that had been painted around the sides of the front and inlaid with mother of pearl all along its neck.

"What an amazing violin, "I said. "I've never seen one like it."

"We call it a fiddle, not a violin," Olaf answered. "A Hardanger fiddle. It's made specially for the kind of music we play."

And without spending any more words, he began to play. The music was simultaneously haunting and frenetic and strangely beautiful. It was almost hard to believe that this instrument was related to the ones used to sing Bach or Vivaldi. When he had finished with his first number he smiled and asked me what I thought.

"I have to say I am amazed," I answered.

He nodded. "It's really quite a different sort of thing." He showed me how additional strings created the sort of droning accompaniment that yielded the unusual sound. Talking about what was clearly a cherished treasure, he became animated, almost loquacious.

"There are many myths about this in my country. One says that you have to be enchanted by a sprite living under a waterfall who is the only being that has ever truly mastered it. Another tells of how it has been used to create near hysteria in the listeners. All of them imply that the art of it is akin to wizardry---and that one must be careful to distinguish the good wizards from the bad wizards."

"But all of our God-given skills or talents can be used for good or bad," added Christina. Olaf and I nodded our assent.

He played three or four other strange pieces and then, as Christina lit the small candles on the tree he played a lovely, but somewhat eerie version of "Silent Night." Even Jimmy would be moved by this, I thought. At its conclusion, Christina extinguished the little flames and Olaf replaced his fiddle in its case. Without further ado, we all donned our warm clothing and they walked me home through the dark and silent forest. They thanked me again for the Madonna. We shook hands, bid each other Merry Christmas and Good Night and I watched from the porch as these simple, complicated people disappeared down the road.

The next morning I returned to my work with a fervor approaching the frenzy that I had heard in Olaf's concert. At one point it occurred to me that I was acting like something of a wizard, but I was too enthralled at that time by what I was doing to reflect much upon it. Since then, of course, I have often had occasion to consider not just the extent to which I have been a bad or a good wizard, though this has often preoccupied me. I have wondered even more about how what I have done has been shaped by my own nature or by the external events and forces that moved me now this way, now that. I wish I could blame a fairy sprite under a waterfall.

By the time Billy returned in the mid-afternoon of the day after Christmas, I had made great progress in sketching in the outlines of the Virgin, Jesus, and the throne. I greeted Billy warmly, told him briefly about my time while he was away, and then we got to work mixing the paints. From time to time, I let him try his hand at applying the quickly drying tempura to the rondo panel. He was nearly as excited as I about the processes and its products, and our days and evenings were spent in the intimate companionship that is reserved for friends happily engaged in a jointly satisfying enterprise.

But as pleasant as these days were, I was, as you would expect, very eager for Judith's arrival. Every few minutes the morning of the last day of the year, I rose from my work, looking out to see if I could spy their car through the bare branches of the trees. Billy had told me that Jimmy's parents had given him a silver gray Chevrolet-6 for Christmas. Now he insisted that it would be well camouflaged in the wintery landscape and I would do as well to sit and listen for it, but I was too excited to sit still.

"By the way, Billy." Billy stopped grinding the vermillion he was preparing as I came back from one of my many visits to the front window. "Your father seemed to want to keep the copy I'm making something of a secret---doesn't want his sister to find out about it. He's knows I told Judith about it, but what does Jimmy know?"

"The truth, of course," he answered, a little too abruptly it seemed. Then his voice returned to normal. "But I've sworn him to secrecy. If he mentioned it to his Mother she would be likely to say something to my Mother and—you know, it would spoil the surprise. And on the subject of so-called secrets, does Judith know about Jimmy and me?"

"Yes. I thought I should let her in on that since the four of us are going to be alone up here. I told her when I spoke with her on the telephone on Christmas Eve."

"What did she say? Was she appalled?"

"Do you want to know exactly what she said?"

"Certainly." He sat back in his chair and crossed his arms.

130

"She said she had suspected for some time that you are a queer."

Billy did not even wince at that brutal term, but threw back his head and laughed. "That is so typically Judith. I can just hear her say that!"

"She said that she had even suggested as much to her roommate, but that Isabel insisted Judith only thought that because you'd never made a pass at her. Judith attributes her perceptiveness and insights to a the class she had on Oscar Wilde last year."

We laughed again. "Then she'll be all right with it?"

"Well, she may be shocked if you make love on the dining room table."

"We'll try to control ourselves."

"Seriously, she can't have been exposed much---I haven't either, except in theory, after all. And Galesburg is Galesburg. There must be some homosexuals there, but I doubt they are any more open about it than you've been. Still, Judith is Judith. I think she'll enjoy the fact that she's been let in on a new side of life."

"Good." And he turned his attention back to his mortar and pestle.

At last we did hear the car and both of us ran downstairs to the front door.

There was nothing disappointing about the sight of my darling alighting from Jimmy's car. She was wearing red slacks and a short fox fur jacket. Her head was bare and a stiff wind played havoc with her mass of black hair. She slammed the door of the car and met me halfway up the porch steps. The fervor of our embrace nearly sent us both sprawling. Billy and

Jimmy also greeted each other warmly, though with more practiced restraint. As if on cue, Olaf appeared and carried two large valises into the front hall.

"Miss Goldenshane will be in the blue room and Mr. Albright in the green," Billy said. After Olaf had gone up the stairs to the second floor, Billy turned to us. "No need to upset the Lutherans. We'll maintain some degree of decorum by making it appear that we're all sleeping alone. Besides, Judith and Jimmy will want their own rooms for dressing ."

"May I see the other woman in your life?" Judith asked as she and Jimmy stashed their coats in the closet.

"There's still a lot of work to be done on her---and especially on her baby. But, yes, I want you to see it."

I had covered both paintings with cloths. Billy, I could see, was as anxious as I to show our lovers the fruit of our labors. First I uncovered the Raphael.

"You need to look at this awhile before we show you what we've done thus far," I instructed. They did as I had asked. I had a momentary impression that Jimmy was about to say something acerbic, but then he seemed to decide that no one in this audience would appreciate it.

"It's amazing," Judith said.

"Why?" I pressed her.

She was accustomed to this kind of dialogue and we often found sparring about opposing interpretations arousing.

"The colors, of course. What did he use for that tunic—cyan or lapus?"

"Good eye, my love. Mostly cyan since it was much less expensive. But he did use some lapus for the highlights. As you'll see, we haven't applied that yet to our copy."

"May I say, without sounding like a barbaric simpleton, that Jesus is simply adorable?" Jimmy injected a bit snidely. "But I suppose they always are."

We all laughed, but Judith quickly added---"Oh, no they're not. You should see some of Crivelli's babies. They all look like wizened little old men."

"They do not," I objected. "The one from the altarpiece of San Domenico is positively cute---I'll prove it to you when we go to the National Gallery in London."

She squeezed my hand.

"Forget Crivelli, let's stick to Raphael," Billy demanded. "Let's show them what we've done, Enrico."

"Not yet. First I want them to tell us what they think of Mary."

Jimmy dropped his cynical pose.

"I think Raphael meant for us to feel sorry for her, in spite of the fact that she was supposed to have been granted the greatest honor that had ever come to any woman."

"Yes, yes, that's absolutely it, Jimmy," Judith said. "But how does Raphael do that? Even though her clothes aren't as splendid as those that most Renaissance artists give The Queen of Heaven, Raphael still gives her these beautiful colors to wear."

"But isn't that just it?" Jimmy answered. "She's got this great baby, she's wearing great duds, and she knows she's going to be famous. Maybe she even knows that she's going to be powerful and worshipped. But she knows horrible things are going to happen. And Raphael shows us that by the way she's looking out into the distance instead of at her son, or at us."

We were all quiet for awhile.

"Christina felt the same way."

"Christina?" Judith asked.

"Olaf's wife," explained Billy.

"She put it quite directly. She asked me if I thought Mary knew at this moment that Jesus would be crucified."

"The Cassandra curse." Judith shook her head. "It would be awful if the gift of the gods came with the price of knowledge of a terrible future."

"But we're all going to have wonderful futures. Unless, of course, I murder Enrico right here and now because he won't let us look at the copy," Billy nearly shouted.

I acquiesced and took the cloth off our rondo.

"Jesus Christ," Jimmy cried.

"Exactly," Billy hugged him.

"I've watched you do this before, of course. But I have no idea how you do it," Judith said. Billy and I both basked in their awe.

"Enrico is an amazing teacher. Maybe he'll give you both a lesson."

"Oh, no," I said, recovering both pieces. "We have even better things to do the next two days." I put my arm around Judith's shoulders and led her toward the door and down the hall toward my room. "Judith and I are going to go have a sandwich in my room. We'll see you later."

"We're going to skip the sandwich," Jimmy chortled.

"Let's all plan to be dressed and meet to begin our festivities fivish, all right?" Billy and Jimmy disappeared behind the door to Billy's bedroom.

Olaf had laid a fire in my bedroom and Judith insisted on lighting it. With increasing anticipation of the pleasures awaiting me, I watched her bend over the hearth, strike an match, and inspect the first flames as they lapped around the logs. She stood up and reached into the pocket of the bulky sweater she wore.

"Before we do anything else---I brought you a present and I want to see if you like it first." She handed me a small box wrapped in red paper with a green bow. "Merry Christmas, darling." I must have looked startled. "We're the kind of Jews that love an excuse for exchanging gifts in December," she laughed.

"Well, I have a gift for you, too. I just didn't know when to give it to you."

"Oh, now, now, by all means." From the bottom drawer of the dresser I retrieved a long, flat box that I had brought with me from Chicago.

"You go first," she said.

I opened the box and looked upon a magnificent gold Swiss watch.

"Daddy helped me choose it. He assures me it's the best---and that it's very manly."

"It is wonderful." She helped me put it on. "But I have nothing so fabulous for you."

"Whatever it is, I'll love it," and she tore off the ribbon and wrapping paper.

135

Angie, my cousin Tommy's wife, had helped me to shop, and had insisted that this was something any woman would love. I followed her advice and purchased a fringed white cashmere shawl. At the end of each piece of fringe was a tiny seed pearl so it made a soft percussive music as one moved. It was quite lovely, made in Italy naturally, and I was certain Judith would like it. But even though I had become accustomed to her enthusiasm for life, particularly all things bright and beautiful, I wasn't fully prepared for her reaction. She held it to her heart and tears streamed down her face.

"I can't imagine anything I would rather have gotten from you. It's perfect."

She kissed me hastily.

"Wait here. Don't move. No, do move----get the champagne ready." And she ran out of the room clutching the shawl.

Earlier I had put a bottle into a silver ice bucket, planning to serve it with the sandwiches and oranges Christina had provided. I popped the champagne cork and poured the bubbling honey colored liquid into the delicate flutes I had found in the dining room.

Judith usually did not take long dressing, and even less undressing, but today she was gone longer than I had expected. My wait was fully rewarded, however, when she appeared in the doorway. She was wearing a long black satin nightgown that clung to her hips. I could not see the top of the gown because she had carefully draped the white shawl around her shoulders. She lifted one arm and placed her hand against the door frame and stuck the opposite hip out----absolutely repeating the stance that Jimmy had assumed the night I met him. As she raised her arm, one side of her chest was revealed, and all thoughts of Jimmy---or anyone or anything else---vanished. A tiny strap, about the size of a strand of linguini held up a triangle of fabric, so narrow that it could not possibly cover her breast---to my great pleasure, of course. She lowered her arm and covered herself again, took a few steps into the room, twirled around and shut the door. Then she faced me again, and with the moves of an accomplished seductress, dropped the shawl slowly and then delighted me with a series of gyrations that magically turned the single shawl into the surrogate for the seven veils of Salome.

I know I have promised not to embarrass you with tale of our sex life, Marco, but I felt I must share this one incident with you in order to give you a complete picture of my wonderful Judith. I will forego description of the acts that followed. Suffice it to say that it was marvelous.

Afterward we indulged in that kind of verbal intercourse that people who truly love one another treasure following the sexual sort. I told her about my work, my time with Billy, my evening with Olaf and Christina. She shared stories of evenings with her friends (Mary, Anne, and Barbara had given her the black nightgown, expecting her to save it for our honeymoon), a movie she and Aaron had gone to with Nochie, plans to meet her Mother in Chicago when she left Minnesota so that they could buy her wedding gown. At one point, she turned on her side and talked with her raised head resting on her hand, her arm bent at the elbow. In my mind I could trace a line across her eyes, down to her mouth, and then down and back across the nipples of the breasts, now completely exposed. It made a perfect elongated S-shape of the sort aestheticians have identified as the most beautiful line in nature. I was in paradise.

"Did you bring boots?" I asked after we had fallen comfortably silent for a few minutes.

"Of course, I brought boots. Only an idiot would come to Minnesota in the winter without them."

"Not true. The sophisticated traveler knows that when one visits the Beauchamp's everything is provided. So let's get up and take a walk before dinner."

"Great idea." She jumped out of bed, threw the shawl around her body, took a large swallow of champagne and ran to her own room.

The door to Billy's bedroom was closed, but as I passed on my way to meet Judith downstairs, I could hear the soft murmurs of conversation that made me think that paradise was inhabited by others beside Judith and me.

The next two days were simply wonderful. Our New Year's Eve celebration was as scintillating as Jimmy and I had hoped. He wore his colorful cummerbund; Billy and I joined him in pinning a spring of holly to our lapels. Judith wore a sleeveless red velvet evening dress with a high front and a low back that formed a point just above her waistline. The hem of the gown was trimmed with white ostrich feathers that magically matched the color of the white cashmere shawl that she wore during all of our waking hours at the lodge. She had a string of perfect pearls around her neck and pearl earrings encircled by tiny rubies.

If someone had painted our group, how would future viewers interpret us, I wondered, as I enjoyed the tasty dishes that Christina had furnished along with several specialties that Jimmy had brought from Minneapolis. Would they think Judith was one of our sisters, one of our mistresses, the sponsor of a salon, an expensive prostitute? Could it possibly occur to anyone that they were looking at two sets of lovers? Could even a Raphael have duplicated the brilliant color of Judith's gown, or could a Rembrandt have adequately captured the way the ostrich feathers glowed in the firelight?

We ate and drank and became tipsy, but not drunk. We laughed, talked, debated issues that I no longer even remember worrying about. After dinner we put on records and danced. I only danced with Judith, but the other three happily changed partners. In their Christmas box to me, my parents had included some Ethiopian coffee and dark Perugian chocolate and I surprised Judith by producing the coffee maker from my Chicago apartment that so delighted her. With attentiveness approaching participation in a sacred ritual, we prepared the coffee and slowly sipped it while tasting bits of the bittersweet candy.

At midnight, our quartet stepped onto the front porch and toasted 1935. Jimmy shared with us a superstition that his Scottish grandmother had always followed: a year of good fortune would be guaranteed if a dark-haired man was the first to enter the home in the New Year. Judith insisted that it had to be a woman. Jimmy warned that it was better to have a light-haired man than any woman. We sparred over which of the three dark-headed people should follow the superstition and be the first through the front door. Throwing caution to the wind we finally gave in to Judith and gave her the honor. Giggling we decided she should be followed by Jimmy, then me and finally the light haired Billy. Perhaps we should have let him go first.

Then, unwilling to waste any of our more private, precious opportunities, we retired almost immediately.

I think, Marco, no, I know, that if I could have two days of my life to repeat, it would be the two I spent with Judith, Billy, and Jimmy in that frozen Eden. We were all innocent then, both in terms of what we knew about the truly dark side of the world, and about how much or how little we ourselves might contribute to it. Two of us would not add to the evil, but all of us would come to experience it.

Judith and Jimmy left on the third of January and Billy and I returned full bore to completing the reproduction. We had a little over a week to finish, but we did. Billy received a telephone call from his father who apologized that a crisis at the St. Paul store precluded his coming to see the copy while we were still at the lodge. So Billy and I left the two Madonna's and two Babies facing each other behind the cloths that covered them. I had done my best work, but I was glad that my Mary did not have to look too long upon the superior colors of the work she imitated. And I hoped that Theodore Beauchamp's sister's eye and memory were not so good that she would be prevented from enjoying her present.

Front of Postcard:

Carlo Crivelli, St. Mary Magdalen, painted for Santa Maria Magdalen, Carpegna, 1470's, Rijksmuseum, Amsterdam

Back: *August 10*

Greetings! Is this a German tankard? If so, where is the thumbpiece that's supposed to attach the lid to the bottom? What's supposed to be in it? Did MM like her ale dark or light? I'm off to DC on the 7th.   Christine

Chapter 8

To Padua, 1935

Judith's graduation (with honors, it turned out) was scheduled for the first week of June, so we set the wedding for June 15. The weeks between New Year's and those events sped by. Judith took an intensive Italian class at a language school in The Loop and all the courses she could find in Italian literature and history at the University. We spent several Sundays with my family in Lake Forest and they were delighted with her progress and enthusiasm for all things Italian. The ease with which she was accepted by them made me even more certain that her Jewishness would not be a problem when we settled in Padova. Angie gave her a wedding shower in May---and Ruth, Anne, Mary, and Barbara came by train from Galesburg to attend. Billy and I joined them for dinner at their hotel. Ruth seemed reconciled to our decision and appeared to be having a good time---without drinking much more than the rest of us. Billy flirted outrageously with the ladies who vied for his attention. All of us, even Ruth, made plans for meeting in Italy as soon as possible.

I continued my classes in American art history and managed to complete three more copies of Renaissance works hanging at the Art Institute---a Caravaggio, a daVinci and another small Raphael Madonna. Billy and Jimmy asked for the Caravaggio (a youth with a floral garland). I gave the da Vinci to the Goldenshane's and, to my happy surprise, Billy's father bought the Madonna---explaining that his sister had been so pleased with her birthday gift that spring that he wanted to have another to give her for Christmas.

Although it was difficult to keep hidden from her, I also worked on a wooden wedding chest for Judith. I had to keep the box small so that it would fit in one of the trunks that we would be shipping to Italy. Following Renaissance tradition, I decorated the panels with symbols of fidelity and scenes depicting things special to the bride. For the former I borrowed from Bassano's painting of Penelope at her loom---substituting black hair for the blond that he gave her. I also reproduced Crivelli's Esther as she brilliantly convinces her husband, King Ahaseurus, to save her fellow Jews. These two paintings constituted the front and back panels of the chest. On the sides, I broke my usual practice of not doing original work---for I wanted to show scenes from Galesburg that had meant so much to Judith, and thus to me: the railroad yard and the geese on the lake at Lincoln Park. I was actually quite pleased with the outcome. On the top I simply entwined a J and an E, and surrounded them with a Crivellian garland of flowers, fruits, and vegetables.

I gave it to Judith the night before she left for Galesburg to make final wedding preparations. I had anticipated glee and this was, indeed, the immediate response.

142

She joked about not wanting ever to have to "unweave" while I was off "gallivanting" around. Then she turned more serious as we briefly discussed Esther's story, and hoped that no such courage would be required of either of us. She made an off color remark about a cucumber I had included in the garland between an apple and a pomegranate. And then she turned her attention to the scenes of Galesburg. She looked at these quietly for a few moments and then turned to me with tears in her eyes. She did not speak, but kissed me lightly on both cheeks-----and then.....Well, I have promised not to embarrass you with such matters. Suffice it to say that what followed was a night of love memorable for its tenderness.

The chest still sits on a shelf in my study. In it you will find a white cashmere shawl, a man's gold watch, and a pair of tin soldiers.

The wedding was an elegant, even lavish affair. My parents disembarked in New York in late May and were able to make contact with more or less distant relatives there. One evening Judith's maternal grandparents, Dr. Isaac Weitz and his wife Rachel, hosted a dinner for my parents and Fred's parents in a famous restaurant. My mother telephoned me the next morning and reported that the evening had been "molto bello," and that they all looked forward to spending more time together in Galesburg. The Chicago relatives insisted, of course, that my parents spend several days in Lake Forest.

The Goldenshanes reserved a large block of rooms for out-of-towners in the Galesburg's Hotel Custer. Mother, Father, and I took the train from Union Depot two days before the wedding, the rest of my Italian-American family arrived the following afternoon. My mother brought Ruth a decanter and set of glasses from Murano---deep green with gold filigree. It was the perfect gift, and Ruth immediately set it in a place of honor on their fireplace mantle.

Billy brought with him another special gift, one from Olaf and Christina. "I had no idea that you had become such a favorite of theirs," Billy said as he handed me a small, flat box. Inside was a red table runner, beautifully embroidered with Nordic designs. A card congratulating us was included, and above their signatures were the words, "For a good wizard and his bride." I tried to explain its meaning to Judith, but there was so much going on that I'm not sure she felt the impact the way I did.

The ceremony itself had been the subject of much discussion. On Saturday morning, Judith and I and our immediate families went for a civil ceremony to the courthouse. one of Galesburg's most impressive buildings—a dark stone affair set in the middle of a park boasting enormous trees. But all of us, particularly Ruth and my mother, also wanted a public affair the next day. That wedding was held in the hotel's ballroom. Judith's dress was perfection. Delicate ivory Belgian lace followed the contours of her sensuous figure to a spot just below her knees. From there a Titianesque cloud of chiffon wafted gently around her lower legs and ankles. From a pearl tiara more lace fell to the back to form a long train. Angie served as matron of honor and Anne, Mary, and Barb as attendants. I can no longer remember their dresses---I think I probably did not even notice any details at the time. I just recall shades of peach and salmon. Billy, of course, was Best Man, with Jimmy, Tommy, and Aaron acting as ushers. Fred had presented Judith with a strand of Balinese pearls, Ruth had given her a handkerchief that her grandmother had embroidered, and the girls had, I later learned, all three ritually placed a blue garter on her left thigh. She carried a bouquet of lilies of the valley and peach-colored roses.

We had not been able to find either a priest or rabbi willing to officiate. Instead, a kindly professor of religion from the college who had been ordained as a Congregational minister eagerly agreed to help out. He helped us choose appropriate passages from the Old Testament and the official service from The Book of Common Prayer. Following our formal vows, Judith, in Italian, recited from the Book of Ruth:

"Wither thou goest, I will go:and where thou lodgest, I will lodge: thy people shall be my people. Where thou diest will I die, and there will I be buried: the Lord do so to me, and more also, if ought but death part thee and me."

I repeated the passage in Hebrew, having worked on it with a friendly scholar at Chicago. I know my pronunciation must have been awful, but no one seemed to mind, if they even noticed. We left out the words that attested to an acceptance of the other's God---we were afraid including them might offend someone and in any case, neither Judith nor I believed that the God we believed in would be an exclusive one.

While pictures of the wedding party were taken, guests were led to a small garden adjoining the ballroom to wait while tables were set up for dinner around a circular space reserved for dancing. During dinner a string quartet played softly, and afterward a small dance band from Peoria provided music for a variety of dancing styles. Over two hundred people had been invited and it appeared that few, if any, had declined. I did not know most of them, of course---only my family, a few of the Goldenshane's immediate neighbors to whom I had been introduced, Ruby and her daughter (who came with other members of Ruby's family whom I had not met before), and Violet and Nochie. I learned later that Ruth had left strict instructions with the hotel's manager that her Negro guests should encounter no difficulties when they entered the hotel or ballroom. If there were any misgivings on anyone's part about our future together, the guest list, or the mixed wedding generally, they were kept concealed. Our feelings of happy optimism were unbounded.

We left Galesburg two days later bound for New York where we stayed for two days with the Weitzs and two with the Goldenshanes before we embarked on a ship for Rotterdam. One evening, while Judith was bathing, I overheard small portions of a conversation between Isaac and Rachel. He said something about thinking he should speak to Judith "about it" but she seemed to be trying to convince him otherwise. She must have prevailed, since nothing unpleasant was discussed. I assumed that "it" referred to the troubles in Europe that seemed closer in New York City than they did in Illinois. Isaac, I thought, must have wanted to discuss his concerns about the future of Jews in Europe. I guessed that Rachel probably thought the topic had been sufficiently addressed already and that these happy days should be in no way darkened. I remember thinking that she was right. I think now that "it" was something else entirely.

Fred had business in New York so he and Ruth arranged to arrive there the day before we embarked. Our send-off was exuberant, our ocean voyage a love cruise. We spent several days in Amsterdam and Paris and then, heeding warnings that we should avoid Germany, traveled on across southern France by train to Venice and arrived in Padova mid-July. Needless to say, these days were bliss. This was Judith's first trip to Europe and both Amsterdam and Paris thrilled her. We walked miles along canals and rivers, down narrow streets and broad boulevards. We ate and drank at every sort of venue. We spent hours in the rooms of the Rijksmuseum and Louvre, taking special pleasure in locating the sole Crivelli in the former--a marvelous Mary Magdalene.

"She looks more like a Queen than a prostitute, doesn't she," Judith remarked.

"I need a necklace like that. Maybe you could copy it and send it to Daddy or Grandpa and he could have one made up for me."

"Let me see," I replied. "The coral beads were very popular in the late fourteenth century and the pendant hanging from it has pearls and a sapphire—a sign of chastity."

"Chastity, that's a laugh."

"True repentance was thought to result in restored purity."

"I'll remember that."

"Please don't."

"I have to admit that this is the most beautiful Crivelli lady I've seen yet. Look at all that golden hair and those lovely facial lines and that perfect skin." Judith could not avoid a critical comment, however. "Still those hands---look how craggy the fingers are---and the palm is all out of proportion. Makes me awfully glad she has slippers on so that we don't have to see her feet." We laughed as we went in search of her preferred Vermeer's in another room.

In the Louvre we spent the longest time in front of *The Raft of the Medusa*. Judith had written a paper on the massive Gericault work and regaled me with details of the story of the shipwreck and its aftermath. In the painting several survivors languish on a raft. In the background is a ship, so tiny it must be missed many viewers who don't know the story.

"We debated for one whole class period on whether the ship is coming to the rescue or has not seen the raft and is turning away," Judith said. "I wanted to think they would be rescued, but I have to admit the ship looks like it's going away from them. Isn't it amazing how Gericault seems to capture both hope and despair in the very same figures? They'd been on the raft for several days---hungry and thirsty and sick. They see a ship and think their ordeal is over, but then it goes away. Don't you think the despair is worse than it was before they saw the ship?"

"Yes, much worse."

Judith's insight was correct. Despair is much worse when it follows hope.

But our somber mood did not last for long, could not last for long, given the utter joy we found and took in one another.

Our last night in Paris we dined at Maxim's. Uncharacteristically Judith put her menu down and said, "You order."

"What?" I asked, amazed.

"You order. Tonight I want to pretend that I am your----I don't know, your---whatever it is that women are who let their men take total charge."

"I'm not sure I can handle the responsibility."

"Just try to imagine that you know what I should want."

"But.....No, this will be fun. I'll try."

The waiter hovered. "We will both start with the white asparagus and caviar. Then Madame will have the poulet avec trois sauces and I'll have the trout almondine. And a bottle of the 1930 Meursault."

How do I remember what I ordered? How do I remember what we said in front of the Gericault? How could I not remember? I could repeat hundreds, thousands, of these conversations, these repartees, these interchanges. What did I order for our dessert? The profiteroles.

"These are just cream puffs!" Judith insisted. And we would laugh and she would talk about how her mother and Ruby could do them bigger and better and fill them with peppermint stick ice cream, and we would laugh some more. On other occasions she would insist upon shocking the waiter by doing all of the ordering herself. "Senor will have the osso buco. Would you recommend the Chianti or the Borolo?" she would ask the waiter, eyelids fluttering, and we would collapse into giggles before the waiter had even turned away. This is who I was with her.

My parents had a medium-sized villa on a hill just outside the Porta Santa Croce on the southern side of Padova. Halfway up the hill stood what I, as a boy, dubbed La Casa Rosso, though in fact it had become more pink than red over the years. It was my parents' guest house but we had all decided that it would be ideal for Judith and me until we found something more permanent. They had updated the kitchen and bathrooms but left redecorating and refurnishing the rest to us. We spent hours engaging in joyful, at times even passionate sparring over colors and fabrics. We wandered through new and used furniture shops in Padova and Venice and Verona. Irena, the daughter of my parents' cook became our maid, and delighted in becoming Judith's language and culinary instructor and friend. I began seriously to work with my Father on his project of establishing a small museum of early Renaissance works, particularly from the school of Padova, in the center of the city. My American bride was a novelty and her outgoing personality quickly earned her great popularity in the shops and markets she frequented.

For a month or so my parents essentially let us play house. Then, during the first week in September the first of

149

what would be several danger signals-- that even we in our state of bliss could not ignore-- sounded. In Germany, the Nuremburg Race Laws were passed, essentially depriving Jews of their rights. Equally distressing for my family, it became illegal for non-Jewish Germans to marry Jews. What made this genuinely frightening was that Hitler offered such a powerful ally to Mussolini. Only a month after the Nuremburg Laws were passed, our leader decided that he must do something to divert attention from his economic and other problems. He invaded Ethiopia; Britain and France, holding out weak hope that Italy might join them against Germany, did little or nothing to interfere. The United States seemed to remain, for the most part, oblivious. Needless to say, my mother and her family were especially worried about their coffee plantation in Ethiopia.

It was soon after the beginning of the war in Ethiopia that my father asked me to come to his study one morning. I was surprised, when I arrived, to see that three of his friends were also there. All were men I had known from childhood and had often been guests in our home and it would not have been unusual for any one of them to stop by for morning coffee. Still, I was struck by the fact that all were together—and from different towns, one each from Venice, Verona, and Vicenza. As we shook hands and embraced, I remarked that it looked like someone had appointed a committee to represent Venetia on some matter of great importance.

"In fact, that is not far from the mark," my father said. "We are a committee and we represent an important Venetian matter, but we are self-appointed." He indicated that I should pour myself coffee and sit down. They had arranged chairs in a loose circle---another sign that this was more than a social gathering.

I won't give you the names of the men. They are all dead now, so they don't need protection; but their families may still be vulnerable in any number of ways. You can perhaps guess who they were. But that it not important to my story.

150

Suffice it to say, they took turns laying out their plans and proposal. They had formed what they were calling "The Institute for the Restoration of Venetian Art"—'Venetian' referring not just to Venice but to the entire state. They had already rented a building adjacent to the museum that my father was establishing.

"There is nothing illegal about what we are doing," one of them quickly assured me. "But we want to make certain that we protect our artistic treasures."

"There will be war. Of that, we have no doubt, and we fear that it will be sooner rather than later. Italy will play a major role----though of course we have no way in these crazy times to know exactly what that role will be."

"What we do know," another asserted, "is that art is always at risk during times of invasion or occupation, and we want to do what we can to avoid the worst."

"The worst being the destruction of our art works?"

The Vicenzian snarled. "The worst being the pillaging of our heritage. Remember what happened when Napoleon was here. The French stole everything they could get their hands on. The Louvre would be only half full, or at least only half as prestigious, if all its Italian paintings were returned to their rightful owners."

For a few moments everyone was talking at once, irately giving examples of cases of villas and museums and churches being stripped of their treasures.

"The point is," my father finally brought the discussion back to some order, "that we have decided to do something. We cannot prevent plundering, but we can attempt to sabotage it. Our Institute will indeed engage in restoration of works---for individuals or institutions, whoever hires us. But our main work will be the reproduction of prized works."

151

"And that, of course, is where you come in dear Enrico. You are the best copyist we know, and we want you to be in charge of the actual work. We will manage things and arrange to hide the originals. Works will be brought to us ostensibly for restoration, but you and your team will copy them. We'll then return the copy to wherever it hung and if it's stolen, so be it. After the war we will make sure that the originals are returned to their owners."

"An owner will be told, of course, where the real thing is being kept. But we will invent a code that assures that we can keep track of where the original rightfully belongs."

"The bonus is that we'll be paid well for our service. After your salary and the wages of your team and expenses are taken care of, the rest will go to the Museo Crivelli that your father is setting up."

"And the team will consist of....?" I asked.

"There are several young people from the University who will, we're certain, want to help. They are eager to use their aesthetic skills for the honor of their country."

"So you'll do this?" my father finally said.

"Of course." I was, from the outset, incredibly excited about the project. "But I will have to tell Judith----and I'm sure she'll want to participate."

"Naturally," my father said and the others nodded in agreement. "We can begin at once. We'll begin with our own treasures---we have each chosen one work from our personal collections. I've chosen the Raphael St. Paul. I know you would have preferred a Crivelli, but a Raphael is much more likely to be stolen, don't you think?"

I had to admit that he was right. The others told me which work they had chosen, and mentioned several friends who had already indicated great interest in the project. We stood in a circle, a bit self-consciously.

"This requires a toast." My father called his butler to bring two bottles of fine Barolo and with that our venture was inaugurated.

Judith was, as I had known she would be, as excited as I.

"Can I help?"

"Can you mix paints? If I call for a sable flat brush, can you give it to me the way an assistant gives a surgeon a scalpel?"

"Aye, aye, sir," she saluted. "At least I think I can learn."

And learn she did, along with a group of eager art students from the University, some of whom had already become quite proficient restorers acquainted and adept with the traditional methods. Le Direttorre, as we called the quartet of managers, set up a small reception area in the front of the building where we offered two or three paintings, described as items acquired by auction and then restored for sale. The large room in back was fitted with a few cubicles where work requiring some privacy could be carried out, but for the most part we felt no need to keep what we were doing secret. I felt at times rather as Rubens must have felt in his "factory," overseeing a team of apprentices, saving challenging jobs or delicate finishing touches for myself. Most of the students could only work a few hours a week, but Judith and I put in long days. We began to bring in quite a lot of money and had things not deteriorated as they did, Judith and I could have lived very comfortably on the income. A real bonus was that my mother and Judith discovered that they not only liked each other (this had been apparent from their meeting in Illinois) but that they worked well together. Both spent hours helping out in the reception area where their main task was devising a system for keeping track of the paintings. I will explain this later.

Then early in December, we were set off on what I can only, admittedly tritely, describe as a roller coaster ride. Judith and I went home for mid-day dinner and found a thick envelope that had arrived from The States with the morning post. It was a very long letter from Fred. We were both famished from our morning's labor and put off reading it until after we had eaten; it was the last meal we would enjoy for a while.

It was an unusually warm December morning, and we decided to take our coffee onto the small veranda that looked out over the wheat fields and vineyards. The letter consisted of five or six pages. Judith began to read aloud but gradually her voice trailed off and she simply passed pages to me as she finished, actually dropping the last ones rather than giving them to me directly.

When a letter writer begins, as Fred did, "This is the hardest thing I have ever written," you can be sure that the words will be the hardest thing the receiver has ever had to read. I don't remember exactly many of the sentences, but the news was incredible as well as awful. He began by explaining that at our wedding Ruth's parents became increasingly concerned about her drinking. After consulting with Fred and Aaron, they agreed that when Ruth and Fred came East, Dr. Weitz would take his daughter to see a psychiatrist. The upshot was that Ruth had been admitted (Judith insisted it was more likely that she had been committed) to a clinic in The Berkshires. That was in early July. That news in itself was upsetting; it is what followed that was incredible.

Fred wrote several pages about how hard his life had been, and how Judith's leaving to seek her happiness had made him think more about seeking his own. He reported that his marriage to Ruth had, for years, been essentially loveless. But his life had not been. For over twenty years he had had a lover and he had decided that it was now time, especially with Judith's security taken care of, for him to end his marriage and go to live with his "true love." He would, of course, see that Ruth was left well-off and he was sure that the Weitzs would take good care of her. But he had begun divorce proceedings and was leaving Galesburg. A friend from Antwerp owned a trading firm in Bali and had offered Fred a position there. He had reason to believe that he and his new wife could live there comfortably and in peace. He planned to depart from Seattle December 1st. The identity of the lover----perhaps you've already guessed this, Marco: Violet Thomas.

There was a final page, and I do, more or less, remember Fred's words.

"I know what a shock all of this is to you. But I have one more and it is best, I think, to get everything out in the open at the same time. Soon after Violet and I fell in love, she became pregnant, and three months after Aaron was born, she also gave birth to a baby boy. He is, of course, Raymond—Nochie. I have tried to care for all of you to the best of my ability. I am certain it will sound brutal to you now, but I hope that at some time in the future you will be able to understand, if not to forgive, what I have decided to do.

"Aaron knows all of this. In fact, when I told him about our affair (and when Violet told Raymond) he claimed that he and Nochie have suspected this for some time. That has not diminished his anger now. Neither had any notion that they were half-brothers. I offered to set up a trust fund for him; he says he does not want it. Still, there will be a bank account here for him when and if he needs it. I have also taken care of Nochie's future. Enrico has assured me that he can take care of you financially. Aaron asked me to say that he will give you a week or so to digest this, and that he will then write to you himself.

"You have brought me nothing but joy, Judith. You are a perfect daughter. Although I was distressed when I learned you would go to Italy with Enrico, I have to admit that I was also relieved. Somehow your doing that permitted me to do this.

"I will write you as soon as we get to Bali. Mail will be slow, but please remember that you will always be in my thoughts and heart. I know that Enrico is there for you now as I always tried to be in the past. I hope with all my heart that we can be together soon.

"Violet also sends her love, but I suppose you won't feel much like receiving that now. Sometime soon, we hope.

"Be safe and happy.

Your loving Father."

I did not know what to say when I finished reading the letter, so for awhile said nothing. I simply moved my chair next to Judith's and put my arms around her while she wept into my shoulder. I also cried. My sorrow was not the same as hers, of course, but it was real nonetheless.

At last she lifted her head.

"I don't want to talk about this now, Enrico. Is that......Oh, God, I'm going to be sick."

She ran to the bushes at the edge of the veranda and vomited. Just then Irena appeared in the doorway.

"Is Judith sick?" .

"She's had some bad news from home. Could you get some water, please."

She quickly returned, and Judith drank deeply. "I just want to go to bed."

"Of course, my darling," I took her arm and led her to our bedroom. She did not cry or speak, just sighed herself to sleep. Until that moment I had not known that one could look so sad while sleeping.

It was several days before Judith could mention the news. Our conversation was limited to pleasantries. She could not eat without becoming ill and she said that the smells in the studio also made her nauseated. Most of the time she lay on our bed, looking at the ceiling.

With Judith's permission, I gave my parents a rough outline of what had happened. My father thought we should call for the family doctor; my mother wisely advised that we give her a few days. I did ask Judith if she wanted to see the doctor, but she just shook her head. Irena found time to sit quietly in a chair in the bedroom, and Judith seemed to take some solace from that.

Finally after about a week, Judith came in her robe to the breakfast table.

"I'm furious," she sat down and struck the table with her fist. "And now I'm ready to talk. But mostly right now I'm famished and want a huge breakfast."

Irena, looking very pleased, proceeded to put platefuls of fruit and bread and cheese in front of her. I actually clapped!

After she had eaten, with no signs of queasiness, Judith announced that she would stay at home that morning to attend

157

to some household chores with Irena while I worked. "We'll talk during your midday break, and then I want to get back to work with you in the studio with you this afternoon."

I happily agreed and stopped by my parents' home to tell them of the improved condition. They were delighted, but my Mother warned that I should do more listening and less talking. I assured her that I had never found that difficult with Judith.

My dear wife ate greedily again at noon. "I really shouldn't be stuffing myself like this. You'd have thought I would have lost weight last week, but my skirt is even tighter than before. Oh, to hell with it, life is too short not to eat more of this lasagna."

Then she became serious. "I have thought and thought about what my Father has done. He has more or less lived a lie----and deceived all of the people he cared most about. Except Violet, of course. And now he's broken all of the most important promises he ever made. I can never forgive him."

"Would you mind if I read his letter again?" I asked.

Judith looked a bit sheepish. "I did something pretty silly. This morning I tore it up in tiny pieces and flushed it down the toilet."

I just smiled. "Probably just as well."

I 'm going to write to him at the address he gave us in Bali---God knows whether it will ever get there. I'm going to tell him that I can't forgive him now and that I don't think I ever will. But I'm going to ask him to write to me once a year and let me know what he's doing. I can't completely write him out of my life."

"If that's what you want to do, that's fine."

"Do you think it's wrong?"

"No. I don't think there is anything wrong here. You have to do what feels right to you."

"Good. And after Christmas I want to go to New York to see Mother."

I must have look as alarmed as I felt.

"I know you can't come with me---your work here is too important. And I won't be gone any longer than I have to. I'll take the train to LeHavre and get a ship from there. I've thought it all out. I'll stay for only a week or so. I should be able to leave and come back in a month, six weeks at the most."

"A winter crossing will be difficult. Why don't you wait until spring?"

"No, darling, I have to go as soon as I can. Do you think your Father's secretary will help me make arrangements?"

"I'm sure he will. And you know that if your mother wants to come live with us, we can arrange that."

"Oh, I don't think that's a good idea. And besides, she's always loved New York. Maybe once she gets better she'll even find someone else. She's really an attractive woman. She deserves a life with some love in it."

Judith had, clearly, thought about all of this while staring at the ceiling in our bedroom. I think she had, in a sense, pictured what the future could be for her mother and that a trip to New York would help her to fill in the details of her image.

"I haven't yet decided exactly how I feel about Aaron and Nochie. I'm trying to wait until I get Aaron's letter. I know I'm angry with them----if they knew about this, why didn't they tell me?"

159

"I would guess they were trying to protect you."

"How do you think they found out?"

I hesitated, but then decided to tell Judith about one of my Galesburg memories that had come back to me with force in recent days.

"They probably saw something, and guessed the rest. I have to tell you that in hindsight I think that I saw something myself that might have made a cleverer, or more suspicious person guess that something funny was going on."

"What?"

"Thanksgiving night---the night after your Father and I had our talk----I had trouble sleeping."

"I think everyone did."

"Yes, but I got up and looked out my window and saw your father go into your garage. I watched for a while, but he didn't come out. I mentioned it to Aaron the next day and he said that your Father often took walks at night."

Judith thought about this. "But you didn't say anything to me."

"No, I didn't really think any more about it. Aaron said he often had trouble sleeping and went for walks late at night." Then I added, "Is there a back door from the garage?" I asked.

"Yes." She shook her head. "Oh, God, and it leads right into the Thomas's backyard---not far from the back door of their house. Do you think my Father used that way to get to Violet's house."

"Maybe."

"But what about Nochie? Surely he wouldn't go make love with Violet will Nochie in the house."

"But wasn't Nochie gone that night?"

"You're right. He went to Peoria to spend Thanksgiving with his grandmother."

"Did he do that often?"

Judith nodded. "Often enough. And he also spent a lot of nights with his aunt who lives on the South side of Galesburg,"

"So if your mother was a heavy sleeper."

Judith snorted. "You mean if she was dead drunk."

I started to apologize.

"No, darling, it's okay. It really is time to face facts. Most nights Mother passed out and nothing could rouse her. We usually didn't even see her until we came home for lunch the next day."

"Well, then."

"And you think maybe Aaron saw something like you saw."

"Yes, that's what I think. Maybe when we hear from him he'll explain."

"Nochie seemed to adore my father. Don't you think he would have hated him if he knew the truth?"

"Feelings are so complicated."

Judith was silent for several minutes. Then, looking as if she might cry, she moaned, " How could I have been so stupid.

This was happening right under my nose. I feel so foolish, along with everything else."

I suddenly remembered something Aaron had said to me that morning that we went for coffee.

"Aaron said something else that morning when we had our talk. I'd forgotten about it until now. I forget his exact words---something about you're being so engaged with living in the moment that you didn't always notice things. Now I remember, he actually said that you didn't realize what was going on in your own backyard. I thought it was just a metaphor."

"But of course he was literally talking about my own backyard." She made a disgusted sound with her lips and then stood up. "I don't want to think about this anymore right now. Let's go to work."

Hand in hand, we walked down the hill and through the city gate to our studio. The number of orders was increasing every day and few of our team stopped for the traditionally drawn out Italian mid-day dinner period. Everyone was happy to see Judith again, but paused only briefly to welcome her back. Happier than I had been for days, I quickly entered that state of concentration and joyful intensity that I felt when I was trying to put myself in the shoes and head and soul of some genius---in this case a young Masaccio. From time to time I looked up to see what my lovely Judith was doing. A few times she had left the table where she was preparing linseed oil to be mixed with pigments, but I was not concerned. It did cross my mind that she was off somewhere more frequently than was typical, but I was so engrossed in what I was doing that I gave it no real thought.

Late in the afternoon, she came to the easel where I had just begun to apply some gold leaf to a halo of St. Anne.

"For some reason, the smells in here are bothering me more than usual today. I think I'll work in the reception area." She gave me a quick kiss and removed her work smock. "Or maybe just take a quick walk. I'll meet you at home, okay?"

"I'll just finish this----it shouldn't take too long." I did watch her walk away, her marvelous hips swaying under her soft woolen slacks. I was tempted to follow her and suggest that we walk quickly home and into our bedroom, but I was at a crucial point in my application and, with a sigh, turned back to St. Anne. I'm sure that lady would have blushed had she known what I was eagerly looking forward to that evening.

But the evening brought even more than I could have hoped for. Judith was waiting in the sitting room when I arrived home. Typically she would jump to her feet and rush to embrace me, but on this occasion she sat serenely in a chair next to our tiled fireplace. And typically she presented a more colorful picture. But this evening she had wrapped her white shawl around her shoulders, and she was dressed in a pale camel colored skirt. Her black hair was pulled back by a brown ribbon and although the light of the flames enhanced the glow I always sensed about her, the overall palette was more earthy than primary. Had I been an sixteenth century genre painter, I would have called the scene, "Woman Seated By a Fire." Though, given what I was about to learn, a more suitable label would have been "Woman With a Secret Seated By Her Fire." She smiled softly and held out her hand. I walked over and, as I took it, sat on the floor in front of her.

"I didn't just go for a walk when I left the studio this afternoon. I asked your mother to arrange for me to see Dr. Inaglio."

"What? Why?"

She laughed at my confusion. "I thought I was so sick last week because of Father's letter. And I'm sure that was part

163

of it. But that couldn't explain why I suddenly can't stand the smells in the studio. Or why I'm having trouble buttoning my slacks. I'm pregnant."

It took me a moment to digest fully what she had said.

"When?"

"When what? When did it happen? Practically any night since the middle of June, I should think! But mostly likely it happened early in December. I can't believe I didn't figure it out until this afternoon. How could I not have noticed that I missed my monthlies? I think your mother knew before I did."

"Have you told her?"

"No, but I think we should walk up to tell them now, don't you."

"Yes, yes, but wait a bit. I want to relish this moment with you. When?"

"You mean when will you be a father? In September, Dr. Inaglio predicts."

I laid my head against her stomach.

"You can't feel anything yet, silly," she laughed.

"It doesn't matter. I just want to be close to him. Or her."

I raised my head with some alarm. "But now you can't go to New York. Tell me you won't try to."

"I promise. I'll write to Mother and the news will please her. And she can look forward to seeing me with her grandchild next year. Maybe I can get her to come here for the birth."

Aaron's letter arrived three days later and we were confronted with another announcement, though one that did not, could not, of course, match the devastation of Fred's nor the joy of Judith's. At first I feared that hearing from Aaron would cause Judith to be depressed again, but her resilience, undoubtedly aided by the almost smug glee with which she regularly stroked her abdomen, was so amazing that her brother's letter seemed almost anti-climactic.

The letter was primarily informative. Aaron expressed his sympathy for the blow his sister had suffered, his relief that I was with her for support, and his hope that her new life offered excitement sufficient to compensate for their Father's "aberration," as he put it. He assured her that he was doing fine and that she need not worry about him. He had been to New York to visit their Mother, and she seemed to be recovering and bearing up better than anyone could have expected. She had decided that when she left the "sanitarium" she would return to live in New York City. She claimed, he wrote, that she had always felt more at home there than in Galesburg.

Nochie was also doing fine. He had rented his mother's place and had moved into "the big house," as he referred to it, with Aaron. The biggest surprise was that Aaron and Nochie had accumulated enough credits to graduate at the end of the fall term at Knox, and had decided to go to Canada to join the Air Force. The Royal Canadian Air Force would accept Nochie, they thought, more readily than the U.S's. A Knox professor whose wife was expecting their third child had eagerly agreed to rent the Broad Street house until Aaron returned, or until he decided to sell it. Aaron would use only as much of the money his father had left him as was needed to execute his and Nochie's plans. He would write as soon as he had a new address.

Aaron wrote nothing of what he had known about his father's affair or when he had known it. Nor did he mention

165

whether he had heard anything from Fred since he left Galesburg. Thus we were left to assume that by the time Aaron's letter arrived her father would be en route to Bali and her brother and half-brother would soon be en route to Canada, if they had not already departed.

Thus Judith's first Italian Christmas was spent in the circle of what had become her only real home. There were times when I saw her looking wistfully into the distance. But for the most part she was her usual lively self. Days were spent at the studio (her body adjusted quickly to the growing life inside her and after only a few weeks she felt no more nausea or aversion to strong odors). Evenings were spent planning our future. We debated about suitable decoration for the nursery that we were setting up in a room next to our bedroom. She claimed to be afraid that I would insist on at least one Crivelli Madonna and Child and wanted to "nip that idea in the bud"--- an English phrase I cannot to this day hear without great sorrow.

Front: Carlo Crivelli, detail of St. Mary Magdalene, from the altarpiece of San Francesco, Montefiore, 1471-3.

Back: *October 23*

Dear Hermann, From harlot to virgin again? Can love really wipe away our sins? Or was it the 30 yrs in a cave? Did C really paint this luscious lass? What's in the jar---booze or a balm of another kind. Detroit in Dec?

Love, Dennis

Chapter 9

Padua 1936-1938

    Judith and my mother worked tirelessly and eagerly with Le Direttore and me to establish a careful record keeping procedure. In the workroom, we proceeded apace---often even with a kind of frenzy that reminded me, when I had time to think about it, of the fiddle music that Olaf had played for me that Christmas night that now seemed so long ago and far away. The copies we prepared would be hung in their normal location, typically the villa of the owner but sometimes on the wall of a museum that was using our service. It was essential, then, to keep track of where the original was being concealed. We had various places of concealment, and the specific identity of each of these had to be recorded. We wanted several hiding spaces, rather than just one, because we did not want "to put all of our eggs in one basket," as Judith put it. Naturally we were worried about bombings and fires. On the other hand we did not want to use too many spots because we needed to keep our operation as unobtrusive as possible. In some of the villas where the copies were hung, false walls were built so that the original could be hidden close by. We also determined that in three buildings in each of our four cities, Verona, Venice, Vincenza, and Padova, we would build especially sturdy and larger hiding spaces. One of these was, in fact, installed in our Padovan studio and some in a space behind the adjacent Museo Crivelli.

We gave our undertaking the code name, "The Crivelli Project," since such a file would not seem at all suspicious given my father's museum work. We linked each of our four cities with towns in The Marches where Crivelli had worked most of his life. Venice was paired with Pergola, Verona with Ascoli, Vincenza with Camerino, and Padua with Fermo. The buildings in each location were simply identified as 1, 2, or 3.

Since Crivelli worked from the 1430's to 1490's we could use the first three digits of those 15th century dates easily without raising suspicion. Thus Ascoli, 1462, would indicate that an original was being stored in building number two in Verona or Pergola, 1473 that an original was being stored in building number three in Venice.

One of our hiding places had formerly been a *scuole*. As you know, Marco, in the fifteenth century, several privately funded lay fraternities were established to do charitable work— run hospitals and alms houses mainly. The Venetian member of Le Dirrettore was also a member of this scuole and arranged for us to use it. On one wall there was a large fresco of St. George and the Dragon, fashioned after one of Carpaccio's paintings on the subject. We hid several originals in a cavity behind that wall. This patron saint of Venice was supposed to protect the city from the plague, and we were proud of ourselves for protecting its treasures from the modern plague we feared was approaching. Beneath the tail of the dragon we inserted the tiny words "Cerca qui." (Look here.)[2]

We also assigned a code name---the name of a Saint --- to each original's owner. Since there were so many saints in the works we were copying, it was easy to associate a customer with a saint in the work he or she had brought to us. These names were kept in a separate file, simply called "Potential Donors." Here we could insert a sheet with a notation such as, "Federico Augusto might be convinced to donate his St. Peter." Or "Spoke with Maria Cassetti about the possibility of buying her St. Catherine." Judith took particular delight in assigning each customer to a given saint---you can guess, for example, why she was so pleased that Augusto had sent us a work that contained a St. Peter. An entry in the Crivelli Project file might thus read, "St. Peter, Camarino, 1472" and that would mean that one of Frederico Augusto's belongings was being held in the second location in Vincenza. "St. Catherine, Fermo, 1481" would show that a piece we had copied for Maria Cassetti was concealed behind the wall in our studio in Padua, building one in our city.

My father, mother, Judith, Le Direttorre, and I were the only ones who knew the code, though our team, of course, knew one existed. One of the students, Tomaso Rio, showed enormous talent both in restoration and administration, and he quickly became my chief assistant.

For insurance, the code was incorporated into the copy we made. Underneath the St. Peter or St. Catherine or St. Whoever we could insert the tiny date. We entertained ourselves imagining how future art historians in countries where our copies might end up (most likely Germany or Great Britain, we speculated) might interpret these little numbers

---

[2] Ariel David, Though fictional, this is based on an actual incident, see, "Missing Leonardo could be in a wall," The Kansas City Star, Tuesday, June 21, 2005, p. A8.

when and if they came across them—particularly when the number clearly contradicted the date when the work was known to have been painted. Two of Europe's most prestigious museums, and four in The States have some of our copies on their walls. I delighted in reading a recent article in *Art Bulletin* in which a scholar argues that a fake is the real thing. We did no Rembrandts; otherwise I am sure they would have been uncovered as fakes by the people involved in the Rembrandt Project. I rather hope I live to see the establishment of a Massocio or a Mantegna Project; the resulting scandals would be delicious!

I must emphasize that we were not forgers, and none of us thought of ourselves as such. Forgery implies intentional deceit, and the owners of the originals were in no way deceived. I suppose some might argue that we *were* setting out to deceive potential looters, so our copies might be technically classified as potential forgeries. But we considered ourselves only protectors and patriots. Whoever stole one of our products deserved to be deceived, don't you think?

There have been the inadvertent consequences. I have not confessed to any of the museums that have our copies on display that their works are not genuine. If people think they are looking at an original and take pleasure in it, who I am to spoil their aesthetic experience? What real difference does it make whether something is real or not if one likes it? Or, rather, even if it might matter to people like us, it certainly doesn't matter to the average museum visitor, does it?

We had about eighteen months of fairly uninterrupted happiness. Or course we were touched by world events. Mussolini's troops had taken Ethiopia in May of 1936. None of our circle thought the invasion was a good idea, but at least now it appeared that our coffee plantations there would be safe. In the studio and around many dinner tables there were discussions, often heated, about the Civil War in Spain that had broken out that summer and continued to be a leading story in all of our newspapers. In the summer of 1937 one of our team went to Paris to attend the World's Fair. He came back with stories of an amazing painting he had seen by the Spaniard Pablo Picasso that depicted the horrors of a German bombing of a small Spanish town. (We all know this as *Guernica* now, of course.) I'm sure it will not surprise you, Marco, that among a flock of artists the arguments about the latest trends in painting, cubism especially, were as, if not more, heated than those about political and social affairs.

Carlo Aaron Zollino was born on September 25th, 1937. Judith and I debated whether Michelangelo or Rubens would have been better able to capture his beauty. He had Judith's mass of black curls, fingers that tapered like mine, and my mother insisted that the dark eyes were exact duplicates of her handsome grandfather.

Ruth could not come to Italy, she wrote, until the spring; her father was not well. But she and the rest of the New Yorkers sent box upon box of infant paraphernalia, much of which mystified Angelina. Aaron sent us a Mezuzah to honor the occasion. He explained that it was not kosher because it did not contain the lines dictated by strict Jewish law. Instead he had written in English his version of words taken from two Psalms: "May your cups always runneth over and may joy always cometh in your mornings." He had enclosed them in a copper case that could be affixed to our doorway, and on the first Friday evening in October we did exactly that. He reported that Nochie indeed was in flight training, but that he had been assigned to a different branch when the Canadian Air force had discovered his mathematical talents. He did not, said he could not, elaborate on exactly what his exact duties were, but he could tell us that he would undoubtedly serve in an intelligence unit.

Carlo was a very happy, easy going child and, we all agreed, immediately showed signs of incredible genius. In six months he was crawling around our feet in the studio, at ten months he took his first steps. These were blissful times. Work went well and we managed to cache scores of paintings in our four cities. Judith put off her plans to visit her Mother; in fact her Mother even began in her letters to talk about visiting us for Carlo's first birthday.

But then in July of 1938 things began really to fall apart. Mussolini decided to imitate the action Hitler had taken when he got The Nuremburg Race Law passed in 1935. We were astonished, given the overall ways in which Jews had been integrated into Italian culture and government; as I had told Fred, many Jews were even members of his Fascist party. Mussolini's former mistress, a Jewess, actively raised funds for the party both in Europe and the United States. Thus Italy's Manifesto Race Laws of that July made no sense; the only explanation we could give was that he wanted to curry favor with the Nazi leader. Suddenly Jews were not allowed to participate in most areas of public life----they were not allowed, for example, to teach in the public schools. Other professions were closed to them and restrictions were placed on their rights to own property. But worst, for us, was a law making it illegal for Jews to marry Christians. And since one's religion was primary defined in terms of the mother's religion, Carlo suddenly became primarily a Jew rather than primarily an Italian.

Still, the laws in Italy were not (and really never were, it turned out) as strictly enforced as they were in Germany. Exemptions were made especially for Jews who had served in the military or who had been active in the Fascist party. Judith contemplated converting to Catholicism and we also discussed moving back to The States. It was obviously becoming too

172

dangerous for Judith (or her mother) to travel for visits, but we really allowed ourselves to hope that things would get better.

Then, in August, came another shock. The family's largest coffee plantation in Ethiopia was attacked and burned down by natives protesting the Italian occupation. Suddenly our main source of income disappeared. Of course, there was still some income from our farms, and a modest amount from our Crivelli Project work, and the trading company had some profits from non-Ethiopian enterprises. But my parents announced that there would have to be real belt-tightening. Since Judith's father had not provided for her financially in any way, assuming that I was well enough off to take care of her, we were now devoid of anything like the wealth we had always assumed would always be there for us.

It was into this set of circumstances that we received a letter from Billy Beauchamp announcing his plans to visit us in early October. He was coming to Italy, he wrote, to put finishing touches on his Ph.D. dissertation. He would stay with us the weekend following Carlo's birthday and then hoped that on the Monday following I would accompany him to Venice to help him gain entry into some of the private collections he needed to visit. (It was even harder then, Marco, for a foreigner to get cooperation without "knowing someone who knows someone," as the Americans put it.)

We looked forward greatly to his visit----the first we had from The States. (Even Judith referred to it that way; she had stopped saying "back home" as soon as she received her father's infamous letter.) The weekend lived up to our fond expectations. Billy arrived at the train station late one Friday afternoon and we were all there to meet him----Carlo, of course, full of excitement as he watched and listened as the steam engines pulled in and out. Judith and I were nearly as uncontained in our enthusiasm as we watched our dear friend alight from his first class compartment.

173

The days went too quickly. The weather was fine in the way that only Padovan autumn days can be, and as soon as Billy had settled in we arranged our seats on the patio so that we could watch the sun set over the wheat fields and vineyards in the nearby hills. It was too warm for Judith to need a wrap, but she carefully hung her white cashmere shawl on the back of her chair. First we sought news about Jimmy.

"He's already in the Navy, doing a residency in surgery at Walter Reed hospital outside of Washington. He will remain there on staff when the residency is finished. And I have also joined up. My commission has already been arranged---but they have kindly agreed to let me wait to be sworn in until after I hand in my dissertation----in January, I hope. I will be stationed in D.C. as well, so we'll finally be really close."

"How in the world did you arrange that?" asked Judith.

"Probably the same way it would be arranged in Italy. One just has to have someone like Theodore Beauchamp for a father."

"And if there's a war and the U.S. enters?" I asked.

"Oh, I think it's a toss-up whether that will happen. Most people in The States want to stay out of it if there is one. After Chamberlain's meeting with Adolf in Munich last month, it's not even clear that the British are going to interfere too much. And in any case, they'll still need doctors at Walter Reed and aides with connections in the Naval Office. I think Jimmy and I will be set for several years. But what about you two? Aren't you worried about what's happening here?"

"Of course we've talked about what to do," I answered. "We've thought a bit about going to The States. But so far we haven't encountered any real problems in Padua. Judith and Carlo are its most popular residents!"

174

"In any case," Judith asserted, "there's to be no more talk about war this weekend. Tell us all the U of C gossip."

We did avoid bleak conversation that weekend. Judith filled Billy in briefly about news from her family---or lack of it. I had written to Billy about the situation, and he diplomatically steered clear of the topic after Judith appeared to have finished saying what she wanted to say about it. He regaled us with stories about working on his dissertation----the thesis being that non-religious art during the Italian Renaissance was far more extensive and influential than most scholars admitted.

We both excitedly described to Billy the work we were doing at our studio. Before he arrived, we had decided that if we could not trust Billy to keep our secret, we could not trust anyone. He was eager to see for himself, and we took him to the workrooms early on Saturday morning. "Still making copies, I'm happy to see," he joked. He was appropriately enthusiastic about what we were doing, and even tried his hand at mixing some pigments with linseed oil. "Just like those good days in Minnesota. If only Jimmy could be here, it would be perfect." We agreed.

That afternoon the three of us went to the Arena Chapel. It was a sunny day, but the blue heaven with its golden stars on the ceiling that arched above these frescoes that arguably changed the course of art history, seemed even brighter than the daylight sky outdoors. We stopped in front of each of the thirty-eight scenes depicting the life of The Virgin and her son, but Billy particularly wanted to see Giotto's depictions of the Virtues and Vices that ran between the narrative scenes and the chapel floor. He especially loved Folly, who looks across the room at Prudence and Temperance. We all laughed at this vice--a bloated figure made especially ridiculous by a short-skirted dress, fat legs, and ridiculous crown of feathers.

"This is one of the examples I'm using to show that Renaissance painters even as early as Giotto could depict the secular as successfully as the pious," he asserted.

"I've always thought all the vices show what the audience at that time must have enjoyed," Judith said. "Obviously they didn't want to just look at Madonna's and Saints any more than we do. And I have to say that in general I've found depictions of the vices more interesting than those of the virtues---and a lot more fun."

"But look---Folly is carrying a staff. I think he's blind. Surely Giotto didn't want us to think of the association of folly with blind ignorance as fun," I objected.

"Okay, not fun, exactly," Judith agreed, "but at least a bit comical, in a contemptuous kind of way. Look at the wine steward in The Wedding of Cana panel. Surely he was meant to be taken as a vulgar buffoon---vulgar in the sense that Aristotle associates with Comedy."

Billy nodded. "There must have been as many asses around then as there are now!"

"One hopes," I joked," that there were also, then as now, plenty of worthy folk---like the faithful young girl serving at the other end of the table."

"That's just what I mean," Judith laughed. "The grotesque steward is way more intriguing than that insipid maiden."[3]

"Where is Usury?" Billy asked. "Isn't that what the Chapel was supposed to atone for?"

"Yes, but it's not one of the seven vices," I answered.

---

[3] Andrew Ladis, "The Legend of Giotto's Wit and the Arena Chapel," *The Art Bulletin,* December, 1986, Volume LXVIII, No. 4.

"Hmmmm, I see. But it's bad enough for Dante to put it along with the most seriously depraved people into one of the lowest circles of Hell----I forget which one."

"The Seventh," Judith quickly responded. We all felt now as if we were back in the classroom in that friendly, but still vigorous, competition to get the right answer. "That's where Mr. Scrovegni gets put with Enrico's maternal ancestor, Signore Vitialiani, for being usurers----or, as Dante conceived it, violence against art."

"I've never quite understood why usury should be thought of as violence against art."

"Oh, Professor Cohen explained it really well," Judith explained. "Dante like others in his time—Christians, at least---thought that the only moral way to earn money was through the sweat of one's brow---honest labor. So usury was disgusting. Dante construed art as a kind of honest craft or work. Earning interest while sitting around sipping wine was violence against work, hence against art."

"But what about forgery and fraud---aren't those violence against art?"

"Dante didn't talk about that," I said.

"So as long as it's hard work it's okay to make copies of artworks and pretend they're originals?" he asked.

"No, people who do that would probably be stuck in the bottom rank of Hell---in the Eighth with other counterfeiters. Thank God we've all agreed that what we're doing in the studio is not really counterfeiting."

"So you escape," Billy said. "But I, of course, will still be in the Seventh----just in another ring. The one reserved for violence against nature. There's no getting around the fact that

Dante would definitely have me in there with the other sodomites."

Judith put her arm through Billy's. "Don't worry, dearest Billy. Enrico and I will build a chapel or temple or something to get you out!"

Monday morning Billy and I went by train and then gondola to his hotel on the Grand Canal. His suite was richly garbed with deep yellow silk wall covering and ivory brocade draperies. The sitting room, furnished with Venetian antiques, led on one side to a lavish bedroom and on the other to a wide balcony. One wall boasted an enormous, gilt-framed mirror above an ornate side table.

"Rather like something out of a Hollywood movie, isn't it?" Billy quipped as he pointed to a rather ridiculous rococo telephone on a small desk. He ordered coffee and rolls and turned to me.

"I'm afraid I lied to you about needing your help to get me into those private collections. Professor Williams' letters of introduction have worked all the magic I've needed—though I may have to call on you for help when I get to Rome."

"Of course, but why....?"

"I have a favor to ask of you----and an offer to make. I want to make it absolutely clear from the outset that my offer stands whether you decide to grant the favor or not."

The coffee arrived and we settled ourselves on two armchairs.

"First, the offer. You have to get Judith and Carlo out of Italy."

"But..."

"No, dear Rico, please hear me out. Mussolini has some obsession about out-Hitlering Hitler. It's not going to be long before he starts doing what they're doing in Germany and Poland and Austria and God knows where else. Jews are going to be hounded, maybe even arrested and sent to some kind of internment camps. You may be, too. Maybe even your parents. In the best case scenario the Brown Shirts are going to start watching you, and all the good work you're doing at your studio will be destroyed. I know you've hit some rough financial times and that it's not going to be easy to get away and settle, shall we say, as comfortably as you're used to."

Billy had put our circumstances and the dangers we might be facing far more bluntly that Judith and I and my parents had dared. I was a bit too taken aback to respond immediately, but it didn't matter as my friend moved on quickly.

"If you want to go to The States, that's fine. I'll do whatever I can to help get you set up somewhere there. But I have another idea—one that assures that your talents will be put to good use. My parents have had lots of dealings with Wilcock's Auction House in London. They always have need of a good restorer, and they've agreed to take you on at a fairly good salary---for the English, that is. My parents own a flat in Kensington and you and Judith and Carlo can live there as long as you want or need."

I started to interrupt, but Billy raised his hand to resist it.

"The National Gallery and Victoria and Albert are also interested in talking with you. I think they may have a program underway something like the one you've got going in Padua. And to get you set up, you'll find that an account has been set up for you at Barclay's, with a not inconsiderable seed fund in it."

I was actually dumbstruck and it was several moments before I could speak. "But, why Billy, why would you do all this?"

He shrugged. "I love you---oh, not like I love Jimmy, of course. But I do love you, and Judith. I told you once that I am not a bad man. That's not completely true. Think of this as my version of Scrovegni's funding the Arena Chapel to expiate his Daddy's sins. There are sins of mine and my father's that need as much expiation as they can get."

"I've never known you to do anything immoral, Billy."

"Sodomy notwithstanding."

"You know I've never thought...."

"I know, I know, I'm just joking. But I have done some not quite admirable things and I'm about to do another. That's where the favor I'm going to ask comes in. But remember, whether you grant it or not, everything is already arranged in England."

"I don't know what to say. Of course anything I can do for you...."

"Don't be so sure." He paused and took a swallow of coffee, as if to steel himself for what followed.

"You know that I want to finish my dissertation up quickly so that I can get to Washington. I've gotten most of it done, but it's rather pedestrian. I need for it to have some more pizaaz. I want to claim that I've discovered something. I've never had an inflated sense of my abilities. Still I'm sure if I took more time I could come up with a solid piece. But I don't want to take the time.

"My thesis is that many of the artists known for their profoundly religious work could also be, should we say, more worldly. Not just that they produced secular things, but often stuff that was downright naughty---even bordering on the pornographic. I've got some examples----Caravaggio, of course, and Corregio and Titian. But everyone knows about those already. I want to expose some new guy."

"Go on."

"I need an artist that is recognized in the profession, but not one that has been or is likely to be too carefully scrutinized or extensively researched."

I began to see the direction, but not the goal, of his remarks. "Is Crivelli the sort of figure you are thinking about?" I asked.

"Exactly. But I don't want to limit myself to his peacocks and cucumbers. I want to be able to argue that he painted a nude."

"That's crazy—he did nothing of the sort."

"Your reaction is just what I want. Everyone in the art world will be astonished with my discovery."

"But you can't discover something that doesn't exist. The very idea is completely incredible."

"No, not completely. He was, after all, jailed in Venice as a youth for committing adultery. It was after he got out of jail that he moved to Padua----he probably had to get out of town. And you know as well or better than anyone that he didn't stay in Padua very long. Why did he leave? Why would a promising artist with a bright future leave one of the centers of art and culture, not to mention money, and exile himself in a remote area like The Marches."

"No one knows."

"And I'm going to provide the answer in my dissertation. I'm going to argue that he got involved in something shady in Padua and in order to avoid going to jail again he fled this time to The Marches and had a conversion and became genuinely spiritual."

"But what possible evidence can you provide for any of this?"

"That's where the favor comes in. You are going to paint the nude for me---that's all the evidence I need to make the rest of my speculation plausible. I have a dealer, who we'll leave unnamed, in a city, that we'll also leave unnamed---to protect you---who's going to uncover a painting in Crivelli's style---a painting of the Paduan woman he was involved with. I've done the research. I have the name of a Paduan merchant that has no ancestors who will object to my claims to protect the family honor. He's going to have hired Crivelli to paint a nude portrait of his mistress. But Crivelli is going to do more than paint her, so he's going to have to run off."

"Preposterous."

"Oh, suppose I grant that there are holes in my story. Still I'll have the painting and I'll have fun watching scholars try to prove me wrong. It'll be a smashing success as a dissertation. You know how people love this sort of controversy. And I promise you this----in a few years I'll expose the dealer myself and claim that I was the victim of a horrible hoax. I will be able to write another paper proving that someone else painted a pornographic copy of one of Carlo's religious depictions. Think of the fun I'll have throwing myself on the mercy of my fellow scholars. Your precious Crivelli's reputation will be restored and I'll have made mine."

"I can't do it It's still dishonest---fraud, forgery, violence against art, even if not in Dante's sense. I can't do that sort of thing."

Billy looked down, took a deep breath and then looked directly at me. "You already have."

"What do you mean? We already agreed that the work we're doing in Padua is not fraud or forgery. No one is being deceived. And if people are fooled in the future it will be due to their own worse crimes."

"I'm not talking about the future," he said quietly. "Or the present. I'm talking about what you've done in the past."

"What in God's name are you talking about?"

But then it struck me.

"The Raphael Madonna? That was a gift for your father's sister—she had to know it was a copy. Again, there was no deception involved."

"God, Rico, you are so naïve. Did you really think my Father wanted that copy for his sister?"

"That's what he said. That's what you said."

"No, I said that he wanted you to make a copy for the lodge, remember? That was a lie too, of course, but then my father changed the story. Both of them were flimsy---I was sure you'd seen through them but were just too polite to mention it."

"Why wouldn't I believe you---and your father?"

Billy just shook his head. "Because he's a businessman and I'm his son."

"You mean there was some sort of business deal involved?"

"Of course. My father doesn't just sell underwear and furniture. He's made another fortune buying and selling art as a silent partner with shady dealers. Lots of it is, shall we say, of questionable attribution. You know how many people want to claim they have originals by great masters. My Father has made some rich hicks very happy. The Madonna you painted at the lodge graces the living room of a Texas oilman. And the copy of the Art Institute Madonna hangs out in the Arizona desert somewhere."

"But surely these buyers had the paintings checked out."

"Yes, by people the dealer works with. There's a whole ring involved----and it's easy to fool people who want to believe."

I put my head in my hands. How could I have been so naïve? I think I must have felt rather like Judith felt when she realized that she had been fooled all those years by her father. I struck out angrily.

"Did you sell the Carravagio I gave to you and Jimmy, too?"

He looked really hurt.

"God no, Rico. Not even I could sink that low. And Jimmy doesn't know anything about this. Oh, he knows about the arrangments I've made for you in London. But he knows nothing about, ah, my request." He paused. "I did try to warn you that morning in the car when we first got to the lodge."

I nodded.

"I know it won't matter," he said. "But I really am sorry. I'm going to try to make it up to you."

"The offer to set us up in England is somehow supposed to compensate for this? Expiate your sins, as it were."

Billy turned pale. "I told you, that offer is not connected to what I'm asking you to do now----or what we asked you to do in the past."

I said nothing but stood and walked out onto the balcony and watched the scene that had so enchanted Canaletto and Guardi. After awhile Billy joined me and we stood just smoking.

"I'll need to think about all this for a few days."

"Fair enough. I have rented a small studio not far from here. We can work there, if you say yes. Of course, I'll help you. Can you find excuses to be up here for a few days? All you need to do is get it started, then I'll do the dog work and you can come back to put on the finishing touches."

I looked at him and said sharply, "I haven't said I'd do it."

"I know, I know. I just want you to do know that it won't take you away much from Padua."

We were silent again and then he put his hand on my shoulder. "Remember everything is already arranged in England. You have to get there as soon as possible. Promise me that you'll at least do that for me, for our friendship."

I let him leave his hand on my shoulder. Looking back I think if I had, at that instant, shaken it off and walked out of the hotel I could have avoided everything that happened later. I would have forgiven myself for my involvement with his father's fraud. I could have severed my relationship with Billy, but instead I didn't even question his friendship. I just said, "I'll discuss your offer with Judith tonight. I won't tell her about---- about the other thing."

"Whatever you think best."

I won't try to make excuses for myself, Marco. That is not my purpose in writing this. I want to be as honest as I can so that maybe you will understand---or, perhaps, so that maybe I will understand it all myself.

In some ways, the most difficult thing for me to confess to you is that already, as I was walking back to the train station, I couldn't restrain myself from imagining how I might manage to paint the nude Billy wanted. If Crivelli had created a nude, what would she look like? Once I allowed myself to go down that path, it was almost easy to rationalize the action. Billy only wanted something for his dissertation. No one really would be harmed. It wasn't as if he were going to sell it to some non-suspecting customer. He had even promised to expose the thing himself in a few years. The whole thing could even be construed as a great joke.

And always there in my mind was my worry about protecting Judith and Carlo. As I crossed the Ponte degli Scalzi I saw a group of Brown Shirts prowling in front of St. Lucia station as if hunting for someone to harass. How could I risk letting my family be victimized, however unlikely it might seem to us now in Padova?

On the train, my brain raced. Thoughts drifted back and forth between Billy's offer and request. I knew he was right; I had to get Judith and Carlo out of Italy before it was too late, before they might not even permit us to leave. How quickly could we make arrangements to go to England? Would Judith even agree to it? Wasn't it possible that she would prefer going back to Illinois, or at least somewhere in The States? To New York to join her Mother and grandparents? Was Tomaso ready to take over for me in the studio so that the work of Le Direttore didn't have to come to an end?

186

And always intruding on these ruminations, hard as I might try to suppress it, was the prospect of doing a nude in the style of Crivelli. Mathematicians and chess players must feel like this, I thought. A theorem that demands attention until it's proven, a puzzle that gnaws even at the sub-conscious until it's solved.

When I reached the door of our house, I paused to look at the Mezuzah Aaron had sent. The copper had turned to green, almost matching the color of our doorframe, and I had become so accustomed to its being there that I had scarcely noticed it for several months. But now it seemed strangely to stand out and thus to emphasize the fact that we were no longer as safe as we had always assumed we would be.

It was clear to Judith as soon as I walked in that much was on my mind. Fortunately news of Billy's offer amply accounted for my demeanor, and that evening I laid out the details of it for her.

"I think we have to face reality, my darling. We've avoided seriously confronting our situation here. You and Carlo are Jews and we can't risk staying here."

She nodded. "Yes, this time I can't overlook----how did Aaron put it to you---the reality in my own back yard."

"England or The States seem our best bets. If you really want to go back, we'll make it happen. But there's not a ready job and we do have to think about our financial situation. The burning of the coffee plantation has had an even more serious affect that we expected."

"My mother and grandparents and Aaron will help."

"Yes, I know that."

"But you'd rather go to England, wouldn't you?"

"It's not that I really prefer it. But everything is arranged, and I have the opportunity to continue the sort of work we're doing here. We've both found that so fulfilling. I don't know if there'd be anything like that in The States."

She nodded again. "It's settled then."

Even knowing her as I did, I was astonished.

"Don't you want to discuss it some more?"

"No. There's no point. You know I love it here---but I'll love it anywhere I am as long as I'm with you and Carlo. The sooner we make up our minds, the sooner we can begin our new adventure. Besides, I've never been to London. You've always wanted to show me all the Crivellis in the National Gallery."

Our new adventure. I sat back and watched as Judith paced around the room, excitedly making plans, speculating about packing and shipping, chattering about what our new life would bring. Her reference to the National Gallery's Crivellis brought thoughts of Billy's "favor" to my mind's surface again, and I was toying with my conundrum while at the same time I watched and listened to Judith.

Suddenly she stopped and turned to me.

"My God, I haven't even said anything about Billy. What an incredible friend. I had no idea that he cared so very much about us. How can we ever make it up to him?"

I rose and put my arms around her. "We'll think of something."

In the middle of that very night I woke with a start and a solution. It was rather like picking up a crossword puzzle that the day before you couldn't make any headway with, but now seems obvious. How could I have not seen it immediately? Now the picture that I could create was vivid to my mind's eye. A nude, yes, but draped---tasteful but still lascivious. Titillating enough to please a man who wanted a lasting image of his mistress. It was all I could do to keep from springing from our bed to begin the work.

My parents were disappointed but completely sympathetic with our decision. We all thought this would be temporary -- that the Fascists' courting of Hitler by imitating his anti-Jewish policies would be short-lived, that Italians would rapidly come to their senses.

Tomaso was eager to assume oversight of the team of painters in the studio. The code was set and my mother more than able to keep records by herself. Tomaso insisted that he could not flatter himself that he could fill my shoes, but would do his best. I assured him that being able to count on him eased my mind.

It was easy to go often to Venice to the room Billy had taken for our work there. Judith was distracted with plans and I could honestly say that details of our settling in England required that I travel often into that city. It took me awhile to convince Billy that my conception was better than his vision of a full frontal nude along the lines of a naked Maja, but once he gave in he took up my plan with enthusiasm.

I intended to borrow from an altarpiece that Crivelli had painted in a Franciscan monastery in Montefiore. Most of the original panels had been sent elsewhere over the years—to The States, England, and Belgium mostly, but a stunning Mary Magdalene still remained. This work had been commissioned during Crivelli's early years in The Marches, and someone he had used as a model in Padova could easily have been the model for this repentant sinner. It would have been especially apt if the real woman had been someone's mistress. Billy could

189

easily argue that if Crivelli had undergone a genuine conversion in The Marches, turning a real life adulteress into this saint would have symbolized his own re-birth, just as it was believed that a repentant prostitute could be reborn as chaste maiden.

The Montefiore Magdalena has long, wavy golden hair. On her slender feet she wears the sandals that signified the poverty advocated by the Franciscans. I would leave these feet bare in my copy. No, Marco, I must be honest, in my *forgery*. My mistress, like Mary, would be in profile, her face slightly turned seductively toward the viewer. My lady's lips, like Crivelli's would be sensuously parted. The overall impression would be that one was gazing at a beautiful woman.

I had first seen the Montefiore work when I was fourteen or fifteen in the throes of hormonal uproar. I fantasized over her for months afterward. I remembered my experience vividly. i did not want or need to return to the site now because I could do a better forgery if I painted from memory rather than from direct perception. I sent Billy to Montefiore, however. He was enchanted.

In her right hand, Crivelli's Magdalene holds a jar of ointment, the traditional way of depicting the woman who will bathe Christ's feet with expensive oil. I could turn the jar into a jeweled goblet that the mistress is offering up, along with herself, to her master. But the best feature of the original, for my purposes, is the way she holds up her red velvet cape with the fingertips of her left hand so that it drapes from a point just parallel to her pubic area. I would give her a naked left arm and a cape to cover this area, but have the cape so delicately held that one knows she will momentarily let it go and expose everything.

Of all of Crivelli's females, this one has the most eroticism---her breasts especially, beautifully rounded and curved and erect. Mary Magdalene is clothed in a saffron embossed bodice. A gauzy fabric reveals the top of her bosom.

190

I would leave this uncovered and reveal its full splendor. I would remove the sandals Crivelli had put on her feet; bare feet would serve as another sign of lasciviousness, for no married woman would appear shoeless to anyone except her husband. A plain gold background served for Mary. I would give her an arch of fruits and flowers---and even a cucumber or two. Prominent in the garland would be apples and pomegranates---the fruit of Eve and later of the Virgin Mary whose son suffered to save mankind.

We completed the work quickly---it was easier to do this forgery than to faithfully duplicate an original because I knew that it was, in a few years time, going to be exposed. I have to admit that I even helped Billy to work out details of the case he was going to make, and I did it with some glee. Art historians are, for the most part, a pompous lot, and as we worked we pretended to be fellows from this or that institute discussing this "discovery," and the subsequent exposé.

By mid-November we were finished—just after news had reached us of the dreadful attacks on Jews throughout Germany and Austria that later came to be called Kristellnacht because of the horrific sounds of breaking and broken glass. I knew then that I had made the right decisions.

Billy somehow managed to ship the painting to his shady dealer and he left soon after. Judith and I stayed in Italy through the Christmas and New Year holidays and then departed for London on January 15. As we left our small villa, Judith turned and kissed the tips of her fingers and touched the Mezuzah. When she saw that I had seen her do this, she looked a bit embarrassed. Then she shrugged her shoulders and said, "You can never have too much help."

And then we were off on our next------adventure.

*Front: Carlo Crivelli, Madonna, 1480, London, Victoria and
Albert Museum*

Back: *January 18*

*Dear Laurie, This baby surely knows what's coming—and bids us
all to share in the sorrow despite M's rich robe and all the
luscious fruit. (2 melons, 3 apples?) A bare tree also forebodes.
Note M's fingers. See you in Chicago. Love, Owen*

CHAPTER 10

LONDON, 1939

Billy had arranged everything, from securing Friendly
Alien status for us to lining up three nanny candidates for us to
interview. How much of what would unfold had he set me up
for from the outset? He could not have predetermined
everything that happened and he always denied any
foreknowledge of our subsequent involvement with ICRA. (I
will explain in due time what that organization is, Marco.) But I
cannot help wondering even now whether he didn't somehow
choreograph that, too.

Our spacious flat was located on a side street between
the Victoria and Albert Museum and Hyde Park. It was a perfect
location. Even before we had left Italy the V&A had contacted
me about doing some work for them. Then, within three days

of our arrival in London, I had been offered assignments at the three most prestigious auction houses in the city and at the renowned Sparry Institute.

During his lifetime, Lord William Sparry had established a foundation that insured that his considerable collection of art and artifacts, along with a substantial maintenance and acquisitions endowment, would provide for a private museum and research library. Both were located in an enormous stone mansion on the edge of Kensington Park, only a short distance from our flat. Nearly every art scholar of any reputation at all had been there at some time to lecture and do research. (Indeed, two of my professors at the University of Chicago had boasted of their sojourns there.) The trustees had wisely set aside funds for the study and practice of restoration. So for me, it was a natural fit and my activities while in England were mostly centered there. The contacts I made were invaluable.

Thanks again to Billy, Judith and I were soon invited into social and artistic circles that it might have taken us years to enter on our own. I was a bit afraid at first that Judith might be bored. The middle-aged nanny we hired was so efficient that, combined with an equally adept housekeeper-cook, she had ample free time. (We did, I hasten to add, as much of the cooking ourselves as we could, as we both felt the need to enliven the English cuisine with our own Italian and American touches.) But, of course, I needn't have worried. Judith's intellect and charm (and what many described as her "sweet" American accent) won everyone over immediately. When the directors of The Sparry discovered that she spoke French nearly as well as Italian and English, they offered her a part-time position managing----"herding," as one of the directors put it--- the visiting scholars. We relished being able to spend time together on the same premises just as we had in Padova. Who else could have fully appreciated my glee when I discovered a small Crivelli St. Thomas in the storeroom?

People so often speak of winds and clouds of war----
these metaphors have become rather frozen. We really did not
feel blown or shadowed. We worried about the impending
conflict, of course, but it did not permeate our lives. We were
distressed when the Germans invaded Czechoslovakia less than
three months after we went to London, but it seemed somehow
distant, probably due to the distractions of settling in. Although
reports and even more rumors reached us about horrific
treatment of Jews and other "undesirables" and "decadents"
especially in Austria, we certainly did not know how widespread
or brutal it actually was.

Carlo thrived. He loved the green spaces, ponds, and
the zoo that were so close to our flat. (Judith felt some of the
sympathy she had expressed for the bears entrapped in the
park in Galesburg. However, our son's enthusiasm for the
animals took the edge off of her disapproval of the zoo.) He
was lively and precocious and showed none of the delays in
language acquisition that children raised in dual language
households are supposed to exhibit. He loved the pigeons in
Trafalgar Square, but was happy to leave them behind to go into
the National Gallery with us. (He once asked if pigeons were
better with English or Italian, but before we could answer, he
decided to be on the safe side and bid them, "Ciao-Bye-Bye."
Will I ever see a pigeon without thinking of this?) Inside the
museum he always insisted that we go first to what he called,
"The Carlos." Has any other child learned as early as he did to
distinguish Crivellis from DaVincis? Even Judith came to look
more favorably on my favorite when she perceived them
through the gleeful eyes of our son. The National Gallery had
acquired several of Crivellis paintings, and the museum kept
them on display, while many of the pieces considered more
important and valuable were moved out of London for safe-
keeping. I looked upon this as one of the few advantages of the
political chaos.

The Board of Trustees at The Sparry consisted of five
people, four men and one woman, plus, as an ex officio

member, the museum's Director, Charles Richmond. Richmond was a solid scholar; he had earned advanced degrees in medieval studies, but was well-versed in Ancient and Renaissance art as well, and demonstrated an unusual openness, for traditional scholars of that period, to contemporary movements and non-European art. (His father had been a diplomat and he attributed his universal tastes to an early childhood spent in India. His detractors attributed it to lack of standards.) He was tall and slender and had sharp features and an equally sharp tongue when with friends. But he had learned—perhaps from his father—to temper his acerbic wit when his position demanded it. He was an impeccable dresser---one rarely saw him in the same outfit for weeks at a time. His conversation was scintillating and his wine cellar outstanding; Judith and I admired him enormously and enjoyed frequent dinners in his eclectically but superbly furnished bachelor flat in Mayfair.

The male trustees, a financier, a shipper, and two others who seemed to do little but watch over their fortunes, were of modest intellect, but this was aptly compensated for by sincere devotion to the arts. We became fond of all of them. It was the female trustee, though, who was by far the most interesting and to whom we became closest.

Lady Sarah Hall was unmarried and, to put it bluntly, unkempt. She was the only child of a very wealthy landowner in Warwickshire. In appearance she stood (and sat and walked) in direct opposition to Richmond. Her body, so far as one could surmise, was solidly rectangular---but it was hard to be certain, for her clothing always hung loosely and was invariably wrinkled and slightly askew. Her daytime uniform consisted of a high-quality but ill-fitted tweed jacket, pale blue or rose jumper, and dark blue or gray skirt---all above sturdy, fashionless flat shoes. Her only nod in the direction of adornment was a short strand of pinkish pearls and matching stud earrings. (Judith was certain that they were examples of the finest the South Seas had to offer and worth a small fortune.) Though still in her early

195

50's, her face was already lined--cross-hatched in the manner of Durer or Rembrandt. Her hair must have had some attention periodically, for it was always the same length, but it was otherwise unstyled. What might have become soft curls with some management stood or sat, depending on the day or area of the scalp, in a wiry frazzle. On evening occasions when formal wear was required, she sported another uniform---a shapeless long black crepe gown with the same jewelry. Only rarely did she add color via a paisley stole gracelessly thrown around her shoulders. (Later, when she and Judith had become fast friends, Judith gave her a long scarf with multi-colored stripes and this became an evening staple—and even occasionally was wound around her throat during the day.) Incongruously, given her failure to nod in the direction of fashion or boldness of dress, when she smoked, which was frequently, she always used an elaborate cigarette holder. She had a whole collection of these, Chinese lacquer, Indian gold, ivory Scrimshaw, silver with onyx inlay, onyx with silver inlay---- and in a variety of lengths. Judith and I took to exploring antique shops so that we could add to her collection---and to this day, even though Lady Sarah has been dead several years---I still find myself on the lookout for an unusual piece that I think might add to that interesting set. It is now housed at the V & A.

In Lady Sarah's case (and in many others, I found, Marco) the clothes fell far short of making the woman. She was, probably the smartest women I've ever known, perhaps the smartest person in terms of breadth of knowledge. There seemed to be no topic on which she lacked an encyclopedic grasp. She had earned top honors in mathematics and logic at Oxford, but could, according to mutual acquaintances, have done equally well in literature or biology or history. She spoke five languages and read seven more. She had a keen interest in politics and, of course, the arts. She had shared with her mother a delight in Chinese ceramics and with her father a skilled eye for Italian miniatures. Pieces of both types from her family's collection had already been donated to the The Sparry, and, as she had no heirs, they counted on many more. Undoubtedly this explains how this eccentric individual came to have a place on the Board of Trustees. But there was no question that the other members had become genuinely fond of her.

Judith made acquaintances her own age---mostly other mothers she met at Carlo's nursery school. However, it was with Lady Sarah that she felt the greatest affinity. Very quickly they become fast friends; something close to a maternal bond grew between them. When the ladies were excused after dinners while the gentlemen consumed their port and cigars, we could hear something approaching raucous laughter from the sitting room. Judith insisted that it was Lady Sarah who most often caused this with off-color remarks or stories, but I suspected that my wife was just as often the source.

Lady Sarah was incredibly generous—insisted, for example, on taking Judith to her dressmaker. (We were amazed that she even had a dressmaker, for we never saw visible signs of it on her.) Judith was provided with elegant outfits at a prices we knew were greatly discounted. It was as if by adorning Judith, Lady Sarah vicariously expressed the flamboyant streak hinted at by her use of cigarette holders.

We spent many evenings at her townhouse near The Sparry. Charles Richmond was nearly always her partner there, and elsewhere, and at her dinners she surrounded herself exclusively with only the most interesting individuals---- scientists, explorers, journalists, and, of course, representatives of all the arts. We spent many weekends at her country home, Stone Corners, near Royal Leamington Spa. On our second visit there, a pony was presented for Carlo's benefit. Lady Sarah herself insisted on overseeing his first riding lessons.

Visits to her residences were themselves like visits to a museum. In some ways, they reminded me of the

Beauchamp's, but Sarah's collections had been more carefully gathered and were exhibited with a greater sense of display. I, as usual, could not resist the impulse to recommend some rearrangements. Even Judith, who was not easily embarrassed, nudged me when I offered my suggestions; but Lady Sarah always said, "Of course, you're right," and on our next visit the pieces in question would have been adjusted: the Gainsborough would have been switched with the David, an Italian miniature would have been moved to higher shelf, or a Ming cat to a solitary spot on small side table.

Politics had never been a central interest of mine, but in the teeming and uncertain atmosphere of those times, it was impossible not to be a party to debates about the issues that so directly affected current affairs. Judith came from a family of avid supporters of the Democratic party in the United States; her maternal grandfather was in fact an active member of the Socialist party in New York. When she spoke about political issues, she mostly disdained and dismissed those who leaned toward the right, without actively doing much in the way of examining her own basic ideas.

Examination of basic political and social and economic ideas was, however, precisely what guests at Richmond's and Lady Sarah's gatherings loved to engage in, and thus Judith and I increasingly contributed our own opinions. The longer we were in England, the more troubled the times became, and the less we could put them to the backs of our minds. Disagreements on these occasions dealt mainly with how far to the left one should go---and just how far the government should take its citizenry. Most of us found Marxist thought exciting; we differed about the extent to which theory could safely become practice. Events in Stalinist Russia made many of us---but by no means all---skeptical. A few (and Lady Sarah seemed sympathetic to them) insisted that what was happening in Russia amounted to unhappy but necessary birth pains for a better world.

These discussions veered into topics about the role of art and artists in society. Most of us may have given both more credit than they are really due for changing social trends. Still, there was some evidence for our position. Judith cited the incredible influence *Uncle Tom's Cabin* had had in changing American attitudes toward slavery. A famous writer lectured us on Tolstoy's including that novel, along with *Les Miserables* and *A Christmas Carol*, as examples of brilliant works that served art's highest purpose---establishing the brotherhood of man. A composer (not so famous) pointed to the ways in which music could rouse the fervor of political demonstrators. I even tried to convince the groups that a minor painter such as Crivelli could intensify the faith of believers, and that the greatest artists could actually bring about religious conversion. (Though when asked for a specific example, I found I could not give one.) I was more successful pointing out that *Guernica*, which had become famous in the months since it's exhibition at the World's Fair in Paris, was certainly an example of how a painting could stir feelings of political sympathy.

"And Hitler has given us the best example of all," said Richmond. "He knows exactly how powerful art can be. Otherwise he would never have put on that show he called the Exhibition of the Degenerates in Munich two years ago."

"But it didn't work, did it?" objected one of the other guests. "He only made the art he hated more popular."

"Maybe here---but thousands of people in Germany are acting as if he convinced him."

As the summer of '39 wore on, the actions of these Germans forced us to give more and more attention to what was coming. Talk of and preparations for war intensified. One result of this---the happiest by far---was the coming to England of Aaron and Nochie. Nochie came just after the end of Spain's

199

Civil War in March and was stationed at Upper Heyford, a base in Oxfordshire. Aaron arrived just before Mussolini and Hitler signed their "Pact of Steel" in late May. He spent a few weeks in London, but then was sent to a secret location. (We now know the place was Bletchley.) After their arrival, Aaron and Nochie were often invited to Lady Sarah's evenings, and they provided something of a novelty for the other guests. A physicist who had a home in The Spa and had known Lady Sarah from childhood was the only one who clearly knew (but of course never publicly identified) where Aaron was working--- though everyone speculated about it with a degree of confidence usually inversely proportional to the degree of accuracy.

Here, Marco, I need to back up a bit to fill you in on what had transpired in their lives after they left Galesburg. Both had indeed moved to Canada—to Montreal since Aaron thought it would be good to learn some French. They used some of Fred's money not only to set up an apartment, but also to pay for flight lessons, on the assumption that it would better their chances for getting into the Royal Canadian Air Force. Judith and I thought this was a pipe dream, but we were wrong. They benefited from the prescient aviators in England and the Dominions who anticipated the importance of air warfare, should full scale conflict break out. These men also foresaw a shortage of experienced fliers, and when two athletic college graduates with pilots' licenses applied, the RCAF snapped them up.

Nochie's color did not seem to matter and he earned his wings with distinction. Color, in another sense, did turn out to matter for Aaron---to his great disappointment, early testing revealed that he was color blind, and so could not enter pilot training. The same battery of tests, however, proved that he had another talent also in great demand (greater and greater as the war progressed) in the modern military. His mathematical skills, not unexpectedly one supposes, were coupled with uncanny linguistic skills. The ease with which he had excelled in high school Latin and college German might have been predictors, but then he excelled in all subjects. He told us later that even he was surprised at how quickly he was able to speak French---though he could never seem to shake his Midwestern accent. The upshot was that he was assigned to a branch of the military specializing in cryptography.

Thus, by early summer, 1939, Judith and her brothers were living only short rail trips from each other. Nochie was not given leave until the weekend after Aaron arrived in London--- or, if he was, decided that his first visit to Judith would be better in the company of his half-brother.

"They'll come mid-afternoon on Saturday," Judith announced after her first telephone conversation with Aaron.

"How was it---talking to him?" I asked.

"We were very formal and polite. It was weird."

"Are you looking forward to seeing them----now that it's real?"

We had tried to imagine what it would be like having these two men to whom Judith had been so close and then so distant so near to her again. She still harbored feelings of anger and resentment about the fact that they had kept her out of their speculations about Fred and Violet. Like all married people, we had conversations that were repeated again and again.

"Why didn't they tell me?"

"They wanted to protect you."

"And I hate them and love them for that. They always preached that the truth would make us free."

"Abstractions are invariably tempered by reality."

"You can be so pompous!"

"All right, all right. I'm sorry. But also remember that brothers aren't very comfortable discussing their parents' sex lives with their sisters."

"And there were certainly a lot of parents involved," she mumbled bitterly. She would sigh and allow or cause the conversation to turn elsewhere.

But now the two she hated and loved would be in our home.

"I definitely want Carlo to meet them----to know them. But I honestly can't say how I'll feel when I see them."

"No, of course you can't."

Strangely, I had not really thought about how I would feel seeing them again. My own personal feelings on the matter had been consumed by my concern for my beloved. I tried to explain this to her, and ended by saying, "I don't know what I expect either."

It was exactly the right thing to say, apparently, since she threw herself into my arms and said, "I love you more than you can know. I couldn't have stood any of this without you."

"Nor would I want to have any life without you."

In spite of our own uncertainties, we did need to prepare Carlo.

"We're going to have some wonderful visitors on Saturday," his mother told him. "They are your uncles from American---Uncle Aaron and Uncle Nochie."

202

"Have I met them before?"

"No---they've been in America, but now they will be in England to be soldiers."

Like all children then, Carlo had become very familiar—and enthralled with---men in uniform.

"Will they fight Germans?"

"We hope they won't have to." We had not tried to explain to Carlo that Italians might also be our enemy.

"We don't want anyone to have to fight, do we?" I added.

"No." He thought for a moment. "Will they speak both English and Italian the way we do?"

"No—only English."

"Then I call Uncle Aaron, Uncle Aaron and Uncle Nochie, Uncle Walnut."

I started to correct him and then thought better of it. Uncle Walnut would be just fine.

The half-brothers arrived with military precision at three o'clock----something they could only have achieved by hanging around outside until the appointed time, as buses had become more crowded and ran less and less according to schedule. Inevitably there were moments of awkwardness as Judith opened the door to our flat and bid them welcome. Tentatively they embraced one another and then turned toward the lounge where Carlo and I were waiting. Judith and I should have known that we could depend upon the child to break the ice. He advanced with his hand held out. "My name is Carlo and I am three years and seven months old."

Aaron responded quickly, "I am Aaron and I am twenty-four years and four months."

" And I am twenty-four years and one month. My name is Nochie."

"Hello, Uncle Aaron and Uncle Walnut."

Shaking their hands, I quickly explained that Carlo understood he should speak only English to them---and that 'noce' was Italian for 'walnut' so he thought politeness demanded translation. He did not question why someone would be named for a nut, but then proper names are never a mystery to children accustomed to having animal and fairy stories read to them.

"It's the perfect name," laughed Aaron.

Both men had brought gifts---a set of exquisite toy soldiers and a small baseball glove and ball for Carlo, and things for Judith and me that were already in short supply in the shops----silk stockings, chocolates, bourbon, and American cigarettes and coffee. (You will be surprised how much I appreciated even this last gift, Marco. Think how hard it was by now to purchase Italian coffee in England, and English coffee is actually worse than the American variety.)

To my great relief, we fell into easy companionship. We walked to the park where Carlo showed his uncles his favorite spots and tried out his new ball and glove. Back at the flat before dinner, while the adults had cocktails, Carlo played with his new toy soldiers, using Judith's wedding box as some kind of fort. As he placed the box with great care, almost delicacy, on the floor he looked up at our visitors and pointed to the sides.

"These pictures are Galesburg," he said. "Mother lived there. She said you live there, too."

"Yes," Aaron said.

"I'm going there when it's safe to go on a boat," he said. "I will come to your house then."

"That will be wonderful," Nochie nodded.

"I want to see the trains. The geese, too, but most of all the trains."

"That will be the first place we visit," Nochie promised.

Aaron delighted Carlo by showing off the fact that he had prepared for this meeting by learning some Italian phrases---and amused his mother and him greatly with his flat Galesburg pronunciation of the vowels. But it was Nochie who had a natural ease with children. It was he who could not resist plopping himself on the floor next to Carlo to participate in the game the youngster had invented. Nochie seemed somehow to intuit the rules.

Still, even with the comfort we experienced with each other, there was a conversation that needed to be gotten through before any of us could truly move on—or, rather, back to the closeness that had existed before Fred's disclosures. Judith and the cook had prepared a wonderful Italian dinner and afterward, with Carlo in bed, we settled with the American chocolate and coffee in our lounge (which Judith always called "the living room.")

"That is without doubt the best dinner I've had since I left Galesburg," Nochie almost moaned in his satiety.

"It may even have outdone one of Ruby's feasts," Aaron agreed.

"Any news of Ruby?" Judith asked. It was an adroit way of getting to the topic that had now become the elephant in the room.

205

"I hear from my cousins in Galesburg from time to time, though not for several months. Sheis fine. She's working in the kitchen at the Cottage Hospital. They say patients have never been so well fed. Or the kitchen staff so well-organized."

"Dear Ruby," Judith smiled.

"And my grandmother in Peoria---she's okay—but she had a stroke last fall and had to move into a nursing home."

"I'm sorry."

Aaron put down his cup. "And I'm afraid I've got some troubling news about Mother. We didn't want to write---thought it would be better to wait until I could talk to you in person."

Judith bowed her head. "Go on."

"She was doing really well. I saw her last August and she looked great---and was in fine form. She never drinks any more. She even started seeing someone, someone she met at Temple."

"Mother started going to services?"

"Yes, she started just about the time that I decided to stop trying to be a real Jew."

"I did notice you ate everything in front of you."

"Oh, well---it was a worthy experiment. Anyhow soon after I saw her she started to have some health problems. They think it's her liver. They're still doing tests and trying different medications, but..."

Judith shook her still bowed head, and without raising it, said, "Will I ever be able to see her again?"

No one tried to answer. We were sitting next to one another on the sofa and I moved even closer and put my arm around her shoulders.

"You know she's one tough cookie," Aaron finally replied. "But I have to be honest---it doesn't look good."

Now Judith's head shot up. "*You* have to be *honest*," she snapped. "That's a good one!"

"Judith…." I started.

"No, Enrico. We have to do this. We've all had more than our share of secrets and things left unsaid." Aaron took a deep breath. "I know you are angry at Nochie and me for not talking to you about Father and Violet. But we didn't know anything for sure."

Now Nochie leaned forward in his chair. "We even felt sort of guilty all those years, like spies or something. We didn't even want to talk to each other about it. We were in the tent that one night and saw your, ah our, father go into my house. But we were only ten. Then we saw things later, tried to joke about it, but mostly we just tried to avoid thinking about it, let alone talking to you about it."

"And I swear to God, Judith," Aaron leaned forward, too. "We had no idea that we were brothers until Father told us, well he told me, Violet told Nochie."

"What things?"

"What things?"

"Yes, what things? What things did you see?" Judith wanted to know.

"You want details?" Nochie sat back.

"Of course she does," it was my turn to snap.

207

"What's the point?" Aaron shrugged.

Judith started to speak, but this time it was I who interrupted. "You should know Judith well enough to know what the point is. She has had to cope with getting this blow thousands of kilometers away from the scene---and she feels as if she missed signs she should have read better."

Judith looked at me with gratitude and took my hand. "Enrico's right. Suppose I accept your excuses for not talking to me about it. Why didn't I see what you saw? Why couldn't I guess at what was going on?"

"Well, for one thing, you weren't in the tent that night. That's the only time we actually saw anything blatant."

"And if Nochie and I hadn't seen that, maybe the other things wouldn't have meant anything to us either. One of the things you learn about cracking codes is that details really matter but they don't make sense without a hunch—a big picture, an hypothesis about how everything might fit together."

"So—what things?"

"Touches, taking more time to fix things at our house than necessary," Nochie said.

"And there were things that may well have been innocent---conversations in the backyards, or Dad's taking apples from our tree to Violet." Aaron paused. "Then, when I got older and realized that Mom and Dad weren't sleeping in the same room any more, well, I wasn't sure it was just because of her drinking."

"Did Mother know? Is that why she started drinking?"

"She says not. She says she suffered some depression after you were born and a glass of wine before bed helped. Then it was worse when I was born."

"But the affair started *before* you were born."

"Maybe her drinking was bad from the start and she just doesn't want to admit it, or can't."

I turned to Nochie. "Did your family know?"

"No---well, maybe Aunt Lou did, but when Mom left Galesburg she refused to talk about her any more. She felt so shamed by the whole thing. Probably more than Mom did."

"What did your Mother tell you?"

"Very little, really. The bare facts---and just that she had a chance for a real life and was going to take it now that I was grown up."

"Humph," snorted Judith. "A real life. And have you heard anything about that real life? I wrote when Carlo was born and a letter and large bank draft arrived several months later. He said they were doing well and hoped that the Japanese would stay out of Bali."

"They don't seem to be staying out of anything else in that area," Aaron said. "I haven't heard from him for nine months. Nochie and I both got letters then, but not another word since. Grandfather's contacts have reported that the company he's working for is still in business, but nothing in particular about Dad."

"If I hadn't married Enrico or left Galesburg......"

"Don't ever, ever blame yourself." Aaron got up from his chair and kneeled on the floor in front of Judith. "You know I was against your marriage." He looked over at me. "But I was wrong. No one could or would have cared more for you. And

Carlo is wonderful. Dad was ready to bolt. If it hadn't been then, it would have come sooner or later."

"And my mother wanted her real life," Nochie mumbled.

Judith stroked Aaron's cheek. "And we have our real lives. No more blame." She stood up, took Aaron's hands, and pulled him to his feet. She embraced him and then reached out with one arm and beckoned to Nochie. I gave them a moment and then stood and worked my way into the circle. Had it been an opera, this would have been the perfect ending to an elaborate quartet.

"And now," Aaron exclaimed. "We can honestly say we've put our deceptions behind us."

"Amen," the rest of us said.

To myself I added, "Yes, all deception behind us." I really meant it.

If only, Marco.

Front: Carlo Crivelli, Altarpiece from San Domenico, Ascoli, 1476. London, National Gallery

Back: *Nov. 19*

Dear Curtis, I am struck with St. D's tenderness—hand on heart and all—as he gazes at J. But St. A looks a bit stern, doesn't he? Probably caused by all those sacrifices he ordered. See you in NYC in June. Best, Isabel

Chapter 11

England, 1939-40

In August of '39, we, with thousands of others, were forced to take the war personally. Civilians began to evacuate London even before the Nazis invaded Poland in September; England, France, Australia, New Zealand, and Canada declared war on Germany a few days later. Given the increasingly frequent skirmishes on the North Atlantic, traveling to The States, we thought, would be as dangerous as staying put.

We agreed that I was needed in London. Officials in the government began to give greater support to the projects for protecting art treasures, and I was increasingly involved in helping with the preparations for this. As an Italian, even one that had been dubbed "friendly," opportunities for wartime service were limited, and I felt grateful to be able to contribute in this manner. I suspect that Billy's influence behind the scenes accounts for the fact that I never experience even the slightest harassment.

211

Trainloads of children were leaving London, but we could not bear to send Carlo off on his own. Judith had heard horror stories about children sent to Wales and beginning to speak that cumbersome language instead of English. And she resisted taking him somewhere herself. She insisted, only half-jokingly, that her aesthetic sensitivities would shrivel on a Yorkshire sheep farm or its equivalent. Ultimately it was Lady Sarah's nagging, and the generosity we had already benefited from so often, that won the day. Among her properties was a house in Kenilworth, "The Rose Cottage," she called it, located only a few miles from her place near Royal Leamington Spa. Kenilworth was easily reached by train from London and Aaron and Nochie were not too far away. The couple who had been living in the cottage---a substantial house, really----had moved into nearby Coventry to work long shifts in the Dunlop works there. The village should be as safe as a farm and it would be easy for me to get there for weekends.

Judith at first delayed until after Carlo's birthday, and then until after Christmas, but finally, right after our 1940 New Year's celebration, she did go to Kenilworth. Once more she quickly made friends, enthusiastically threw herself into the activities available, and created opportunities for herself. One day a week she assisted at Carlo's kindergarten.

"You won't believe *this!*" she wrote in one of her almost daily letters to me. "I am learning to *knit*. I've finished nearly half a scarf and am attempting a pair of socks. I wanted to include some colorful stripes in the scarf, but the Knitting Club "Commandant" dissuaded me---something about camouflage. The scarf is just *knit* stitches, but the socks also require *purling*! I kept getting lost at first and dropped a stitch or two in every row. So I started concentrating, and saying out loud to myself, 'Knit one, purl one, knit one, purl one.' Carlo must have been listening, because when my neighbor told me that I was progressing amazingly well, Carlo said, 'Oh, it's easy----you just knit one then purl one.'

The story had spread all through the village by the time I went to the shops in the afternoon. Carlo is a hero!"

She folded bandages, organized paper drives, arranged fund raisers. The winter of 39-40, while the so-called "pseudo war" in France went very haltingly, was the coldest in almost fifty years. Food rationing began a few days after Judith got to Kenilworth. She helped to make sure that the elderly in the village had enough food and fuel. There were coal shortages, and digging trains out of snow drifts caused frequent train delays, to my great horror on Friday afternoons when I was trying to get to my family.

"Lady Sarah is a Godsend. As usual her generosity never lags," Judith wrote. "Once a week a man from her estate (Carlo calls him Nonno John) delivers a stack of wood from her forests. It has been carefully aged, and Carlo and I are warm and toasty in our 'lounge.' We essentially live there now; last night we made our beds on the floor in front of the fireplace instead of braving our frigid bedrooms. Don't worry about us being hungry or thirsty. Nonno John also brings eggs and butter from their farms, and even bottles of wonderful wine from Sarah's cellar. (Never fear, my darling, I save the best for my evenings with you.) Nonno delivers boxes to others in the village---but I doubt they contain the same wine we are blessed with. Sometimes he takes Carlo with him and calls him his 'assistant'. Lady Sarah herself visits often, never empty-handed."

Rose Cottage could easily have been the subject of the most sentimental of rural landscape paintings. The stone façade was adorned with vines and the eponymous rose bushes. A requisite babbling brook, frozen that winter, edged the back garden. We were informed by several villagers that many prize-winning blooms had been harvested there. We planned to plant vegetables in the spring, and Carlo promised to help in the garden. The house itself had been refurbished in the early 20's and, although it was difficult to find a room where the line of the ceiling was strictly parallel to the line of the floor, it boasted indoor plumbing and a charming kitchen. In those days, refrigerators were still few and far between, but the ice box was well-constructed, and in any case during that frigid winter there was little need for it.

I loved my weekends there. Judith had brought with her from The States the short fur jacket she had worn to the lake lodge in Minnesota. Some evenings, after Carlo had fallen asleep upstairs, she would stand in front of our fireplace clad only in that jacket and negligee and undulate rhythmically to a tune played on the radio. On my trips back to London on the train (and in trips in my memory) I have visualized what Rembrandt might have done with my Judith had he used her as a model for that lady in a sequel to his Elders painting. This painting would communicate no doubts whatsoever about what she wants.

"How did my mother endure all those loveless years?" she once wrote. "I can scarcely bear the nights here without you. It's only by imagining how we'll spend the evenings when we're together that I manage. She must not have had any such thing to look forward to. That was left for Violet."

For about six months we wondered whether Judith's move had really been necessary at all. There was plenty of activity on the continent, but we continued to feel safe on our island. The occasional rehearsals of how to respond to an air raid warning were often something akin to parties. Finland fought valiantly, but capitulated to the Russians in early spring. The Nazis invaded Denmark, Norway, France, and the Lowlands. And things did not all go well for the Brits. Churchill became Prime Minister just three weeks before the evacuation of Dunkirk---an event that mixed feelings of national pride and humiliation. Still, London seemed safe.

As for my national pride---it essentially ceased to exist. I had never been a great supporter of Mussolini, and my ambivalence toward my government quickly morphed into a bitter anger. Mussolini would have been a mere buffoon, had circumstances not made him so dangerous. He seemed to empower himself by aping the actions of other tyrants. It was almost as if he had taken a leading role in a drama that called for skills just beyond his abilities to carry it off. In May of '39 he and his ministers---one of whom was his own son-in-law--- signed the Pact of Steel with Hitler. Formally titled, "The Pact of Friendship and Alliance," the two countries pledged economic and military cooperation. Most Italians opposed it (certainly my parents found it disgusting) and Mussolini at first did very little to hold up his end of the steel rod. He waited a full year to join Germany in declaring war on France (which only gave us false hopes that he might have re-thought his alliances), and then botched an invasion of the southern part of that country. I was happy, of course, that the armies had flailed and failed so badly, but at the same time couldn't help feeling some shame. In September of 1940, Italian troops invaded Egypt and had some initial success, but that turned out to be a disaster as well. They couldn't even manage to succeed on their own in Greece! At every turn, Mussolini and his armies seemed not so much concerned with actually winning campaigns as they did with making sure Hitler would share the table crumbs with them. I know you know some of this from your history classes, Marco, but I fear your teachers too often gloss over the truth.

At any rate, from January to June, my little family was as happy as we could be given our separation and general fears about the world. Every three of four weeks, Aaron managed somehow to get a car and drive from Milton Keynes (since we know now that he was at Bletchley I won't bother to refer to it as X!) to Banbury (close to Nochie's base) and then to the cottage. The treats they brought so supplemented Lady Sarah's largess that we felt almost guilty about the mini-feasts we enjoyed while others were beginning to suffer real shortages.

On one of these visits, when Nochie had not been able to get a pass, Aaron asked us to participate in what he called "a little experiment." He said he had been devising it since a visit we had made to the National Gallery before Judith had left London.

On that visit, Aaron had been duly impressed with Carlo's ability to identify paintings and painters. He was also fascinated by the fact that Carlo could "read" the pictures.

"See the man with arrow stuck in him----that's St. Sebastian." Or "The lady in blue is Jesus's mother." With a Dutch genre painting he would explain, "That little dog means that these people are good."

Aaron quickly fell into the game of identifying who was who and what was what. "It's like reading a code," he said.

"Not *like* reading a code," I replied. "It *is* a code. There are whole compendia or dictionaries that gather together explanations of all the icons."

So on this particular visit, Aaron said, "I want to show you some images----and I'd like to do it before Carlo has to go to bed. Maybe he'll see something we don't." Out of his satchel, Aaron pulled several heavy sheets of paper.

"Close your eyes," he directed. "I'm going to put a page on the table in front of the couch. Now when I tell you to open your eyes I want you to tell me what you see. One, two, three, open!"

"I see a bunch of lines of 0's and 1's," Judith said immediately.

I nodded. "Me too"

"Anything else," Aaron asked. "Carlo?"

"I see a duckie."

Judith and I looked at him as Aaron clapped his hands. "Good boy! Can you show Mommy and Daddy."

Carefully Carlo moved his hand to the sheet. "Here." And he traced the outline of a duck formed by an arrangements of 0's in the middle of the 1's.

"Oh, you're right, darling," Judith exclaimed with glee. "And look, it can be a rabbit, too." She showed us how the beak could become ears and the back of the duck's head the profile of the rabbit's face. "I remember this figure from a psychology class. It's a famous ambiguous shape."

"Right," nodded Aaron. "Now close your eyes again."

The next sheet showed the same ambiguous figure, this time via an arrangements of S's among an apparently random collection of letters that filled the page. The third sheet showed an apparently innocuous picture of three bears having tea.

"I see some bears drinking and eating," said Carlo. Then he smiled and looked up slyly at his Uncle. "But are you fooling us? Are there some hidden pictures?"

One of Carlo's books, like the magazines Judith had as a child, was full of puzzle pictures where one is instructed to find hidden objects in the drawings---a spoon or a pencil or a sailboat.

"Bravo, Carlo. But I'm not going to tell you what to look for. Let's see if you and your parents can find anything by yourselves."

Quickly we did find a kite, a cup, and, yes, a sailboat.

"There are some other things, too," Aaron said. "I'll give you a hint---there are two things you haven't found yet."

We were rapt. We turned the sheet upside down and sideways and eventually found a shovel and a needle.

217

"Close your eyes again." When he gave us permission to look at the new sheet, it was harder to decipher. It looked at first like a design page for military camouflage. (I had been involved in London in some discussions about creating such designs.) Again, it was Carlo who had the first success.

"Look---there's a little girl with a balloon." As he pointed to the relevant areas, slowly but surely, Judith and I also picked out the image.

Aaron shook his head. "No matter how hard I try, I can't see it. In fact, this is one of the images they use in tests for color-blindness. The way the colors are arranged makes it impossible for me to see anything but splotches. Obviously, Carlo didn't inherit my weakness, thank God." He ruffled Carlo's hair.

"Now eyes closed one last time." We could hear him arranging three more sheets. "Okay, open."

The pages again consisted of seemingly incoherent display of letters on one, 0's and 1's on the next, and random numbers on the third. We tried, but all failed to see anything.

"Where's the picture?" Carlo asked.

"I don't know, buddy. I don't see anything either. I don't even know if there is a picture. I just thought one of you might see something."

We continued to study the sheets, but nothing emerged in spite of our turning them upside down and sideways. Nothing.

"Oh, well," Aaron said. "It was worth a try. I just hoped you people who spend your lives looking at coded pictures of saints and stuff might see something we Cretins miss." He laughed and returned the pages to his satchel.

Later that evening, as we were finishing the last of the evening's wine, Aaron gestured with his head in the direction of the satchel.

"I'd rather you didn't mention my little experiment to anyone, not even Nochie. The work I'm doing is really hush-hush. It's not that I've shared state secrets with you or anything. But some people might not appreciate my even saying as much as I have about my work. I just didn't want to overlook anything in our attempts to….well, in our attempts."

"Of course," Judith and I said in unison.

Sometimes, Marco, no matter how much I try to put it aside, I worry about what that fine young man would have said had he ever learned about my own involvement with codes. Aaron was so, so good---like Judith and Carlo and Nochie and Jimmy. Maybe if there'd been more time, more of their goodness would have rubbed off on me.

The cold winter finally gave way to spring. But just as the tulips behind the Rose Cottage began to turn brown, Denmark, Norway and then the Lowlands were invaded and quickly, unimaginably quickly, fell to the Nazis. The June entry of Hitler's troops into Paris left us all so depressed that we could hardly discuss what was going on, and we felt less and less safe on our island. We prided ourselves now on our decision to have Judith leave London. In mid-July, with the onslaught of the now-famous Battle of Britain, it became more and more obvious that we had done the right thing.

As the air raid sirens droned destruction's symphony, I asked myself what circle of hell I had descended into with all these other poor souls. The all-clear signals were little solace, for they often provided only a kind of trumpet voluntary annoucing a procession through rubble leading only to a deeper descent through the rings. The percussive crunching of glass beneath our feet is the background of nightmares. Could a collaboration of Piranesi and Goya have captured the horror? During the first weeks of the attacks and defense, the only victor was confusion. Neither side appeared certain about what they were doing or what was happening.

Many weekends I was unable to travel to Royal Leamington Spa, and the mail was irregular. I distracted myself by spending longer and longer days at The Sparry and the V&A, where greater and greater efforts were directed at protecting the holdings. In 1939 the V & A was actually closed and much of the collection removed to safer locations. But it reopened in 1940 with a few things on display, to provide, said one advertisement, an hour or so of relaxation and reprieve from the public's obsessions with war. There was some bomb damage, but miraculously most of the museum was spared. The Sparry also received only minor damage.

On September 7, over a thousand bombers attacked London. The Brits, rather than being demoralized, felt vitalized. It wasn't that anyone was enjoying themselves, but rather as if they had decided that if they had to be in hell, they would make a party of it. People brought food and tea and ale to air raid shelters. Card games were organized, guitars strummed and accordions squeezed. Anyone with a voice and an ego led sing-a-longs. Although I could never find the source, and hence I am not completely certain that anyone but me heard it, one night I thought I heard someone playing a Hardangar fiddle. Was a wizard trying to ease our strife?

Or perhaps the uncanny tunes only declared the arrival of a letter in mid-September. It was from Billy.

Dearest Rico,

Your letter of March reached me. (Does a more recent one lie at the bottom of the sea?) I am relieved that Judith and Carlo are safely out of London. I worry about you but will soon be there myself to protect you.

Our best laid plans have gone the way of all such. At first, all went according to our designs. I became both Dr. and Lieutenant William Beauchamp in June. My dissertation caused the hoped for stir---the sequel (one hopes for an every bigger stir, perhaps even roil) must wait until this mess is over. By mid-July I had settled in D.C. and for a few sweet weeks shared an apartment with Jimmy between the Pentagon and Bethesda Naval Hospital.. Then things fell apart. In its wisdom, and despite our best string pulling, the Navy decided that Dr. Albright is needed at a base in Hawaii and that only someone with my charms (and, one must admit, my father's connections) can fill a naval aide slot in our London embassy. I suppose Jimmy and I could be farther apart, but only if he were sent to Fiji. At least dear Jimmy will be safer in Hawaii than in Fiji or London.

So---I may see you before, and certainly soon after, this letter arrives. I will take solace in the company of my dear friends. I look forward to helping you celebrate Carlo's birthday. And you can expect that I will count on you and Judith to get me through New Year's Eve without Jimmy.

Love as always,

Billy

The call informing me of his arrival did come soon after. He reached me at The Sparry.

"Is your apartment still standing, dear boy?" How could I have failed to be delighted by the sound of his voice?

"Yes, dear friend."

"Good---then if it's still standing at 6 PM I'll be there for drinks. I've already made dinner reservations for 8."

"Where?"

"Need you ask? At The Café Royal, of course. The maitre d' promised to give me Oscar's old table."

"Aren't you afraid that your bosses will frown on the Naval Attaché's identifying himself too closely with Wilde?"

"I'm only an aide. In any case, most of my bosses will probably be dining at the same place."

He was, of course, dashing in his uniform, though he insisted that he could not hold a candle to Jimmy. He arrived carrying a large bag containing several bottles of wines and spirits. He explored our flat, quickly consuming the first whisky I had poured him, and held his glass out for more.

"You've done wonders with it."

"You've been here before?" I asked with surprise.

"Oh, yes. Didn't I tell you. My father owns the building. He kept several apartments for his best associates. I especially like the Crivelli in the front hall. One of your copies, I presume."

"Yes. The original is in the NG. I've had more time to do some pieces since Judith and Carlo went away. I have a great workroom at The Sparry." I described in some detail the various things we were doing around the city to protect the artworks.

As we moved from the flat to a taxi to dinner, conversation moved, as it always did with Billy, easily from one topic to another. But that night we did not broach details of the "favor" I had done for him. Instead, he blithely spoke of his dissertation and the frantic discussion it had generated at his oral doctoral exam. A leading journal had promised to speed publication of a paper based on his Crivelli chapter. However, Billy did not linger on the subject. It was as if he knew he needed to protect me from having directly to confront the role I had played in the deception. He even waved me off when I tried to thank him for everything he had done for us in England.

Instead we talked about Jimmy and Judith and Carlo. He so charmed the waiters that they practically fought over who got to serve him. In short, it was a night with Billy and more than welcome relief from the blitz. Even the Germans, or at least the weather, cooperated. It was so overcast that flying that night was out of the question. We were spared having to interrupt dinner with a run to the nearest shelter.

We were the last to leave the restaurant with its elaborate food and more elaborate decoration---all mirrors and gilt and velvet and crystal. We stood for several minutes in front waiting for our cabs.

"Next time we'll have to dine at the Cadogan. Maybe I can arrange a private supper in Room 118."

"Room 118?"

"Oh, dear boy. That's where Oscar and Lord Douglas always stayed. It's where he was arrested. Now don't look like that! You know if it still existed you would love to stay in the room in Milan where Crivelli was arrested for adultery."

I could only laugh.

"Now to another subject close to your heart. Carlo's birthday is soon, right?"

223

"Yes, October 5th."

"That's what I remembered. I have already arranged for a two-day pass and a car to drive us to Kenilworth."

"You're a wonder!"

"Of course I am."

We spent more evenings like this together and on one I gave him an after- hours tour of The Sparry. We had boarded up the windows and many works had been removed, taken out of London, like the children, for safe keeping. The walls had a new rhythm. Spaces lighter than the surrounding areas showed where the previous inhabitants had resided.

My workroom in the attic, in contrast, was crammed. Several pieces in various stages of restoration stood or lay on easels and tables. We were attempting to keep the gallery open, but with hours reduced, naturally. I was working furiously to prepare pieces that had been in storage for display. (Many, I fear, were of dubious quality.)

On two easels were copies of Crivelli's that I tried to find time for. It was working on these that provided my best means of easing the separation from Judith and Carlo.

"They're both after sections of that huge altarpiece at the National Gallery, aren't they?" Billy asked.

I nodded.

He pointed to the one on the right. "That's St. Peter with the keys, I know. But who's the guy on the left? One's accustomed to seeing a lot of produce in Crivelli's pictures, but I don't remember any saints who have apples on their heads and shoulders. Am I forgetting one of the conventions? Or maybe those are melons."

I laughed out loud. "No, no, no, Billy. They aren't any kind of fruit---but I can see how you might think so. So far I've only sketched them in. They will be stones, I hope, when I'm done."

"Aha, St. Stephen, then---one of the many whose martyrdom involved stoning."

"Carlo calls him St. Stones. This painting is one of his favorites. I hope to finish it by his birthday. I haven't had the heart to tell him that people killed him by throwing rocks at him. He thinks he suffered by having to walk around all day balancing heavy rocks. It will take me much longer to finish St. Peter. I haven't even started the details on his mantle. The trim contains images of six saints---some of them only partial views, thank God. And the embroidery is incredibly intricate even for Crivelli. I'll have to use a magnifying glass to get it even approximately right. It's by far the greatest challenge I've set for myself."

"Do you expect people to look at him with a magnifying glass?"

"No---but...."

"But you would know." He looked surprisingly satisfied, patted my shoulder, and turned back to St.Stephen. "And you could make those stones apples or melons or even cucumbers, couldn't you?"

"I could make them anything."

We were too close to the topic of my "making anything" out of Mary Magdalene. We both busied ourselves looking at other artifacts in the room.

"A real mess, isn't it?" said a voice from the hallway. I turned to see Richmond.

225

"Charles," I called, "You're working late again."

"Yes, trying to pack a Ming vase that I'm going to drive myself to a farmhouse in Wales this weekend."

I know we can all be accused of distorted memories, Marco, but I do not think it would be apt in this case. I am certain that something passed between the two men. Richmond paused, just a touch awkwardly, before moving into the studio. Also Billy hesitated, as if deciding how to handle their meeting.

Still, quickly enough so that I dismissed my sensation, Billy stepped toward Charles, who had now in turn approached Billy.

"Good evening, Mr. Richmond. You may not remember me, William Beauchamp. We met several months ago at a dinner---Sir Edmund Crane's, I believe."

"Yes, yes, of course, William. I thought you looked familiar. I recall that you were working on your doctorate. University of Chicago, right? Ronald Moore is our mutual friend there."

"Yes. I have the degree now, but I've put my academic career on a back burner for a while. I'm in the Naval Liaison Office at our embassy here."

"Oh, you know Enrico from Chicago then?"

"Exactly. So I've been aware of his talents, and his strange obsession with Crivelli, for years."

"We may persuade him to let us put one of these on display. Our walls are sadly depleted."

"I'm sure no one will be able to tell it from the real thing," Billy insisted.

"Oh, but of course we would explain that it's a copy," Richmond replied.

"Naturally."

"Can you join us for a drink, Charles?" I asked as I began to replace covers on the various projects.

"I'd love to, but I'm afraid the vase will keep me here for several hours yet. Enjoy yourselves, and keep safe." He took Billy's hand. "Til we meet again, then."

"Good seeing you, " Billy bowed slightly. (And a bit ironically, perhaps?)

Lady Sarah wanted to host Carlo's birthday party, but so did Judith. She wanted village friends to attend, and Carlo, already able to discern its superiority, wanted Italian treats that, under Judith's tutelage, a neighbor had become quite expert at preparing. The Rose Cottage was a bit crowded, but the day was fine and we pleasantly spilled out into the garden.

As promised, Billy had obtained a car (as had Aaron who brought Nochie with him---happily he had obtained a rare pass) and fetched me early on the morning of October 4. Since the 5th fell on a Sunday, we decided to have the party a day early. In the back seat of the car sat a shiny new red wagon with the words "Radio Flyer" in lovely white calligraphy along the side.

"Where in the world did you get that?"

"Where does a Beauchamp get anything?' he laughed. "I actually brought it with me one the ship from Norfolk. That took some string pulling, may I say?"

It was, of course, the hit of the day. Carlo generously allowed playmates to take turns with him pulling and being pulled across the lawn. He appreciated the truck I had brought, but it was the wagon that he demanded be placed next to his bed. (I had not had time to finished "St. Stone," reconciling myself to finishing it for Christmas instead.)

"I shall name it my *carro rosso*," he announced joyfully.

Richmond was at the party, and Lady Sarah, of course. When I introduced Billy to her, I once again had the strange sensation that she and Billy already knew one another. Apparently not, though, since neither referred to having met previously. Nonetheless they seemed oddly intimate during the party. At one point I had gone into the kitchen to refresh a platter of antipasti and heard them talking in the garden just outside a window. I did not hear much, for Lady Sarah was standing with her back toward the house and the wind carried her voice away. I did hear Billy say something about it being too early. "I want to be allowed to do this in my own way and in my own time." I was too busy to think about it then, but now I know that they were already plotting out their strategy and tactics.

Although it was a weekend, all of the guests left shortly after tea. The children were exhausted and Carlo's uncles had only one day away from their duties. Richmond left with Lady Sarah, as he was to stay with her until Monday. This meant that Judith, Billy, and I could fall into our easy familiarity.

"The wagon is the cherry on the top, Billy." Judith glowed. "You have done so much for us. You were right, of course. We did have to get out of Italy. We hear such horror stories about what's happening to Jews."

"I fear it is only the tip of the iceberg. Evidently it's not just Jews---gypsies, the mentally retarded, cripples, political misfits, all sorts of folks that don't fit the Nazi ideal of a real mensch are being rounded up."

"Will the US join Britain in the fighting?"

228

"Hard to say. Roosevelt wants to, but there's still a lot of resistance. Some people are counting on Stalin and Hitler to fall out so that Russia will turn out to be Britain's ally."

"Would the British allow Churchill to align himself with a Communist?'

"They may have no choice. Would it be so bad? Lots of people think Marxism holds out a lot of hope."

"Do you?"

"I've thought about it."

"Your father must go crazy," I laughed.

"Oh, I'd never discuss this with him. But let's talk about brighter subjects. Lady Sarah kindly invited me to join you all for Christmas day at her castle."

"She would never call it that," said Judith quizzically. "Why do you? Have you seen it?"

If Billy had misspoken, he quickly recovered. "Oh, I just imagine those pearls and cigarette holders and tweeds must inhabit rooms lined with armor."

"I've never seen a single piece of armor there," I chuckled.

"Mostly I want to insure that New Year's Eve will be just us----and Carlo, naturally. I shall begin immediately hoarding all the fancy foods that I can filch from the embassy stores. I hope you brought your red dress," he said to Judith.

As Billy and I drove back to London late the next afternoon, we were mostly silent. I was always blue when I had to leave my family, and Billy was clearly lost in thoughts of his own. We pulled up in front of my building just as the abominable sirens began to blare.

"Get to your shelter," he urged. "I'm going to hightail it back to headquarters so that I can get the car underground. I'll call you later in the week----and give you a report on my success at pilfering savories."

I was able to get to Kenilworth two more weekends in October and the first in November. I could almost feel my arms becoming stronger as I pulled the *carro rosso* up and down the village streets. Evenings, before making love in front of the fireplace or in our bed, Judith knitted those drably colored stockings and scarves while I read aloud to her. Lady Sarah had brought several volumes from her library and we enjoyed the variety that they provided. One evening I happened upon a translation of a poem by Rainer Maria Rilke in a poetry anthology.

"Here's one about a sculpture," I said. "It's called *Archaic Torso of Apollo*."

We do not know his unheard of head,
in which the seeing of his eyes ripened. But
his trunk still glows like a thousand candles,
in which his looking, only turned down slightly,
continues to shine. Otherwise the thrust of the
breast wouldn't blind you, and from the light twist
of the loins a smile wouldn't flow into
that center where the generative power thrived.
Otherwise this stone would stand half disfigured
under the transparent fall of the shoulders,
and wouldn't shimmer like the skin of a wild animal;
it wouldn't be breaking out, like a star, on
all its sides: for there is no place on this stone,
that does not see you. You must change your life.

" How could Hitler and Rilke speak the same language? I like that line about the trunk glowing like a thousand candles," Judith said. "Don't you?"

"Yes."

"I think Crivelli shines like a thousand candles for you, doesn't he? Carlo shines that way for me."

"You and Carlo shine like a million candles for me."

"But what does he mean that the stone sees you? And that you have to change your life?"

"I think he means that when we look at great works of art they look back at us. Not literally, of course. But just as we make demands of them, they make demands of us."

Judith stopped knitting and look at the fire. She nodded. "That's good. They demand us to cherish them and care for them. That's why what we did in Padua and what you're doing here is so important."

"You must change your life," I repeated. "I think he means that we have to be true to art and that the only way we can do that is by being truer to ourselves and each other." As I choked back a sob, Judith ran to my chair, kneeled and hugged my legs.

"Oh, my darling, you are so true to everything."

I came very close to confessing to her what I had done for Billy. But I needed more than anything at that instant to make love with her. Afterward it was too late.

On the first Saturday evening in November, Judith stood in profile in front of our fireplace. She was wearing her slinky black satin nightgown.

"Tell me what you see," she teased.

I saw the most beautiful woman in the world. Her sensuous contours blurred in the chiascuro created by the firelight behind her. Her mass of hair fell beyond her shoulders. She had placed the tips of her fingers on her shoulders, tightening the satin across the orbs of her raised breasts.

"I see a vision that could not be captured with any degree of adequacy even by the likes of a Rembrandt or a Rilke."

"Look more closely, my darling. In a few weeks you may be reminded more of Rubens or Botticelli."

"They could never have gotten the light right."

She reached down and picked up a cushion lying of the floor and threw it at me.

"I really had not intended to spend the evening cataloging artists. Look again----look at my belly, damn you."

She resumed her profile stance. My eyes now traveled beneath those lovely breasts as Judith stroke her abdomen. "Can you see the bulge yet?"

I leapt to my feet. "A bulge---you mean...." We clung to each other.

"Yes, yes, yes."

"How long have you known?"

"Just since Thursday. I finally realized that I hadn't had my monthlies for a while, and when I did I really couldn't

232

believe I was pregnant again. I feel so good, nothing smells bad, and everything still tastes wonderful. It's nothing like with Carlo. It must be a girl."

"When?"

"The doctor and I estimate late June."

Lady Sarah joined us the next day for luncheon and she nearly began redecorating one of the upstairs rooms for a nursery before the pudding was served. Carlo asserted that he would be very careful with his sister in his *carro rosso* I hoped aloud that perhaps by then we would all be back in the London flat. Lady Sarah accused me of combining Pollyanna-ism and Italian refusal to confront reality. We all laughed and talked at once. Nothing that day could dim our bright picture of the future. It was a Jan Steen *Merry Family* with no hints of a warning.

Postcard

Front: Carlo Crivelli, St. George and the Dragon, 95-33cm, New York, Metropolitan Museum of Art, Rogers Fund

Back: Oct. 15

Dear Morris , This Geo doesn't look ferocious enough to protect himself, let alone a whole nation. Great placement of the lions, however. Red and white lance to signal Crusaders? Did he get to Jerusalem? Will you get to NY? Love, Emma

Chapter 12

England, 1940-41

I find that I have tried to put off writing about these next events, the ones that probably more than anything determined my fate. Judith used to quote lines from a poem she memorized in high school---something about "a road less traveled." Did I take a road more or less traveled? I do not know.

You have been told, Marco, about what happened; but I have never been able to spend more than one or two sentences discussing it with you. My story now demands the details.

On a clear, crisp night in mid-November, I returned to the flat later than usual. I had been working on one of the panels of St. Peter's mantle, the one depicting part of the head and knife of St. Batholomew. It had gone very well and I lost track of time, the way one does when the task at hand yields that rare balance between the level of challenge and the level of one's skills. My happy mood was heightened when I saw a letter from Judith waiting for me.

My darling,

I have to be brief today, as I am madly trying to finish a pair of sox and 2 caps. Our knitting group is joining up in Conventry with several other Warwickshire clubs for a Red Cross money raiser. We will have booths in a hall near the cathedral—"selling"goods to people who will then give them back. There is to be a special area set up as a play room, so several of us plan to load the kids on the bus and spend the day. We'll have supper there, too, and Carlo is very excited.

Don't worry: I'll get back in time to get a good night's sleep in preparation for your arrival on Friday.

I don't think I'll have to stand in profile in something slinky for you to see my big belly---I swear I've put on 6 inches in the last 6 days. But I feel so good. Only having you here every minute would make me happier.

C sends hugs and kisses. Me too. As usual, I pine for you.

Love, Judith

I smiled, picturing my darlings at their fair and anticipating hearing their stories about it the next day. As I began to re-read the letter, the telephone rang. That was November 14. It was Aaron on the phone.

"Thank God. I've been trying to reach you."

"I just got in. I was working late on…."

He interrupted me. "And I've been trying to get ahold of Judith in Kenilworth. She doesn't answer."

"That's strange. She should be home by now. She and Carlo and some friends were going to spend the day in Coventry."

"No, God, no," Aaron moaned.

"What is it, Aaron?"

"It's Coventry. It's being horribly bombed. Where the hell did she go? Please tell me she didn't go near the center."

"To a hall near the cathedral?"

"It's destroyed."

"What's destroyed----surely not the cathedral."

"Get to Kenilworth as soon as you can. You probably won't be able to get there tonight, but as soon as you can. I'll meet you there tomorrow. At the Rose Cottage. We have to find them. They may have trouble getting back."

But, of course, they didn't ever get back.

Bombing raids in Britain's industrial areas throughout the summer and early fall had been relatively contained. But on November 14, 1940, soon after 7 PM, five hundred German planes armed mainly with incendiary bombs hit Coventry. The center's beautiful Cathedral of St. Michael succumbed to flames. By the time Aaron's call came, the roof had already fallen in and much of the city center was burning. The hall in which the fair was being held, according to reports we got the next day, was among the first buildings destroyed, and most of the people who had taken refuge in its cellars died when it collapsed.

The bombing continued until dawn. Fire fighters concentrated efforts on the historic church, but to no avail. Through clouds of smoke the next morning, the incredible destruction became evident. Literally thousands of buildings were gone and most factories badly damaged. Tram tracks twisted around and over hills of rubble. Rescue parties worked for days around the clock.[4] A member of one of these was the husband of a Coventry Knitter and knew about the fair. He was with his colleagues when they discovered the bodies of the women and children.

Many details of those days are hazy for me. Somehow Billy appeared at the flat with a car soon after Aaron's call and took me to the cottage. Aaron was already there, and one day Nochie appeared as well. Lady Sarah and Nonno John were in and out. None of us could get into the center of Coventry the first day after the bombing. On the morning of the 16th, the husband of a neighbor came to tell us that the bodies had been uncovered. We discussed the logistics of identifying and fetching ours. One of my clearest memories is of how *quiet* this discussion was. Had this been Italy, everyone would have been making suggestions, demands, predictions, objections---all at once. But this was so civilized, or perhaps so uncivilized; who can say, really, which it was? I participated in this and all the other activities in a kind of stupor, going through motions, registering and reacting almost unemotionally.

Finally a high ranking Home Guard official, a friend of Lady Sarah's, appeared at our door with Nonno John and his truck. Aaron, Nochie, and I were driven to a make-shift morgue. We were lucky, I suppose. Throughout Coventry there were

---

[4] "The Coventry Blitz," *News and Information of Coventry and Warwickshire*, www.cwn.org.uk/heritage/blitz. The knitting fair is my fiction.

many victims who could not be identified. Those who perished in the hall basement were killed by debris that ultimately protected them from the conflagration. Judith and Carlo had been found next to one another. Neither, thank God, looked especially frightened, or even perturbed.

Billy contacted the embassy and arranged for a Rabbi to oversee the funeral, and Lady Sarah provided space for the burial in the mausoleum on her property, with the understanding that reburials could be arranged later. Afterward our small party gathered for tea in the mansion's morning room.

I turned to Aaron. "Did you like to stand on that railroad bridge the way Judith did?" I asked him.

"You mean the one over the switch yards? Yes, I think it was a favorite place of every kid in Galesburg. What made you think of that?"

"When I was there---that Thanksgiving when I met you all for the first time---she took me there. Said it was one of her favorite places---that she liked to watch the dance of the trains. She also said that people claimed that it would be one of the most important targets for enemies if there were a war. I keep thinking about that. I took her out of Galesburg. I don't think I'll ever forgive myself."

I was grateful that no one tried to point out that I was not to blame for what had happened.

"There will be a memorial service in Kenilworth next Sunday," Lady Sarah said. "Four women and six children from here died. Carlo was the youngest."

"No," I corrected her. "Sarah Ruth was the youngest."

The others turned to me, puzzled.

238

"Sarah Ruth. That's what we had decided to name the baby." And, at last, I dissolved into tears.

I spent the rest of the month in the cottage. I more or less allowed Lady Sarah to take care of gathering up Judith's and Carlo's belongings. She was deep into her own grief, but seemed to take some consolation in collecting and organizing things. I saved a few items---the white shawl, a few of the toy soldiers Carlo had led to various victories in his imaginary games, the jewelry, the wedding box, a teddy bear. The rest was taken away in Nonno John's truck. I really wanted to keep the red wagon, but in the end realized that it would be better to give it to one of Carlo's playmates. I found the image of the village children continuing to pull the *carro rosso* along the roads somehow helpful.

Lady Sarah spent several evenings with me. Billy came one day, so did Aaron, so did Nochie. Food and wine appeared somehow. Whatever the company, we sat quietly, sometimes with the radio on, often just staring at the fireplace. All of us tacitly agreed that there was nothing to be said.

Then on December 6th The Sparry was damaged by a bomb that fell on the street in front of it. Lady Sarah came to tell me the news.

"Can you face getting back to work?"

I remembered how Judith had dealt with the blow about Fred and Violet---taking several days to grieve and then announcing that she wanted to get back to work. I knew my own sorrow was greater and would not begin to diminish for a very long time, but I could almost hear her tell me to "get on with it."

"Yes. I can't stay here forever. Going back to Italy is out of the question. I might as well do something useful. I think

239

Judith would have wanted that. I even think Carlo would have wanted that."

"Good, they need every hand they can get to help with repairs and restoration. The Board is determined to reopen as soon as possible."

We left Kenilworth that evening. Although I have been many times to Lady Sarah's estate, I have never returned to the Rose Cottage.

To my great relief---the first positive emotion I had felt for weeks---the attic studio had not been touched by the bombs. But the southwest corner of the museum was severely damaged. The building's superstructure remained intact, but it would be impossible for visitors to use the main entrance for several weeks, so we had to set up a new entrance from the back. Two minor French works were destroyed, as was a large Delft vase. But the other damaged works, less than a dozen fortunately, could be refurbished. It sounds brutal, I know, Marco, but I almost felt as if the challenges were a blessing. I was able to lose myself once again in my work. I often spent the night on a cot I had brought into the workroom so that I could avoid facing the flat, where trying to lose myself was a losing battle.

We did not spend Christmas at Lady Sarah's. Instead Aaron and I went to Billy's flat for Christmas Eve. Nochie could not get a pass. The desert offensive that Britain had begun in North Africa meant that bomber pilots were given shorter and shorter resting periods between flights. The three of us decided that we would spend the night getting very, very drunk. Billy set out some of the fancy food he had pilfered---some fine Gouda cheese, a ham from the Ardennes, a fruit cake soaked in calvados, a mango chutney nearly vermillion in color, a plate of assorted olives, and even a small jar of caviar that he claimed to have pocketed at a reception at the Russian Embassy.

These delicacies provided the one period of near-hilarity. Already tipsy, I insisted that we create a still life arrangement with them. Like little boys we shoved each other about as we argued about whether the chutney should be in front of the cheese or the ham, the fruit cake centered or marginalized. Billy wanted to add a rose; I objected that it would be too sentimental. After that we ate a bit, but mostly sprawled in Billy's overstuffed leather furniture and sipped, and then gulped, some of Scotland's finest whiskey.

Inevitably, I suppose, we became more morose than gay.

"By the way," Billy said. "I saw Ambassador Kennedy at a reception yesterday and he sends his condolences."

"Be sure to thank him," Aaron replied moodily.

"Do you think this war could have been prevented?" I asked Billy. We had raised that question, of course, many times before, but it never failed to be asked when more than two people gathered together.

"Maybe. There are plenty at the embassy who say, now, that things might have been different if Chamberlain and Daladier had been more firm in the beginning with Hitler and Mussolini. Or suppose the U.S., France, and England had interfered in Ethiopia or Spain or Austria or even Czechoslovakia."

"They all claimed they had to build up their forces first."

"They were strong enough," Billy asserted. "France had more tanks and planes than Germany in '38. The Brits had more bombers. But I'm afraid even if they had gotten involved they would have fucked it up as badly as they did in Norway. They

241

seem always to make the wrong assumptions. Somehow they keep being out-witted by the German military masterminds."

"Well," I said, "in any case Hitler and Mussolini are garden variety bullies. They wanted war and would have started it no matter how much Britain or the US or anybody else gave in or stood up to them."

"And Chamberlain is a garden variety gentleman who believes people will keep their promises," Billy said scornfully. "The best thing the English have done so far is to get men out of Dunkirk. Then it wasn't the military, it was civilians with their little fishing boats and dinghies. Maybe the Russians are the only ones who'll be able to handle the thugs in the end."

"But they hardly acted admirably themselves in Finland."

"I suppose it's too early to tell who will deserve to be admired," Billy replied.

"We can't blame the Blitz or what happened in Coventry on Chamberlain," I said bitterly, and took a large swallow of my drink.

Aaron had been silent during our conversation, and, as his head was down, I thought he might even have fallen asleep. But now he raised he head and said loudly and angrily, "Who cares? What the fuck does it matter?"

Billy looked at him with some concern.

Aaron stood up and walked to the bottles and re-filled his glass.

"German and Italian bullies. English gentlemen. American ostriches. Do you really think it's like that? They all make assumptions and mistakes and don't care who gets sacrificed as they try to get something right. They've sunk

French ships just so the Germans couldn't use them. They even shot down a German rescue plane carrying Red Cross workers. Real humanitarians. And now Coventry." He paced back and forth.

Billy leaned forward. "Be careful, Aaron." And in the ensuing moments he tried several times to interrupt Aaron's flow of words. To no avail.

"It didn't have to happen," Aaron shouted. Then, more softly, as he sat down, "Everyone at Bletchley is talking about it. Not out in the open, but in little groups. We've been having luck breaking the German codes lately. People are saying that one message indicated that Coventry or maybe Birmingham would be bombed that night. The people could have been warned---but that would have meant that the Krauts would have figured out that the code had been broken and would have re-coded everything. Our deciphering efforts would have suffered a severe setback. So they sacrificed Coventry for what they saw as the long term gain. They sacrificed my beautiful Judith and Carlo so somebody else's Judith and Carlo would live." He put his head in his hands.

"That's only a rumor, Aaron," Billy objected.

Aaron raised his head. "It's a rumor that I believe. You don't know how ruthless they've all become."

Most scholars now say, Marco, that this was simply a rumor; the British War Ministry had no foreknowledge of a raid specifically on Coventry. But then, and for many years after, it was a story almost everyone believed and repeated---one of the specters in the fog of war.

When Aaron's outburst was over, he stood, looked at us for a long moment, shrugged his shoulders, and left the apartment. It was the last time we would see him.

Billy rose and stood at the window staring down at the street several minutes before turning around.

"He'll be all right."

We were, amazingly, both completely sober now.

"What he said---it's really just a rumor, Rico. I heard something along those lines at the embassy, but people who really should know deny it."

"People deny lots of things," I said. "Could it be true?"

"Of course, it *could* be true. But it's not going to do any of us any good to believe it, or even to think about it. What happened is horrible. I fear it won't be the last horrible thing that we have to face."

"Sometimes I think I can't go on—that I don't even want to. The only time the pain eases a bit is when I'm working. And then I turn and see St. Stone and it's as if it's happening all over again."

"Get rid of it. Better still, give it to me. I'll keep it out of sight here until you're ready to work on it again."

"Will that day ever come? If I really thought they could have warned people about Coventry, I couldn't forgive them. I'm not even sure I'd think anything anyone does is worth anything."

Billy walked over and stood directly in front of me and looked down into my eyes.

"There will always be things worth doing. For every scoundrel there's a Judith. For every bully, there's a Jimmy. For every botched battle, there's one that works. No matter how much we've done ourselves that we're ashamed of, there will be things we can try to be proud of. What you're doing at The Sparry now has to be one of those. It matters. If it doesn't….." He leaned down and kissed the top of my head.

"There will never be another Judith or Carlo," I said softly.

"No."

"I'm going to walk back to my place now."

"Whatever you want," Billy replied.

"Maybe Aaron will have gone there."

"Right."

He walked with me to his front door. Neither of us was callous enough to wish the other Merry Christmas.

Aaron was not at my flat. I do not know where he spent the next days. He was in London, however, four nights later when the Germans launched another massive air raid on us. His body was not recovered until the first day of 1941. He had been badly burned. Although Jewish law forbids cremation, exceptions can be made, and in this case one was made. The same Rabbi who had officiated a few weeks earlier, came with Nochie and Billy and me to Lady Sarah's. We placed the urn near Judith and Carlo. Several people from Bletchley attended the short ceremony there. I was surprised at how many came, for Aaron had had to keep that part of his life a secret. Person after person shook my hand and remarked on what an exceptionally fine man he was.

Afterward I sat alone in the small stone building and attempted to benumb myself. Billy had predicted that we would face more horrors. I could not allow myself to face the future any more than, at that time, I could fully address the immediate past or present. I determined that I could not, would not concern myself with either shame or pride. I would simply do what it took to abide the horrors.

Ruth could not discover ways to abide the horrors. In February, I received a telegram from Judith's grandfather.

"Sorry to inform that Ruth died yesterday. Letter follows."

It would take the letter almost two months to get to me.

"Dear Enrico,

When we received the snapshots of Carlo's birthday party, my daughter Ruth was full of optimistic plans for visiting all of you. In spite of her illness (a liver cancer we believe), she had rallied and we were all hopeful that she would steadily improve. The tragedies in England, however, took the fight out of her. She began to drink again and she succumbed on February 9. Fortunately her physical suffering was minimal.

She was sufficiently of "sound mind" to prepare a final will a week before her death. You and Raymond Thomas may already have learned from lawyers here that you are her sole and equal beneficiaries. Arrangements have been made for her estate to be administered until the two of you can take over.

This may come as a surprise—particularly to Raymond. Ruth knew, however, that he was Aaron's sole heir, and

I think sharing in his wishes gave her some small measure of comfort in her last days.

Rachel and I appreciated deeply your last letter. We did not tell Ruth that Judy was pregnant. There seemed no point. We hope that God is granting you some respite. We regularly take tea with Fred's family here, and with your mother's cousins in Brooklyn. These gatherings bring us all some succor. We seek it where we can. We pray that time will yield more comfort to us all. You know, I think, that we will assist in any way we can.

Keep safe,

Love,

Isaac Weitz"

A note was added at the bottom of the page.

"Judy always loved to go to museums when she visited us. A particular favorite of hers was Vermeer's *Mistress and Her Maid* at The Frick. I go there often to look at it. Vermeer's humanity brings me brief periods of hope and reconciliation It also makes me feel closer to you, dear boy. Remember always that you brought our dear girl great joy.

Love, Rachel"

Nochie and I did hear soon thereafter from attorneys in New York and Galesburg. Billy set up a meeting for us with a lawyer at the embassy who guided us through the necessary paperwork. Later, in a pub, we tried to speak of the future.

"We are rich men, Nochie. Not as rich as Billy, of course. Still what will you do after the war?"

He thought for a moment. "Every night at least one plane fails to make it back to base. We've all stopped talking about what we'll do if this ever ends. You?"

"I still can't picture any future without Judith and Carlo. I haven't heard from my family in Italy since the fleet was badly destroyed at Tarant. The family business depends so much on shipping---it may not even exist anymore."

We sat quietly for several minutes.

"Have you, ah, heard anything from your mother, or ah, father. Is anything getting here from Bali?"

"No, I haven't heard from them for months---maybe it's even been over a year now." He took a deep swallow of his ale. "May I ask you a favor?"

"Of course."

"If something happens to me---will you try to get the news to them? Maybe Billy can help."

"You can be sure I'll do what I can. I did write to Fred after...."

Nochie nodded.

We finished our drinks without saying much more. Nochie wiped his mouth and, to my great surprise, took my right hand in his two large dusky ones.

"Let's be sure to meet at least once a month. Not just to review the reports the lawyers said they'd send us. I just want to sit like this---stay connected, you know?"

"Absolutely."

But that was not to be either. The next week Nochie's plane took heavy flak. He managed to get the plane and his crew back to his base, but he had serious upper body injuries. He was sent to a hospital in Oxford for two months and I visited him there when I could. Billy went with me when they decorated Captain Raymond Thomas with an assortment of medals. Then he was sent back to Toronto. He recovered slowly, but could no longer engage in combat aviation. He finished out the war as a flight instructor and then returned to Galesburg. We corresponded, but it would be several years before we really connected again.

Something else happened during these years, the consequences of which we have only been able to surmise. Nonetheless, nothing has ever come to light to cause us to doubt our inferences. In February, 1942, the Japanese invaded Bali,

"Do you know where Judith's father has been living?" Billy asked when he called to give me the news.

"I haven't heard anything since long before Judith's death. In my last letter from Nochie---a fortnight ago---he mentioned that he still hadn't heard anything since then either. Our last address for them is a place called Densapar. That's where the shipping company had its offices. What do you know?"

"Very little. A Dutch admiral tried to defend the island, but it's fallen like all the others in the area."

We would never learn the fate of Fred and Violet. Suffice it to say that I do not think, whatever their sins, that they deserved what they undoubtedly suffered.

From your studies, Marco, you know that '40 and '41 were humiliating years for the Italian Army and Navy in the Mediterranean. I did try to get some news about my family; Billy helped. But to no avail. 1941 is mostly a blur to me. When

249

I remember it, it is tinted the way dreams are tinted---with a kind of shadowy overlay. I spent as little time at the flat as possible. Even on my cot at The Sparry, I had trouble sleeping and often I would work in the middle of the night for an hour or two before falling back into a fitful slumber. There were some assignments elsewhere and I even did some work on camouflage painting. Billy, too, threw himself into his work. Indeed, I had never known him to work so hard. He could not talk much about what he was doing. He did tell me it was connected to President Roosevelt's Lend Lease program---that rather under the table way of coming to the aid of Britain. We saw each other often, of course, and he went occasionally with me to dinner at Richmond's or for a weekend at Lady Sarah's estate. But they, too, were busy. Lady Sarah had taken on--- some would say over---several programs designed to help orphans and the wounded. She not infrequently engaged in tirades against the government's apparently deciding that they could ignore the poor and sick even more than they had before, given the excuse of the war.

My memories of the last month of that year, however, are quite vivid. Billy and I spent the first weekend of December at Lady Sarah's. We took a late train back, and I returned to my flat to sleep. My exhaustion must have taken a rare upper hand, for I was sleeping deeply early the next morning. The telephone rang several times before I could get to it.

"Who's this?" I said groggily.

"Me," Billy replied. "We're at war. I mean the US has entered it. The Japs bombed Pearl Harbor yesterday. I'm praying that Jimmy's okay---but communications are completely screwed up and I may not know for sure for days."

He filled me on the few details he had, and on Roosevelt's declaration of war on both Japan and Germany. We were both actually excited—and hopeful now that with America's help the war would be over sooner.

A few days later, however, another horror sent us reeling back into whatever level of The Inferno we seemed doomed to inhabit.

This time I was in my workroom and a secretary came to tell me there was a call for me in the office. On the other end of the line I heard someone taking, or trying to take, a few deep breaths. Then Billy's voice, a few words almost drowned in sobbing.

"You.....must.....come....to ....me."

Then another voice.

"Mr. Zollino?"

"Yes."

"This is Commander Thompson at the U.S. Embassy. I'm one of Lieutenant Beauchamp's superiors. He's had some very sad news His friend--the doctor stationed at Pearl Harbor—was killed there during the bombing."

"My God!"

"Yes—a Dr. James Albright. I'm afraid he was killed trying to attend to some of the wounded at the docks. Billy is quite broken up. I wonder if you could come and take him to his flat, or perhaps back to yours. We'll need him here, of course, but I think he requires a few hours to pull himself together."

"I'll be there as soon as I can."

A few hours? A few days? A few lifetimes? What does it really take?

Another Christmas, and another invitation from Lady Sarah—this one turned down. Billy and I sat alone in his flat on Christmas Eve. This time there were no fancy foods---only some bread and cheese and whiskey on the table, and neither of us was in the mood to arrange a still life.

"When we were kids," Billy reminisced. "Jimmy had a lab in the basement of his house. I didn't understand half of what he was doing. Sometimes he built models of cars or planes and I would try to do some myself. But he would still be sanding parts when I'd already clumsily glued all my pieces together---and some always fell off within minutes. He'd laugh, but never cruelly. He'd reassure me that I had other talents. I could draw and write well, so he'd let me make labels.

"His favorite thing, though, was his chemistry set. He did all the experiments that were described in the little booklet that came with the set, and then he'd read some other books and make up variations. As I said, I didn't understand much of this, and I didn't really want to. All I wanted to do was to sit next to him in that basement and watch him. His hero was Einstein. I don't know how many times he told me that science was going to save the world.

"Sometimes I'd take a book, a mystery or an adventure, and read out loud while he puttered."

"When did you, ah,...?" I hesitated.

"Discover sex?" He smiled. "When we were sixteen. One rainy summer afternoon in that basement. The amazing thing is that we never felt any guilt. That was because of him. He said if we wanted to do it, it must be natural. It was soon after that he gave up airplane models and chemistry for biology."

"But you couldn't act, ah, naturally, in public."

"No. I think that's why we took on the role of cynics. We read a lot about Oscar Wilde together. Have you ever read his long letter to Lord Douglas—the one he wrote from prison?"

"No."

"He rails against sentimentality---calls it the cynic's bank holiday. We decided when we read it that cynicism was the way to go."

"But he wasn't really a cynic, was he? Certainly not as a doctor."

"God, no. But he wasn't sentimental either. He mastered some combination of realism and optimism. He thought he could help people---really help them."

We had turned off all the lights in his flat because of a blackout. But we allowed ourselves a few candles and a fire. Together we watched the flames and listened to the spitting of the logs. As customary, I fell into speculation about how some artist or other would handle the room's lighting. Billy interrupted my musings.

"I want to do something to help people, Rico."

"But you are. Your work at the Embassy...."

"Peanuts. There are people really helping, working to make a world after the war where people, all of them, can make a decent living and have doctors like Jimmy to take care of them. I want to help the people who are trying to make a difference."

"Well, there are organizations here that..."

"No!" he almost shouted as he stood up and began to pace---much as Aaron had done the year before.

"This country won't let it happen. Neither will the U.S. Believe me, I know what the people in charge are like, what their real goals are. Roosevelt is different---but already people are getting ready to put things back the way they were after he's gone. The people who really run things are bound and determined that they will protect what they have—and see that they and their friends get more of it."

"Then who can you trust? Where are they? Russians?"

"Russians, yes. But not just Russians. Others with dreams like they have."

"But surely Stalin is no better than...."

"You're right. But he's put the country on the right track, and he won't be in power forever. There are people there who will work to set up a more democratic socialist nation."

"I've never heard you talk this way, Billy."

"I know----but I've been thinking this way for some time. And I've been doing some work with these people for a while. When I first got involved with them it was mostly, well, for the fun of it. I know myself pretty well---better than most, I think. I've always known that I'm not like Jimmy, or you, or Judith, or Aaron, or, God help me, even Carlo. I'm more flash than substance. But I have a redeeming virtue: I'm flash that admires substance. And I think I'm really, truly capable of love. I've often felt that the people with substance that I love like to have me around. Maybe they get some kind of energy from me, or can relax and recharge. That used to be enough. But now, I need more. I want to try to be, well, substantial."

"And you think you can help---how?"

"I'm not quite sure. By making sure they get the finances and equipment they need----and the science that Jimmy thought could save the world."

"You want to get science to them?"

"I don't have any information myself, but I can help those who do to get it in better hands. Everyone here and in America is so secretive. We don't even share a lot of stuff with each other. We're hoarding the knowledge, and the money, of course. Artists and scientists don't keep secrets. It's not in their nature."

"But you wouldn't want to give away things like troop movements or weapons programs."

"Probably not. But if someone at my embassy whose judgment I trusted had a piece of information that might help, say, people in Stalingrad, I might be willing to pass it on. Or if British Intelligence somehow found out when or how Nazis were going to attack, let's say Odessa, surely it wouldn't be wrong to get that information to those in a position to use it to save Russian lives. If the rumors about Coventry are true, don't you wish someone had been able to get a warning out?"

"Have you talked to others about this?"

"Some." He leaned forward with his elbows on his knees. "Do you want to help? Don't you think Judith would approve? Remember how highly she valued generosity?"

"But even if I want to, what could I do?"

"Provide a language for sharing."

Thinking about this later, I realized that the phrase, 'a language for sharing', was too carefully tailored for it to have been a spontaneous remark that night. I was, however, too caught up in our discussion, and my surprise at Billy's intensity about this kind of thing, to notice.

"I don't understand."

Billy stood again and freshened my drink.

"You are a master of secret codes. Not like Aaron was, of course. But you speak in one all the time---your Crivellis and Steens and Velasquezs---all those painters that use symbols that speak to the people who share their language."

"They're hardly secret."

"But we can use them to communicate in ways that only insiders understand. You can manipulate elements to give signs."

"What kind of signs? Secret information?"

"Maybe. But mostly the people who want to pass information need safe means of exchange---need to tell and be told where to pick things up, for example Wasn't it Mirandola who said that divine things have to be concealed under enigmatic veils?."

"You think the information that is getting passed falls under the category of the divine?"

"Well, no. But I do think passing it falls under the category of good works."

"And my role would be?"

"Wait here." He left the room and returned with a painting, carrying it so that I could only see the back. Slowly he turned it around and moved it into the candlelight. It was the St. Stephen, the one I had been working on when Judith and Carlo were killed, the one he called St. Stone.

"Is it okay? Can you look at the now?"

I swallowed and nodded.

"Look at these stones---the things I thought were melons. Do you remember when you showed this to me when you were working on it? You said you could make the stones melons. You could, or if that's absurd you could turn the palm he's holding into a rose. Then you could hang it at The Sparry. Lady Sarah and Richmond will make that happen."

"Lady Sarah and Richmond?" I asked, astonished.

"Yes, yes. They're part of this."

Billy continued excitedly, leaving me no time to express, indeed really to feel, my amazement.

"Suppose someone comes to The Sparry and knows to look at that Crivelli---and knows that it's a copy of the St. Stephen at the National Gallery. It would, of course, be openly labeled as a copy. And suppose that person knows that if a stone has become a melon, then it's okay to leave a package in the cloakroom. Or if the palm has become a rose, it's okay to give an envelope to a person that's, say, standing in front of the Titian in the next room."

"But I'd have to keep changing the painting."

"You could do that, couldn't you?"

"Yes, yes, I guess I could. But there would have to be a whole network of people, well, who share the language."

"There is, dear boy. Or there will be. Don't you see, we have to join in. We have to do this so that the lives of Jimmy and Judith and Carlo and Aaron---and the pain of Nochie---so that all of it makes some kind of sense. I can't go on unless I have something like this. I don't think you want to either."

257

What did I want, Marco? To help, to compensate my loss, or just to do something that would make me feel less numb? I did not take time to think about it; I simply agreed to join with Billy and Lady Sarah and Richmond---and the others, many of whom I would never meet or even know the names of.

Postcard:

Front: Carlo Crivelli, St. Stephen, Panel from Altarpiece for San Domenico, Ascoli, London National Gallery,

Back: *July 9*

Dear Catie, This unfortunate soul was assigned to help the poor only to end up being stoned. His feast day is 12/26—Boxing Day, I guess. Is this who inspired King Wenceclas? Love, Kirrie

Chapter 13

England, 1942-45

      Billy, Richmond, and I saw in 1942's New Year in the country with Lady Sarah. Our older friends were extremely excited that Billy and I had decided to join them in their "undertaking," as we called it. (Billy, of course, had decided earlier, but I did not ever find out exactly when---he always remained very vague about this.) We sat for hours in the dining room and sitting room discussing possibilities. Naturally, they were eager to fill me in on some details, but readily admitted, more comfortably than I would have thought, that there was much about the project that they themselves had not been told.

*Indeed, Marco, there was much none of us ever learned,
though I have a hunch that Billy, Richmond, and Lady Sarah
always knew more than I did. Some of what I did learn I still
cannot reveal, even to you now. Some of the people involved
are still alive; many of the participants have descendants who
might be harmed should I write too much here. I will try to give
you as clear a picture as I can. Some elements of The
Undertaking are no longer active. The rest, I believe, will cease
to exist when I die, and, hence, when you read this will have
been discontinued. Still, I think you will realize that this
document is sensitive, though you may want to share some of it
with your mother. I leave that to your best judgment. She, I
know, would not want any of this made public. She takes family
reputation and status so seriously.*

My activity was initially centered at The Sparry. I did
continue to do some work for other museums and galleries that
were in no way connected to The Undertaking, but less and less
as time went on. In the beginning, my only task was to produce
copies of Crivelli's that could be displayed in various rooms in
The Sparry, with agreed upon iconic substitutions when
necessary. By this time, the collection's great works had all
been removed for safe keeping, and there was ample space for
displaying my re-creations. It would have seemed odd to a
viewer with any knowledge of art history to have too many
Crivelli's on display even under war time conditions, so the
number on display at any given time never exceeded three.
Naturally, we could keep re-hanging the works as I finished the
necessary revisions. There was the St. Stephen, of course. I
thought that Carlo would have been proud of the fact that a
work intended for him was being put to such good use. There
was also the St. Peter---a work with such elaborate detail that it
was easy to make alterations.

These were the only two copies of works that hung in
The National Gallery. I spent several hours going over the

originals with the individuals who would use the works at The Sparry to garner information. All they needed to familiarize themselves with, however, were a few key elements that I could then provide substitutions for in such a way that the necessary signals could be provided.

Artists in every culture and era have used symbols to communicate ideas and emotions. The degree of codification, however, was rarely higher than in Crivelli's time. As I had told Aaron, whole dictionaries in the Renaissance were devoted to "defining" what an animal or jewel or plant or color or number or whatever denoted. Because Crivelli's works are so packed with details, it was easy to manipulate them to our ends. A crown of pearls that symbolized The Virgin's purity in an original could easily become one of sapphires---signifying chasity---without altering the overall message, and hence without arousing suspicion on the part of even the most sophisticated gallery visitor. To a member of our circle, the substitution would alert him or her to an imminent exchange or deposit.

I could turn a cucumber signifying a life force into a bunch of grapes symbolizing Christ's blood; an apple into a pomegranate signifying Eve's redemption as Mary. Crivelli made extensive use of all the instruments of The Passion---the rod of flagellation, the scourge, the crown of thorns, a bucket of vinegar, a sponge, a ladder, and, of course, the Cross. Carried by an angel, a crown of thorns could with little work become a trumpet or garland of roses. The possibilities were essentially endless; I was limited only by my "readers'" grasp of a particular vocabulary.

For the most part I had no idea of what kind of information was being exchanged, or what kinds of actions were or were not taken as a result of the alterations I made in the copies that were moved in and out of the galleries of The Sparry. But from time to time we did get news of some success. On the evening of December 17, 1942, Richmond hosted a celebration at his flat. At that elaborate dinner (one would not have had a clue that night that rationing was taking place), I met some players that I had not seen before, including a two Americans besides Billy, two Poles, two Russians, and three Frenchmen. The British Foreign Secretary, Anthony Eden, had addressed Parliament that day with a stirring speech that many argued solidified his political future. Documents had been smuggled out of Poland and Germany that proved that Hitler had moved from eliminating rights of Jews as citizens to actually transporting them to camps where they where enslaved and even exterminated. Eden read a statement condemning these acts that was, that same day, read in a dozen other countries, including the USA.

Why did we have cause to celebrate? We prided ourselves (whether correctly or incorrectly I can't be certain) that some of the pictures and documents that proved the atrocities were taking place would not have gotten to England if some of our project's tactics for exchange and delivery had not been in place. We truly felt that we now had hard evidence that our efforts were affecting public opinion and influencing public policy.

Billy embraced me and said, "At last. Something more than a bit of fluff. Judith and Jimmy and Aaron would be proud of us, wouldn't they?"

As often happened, after the others had left an evening gathering, Lady Sarah, Richmond, Billy and I remained.

"You seem quiet," Billy said to me as we sat sipping cognac.

"Those horrible pictures are enough to make any one quiet," Richmond stated quietly.

"Of course they are." Billy spoke with much more animation. "But Rico should take great satisfaction in what was achieved today. More than the rest of us."

262

"Because?" I pushed him.

" Because it's precisely people like Judith and Carlo who will benefit. What if you'd stayed in Italy and they had ended up in one of those awful places?"

"They did end up in an awful place," I replied, struggling to maintain control. "Sometimes I really don't see that it matters very much which awful place one gets to."

"Of course it matters." Lady Sarah set her glass down so sharply that it should have cracked, but somehow it stayed intact. "Of course it was terrible what happened to them. But until the very end they were blissfully happy. You gave them that. I hope I did too. Surely it was better to die the way they did than to spend their last months in the hell of those prison camps."

"Still---I shouldn't have insisted that Judith leave Illinois; I should have listened to her family."

This was a conversation that I had had with all of them, together or separately, but they always managed to repeat themselves patiently.

"You didn't insist," Billy pronounced as he had in the past. "She did it of her own free will. Wild horses couldn't have prevented her coming to Europe with you."

"I could have stayed there."

"We can't change the past," Richmond said, quietly.. "All we can do is use it---to try to learn from it and make things better. And that happened today."

"Okay, I grant that. But there's another thing I worry about sometimes," I said. "Here we sit, surrounded by opulence and we claim to be working for a world in which everything gets distributed fairly. Why haven't we—and all the others we meet with---sold everything and given our money to the poor and hungry?"

"Because until the world is changed we can be much more effective staying the way we are," Lady Sarah insisted.

"Besides, it's human nature. People aren't going to give up their advantageous perches until they're forced too. We're no different that way," Richmond added.

Billy nodded. "Remember how the monastic orders fought about whether they should own property? When your friend Crivelli painted for those who preached the simple life, he put his saints in sackcloth and sandals. When he painted for the ones who argued they could only do God's work if they amassed and kept enough to build glorious churches so they could pass the word to the masses, he put them in ornate robes."

"The church is as hypocritical about serving the poor as the Tories," Lady Sarah snapped.

"So you think 'come the revolution' we'll have to put sumptuary laws in place again?" I half joked.

"Sumptuary Laws?" she asked. "What are they? What a great term."

"We haven't had them in England for centuries, but we did have them once. Only knights and other nobles, for example, were allowed to wear fur in the fourteenth century," Richmond explained.[5]

"They go back at least to Rome. Limits were put on how much gold women could wear, for instance, and no man could wear silk," I went on. "In the Ottoman Empire the number of folds in a turban was even decreed. Savanarola managed to get

---

[5] "Dress," Doreen Yarwood and Diana Julia Alexandra de Marly, *Encyclopedia Britannica,* 2007 EB Online, 12 March, 2007.

264

people to take them seriously for awhile. No one could wear fine cloth or scarlet in public. That's one reason red is a color for The Virgin. She wears the blue of purity on earth, but red robes when she becomes The Queen of Heaven."

"Of course, laws like that would never work for very long," Billy scorned. "At least not anywhere except in some utopian or religious communities. My father made all his money precisely because people want to show off. Your cigarette holders, Lady Sarah, would certainly be outlawed." He pointed to the delicately scrolled gold and lapis lazuli cylinder she held. "The revolution will have to settle for what's possible."

"Once we discover what that is." Richmond rose and offered us more cognac. "More of this sumptuous stuff, anyone?"

We all declined.

"Until Sumptuary Laws are passed, I suggest we all find cabs and go home to our comfortable beds." Lady Sarah yawned as she stood up and tied her striped scarf more securely around her neck.

"You two go on," said Billy, remaining in his chair. "I'm spending the night."

Richmond smiled fondly at him.

I managed, I think, not to show my surprise, but expressed it a few moments later when Lady Sarah and I stood in front of Richmond's building.

"I had no idea---and usually Billy tells me everything."

"It has only started. Billy wanted to say something to you but worried that you might disapprove of his not remaining as faithful to Jimmy's memory as you have to Judith's."

"Is it serious?"

"It is a happy arrangement. It provides a healthy outlet for both of them. And, need I say, a safe one. Will it last forever? I seriously doubt it."

"Actually I'm glad for both of them."

"You need something of the sort for yourself, dear Rico."

"No, not yet. Sometimes I think I'll never need it again. After seeing those horrible pictures----Mostly I just need to do what it takes to stay numb."

A cab pulled up.

"You go on. I think I need to walk."

We embraced rather fervently. "She was the love of my life, too. And I didn't even need to be the love of hers. Isn't that odd?"

Leaving me surprised for a second time, she rode off.

Billy and I were both troubled, when, early in 1943 he came to me where I was working at The Sparry in my workroom with an assignment quite different from the ones we had been given earlier---the ones that seemed to deal only with providing a shared language for facilitating exchanges.

"They want you to insert an extinguished candle somewhere in the St. Stephen."

"An extinguished candle? That's a symbol of Death. Why?"

Billy looked uncomfortable. "Someone has been disloyal."

It did not take me long to grasp the implication.

"And that someone is to die? We're supposed to cooperate in an assassination?"

Billy nodded.

"Billy, we can't."

Agitated, Billy picked up a pestle and began to grind a piece of vermillion that I had placed in a mortar on one of the tables. "I don't like it either, Rico. But they told me we can't afford the luxury of such scruples when we are at war."

"Who are they? Richmond, Lady Sarah?

"No. Others. I can't say."

"But you trust them."

"Of course. I wouldn't even have come here otherwise."

"But death..."

Billy stopped his grinding. "We know people do what they think they have to do."

"Coventry, you mean?"

"Coventry---and other things. Things we don't even know about. They assured me that this-- this disloyal person has been responsible for many deaths himself and that if he's not eliminated, our work will be seriously curtailed."

"I don't like it."

"They promise it won't happen again."

I walked to the window.

"If you want," Billy said, "I'll try to do it myself." He walked over to St. Stephen.

"No. We'll do it together. Mix some of that bituminous yellow with the linseed oil."

So, for a week, St. Stephen hung in Gallery Three with an extinguished candle in his hand instead of a palm frond. I had taken another step along my path. And when "they" did not keep their promise not to ask us to do this sort of thing again, it became easier to take my subsequent steps.

Not long after we gave St. Stephen an extinguished candle, Billy and I spent a weekend with Lady Sarah in the country. Richmond was there as were two couples that I had met earlier, though had not known then that they were involved in The Undertaking. Both were part of the art world, but I shall not identify them. Suffice it to say, the currents of our lives would mingle again.

On Friday night, we dined and played bridge and gossiped; there was no mention made of our secret work. One of the couples---I'll just call them Donald and Donna Smith—was American. Donald appeared to be involved with armaments as well as art, but exactly how I never learned. Donna was a former model and quite a beauty, with an eye not just for quality in paintings (she was an avid collector of Impressionist works) but for adorning herself exquisitely. Both had been raised in Wisconsin, and their accents filled me with nostalgia and longing. Donna wore a dress that, although black, was of a style similar to Judith's red one, cut high in the front and low in the back. Instead of ostrich feathers, red brocade ribbon formed a border around the hem. She had draped a crimson velvet shawl around her pale shoulders and ruby earrings that reminded me of a pair I had seen on display at the V&A hung delicately along a long, slender neck. Lady Sarah was wearing the colorful striped scarf that Judith had given her. Somehow, everything seemed to remind me of Judith.

Donna was quite the opposite of her, physically:, straight blond hair, every strand of which stayed in place, peach complexion, a tall, thin body carried with willowy grace whenever she moved across a room. On previous meetings, I had been impressed with her wit and intelligence, but for the first time that evening—indeed for the first time since that awful November night, I found myself sexually aroused.

The attraction was mutual. Shortly after I retired, there was a soft knock at my door. Donna, now in a champagne-colored nightgown, but still draped in crimson velvet, entered when I opened the heavy door. There were few preliminaries.

"Don't worry, Rico. My husband and I have an open marriage—but a very happy one. I don't want anything except what I believe will be a pleasurable hour or so. I like you, and I think you like me. If I'm wrong, just say so, and I'll leave with no hard feelings."

"You are not wrong."

The next hour was quite pleasant. There would be many hours like it during the next few years. We never exchanged letters or gifts. She made no demands, nor did I. We simply enjoyed each other during our encounters. I have no doubt that she spent similar hours with other men; I felt no jealousy. For me, however, these outlets sufficed. The activity was of a different category from what I had with Judith, and from what I have had with your mother, Marco. I'm sure Billy would say the same about his relationship with Jimmy and the others in his life. I consider it a serious mistake to lump all sexual activity together, just as I consider it a serious mistake to lump all artistic activity together.

269

On Saturday, a kind of informal seminar took place. Donald called it "brainstorming," an American expression I have never quite taken to. The topic of our discussion was, not surprising, the work of The Undertaking, primarily funding it and related projects.

"Perhaps we could sell some of The Sparry's works," John suggested.

"Out of the question," and "Absolutely not," were the simultaneous, indignant responses of Richmond and Lady Sarah.

"Too bad," Donald held up his hands apologetically. "There's a real good market in American now—and the supply of the most popular European artists is drying up."

"Then we moisten it," Billy said, matter-of-factly.

"How?"

"With what?"

"With Rico's wonderful copies," Billy replied. "There were plenty of people before the war who could be fooled into thinking they were buying originals. There'll be lots more now."

"That would be dishonest," said Richmond.

In the context of what we had all been engaged in for several months, this remark was ludicrous, and everyone, including Richmond, recognized that at once. We all broke into peals of laughter. From then on, whenever one of us said, "But that would be dishonest," hilarity ensued.

The other couple at Stone Corners that weekend was a French pair, let's call them Jean and Marie.

"We may even be able to take advantage of the fact that there is a new source of art works becoming available in Europe---however sadly," Jean pointed out.

The group turned to him.

"The Germans, wherever they go, are looting everything in sight, and when they evict Jews from their homes, they simply take what they fancy. Many of those people were wealthy and sophisticated collectors, n'est-ce pas?"

"Fortunately some of them were able to sell their treasures themselves to raise funds for escaping," Marie added.

"So it would be easy to explain how a substantial number of works suddenly became available," Lady Sarah nodded.

"And harder," I added, "to investigate the provenance and legitimacy of the sale."

"How many can you turn out, Rico," asked Richmond. He knew, of course, about the workshop we had set up in Padova.

"I'll need time to keep doing the substitutions at The Sparry, naturally. But if I could get some assistants we could probably do five or six a month. There are plenty of photographs in The Sparry library that we could use. Not as good as the originals, of course, but we might be able to manage."

"Why not just do a bunch of Madonnas," suggested Donna, "in different styles---ones that would fool the unsuspecting? As long as we're careful who we sell to---not sell two works too much alike in the same town, for example. Wouldn't that work?"

"Where will we find dealers to help?" asked Lady Sarah.

Billy chuckled. "Leave that to me."

So a new phase of my work unfolded. I made a copy or two of Crivelli's, to scratch that itch, as it were. Mainly, though, with the help of some skilled craftsmen that Richmond miraculously found (two men too old for military service and two who were of the right age but not qualified for reasons of health), I turned out a series of Titians, Raphaels, Leonardo's, and a Botticelli or two.

Happily, I can assert that none of these are now hanging in museums, unlike some of the pieces we produced in Padova. Some have been declared forgeries. Some have been (and for this I do feel a bit a guilt) "restored" to the heirs of Jews whose homes were plundered. Most still grace the houses of individuals who continue to enjoy them in their ignorance.

Yes, Marco, it *was* dishonest. But it was in a good cause. We were always able to rationalize that our activity was (and is) not dishonorable or despicable. We often contrasted ourselves with forgers whose actions were intended only for their personal gain---to Van Meegeren, for instance. He, you remember, was an embittered painter who deeply resented that fact that his own work was never critically acclaimed. So he turned to producing Vermeers---not copies, but works in the style of that fine artist. Though it's hard to believe now (the pictures are so inferior) he managed to pass them off as the real thing. He might never have been discovered if he had not been tried as a Nazi collaborator in Holland. He then smugly confessed what he had done to make fools of the people he had tricked---including some curators at very prestigious museums. He was a scoundrel, we maintained. We were heroes.

The postcards were my idea. Like most ideas it was born of necessity. In May of '43, we saw the demise of the Comintern—the international association of Communist parties that had been founded two decades earlier. It was supposed to unite Socialists around the world, though many saw it primarily as part of Russia's strategy to keep control of the global movement. The Allies were staunchly anti-communist, of course, and as the war progressed, Stalin believed he could gain ground by appearing to be cooperative. He decided to disband the Comintern. At the same time, he increased his support of more informal "popular fronts" wherever they sprung up.[6] All of a sudden, a greater need arose for exchanging resources and information in locations far beyond the reaches of The Sparry. That is when the Crivelli Research Council, was established—in September of that year--and the reason the postcards became so important.

"We know how to communicate using The Sparry, but how can we use our know-how abroad?" asked a man who looked uncannily like Crivelli's painting of St. Thomas Aquinas in the upper tier of the National Gallery's San Domenico altarpiece. His face was somehow round and sharp at the same time. Deep lines traveled from his nostrils past his mouth where they met similar ruts that looked as if they had been carved into the inner sides of his cheeks. The tight bow that formed his lips was almost always pursed, and led one's eye upward along a long beaked nose to piercing walnut colored eyes beneath busy eyebrows that nearly met at the nose's bridge. Incredibly long and sinewy fingers contrasted with a short, squat body. He did not quite have St. Thomas's tonsure, of course, but he was essentially bald except for a narrow horseshoe shaped ridge of black hair that looked as if it has recently been dyed. When I mentioned the resemblance to Billy later, he laughed and accused me of seeing Crivelli saints everywhere, but, after a visit to the museum, had to admit that I was right. We took to referring to him as St. Tommy.

However, that early fall weekend at Stone Corners, he introduced himself as Dennis Jones. No one believed that this

---

[6] "International Third," *Encyclopedia Brtiannica, 2007 Encylopedia Britiannic Online*, March 15, 2007, http://www.britannica.com/eb/article-9042565.

was really his name. He spoke rapid English, flawlessly grammatical, I was told. I attributed my inability to place his accent to the fact that I was not a native speaker, but Lady Sarah, Richmond, and Billy were also unable to guess at his origins. He became the self-appointed leader of our discussion.

"I would like us to come up with ways of insuring that the contributions we've made in England can be duplicated or at least emulated elsewhere," he asserted.

"Unfortunately," said Donna, who had come without Donald that weekend, "we can't hope to find enough Rico's around the world to keep changing works in museums."

"Let alone enough museum directors to cooperate," said Billy.

"Oh, that might not be such a problem," said Richmond. "There are more of us sympathetic to the cause than you might think. But I agree that there are not enough Rico's."

"I'm flattered." I was, naturally, very pleased.

"We also have to worry about having a Rico ourselves," Lady Sarah interjected. "The Americans are advancing from Sicily and it's only a matter of time before Italy is free of the Nazis. Their surrender should speed that up."

Indeed, it would only be a month later that my country's leaders switched alliances and declared war on Germany. I would become more and more anxious to return to Padova to see what had happened to my parents and our home. As you know, of course, it would be two more long years before I could go back.

"We do have one thing on our side. After the war, travel will become easier again. Someone from here will be able to travel, say, to Boston and maybe we can think up some way to make use of the Boston Museum or The Gardner," suggested Richmond.

"But wouldn't that be awfully inefficient?" objected Donna.

"It would be easier to send a painting---or a copy of one," Lady Sarah said.

"Would it? How? They'd have to be boxed up. And it would be so bulky. If it were done too often it might arouse suspicion," Billy said.

Who knows where ideas really come from? Probably some combination of memory and imagination, as David Hume had suggested. At any rate, at that moment my eyes fell on one of the Italian miniatures that Lady Sarah's father had purchased and that she and I had moved from room to room, and shelf to shelf in an effort to find the perfect spot for it.

"They wouldn't have to be bulky if we made the copies small enough. And they wouldn't have to be boxed, or even concealed in baggage. We could reproduce them as postcards. I've always been irritated that I could purchase postcards of Michelangelo or Turner or Vermeer, but none of Crivelli's. There's nothing to stop us from making Crivelli postcards and mailing them wherever they're wanted or needed in the world. Just receiving one would be a sign that information was about to be exchanged." I was thinking out loud, and immediately everyone joined in.

"Or that the information could be found right there---in a coded message on the other side," someone said excitedly. Everyone later took credit for being the first to make this suggestion.

Jones sat back and listened as suggestions shot around the room. From time to time he took notes in a small burgundy leather notebook.

"The number of cucumbers or roses or sapphires could signal the date of a meeting."

"It wouldn't even have to be that obscure. The same postcard could be used over and over if the date on the card stood for, say, the same date but a month or two later when an exchange was to take place."

"A dragon—which everyone knows refers to something evil—could be a generic sign for an enemy."

"But, of course, not everyone does know that. It's part of the beauty of Rico's plan."

"Crivelli often gave his saints blond hair since that was a sign of nobility. We could use blonds as a short hand for Germany---or just to indicate North."

"Right. A blond saint holding a cross surround by a garland that includes two cukes could mean you were to meet someone at Old North Church in Boston at two o'clock. Dated June 1, it would mean to be there July 1."

Some ideas were so silly that we laughed with glee at and with one another. Others made us more somber, as when someone pointed out that there were almost limitless ways to indicate death: a Judas or a skull or a snake or a Pieta or any of the instruments of The Passion that Crivelli was so adept at utilizing. But mostly we stuck to suggestions for ways of setting up meetings.

"We could use a dove to warn someone to flee, and a peacock to mean you should stay put."

"If one of us needed a meeting in New York we could send a postcard of The Met's Madonna. We could say, '9/25. Dear X, I was impressed with this. I love the central theme of integrating two virtues. Best, Y.' That would announce a meeting in Central Park at 2 PM on November 25."

276

"Or 'What a Grand Dragon just left of center. And three saints!' That could mean it's time to erase someone who's been disloyal at three o'clock in Grand Central Station," Jones said coldly.

That silenced us for awhile, but our excited imaginations did not allow us to remain that way much longer than it took Richmond to help Lady Sarah refresh our drinks.

My own experience in Padova allowed me to provide the plan we eventually used for a city cipher. Art postcards always provide the city where the picture they reproduce is located. A list of these venues was paired with a list of cities in which the group and its associates were active. London stood for New York, and vice versa, Berlin for Boston, Brussels for Moscow, Paris for Rome, Amsterdam for Detroit, Chicago for Milan, and so on---these were our primary meeting places. As busy museums were natural and safe places to make exchanges, with cloak rooms providing ready depots for deposits, we also paired these. Thus New York's Metropolitan Museum and London's National Gallery referred to one another, Berlin's Gemaldgalerie to Boston's Museum of Fine Arts (chosen over the Gardner because it was bigger), and so on.

If necessary, it was easy for me to "fake" a Crivelli--- paint something in his style and state on the postcard's printed information that it was, say, St. Priscilla from The Minneapolis Institute of Art. If the painting did not in fact exist and that museum did not in fact own a Crivelli, mention of another city within a card's message could be taken literally.

We were all confident that authorities would never be suspicious of art cards sent openly through the mails. Our sense of security was heightened, of course, by our admittedly snobbish confidence that most individuals would be utterly ignorant of medieval iconography.

I had a reasonably large collection of photographs of Crivellis from museums outside of Great Britain. In the beginning these had to suffice. After the war, when I was able to travel again, I could make copies of more and more originals without arousing suspicion. Curators, even those not in cahoots with us, were delighted to allow the Director of Museo Crivelli in Padova set up an easel in their galleries.

It goes without saying, Marco, that I cannot give you any instances of the actual correspondence that passed between our agents. I am, however, affixing "demonstrations" at the beginning of each section of this memoir. I leave it to you to decipher them on your own. There are no "right answers." Use your imagination. I will, however, decode one for you. I'll show you how it worked for the one for Chicago, 1934—the one that shows the Chicago Art Institute's Crucifixion. This is the painting I was working on when I first met Judith.

This postcard shows that the painting was acquired by the Art Institute in 1929. Since Chicago was paired with Milan, one could already determine that the time of the meeting would be 7:29 PM somewhere in the Italian city. Jerusalem refers to the Synagogue on Via Guastalla—a place we had pre-arranged if exchanges were to take place after museums had closed. Six (trees) means the meeting is to take place in the 7th month---and two (people) indicates the second day. The Virgin means you should look for a woman; the sailboat tells you she'll be wearing a boater hat. The postcard would, indeed, be mailed to me--- "Nancy" is, of course, a fake name.

We now called our undertaking The Crivelli Research Council. From the time of our establishing CRC to the time when I returned to Italy, I was kept incredibly busy doing substitutions at The Sparry, producing copies in our workshop, and preparing paintings that could be photographed and taken to a printer (one of our own, naturally) to be turned into art postcards. Memories of this period are blurred across these activities, but I was not really unhappy. The work provided a great deal of satisfaction. I convinced myself that Judith would have approved. I know it is a contradiction, but I was excited and numb at the same time. I met many people, but Billy, Lady Sarah, and Richmond remained the only ones to whom I was truly close. There were the occasional, pleasant hours with Donna. Some of the people involved later became famous, that is to say, notorious. Most remained determinedly anonymous. A few would continue to affect both what I did and what was done to me in Italy and beyond.

Front: Carlo Crivelli, The Madonna of the Songbird, 1480, Egg on paper, Bruges, Groeninge Museum

Back.

Dearest Rico,   *Sept. 25*

I plan to be in Venice soon, and I would be as happy as this little lark to see you. Or should I say happy as this little dickens? I count 20 jewels but only 2 melons. You taught me to pay such close attention. It is repaid. And will be.

Love, Donna

Chapter 14

Italy and Elsewhere, 1945-Present

With everyone else, I was swept up into the euphoria that came when the war ended. When the confetti had settled, however, we had to reconcile ourselves to the fact that reconstruction would be painfully slow. Travel outside of Britain remained essentially impossible; mail from the outside still only trickled for months. In July, Billy did manage via his networks to get some news of my family, but only that my father had been living in Venice before returning to Padova. My friends sympathized with my desire to get back there myself as soon as possible; as usual, they managed to arrange things.

I had to leave almost everything in England with Lady Sarah, including the remains of my loved ones. Richmond held a farewell dinner for me in Gallery Three at The Sparry, the room in which three of my Crivelli reproductions hung. (They still hang there today, identified, of course, as copies of works at The National Gallery.) It was, as one would expect from that gentleman, an utterly tasteful affair, appropriate in every way. I looked around the room at my friends, both the humans and the artifacts, and both hoped and worried that Aesop had been correct about our being known by the company we keep.

Between them, Billy and Lady Sarah arranged for me to hitch a "ride" on the yacht of a Greek shipping magnate who had spent the war years in Liverpool. He got me to Calabria and from there I slowly made my way north by bus. To my enormous relief, Padova had not been badly damaged. There had been bombing in the northern part of the city, but our property had not suffered any direct hits. That is not to say, however, that it was unharmed. The Germans who occupied the city had taken over our family's villa and the smaller house where Judith and I had resided. The Nazi officers were not pigs, but neither did they give much attention to repairs or upkeep of the grounds. Furthermore, when they departed, the had helped themselves to whatever they fancied—china, silver and some of our works of art. (Their plunder included the copies we had substituted when we hid the real things; I take pride in their having been so fooled.) The Americans passed by our property, so it had sat empty for several months; there were the expected signs of neglect, but nothing that could not be fixed, thankfully. Unlike many of my Italian friends, I also returned with a substantial fortune, thanks to my inheritance from Judith's mother, and was able to refurbish things more quickly than most of our friends.

The worst loss was my mother. She had died of pneumonia during the winter of 1944. When she and my father were evicted from their home, they moved in with her family in Venice. They were safe enough, but could not prevent my mother's falling ill. I was greatly saddened when I learned this, of course. I felt even sadder about my father's condition. The war and Mother's death had essentially taken the life out of him. He had become an old man; he shuffled rather than walked, mumbled rather than spoke, and seemed to find it difficult and exhausting to concentrate. One of our old servants was living with him in the villa. He kept the shades drawn and spent most of his time staring into space.

As in other countries that had been occupied by the Axis powers, there were, following the surrender, several purges of collaborators. Those in Italy were rather less radical and shorter-lived than elsewhere, but alarming nonetheless. My parents had, like most of their compatriots, been forced to cooperate with Mussolini's and then Hitler's policies. Their shipping business had dwindled, but the company kept active in the delivery of supplies. I was never informed of the details of this operation. Whatever its nature, there was considerable worry that members of the family might be considered war criminals.

Instead, when investigations ensued, my father and other members of Le Direttorre became heroes for protecting Italian treasures. After I had left for England, their work had greatly expanded. They hid not only artworks, but wine, jewelry, gold, and anything else that needed protection. As soon as it was safe, they had begun to return these items to the rightful owners---or, in many cases---to their heirs.

My father could no longer do much in the way of contributing, but upon my return I quickly became involved. Fake walls were torn down and other hiding places uncovered. Almost all of the works were returned, though a few do hang now in our museum.

Needless to say, I expect that you, Marco, will return them should the real owners ever turn up and make a valid case for ownership. The Crivelli Project file is still in the office and will aid in distinguishing authentic from inauthentic claims.

At any rate, I gradually became something of a local hero myself. The work of LeDirettore was the subject of several newspaper and magazine articles. I assumed that I would be able to spend my time running Museo Crivelli, doing restoration work, and engaging in the detective work that was required for tracking down owners of originals that we had hidden. I had provided a sufficient number of works for making postcards before I left London. I thought that my work for The Crivelli Research Project was over. I was wrong.

Few democracies have experienced greater political turmoil than Italy. Both inside and outside the country, the very term "Italian politics" most often produces derisive laughter. Coalitions form, fall apart, and new ones form, as short-lived as the last. Factions have sub-factions, and sub-sub-factions. During the war, anti-Mussolini groups had a common bond. Post-war, these frayed and broke apart. The Communist Party was one of the most stable and powerful. Even now, as you know, Marco, it is influential; it was even more so a few decades ago. It was probably for that reason that agents from the Crivelli Research Project felt freer to travel and meet in Italy than in other Western countries.

I had returned to Padova in early January, 1946. For about nine months I was able to concentrate fully on my home, my museum, and my own artistic projects. I was told later that Lady Sarah insisted that I be given that amount of time to re-establish myself. They did not give me even a full year. Around the first of October, I received one of my own postcards. The front showed what you see affixed to the first page of this section. This painting does not exist and there are no Crivelli's in Bruges. (There is a Madonna of the Swallows at the National Gallery and I used this as inspiration.) As I explained earlier, when the museum named did not own a Crivelli or a painting was non-existent the city mentioned in the message was to be taken literally. 'Dickens' refers to the fact that the author stayed in the Hotel Danielli when he once visited Venice. You should be able to figure out the rest.

I followed the instructions I decoded from the postcard's message. Thus on October 25, a beautiful, warm fall day, I went by train to Venice and knocked on the door of Donna's suite. As usual, she was dressed superbly. Dior's so-called "new look" would not be unveiled and dominate the fashion world until the following spring, so her skirt was still short and revealed her long, beautifully shaped legs. The fabric of her dress was suitably thin for the hot, humid day, and after a brief greeting, she unzipped it and let it fall. Still standing in the white gauzy cloud it formed she undid her bra and I stood a long moment admiring the slender body that had been browned in the sun--undoubtedly at some expensive resort on the coast of Portugal or Spain or perhaps on the deck of some lavish boat. (A few years later I saw a Modigliani nude for which she could easily have been the model.)

We made love, dressed, and ordered lunch to be taken on the balcony off the sitting room. Venice had, thank God, escaped damage during the war. Even the least sensitive thugs seemed to have sensed that there are some limits to what is allowed. The view was similar to the one that Billy and I had looked upon---was it only eight years before?

"I was not really sure that I would ever see you again," I smiled at her. "Needless to say, I'm very glad you're here."

Over lunch we chatted lightly about what we had been doing since we had last been together. It was all very relaxed--- until she suddenly looked at her watch, wiped her mouth, and firmly but neatly replaced her damask napkin next to her coffee cup.

"I think we should take a stroll, my dear," she said. It was not exactly an order, but it was definitely more than a suggestion. "I understand the Galleria dell'Academia here has several of your beloved Crivelli's."

We walked from the hotel to St. Mark's Square, then passed by La Fenice on our way to the Ponte dell'Academia. We paused on the bridge and watched the gondolas and vaporetti passing below us on the Grand Canal.

"Surely, dear Rico, you knew one of us would come," Donna said softly.

"One of you?"

"Someone from CRC."

"I thought my work for them was finished when I left England."

"Oh, no. There's still much to be done."

"I'm very busy with my own affairs now."

"Yes, I know. We've gotten regular reports."

I know you probably think me naïve, Marco, but I was genuinely surprised. She took my arm and we walked without speaking into The Academy.

"Where is the dread St. Sebastian? I think that would be the perfect place for our little chat."

The painting she had chosen was not one of my favorites. The Saint's body is almost a parody of the artist's style: elongated, sinewy limbs in uncomfortable positions, a distended stomach, a face that looks more nauseated than pained. And pained he should be due to the ten or so arrows that pierce him---one presented as having gone completely through his right arm. He is accompanied by only slightly less unappealing companions---Sts. Roch, Joseph, and Emilio.

"What's the deal with this guy's tights?" Donna asked a touch scornfully.

"He's lowered one leg and raised his tunic so that you won't miss his wound."

"Since he's pointing to it and it's a pretty big bulge I shouldn't have thought there was much chance of that."

"The story goes that he gave up all his worldy goods and went from town to town healing plague victims. Finally he had a vision in which Jesus told him he must suffer physically. When he woke up, he had a sword wound in that thigh and gave thanks to God for permitting him to suffer for Him. Crivelli has another version in the Wallace Collection---I'm surprised you never saw it."

"I must have walked right by it. I'm surprised you didn't make a copy of it for our work."

"Actually I wanted to, but the directors of that collection had some kind of grudge against The Sparry, or maybe just Richmond. In any case, they wouldn't let me set up my easel there, or even take a photograph."

"Nasty, nasty,"

"I think there are some works in another room that you'd prefer."

I took her to a Lorenzo Lotto portrait of a gentleman seated in his study.

"Much nicer."

She sat on a bench and I joined her.

"How did you get reports about me."

"From people who went to Padua from time to time. Lady Sarah insisted that no one contact you until you'd had time to settle back in."

"And it has been determined that I've settled?"

"Yes."

"So now?"

"Dennis Jones wants to meet with you."

"Jones? You've seen him again?"

She put her hand on my leg.

"Rico, there are things we can't tell each other. It will be safer that way----and better for everyone. I'll be contacting you from time to time. That won't be unpleasant, will it?"

I smiled, took her hand, and lifted it to my mouth. "Quite the contrary."

"We have no reason to think we're being watched, but if we are we have great cover. No one will suspect anything except a harmless affair."

"And Jones?"

"That's a bit more tricky. He's set up a new cover---he's opened an art gallery in Amsterdam and will become a reputable dealer. Well, apparently reputable anyway. So maybe it won't be strange for him to meet with you from time to time. Still, this first meeting is to appear accidental. He will be at the Arena Chapel next week---on the 18th----when it opens. You should plan to get there thirty minutes later. Can you do that?"

"Yes, of course. But what does he want of me?"

"I don't even know." She turned to me. "You believe that, don't you?"

"I do."

She pointed at the painting. "That gentleman looks a little like Billy Beauchamp, don't you think?"

"A little, maybe."

"How is he?

"Are we allowed to discuss him?" I asked rather sarcastically.

"Oh, Rico, don't. You want to continue to help us, don't you?"

"I hadn't really thought about it much during the last months. As I said, I thought my role had come to an end. But, yes, I suppose I do."

"So----how is Billy?"

"He's out of the Navy and back in The States. He landed a job as a Professor in the Art History Department at the University of Minnesota. His parents are ecstatic. Is he, ah, still involved?"

"I honestly don't know. But if he's in an art circle, it wouldn't surprise me. They will probably arrange meetings of The Crivelli Research Council periodically. I'll bet we'll find that Billy is a member."

"And we are members."

"Oh, yes."

"Then I have good reason to look forward to Council meetings." I squeezed her hand.

"As do I."

She stood up. "I'm going back to the hotel now. I have a train to catch. You wander around the museum for a while and then go back to Padua."

I stood as well, and we embraced as friends do.

"We're going to do good, Rico," she said over her shoulder as she left.

"I certainly hope so, caro mio."

I sat for a while looking at the Lotto, thinking of Billy and, inevitably, of Judith. I wandered back into the gallery that housed St. Sebastian and remembered my first visit there with Judith, only a few days after we had arrived in Italy.

"St. Roch looks more like he has a hernia than a knife wound," she had said. Would I ever look at the paintings we had seen together without remembering them through her eyes or thinking of them without hearing what she had said?

No.

The chapel opened at ten. It was only a short walk from our villa, but I either had allowed myself too much time or my nerves had caused me to walk faster than usual. The chapel itself had miraculously escaped the bombs that fell in its neighborhood; the Eremitani church next to it had not. In years to come, the city would devote considerable resources to restoring the frescoes inside----the Mantegnas that had probably had such an influence on Crivelli were, among others, pieced back together. But that morning, I had to stroll about the grounds to insure that my entrance into the Scrovengni would be timed precisely. Thus I was forced to confront this example of the human tragedy. Did I really see the eye of St.

289

Christopher staring at me through the rubble---or did I only imagine it?

At last it was 10:30 and I entered the building so familiar to me. I had visited it several times since returning to Padova, and on this occasion, as on those, remembered vividly the autumn day when Judith and Billy and I had discussed folly and violence against art.

Jones was standing at the far end, staring at the wall depicting The Last Judgment. I was not sure what was expected of me, so I paused near the entrance and tried to appear to be studying the panel that depicts The Ascension. Apparently I had acted appropriately. After a minute or two, Jones looked over at me, feigned pleased surprise, and walked toward me.

"Excuse me. Aren't you Enrico Zollino? Dennis Jones here. We met in London---at the home of Charles Richmond, if memory serves me correctly."

He extended his hand and I shook it.

"Of course, I remember you Mr. Jones. I believe we may also have both been guests of Lady Sarah Hall."

"Indeed. I remember how cleverly you explained her Titian in the dining room—the one showing a Venetian fair."

"My, what a good memory you have."

"Not at all. You made a strong impression on all of us. So, you're back in Padua. Did you find your family and the museum safe?"

"Unfortunately my mother died while I was gone. And my Father is a bit ill."

"I'm sorry to hear that."

"But Museo Crivelli and our home suffered only minor damage---more from neglect than intentional destruction."

"Excellent." He gestured around the room. "You are lucky to be able to come here whenever you like. What an inspiration."

"Yes, it is."

"Do you have a favorite panel?"

"Well, I love this one," I replied, turning and pointing to the depiction of Anne and Joachim meeting at The Golden Gate. "Giotto has always been praised as one of the first truly Renaissance painters---for the ways in which he began to depict his subjects as real human beings. I think this one is just about his finest. The way they share the miraculous moment when the elderly Anne tells him that she is expecting a baby. I think their embrace is one of the most moving in all of art."

"It is lovely. They seem almost to have melted into one whole."

"Exactly. And so different from this embrace." I led him to the panel in which Judas is about to bestow his traitorous kiss upon the lips of Christ. "Where there was total harmony between Anne and her husband, here, though the volumes are so simple, everything screams tension and betrayal."

"A remarkable achievement, yes."

We spoke a bit more about a few panels and then Jones looked at his watch.

"I'm afraid my time in Padua is brief. I've opened an art gallery on P.C. Hoofdstraat in Amsterdam. I hope you'll be able to visit it one day. I'm negotiating some purchases in Venice and only have a few hours here. I do want to spend more time in this chapel, and I know you'll understand that I want to be on

291

my own---though please understand how much I've enjoyed talking to you."

"Of course."

"But I would also love to see your little museum. Perhaps I could meet you there later?"

"I would enjoy that. What time would be convenient for you?"

"Could we say 1 o'clock?"

I considered suggesting lunch, but decided it was best to let him take the lead. So I simply gave him directions to the museum and left him studying the Giotto's.

Museo Crivelli was closed for the midday break, so Jones and I were sure to have it to ourselves for the hour between one and two when it would re-open. He must have known that when he suggested the time for our meeting. There were, in any case, very few visitors in those days; and most of those came not to look at the Crivelli's but to see if I could help them to reclaim a lost work.

Jones arrived promptly.

"I hope you won't be insulted if I find the Crivelli's a bit jarring after the Giotto's."

I laughed. "I would be surprised if you did not. They are separated by almost a century and a half. And by quite different religious and aesthetic outlooks, of course."

He nodded. "Are we alone?"

"Yes. I have only one assistant and she won't be back for at least an hour."

"Then I won't waste time. Donna told you that we need your help."

"Yes, though frankly I was surprised. I thought I had completed my assignments when I left England."

"Your talents are too valuable to be wasted. We do have enough post cards to last us for a while. We may need you to do more in the future, but for now we have other projects."

"I have some coffee in my office."

"Excellent."

We settled in a pair of chairs that flanked a small tarsia table that my mother had purchased in Florence as a wedding gift for Judith and me.

Jones stoked the table's geometrically designed surface appreciatively. "Amazing, as is this coffee."

"I'm glad you like the coffee. Foreigners sometimes find it a bit too strong."

I hoped that he would accept the opportunity I had given him to identify his origins. Instead he got down to business.

"The Red Army did its share of looting, of course. And many individuals kept what they grabbed for themselves. But a fair number---a surprising number, actually, given human nature---turned them over to their superiors for the good of The Motherland. The leaders intend to return some of them. That should earn them points both at home and abroad. But they also want to sell some, and hide others. Rather like putting deposits in a bank for a later day. Several are already stowed away in Leningrad and Moscow. But they want some on this side of the curtain."

"And my role is...."

293

"Many of the works have been damaged and need restoring before they are sold. That's one job for you. Others need to be, shall we way, put in cold storage. You have suitable space for that here, I believe." He gestured generally in the direction of the galleries.

"I can do that."

"There's a whole history of statesmen selling paintings to raise money for their causes, you know," he said, as if to rationalize the enterprise.

"Of course. Mussolini oversaw quite a lot of it."

"And Lenin even sold some of The Hermitage's works--- quite openly, in the early 20's. You probably know that Andrew Mellon bought several. They're in the National Gallery in Washington, D.C."[7]

I nodded. "Those sales were quite public. I take it that ours...."

"Yes. Our sales will be a bit more private."

I nodded again.

"There's something more."

Of course there was.

"We need couriers. Not just for messages, but for other things---the paintings, documents, maybe other things. Billy Beauchamp is arranging to have the CRC hold annual meetings. The Council will become a satellite of the International Renaissance Art Society, and will hold its meetings at the same time---the third weekend in August. You'll go to those meetings."

---

[7] Stanley Meisler, "The Hermitage," *Smithsonian Magazine,* March, 1995, pp. 40-55.

"But...."

"Please wait. Once a year will not be enough for us to get together. So Lady Sarah and Richmond---and some others you know----are establishing another society. It's called The International Committee for Returning Art---ICRA. Ostensibly its mission will be to facilitate just that---getting stolen art back into the hands of the rightful owners."

"And its hidden agenda is....?"

"Varied. You don't need to know much more than that right now. Suffice it to say that with the reputation you've gained for the work you and your father have done here, you are a natural choice for membership. You'll be getting an official letter in two weeks inviting you to join and laying out details for the inaugural meeting."

My head was spinning.

"Look, Mr. Jones. I'm glad to do what I can to help. But I have so many questions."

"Ask them. I'll answer what I can."

"First, the restoration and, ah, storage work. I can do that, but how will I get the works and return them when I'm supposed to?"

"Easy. Paintings will either be shipped or hand delivered. If there's a note telling you where to ship them back, do so. Otherwise you will keep them until you get further instructions."

"Which will come to me how?"

"That's one of the things you'll learn at ICRA meetings. Occasionally you'll be carrying a painting with you. Mostly someone will fetch them here, though. You'll be informed in advance when and who and what and...whatever."

295

"And if someone gets suspicious?"

"Why should anyone be suspicious of the Director of Museo Crivelli belonging to ICRA? I've already explained that your heroic actions on behalf of Italian art treasures make you a natural for membership. It would be strange if you were not asked to join."

He poured himself another cup of coffee.

"Your expenses will be paid; that goes without saying. Both organizations will have substantial endowments. I expect you'll want to donate some of your own fortune—but that's by no means a requirement. We'll be doing a great deal of legitimate work with Jewish organizations trying to help people find stuff stolen from them. You might consider a memorial for your wife or mother-in-law. Perhaps your wife's half-brother will want to donate, too."

"I absolutely do not want Nochie involved in this," I said forcefully.

Jones held up his hands.

"As you wish."

Thus my life in the studio began regularly to be interrupted with frequent trips to meetings all over America and Western Europe, occasionally Japan. You know how often I have been away from home, Marco. As far as I know, no one has ever suspected me of anything but the noblest public works.

Most of what we did was, in fact, noble, if not always public. But some, I fear was not. I believe we all tried to fool ourselves that the ends justified the means, but I don't think any of us really succeeded in deceiving ourselves—at least when we allowed ourselves actually to reflect on our activities.

296

Unquestionably some of what we did was admirable, especially returning works to people (or their heirs) whose prized possessions had been taken from them, or pulled off walls of the homes of people who had been shipped off to God knows what kind of horror. However, for every work we helped to return there was another one that went elsewhere. Sometimes an item went to otherwise reputable museums whose directors---in the interests of amassing prestigious collections---were not always conscientious about checking its provenance. At least those works were made accessible to larger audiences than otherwise would have been able to see them. The sheer quantity of aesthetic pleasure in the world was undoubtedly increased, and that cannot be a bad thing. But often the items in question found their way into the private collections of individuals who had no right to them and who, often, were capable of very little in the way of genuine aesthetic response. It was hard for me to justify this to myself.

The worst thing ICRA did, however, was to become a kind of Gun for Hire in the art world. We didn't commit any murders, at least not to my knowledge. But in order to raise funds for the various undertakings of our groups and others with which we were loosely associated, we did become part of ring that oversaw the "redistribution" of art. We assisted and abetted art thieves, in other words. The sort of thing I had done for Billy's Father was the norm. Some of the undertakings were devilishly clever. One of my favorites is this. In Florida there are countless mansions that are second, even third or fourth, homes of millionaires. They stand empty for all but a few weeks a year. A thief can go in, lift a masterpiece, have it copied, put the copy back in place of the original and make a fortune selling the original. The millionaire almost never even notices what's happened.

I love art, Marco. You know that. Still, the extremes to which some people are willing to go to possess particular works never cease to amaze me. It is, I believe, a kind of addiction for some people. They must, simply must, own a piece for themselves. One can understand the economic urge to own a valuable work; but most stolen art can only be sold at a price far below what it could bring on the open market. And, I suppose, one can understand the desire to complete a collection---one that, perhaps, can't be completed without taking drastic measures. But is there such a thing as aesthetic obsession? A hunger for beauty that is not mingled with a desire for money or status or some other kind of deep longing? And even if there is, could this justify or even explain robbing someone else of a thing of beauty? Is there an aesthetic itch that can only be scratched by gazing upon something that one owns oneself? If I thought there really was such a thing, I might not regret having cooperated in this aspect of ICRA's mission.

Our responsibility was two-fold: providing information and, once again, "providing a language for sharing," as Billy has so euphemistically put our work with codes. Between the CRC and ICRA (the membership intersected a great deal, of course, but not totally), we were able to disclose the locations of works held privately that someone, for whatever reason, wanted. One of us always knew, or knew someone who knew someone who knew, who owned what. Since we were never asked to participate in the theft of a Crivelli (a fact that did, I confess, miff me a bit), I can use him as an example. Suppose in an article about him an illustration of a work under discussion was attributed to a private collection. Chances are that I would know who owned it; let's say it was Baroness LaFarge and that the painting hung in the library in her townhouse in Paris. We could not use the post card code we had already developed for the CRC since it was being applied elsewhere. Instead I would write to our contact along the following lines---using anything but a postcard showing a Crivelli work.

Dear Professor Smith,

I am happy you enjoyed your visit to Museo Crivelli. I found the citation for the article I mentioned to you. It is in Revue Parisian de Arte de la Renaissance, Vol. XXI, No. 45 by Jean LaFarge.

Sincerely,

Enrico Zollino

I think you get the idea, Marco. On occasion, we could also notify our contacts when Baroness LaFarge was going to be out of Paris, but the professionals who handled the actual theft usually were quite capable themselves of managing the details of their trade.

After a work had been taken, it would sometimes find its circuitous way to one of CRC's storage bins, including the one at our own institution. I have to say that I enjoyed the opportunity to spend time with some incredibly brilliant works. I only wished that I could put them on display so that others could take pleasure in them as well.

These days the work of CRC and ICRA that involves sharing information is done primarily by electronic communication. Much of the drama, not to mention hands-on aesthetic appeal, has disappeared. We do occasionally still use the Crivelli postcards. We still use our iconic codes. And, I am happy to say, much of what we do is legitimate, worthwhile activity. A great deal of reclamation work remains to be done around the world---not just returning works that have been stolen from Jews or others. Institutions, even whole nations, increasingly argue that works taken from them should be returned, with some success. Curators have been tried and found guilty of cooperating with dishonest art dealers and the works in question have been restored to their proper homes. Museo Crivelli still displays works that were, for some reason, not reclaimed after the war. I regularly advertise their existence and whereabouts in art journals and other appropriate places. I am always genuinely delighted when someone can authenticate right to ownership.

On one of my trips to England to attend a meeting, I was surprised to discover that Lady Sarah was not in attendance. Richmond pulled me aside after the meeting.

"Lady Sarah would like you to go to Stone Corners."

"I hope her absence is not due to illness," I said.

"I'm afraid it is. In fact, she is seriously ill. This may be the last opportunity you have to visit her."

I knew she was considerably older than I, but somehow she had seemed ageless. I could not believe that she was dying. Needless to say, I went immediately.

In some ways, she looked the same. Same costume, hair consistent in its inconsistency, same rose colored pearls, same cigarette in an extraordinary holder. But she was pale, and had lost quite a bit of weight.

She was seated in the parlor where, on one of my visits, I had convinced her to move a Rembrandt so that it could be lit from above rather than from the side. It was early September. The days had not yet become chilly, but a fire burned in the fireplace. She had drawn her chair close it, her striped stole pulled tightly around her shoulders. She drew deeply on her cigarette.

"They always said these would kill me. But they were wrong, of course. It's something else entirely."

Richmond had not mentioned the cause of her illness, and I did not feel the need to pry now about details. They were unimportant.

"Did I miss anything interesting at the meetings?"

"A couple of nice tidbits. A Monet will have to give up the Rivera for a less sunny clime."

"Pity. I hope it's not going to that scoundrel in Detroit."

"I'm afraid so. And the lead we had on the Weisman Durer turned out to be a dead end."

"I warned them that it would be."

"We missed you."

She smiled rather sardonically. "Good. I like to think I'll be missed at least for a few months. I have no delusions of grandeur, however."

She continued to smoke without saying anything for several minutes. I got the impression that she felt the need to regain some strength. Then she continued.

"I want you to have the Rembrandt," she moved her head slightly in the direction of the painting on the wall, "and the little miniature we had such a time finding the right spot for. Then I want you to choose something---anything." Her gesture managed to indicate the entire estate. "Something you want for yourself---or for Museo Crivelli. The rest of the stuff will go to London. Mostly to The Sparry, but people at the V&A and National Gallery have flattered me sufficiently to insure that they will get a few things, as well."

She paused again.

"The house and the grounds are to become a school. I have more than enough to endow it and still leave substantial amounts to The Sparry and ICRA. There will be several scholarships for children whose parents were killed or injured in the war. It is to be strictly non-denominational. With your permission, I want to call it The Judith Carlo School."

301

I bowed my head. We both sat silently. The sun had set while we had been speaking and the outer edges of the room had become dark. We sat in the chiascuro circle created by the flames of the fire.

"I had a lover when I was very young. Her name was Joy---and that's what she was to me for one beautiful summer. I met her at University and we spent one summer on a grand Grand Tour. Then we came back and she decided that she preferred men. And I decided it was easier to do without sex. I told you that Judith was the love of my life. That's true; but my love for her was far more complex than what I had with Joy. I was attracted to Judith, of course. Who wasn't? But she was friend, daughter, companion.....It was a kind of blessed state. One utterly devoid of appetite or jealousy or any of those other things that goes with ordinary passion. It was enough for me to be with her, and with her when she was with you or Carlo or our friends or the villagers."

She paused and took a deep breath. The cigarette in her holder had turned to ashes that now fell onto the hearth.

"My only regret is that I could not have died in her place." She looked at me. "Can you believe that I truly mean that?"

"Yes, I can. She would love having a school dedicated to her and Carlo."

"I do have a favor to ask of you." She paused again and looked directly into my face. She leaned forward, in order, I believe, to make sure she could read my expression. "I will be buried in the mausoleum, of course. Would you consider leaving Judith and Carlo and Aaron there? Not forever. Just for a few months. It would make things somehow easier if I knew I could lie with them for a short spell. I know it sounds horribly sentimental. Out of character. I think perhaps character changes under these," she hesitated, "ah, circumstances."

302

"I'm actually glad there's something I can do. Just as long as I know I can, how should I put it, come for them some day."

"I will make it crystal clear in my will that you can do that whenever you wish."

With great difficulty she stood up. "You'll find a cane behind that screen," she pointed to an elegant black lacquered screen that stood in one shadowy corner of the room. "I haven't completely lost my pride, so I have it concealed there."

I fetched it for her.

"I would like to walk down to the mausoleum now."

"So would I."

We strolled through the twilight down a path behind the house. Inside the stone building candles had already been lit in preparation for our visit; or perhaps she had them lit every evening.

We sat without speaking until Nanno John came to tell me the car was ready to drive me to the station. Lady Sarah did not try to stand up. I bent and kissed her on both cheeks.

"Arrivederci."

She died four days later. Richmond would follow her not long after. I saw Donna one evening before I left London, but that would be our last encounter. Dennis Jones was replaced by someone else who took over as my "supervisor." (As you will soon learn, I saw Dennis only one more time.) That supervisor was also replaced; I forget how many there have actually been. There is an occasional mission for me, but now that Billy is also gone, I fully expect that whatever remains of the secret activity associated with those committees will cease with my own death. That is one of the reason I will feel comfortable turning this memoir over to you.

And life changed here.

Your mother, as you know, was born in Venice. Barely out of school, she fell in love with a dashing young soldier who had the great misfortune to be assigned to the ill-fated Eighth Italian Division that suffered such heavy casualties on the Russian front. He died there soon after their marriage.

When I first saw her in a café in St. Mark's Square, I felt eerily as if I were looking at DaVinci's portrait of Cecilia Gallerani. Long brown hair was pulled tightly back from her perfectly proportioned face. Large dark almond eyes would have held one's gaze, if the subtle curve or the ivory smooth skin of her face had not drawn them to the superbly shaped chin. She wore a blue blouse with a squared bodice that revealed more of that incredible skin. Cecilia holds an ermine; your mother held a small dog, and stroked it with long tapered fingers. She did not, of course, pluck her hair line as ladies of the Renaissance did in order to achieve the extended forehead that they considered an element of their vision of beauty. But the eyebrows were the same. She always denied any intention of mimicking Cecilia, but I never believed her. The resemblance was too striking. You are the male version of her beauty, Marco.

Her family had suffered greatly in the war—had more or less lost their entire fortune. Still, you must never think that she married me solely for my wealth, or I simply because of her resemblance to Da Vinci's painting. Ours was a marriage based on genuine affection, respect, and mutual interests. Her intellect and wit and sense of dignity and decorum have been great assets in my work. Just as your clever and innovative management skills have been far more valuable to me than a desire to arrange and rearrange art works would have been.

Naturally she knows nothing of my other "activities." (As I already said, you may, if you choose, share this manuscript with her; I have total trust in your judgment concerning what to do with it.)

I want you to know that I have been completely faithful to our marriage vows. The needs that Donna had met were amply satisfied within the walls of our home. And since the day you were born, my family life has lacked for nothing.

You will, inevitably, wonder how your mother and you compare with Judith and Carlo. All I can say is that, in my experience, Tolstoy was wrong: it is not the case that all happy families are happy in the same way. The fact that I care enough to write this for you is, I hope, sufficient evidence of the happiness you have brought me and the deep regard I have for you. I believe I have done work that is good. I do not fool myself, however, that all of it has been admirable. We all, I believe, are kept in a state of ignorance about most of the consequences of our actions. Who knows whether that is ultimately our damnation or our salvation? Who knows if the wizard behind the waterfall that moves the violinist is benign or devious?

Chapter 15

Padua and Copenhagen, 1951

Postcard

Front: Vinbeholder: Triptolemos mellem Demeter og Persef, Ny Carlsberg Glyptotke, Kobenhavn

Back: *4/22*

Thanks for rec about Den Sorte Ravn. Had the sole in white wine with a Chardonnay, though not in as fine a vessel as this one. Hope we find something as good at our 7th annual meeting in Oslo.

Kisses, Maureen

To say I was surprised is an understatement.

In early May, a postcard came from our own Arena Chapel. It showed Giotto's version of the Final Judgment and using a rather crude form of our code, asked me to stand near it at 11 o'clock two days later. I walked to the door of our museum and looked to see if someone might be standing somewhere nearby, but the road was empty. The postcard had come with the regular mail---and indicated that it had been sent two days earlier from Milan. Since no one had communicated with me in this way for some time, I was naturally suspicious. Nonetheless, I did walk to the Chapel on the appointed day, feeling a bit silly as I kept glancing around and behind me to see if someone was watching or following.

I arrived shortly before eleven and stopped wistfully in front of the Folly panel that Judith and Billy and I had discussed in what now seemed another life time.

"Perhaps it is a folly for us to meet here," someone behind me said softly.

I did not at first recognize the speaker. Was it seven or eight years since I had seen him? He had aged at least twice that many. He had lost a great deal of weight and his hair, which I remember as dark and always well-trimmed was now grey and rather ragged. His clothes, although obviously expensive, were wrinkled. He wore a short raincoat that even had a coffee stain on one sleeve.

"I'm fairly sure no one followed me," he said quietly, but there was an overtone of urgency in his voice. "We'd better go to the park."

The grounds surrounding the chapel were not as lovely as they had been pre-war; nothing in Italy was. But they were green, and a stone bench near the river offered us a good spot for conversation.

"I know you are surprised to see me. I didn't think we'd meet again either. But I need your help. They killed her."

"What? Who?"

"Donna," he spit out.

I was literally speechless, and Donald allowed me some time to recover before he continued—more urgently and angrily than before.

"I know about you and Donna."

I started to speak, but he interrupted me.

"Don't worry. We gave each other a lot of freedom. She probably told you that herself. But she was always mine. And I would have done anything for her. I did do----all those things we did in England. And elsewhere. I would never have gotten involved on my own. All I ever wanted to do was live with Donna and make rope."

"Rope? I thought you made ammunition."

"No—not bullets. We made cable for war machines and ships, but we never stopped making the best rope in the world. I'm probably the only one in our circle that made my fortune legally."

"But Donna?"

"Yes, yes. I'm getting to that. She finally just wanted that, too. Not to make rope, of course. But she just wanted to live with me in Baltimore and do good work. She became disillusioned with what was happening behind the Iron Curtain, and with what we were doing to support it. She just wanted to play tennis and golf and help orphans and Negroes."

"So tell me what happened."

"They said they still needed her. They wouldn't leave her alone. They didn't care about me. I wasn't clever enough for them anyway. They just tolerated me because of Donna--- and my money. Sure, they wanted that. But it was Donna who could travel around and take things from one place to another without being suspected of being anything but a beautiful, rich woman flitting from one glamorous spot to the next."

"And.....?"

"Six months ago, she told them she was finished. She came back to Maryland. But they came, too. And they killed her."

"But how?"

"They made it look like an accident. Her car went off the road one night when she was coming home from an NAACP meeting. "

"How can you be certain that it wasn't really an accident?"

"Because she'd had warnings."

"What kind of warnings?"

"What difference does it make? She told me she was scared. But she refused to give in—and they killed her. I know it."

And I knew it, too. I didn't need any real evidence. We both knew it.

We sat without speaking for a long time.

"I'm sorry," I finally said simply.

"I knew you would be. And I knew you'd help me. You're the only one left that I can turn to."

"But what can I possibly do?"

He looked down at the ground, and then turned and looked directly and piercingly into my eyes.

"I've been waiting. I know they were watching me." He waved his hand in dismissal of any questions I might have about how he knew this. "But they stopped---after about four months. I've waited another two months and now I've got my plan."

At this point I just wanted to get up and walk back to my quiet museum. But I knew I couldn't and wouldn't. It was like that other time---when Billy asked for his "favor." I could voice objections, all the time knowing not-so-deep-down that I was bound to cooperate.

"I don't need much from you."

Donald sensed, probably had known in advance, that he could count on me.

"My company has a factory in Copenhagen. I just need you to get him there."

"How? Who?"

Donald looked at me with surprise.

"Who? Dennis Jones, of course."

"Dennis?"

"He's always been the chief of this end of things."

"Did he come to Baltimore?"

"Don't be so naïve. Of course not. As usual he had others do his dirty work. But he was behind it. And I'm going to kill him."

His blatant statement caused me to start.

"How else can I get the revenge I need?" he asked, as if this must have been clear from the moment he uttered Donna's name.

"But...,"I began.

Again he held up his hand. "Just listen to my plan."

He took a deep breath.

"You will get him to Copenhagen. Then I will do the rest. I'll take him----elsewhere. You won't even know where. His body will be found weeks later and miles away. There's no way you'll be suspected. You'll be back in Padua before he's even disappeared."

"But how will you get him out of Denmark?"

He smiled cynically. "Our factory makes rope for a yacht builder."

I shook my head. "Maybe you are the cleverest of us, after all."

"Time will tell."

"And I supposed you've figured out how I'm going to get Dennis to Copenhagen?"

Donald reached into the breast pocket of his coat and showed me, what else, a postcard. I held out my hand for it, but he pulled it away.

"Just look. Don't touch. We don't want your fingerprints on it. I'll take care of putting it in a mail box."

He held it where I could see it. It was the one from the Glyptotek that I've affixed at the beginning of this section.

"It's not a Crivelli," I objected.

"It'll work." He turned the card around so that I could see what was written.

"Believe me he'll be at the Black Raven on May 22nd at 7 o'clock. I've made a reservation in the name of Marco Alberti. I thought it was appropriate to show a meeting. " He turned the card over so that I could look again at the work reproduced on the front. Demeter and Persephone are meeting with Triptolemos to discuss how he's going to bring agriculture to the

Greeks. "Even though it's not a Crivelli, Dennis will be curious. He'll come. And if he doesn't, I'll go back to the drawing board."

"So I meet him at the restaurant, and then what?"

"You have the sole and white wine sauce and tell him about a project you have."

"What project?"

"Make something up," he replied impatiently. "Tell him you've found something or someone and need his help."

"Yes, I can do that. And after dinner?"

"You leave The Black Raven. Then you walk to the end of Nyhavn where it stops at the harbor. Turn right and walk to another restaurant called the Fiskhuset. Wait there-- a few doors away. I will be dining there with someone who looks like you. You probably won't need an alibi, but if you do, I'll swear you had dinner with me. When you see me leave the restaurant, hail a taxi and go back to your hotel. Then come back to Italy the next day."

"And you will...?"

He shook his head and shrugged he shoulders. "Do the rest."

Just as I had begun to imagine the details of creating a pornographic Madonna for Billy on the way back from our meeting in Venice, so I began working out the details of my visit to Copenhagen as I walked back to the Museo Crivelli.

During World War I, Wilhelm and Henny Hansen built a mansion north of Copenhagen's Deer Park. With several other collectors and dealers they made it their mission to purchase

312

and display nineteenth century French art. In the early 20's, however, the Hansens suffered severe financial losses; many of their works had to be sold. Some of these were confiscated by the Naz's when they occupied Denmark. After the Hansens deaths, the beautiful home and surrounding English gardens were left to the Danish nation. While the collection now includes mainly Danish works, Ordrupsgaard Museum is a lovely showplace.

Because of the Nazi confiscation, one of the curators of Ordrupsgaard, Foge Asmussen, served with me on IRCA. It would not be at all out of the ordinary for me to visit him. I also concocted a scheme that could connect him and Dennis Jones. Furthermore, I was afraid that Jones might stay at L'Angleterre Hotel in central Copenhagen—the hotel where I usually stayed when I visited that city. I wanted to avoid being in the same hotel. Visiting Asmussen, it would be natural for me to stay in the equally comfortable Park Hotel in Hellerup, not far from Ordrupsgaard.

But Foge would not hear of it.

"Nej, nej, nej," he nearly shouted when I called to set up a meeting. "You must stay with Charlotte and me."

"I don't want to impose. I do have other business in the center."

"No imposition. Charlotte has been studying Italian and will kill me if she doesn't get this chance to practise."

The mention of killing was, to say the least, unsettling.

He hurried on. "We're a stone's throw from the Hellerup train station and a there's a tram stop just a hundred meters from our doorstep."

"That's very kind of you."

"So you're coming on the 20th. Just let me know what time you're getting in, and I'll meet you."

"No, no. At least let me take a taxi. The trains are so often delayed now---and I'll have to make several change overs."

"All right, then. Just call me when you get into the station."

The Asmussens were perfect hosts. Their stately home stood on Standvejen across the road from a rocky beach. Charlotte's Italian, spoken with a heavy Danish accent and rhythm, was utterly charming. Both she and Foge spoke perfect English. Charlotte was tall, as was her husband, and large-boned. But her blond hair and complexion was reminiscent enough of Donna's to make it unlikely that I would forget the reason for my trip. After a short drive up the coast to Hamlet's castle in Elsinore with them both, Foge took me to Ordrupsgaard, where we had a tour of the museum and grounds and then went to his office to discuss our "business."

Foge was so kind and thoughtful that I felt guilty that what we were discussing was a total sham. It took considerable effort on my part to temper my remorse by reminding myself that the end of my visit would, if all went according plan, justify the means.

"I think I may have a good lead on a Monet water lily that may have been purchased in 1921 by someone in Copenhagen," I began. "The timing is right for the Hansen sales. I have to check with some other sources in the center, but first we should look at your records."

"Naturligt." Foge opened a lower drawer of a tall wooden filing cabinet and extracted a thick folder. "Most of the

Monets went to the Glyptotek or Statsmuseum or other museums."

He carefully leafed through the documents. "Aha--- here are two Monet's. A water lily and a hay stack. Both, in fact, were purchased by Solomon Shapiro in September of '21. That fits."

I could not believe my good fortune. I really didn't expect Asmussen to find anything. It was not totally out of the realm of possibility for the Hansens to have sold works to a Jewish family in Denmark. But this coincidence seemed almost fated.

"Is there an address?" I asked.

"Only a business. Shapario og Sønner Guldsmed. Købmagergade 52. "

I wrote down the information.

"What more can you tell me?" Foge asked excitedly.

Having worked on IRCA, he knew that the majority of our attempts to recover and return art works to rightful owners came to naught. He was also aware that many of our investigations had to be kept private, especially in their initial stages.

"Very little," I replied. "Recently a water lily of questionable provenance appeared in a gallery in Munich. You may know which one, but I'd better not divulge that yet."

He nodded knowingly. All IRCA members had a list—a rather long one I'm afraid—of disreputable dealers in the United States and Europe.

"Of course, I hope this turns out to be the one we sold," he said. "and, of course, I want the Shapiro's to get it back. But

315

they may not..." He paused and looked down at the file on his desk.
"You know—the family may not be traceable. In which case, Ordrupsgaard may get it back."

He put his fingers to his forehead and shook his head.

"Listen to me. I shouldn't even think of such a thing. Of course, we want to be able to trace the family."

Again, I felt a twinge of remorse. Asmussen was such a truly honorable man. He sat up straight, as if an inner moral rod had been re-straightened. "Do you want me to go to the center with you tomorrow?"

"No, thanks. I think it's better I go alone. I'll check out the address, and then I've arranged to meet..." I waved my hand. "Well, you know....ah, someone.....for dinner tomorrow night. He may be able to provide more help."

Foge chuckled. "I hope I know enough not to press you about the source. But at least I hope you'll have a good dinner."

"Oh, I can certainly tell you that. We're meeting at a place called The Black Raven."

"Ja, ja. Den Sorte Ravn in Nyhavn. Be sure to have the sole in white wine sauce. It is delicious."

"So I've heard."

It was perhaps foolish of me, but I went the next day to Købermagergade 52. Not surprisingly, there was no jewelry store. It had been replaced by a delicatessen. None of the persons working there had ever heard of the Shapiros or a jewelry store. I chose two small open-faced sandwiches and, with a cup of coffee, sat at a counter that ran along the window facing the street. Suddenly I had the feeling that I was being watched. I was relieved that I had done nothing that could not easily be explained. Still, I spent the rest of the day doing things that could in no way be thought suspicious. I spent the afternoon at the Glyptotek. I was a bit nervous that I might see someone who knew me, but my luck held out. When the

museum closed, I followed Strøget back to Kongens Nytorv and went into Magasin du Nord where I purchased a pair of Georg Jensen silver earrings for your mother. Then I sat in a nearby café. I ordered a beer and tried to read a day old copy of the *London Times* . But mostly I went over again and again the details of what I would say and do. At last it was time to walk across Kongens Nytorv square and follow Nyhavn to The Black Raven.

I have reflected often , dear Marco, on the ways in which my attention, indeed, I must acknowledge, my obsession with the fine tactical points made it possible for me to ignore the larger picture of the admittedly nefarious actions in which I had become involved. When looking at a painting, I don't think my perception of details ever detracted from my observation of the whole. Great art, I believe, requires that one go back and forth between the parts and the whole. I suppose the obvious explanation is that what I did, beginning with my favor for Billy, simply was not great art.

"God aften. Velkommen til Den Sorte Ravn."

I identified myself to the receptionist as Marco Alberti. Looking around, I explained in English that my dinner companion had not arrived yet. He obligingly seated me at a table near the entrance and next to a window. There were only a few other tables in the small, rather rustic but very pleasant room. The restaurant was located at ground level; one could

317

watch passersby and look across the narrow canal that divided the two sides of this famous street. I was seated in one of the buildings on the elegant side. Across the canal was the bustling seedy side, boasting seamy bars, cafes, brothels, and a string of infamous tattoo parlors. A tasteful brochure informed me that Hans Christian Andersen had resided in the building next door. I was trying to remember if he had been the author of that story about an ugly duck that in reality is a youthful swan, when Dennis Jones came through the doorway. Only two other tables were occupied and, as couples were seated at both of those, he spotted me immediately. I must say that I was gratified at the surprise that registered on his face.

I stood up and held out my hand to greet him. He took it, and to my surprise, also air-kissed both of my cheeks.

"My God, Enrico, you are the last person I expected."

"Does that mean no one has been watching today?"

His laugh was exactly the cynical chortle I remembered. "Of course, I've been careful. But I wasn't really worried about anything untoward happening to me in this quaint place. In any case, we couldn't look for you since we didn't know who 'Maureen' was. Not a name we've used before, I think. How long has it been? I hope you've been well. I know you've been doing good things for us."

"I'm fine, thank you. I was surprised when someone else took over your meetings with me."

"Yes, yes. Well, I was given other assignments. I still have my gallery in Amsterdam, of course. And I've been involved with our sales and acquisitions."

I was struck by the ease with which our conversation would have sounded like a perfectly normal business discussion had it have been overheard.

We paused to order---both of us had the special fish, what else--and a bottle of Chablis. Dennis oversaw the tasting of the wine the waiter brought and then continued.

"I take it you wanted to see me about one of these acquisitions?"

"Yes, and I needed to see you in person. One of your colleagues has discovered a client who is interested in a Monet."

"Who isn't these days?"

I smiled. "There are still some of us who remain loyal to Crivelli."

The strange laugh, again.

"My client has more than just an interest. It's more like an obsession. He's willing to pay a lot."

"And just why is it that we are in Copenhagen?" Dennis asked, his voice slightly softer.

I, too, lowered my voice and leaned in slightly.

"I thought it was best for us not to meet in Amsterdam for now. You will understand in a bit, I hope. "

"All right. Go ahead."

"I think in this case, much as I would like to avoid it, I will have to involve IRCA.'

Dennis raised his eyebrows. "Surely that's been done before."

"Actually, not to my knowledge. I've tried to keep it separate. I don't know about others. Billy perhaps has....."

He shook his head, making it clear that this was not a subject to be broached.

"In any case," I continued, "this time I will need to present a case to the IRCA proving that the interested party is in fact someone who deserves to possess the work. I've made some real progress in that direction. But that made it necessary to come to Denmark to see Foge Asmussen."

"Should I know him?"

"No. He is curator of a small museum here and a completely independent member of IRCA. The people who established the museum had to sell off some paintings in the early 20's. Fortunately one of them was a Monet water lily."

"And my role is....?"

"You need to find me one of those. And help me, shall we say, produce the documents that I can take to IRCA. The Monet was sold to a jeweler by the name of Solomon Shapiro. His shop no longer exists, and I've checked in the phone book. There are no Solomon Shapiros and no jewelry stores under that name. We will have to have papers that prove that we have found a descendant who has an authenticated right to get the painting back."

I actually felt pleased that I would not in fact have to take any such case to ICRA. That committee has done so many admirable things.

"Then the painting will be returned, so to speak, to our client. And he will pay us very, very well for our efforts."

"I see." Dennis whispered now. "Does it have to be a real Monet?"

Now I laughed. "Let's just say--real enough."

"There are so many of them----I think we can get something that will work."

He held up his wine glass. "To returning art to the rightful owner."

I clinked my glass against his.

When we left the restaurant Dennis asked if I was staying at L'Angleterre.

"No, I'm actually staying at Asmussen's home. I'll just walk down to the harbor and get a taxi."

We shook hands.

"Very well, then. I'll wait until I hear from you again. Should I expect another postcard?"

"Yes, but it may be a while."

A long while, I thought to myself.

I turned to the right, Jones to the left. At the harbor, I turned right again, as Donald had instructed. A sign announced that a ferry was about to depart for Oslo. I passed a variety of shops catering to tourists and sailors and soon caught sight of the Fiskhuset. I stood by a short wall and looked out at the vessels of all sizes and shapes moving through the water as if some invisible hand were choreographing their movements. I did not have to wait long. Donald emerged with a dark-haired man about my height and build, looked around and, when he caught sight of me, nodded slightly. I then walked toward a taxi stand that I had passed on my way.

But just before I reached a waiting cab, I noticed a large blue poster tacked to an advertising post. On it was a stylized picture of a colorfully painted violin and the announcement of a concert that very evening.

Koncert 22 Maj

Grøn Nat, Strøget 71,

Hardanger Violinist Karl Jensen.

That such a concert should be advertised so close to the ferries to Oslo was, naturally, not improbable. But certainly it was an eerie coincidence. Another reminder of my own enchantment.

Memories danced as frenetically as Olaf's music as the taxi took me out of the center, back to Strandvejen and then along the coast to the Asmussen's. Foge and Charlotte were waiting for me with coffee, akavit, and small cakes. They were eager to hear a report of my day's findings.

"The jewelry store is no longer there," I explained. "It is a delicatessen and no one who works there had any knowledge of a Shapiro family."

They were disappointed but not surprised.

"So now" Foge said, "we will have to rely on our usual procedures for tracing families."

I nodded.

The remainder of the evening passed pleasantly--- Charlotte determinedly attempting periodically to converse in Italian while Foge looked on contentedly.

In spite of all my attempts to silence them, strains of haunting tunes in my brain provided background music.

Chapter 16

Washington and Galesburg, 1952

Postcard

Front: Madonna and Child, Carlo Crivelli, Italian, Venice (?), ca, 1489, Tempera and gold on wood, The Jules Bache Collection, 1949

Back: *June 16*

Dear Enrico, I was in NYC last week and thought of you immediately when I saw this. Our Lady has certainly enjoyed a good harvest. One would have to look very closely to spot the Turks! Hope this finds you healthy and happy.

All the best, Donald

IRCA met in Washington, D.C. in the fall of 1952. Foge could not make the trip, and I was relieved that there would thus be no mention of the missing Monet. I had written to him after the postcard from Donald (see above) telling him that all of my leads and searches had come to nothing. Still, I had been worried that he might mention it at one of our sessions.

Billy did attend, and we arranged a dinner for just the two of us in small restaurant near The National Gallery. We caught up on family and professional news. He was in the final stages of preparing a book on his "Crivelli Saga," as he put it, and in the initial stages of a new love affair. I showed him some recent photos of you and your mother; he displayed appropriate enthusiasm.

323

We did not discuss any current CVC business. But he could not resist sharing what he believed was some news that would interest me.

"Did you hear that Dennis Jones has gone missing?"

"No. But then I haven't seen him for a long time. I did hear something about a work that his gallery in Amsterdam had acquired."

"Well, he left the gallery around the end of May, but didn't tell anyone where he was going. And no one has heard anything since."

"Are the authorities involved?"

"Oh, yes. But Dennis never was one to leave a trail. He must have had a half dozen passports. Maybe more. My sources say that even Interpol has just about given up." He paused. "One assumes, of course, that some others are still looking. Someone even came to Minneapolis to talk to me. Has no one come to Padua?"

"No. Not yet, anyway."

"Then there's Donna's death. Do you think there might be a connection?"

"Donna's death?" I feigned great surprise.

"You hadn't heard about that? She died in a car wreck in Baltimore last fall. Surely someone let you know?"

"No. No. That's awful. Of course, I hadn't seen her for years either. The last time was....."

I stopped and Billy nodded. Details of this sort were never to be exchanged.

"So what do you think? Could there be a connection? Might Donald have done something to Dennis?"

"But why would he? You said she died in a car accident."

"Well, that was the official report. But even Donald would have been suspicious."

"*Even* Donald."

"Well, you know, he was never the brightest light on the tree."

"I didn't ever get to know him very well."

"I suppose not. His money was nice, but he always just sort of hung around. Didn't seem to do much but give Donna what she wanted." He shrugged. "No, he probably wouldn't have been able to do anything even if he was suspicious that the accident wasn't really an accident."

I also nodded. "I suppose not. And we don't, after all, know that her death wasn't an accident."

Billy shook his head. "You're right. Probably Dennis's disappearance has nothing to do with it in any case. So Dennis must have done something that really pissed somebody else off."

"Probably. In any case, I can't say I'll miss him."

"No, I'm not sure anyone will."

We finished our dinner speaking only of the happy times past.

"Does that Norwegian couple still work for your family?'

"What?" Billy asked, surprised. "You mean Olaf and Christina? What in the world makes you ask about them?"

"I actually think about them quite often. They were very nice to me. Olaf played his violin for me."

"My God, I don't think you've ever mentioned that."

"Yes, they had me for Christmas dinner that year when we were working on the Raphael."

"I do remember that. But he played his fiddle for you?

I nodded.

"He must have really liked you."

"I hope so. They told me the story about the wizard behind the waterfalls. I often think that I became enchanted by something like a wizard. It all really started then, didn't it?"

Billy did not bother to try to speculate about how things might have been. He knew that, between us, it was neither necessary nor beneficial.

I am preparing a copy of this memoir for Billy, Marco. It will be up to you to decide whether to give it to him or not. If you are reading this, Billy, you will, I hope, always remember that I have never stopped loving you.

On that trip to the states, I went to Galesburg for what will be the last time. I had written to Nochie to let him know that I would be in Washington and he pleaded with me to come to visit him and his family--in the Broad Street house where they now lived.

My train arrived late morning, and Nochie met me at the station. He had taken a job as basketball coach at the high school, and had to teach and attend practice all afternoon after class. He lent me his car so that I could revisit the town and my memories on my own. After I dropped him off I went to the Coffee Corner where one could still get a hamburger, French fries, and a Coke for under fifty cents. I walked down Main Street, past the jewelry store----now a luggage store----and stood briefly on the curb thinking about the meager Christmas parade seventeen years before. I drove up Broad Street, past the donut shop where Aaron had seemed to reconcile himself to Judith's and my marriage, then up past Judith's---now Nochie's---home and around the corner to the little house where Violet and Nochie had lived. Between the two houses I could see the garage with the back door that had provided Fred an escape into the arms of his lover.

Then I drove north to Lincoln Park, but it was too early in the season for any geese to land in the lake. The Bear House was there, but the bears had been sent away; Judith would, I am sure, have said that they had been let out of their prison. I watched some toddlers swinging, sliding, and riding on a kind of small merry-go-round powered by their mothers' arms. I thought to myself that Carlo would have been 15 that fall. His sister would have been twelve. If I had agreed to stay in Galesburg, he would have been a student in the High School. Perhaps Fred and Ruth would still be in the Broad Street house, and the luggage store would still sell jewelry. And maybe Judith would have been here in the park with yet another one of our children.

The geometric grid of streets that defined Galesburg's landscape enabled me without difficulty to find the 4th Street Bridge that crossed the railroad yards. I parked at one end and walked to a point near the middle. Looking out over the tracks and the eponymous roundhouse at the center of the activity, it was almost as if nothing had changed. There were several newer freight cars, naturally, but those only emphasized an impression that the war had not adversely affected this spot. It had not, after all, been bombed.

My memories of that chill November day in 1935 were interrupted by the approach of a young girl on a bicycle. She leaned her vehicle against the railing and stood only ten or so meters from me. She was a bit plump and her dress, though clean, was faded and a size too small. A pair of scuffed brown oxford shoes were run down on the outer sides. Her long but thin light brown hair had been braided, but one of the braids was coming loose. Her overall appearance, nonetheless, belied a kind of control in her general character. There was something about the way she stood with her hands firmly on the railing of the bridge, head moving quickly so that her eyes could dart from one point of the rail yard to another that conveyed sharp, intense engagement with what she perceived.

Out of the corner of my eye, I could see her curiously if furtively glancing at me. Aware that she had undoubtedly been warned not to talk to strangers, particularly men, I nonetheless risked bidding her a good afternoon.

She was also willing to take a risk, and clearly enjoyed the opportunity to appear sophisticated by carefully nodding her head in my direction and saying as formally as she could muster, "Good afternoon, sir. It's a lovely, day isn't it?"

"Indeed it is, and this is a wonderful spot."

"You aren't from around here are you?"

"No. I come from Italy."

Clearly she had not been warned that foreign men in particular might be dangerous. Indeed, my being Italian seemed to make it more permissible to speak with me.

She moved a bit closer. "Really? That's amazing. I've just been looking at some Italian postcards."

You can imagine, Marco, how this announcement affected me, but she seemed not to notice the look of astonishment that must have marked my face.

"A friend of my father's is storing some things in our garage. They were his mother's. She just died. He gave me a big box of things she collected on her travels, mostly postcards. She was very rich and went everywhere."

"Even Italy?"

"Yes. A long time ago---twenty or thirty years."

She paused and we both watched a string of cars coupling at the bottom of one sloping track.

"Could you tell me where Firenze is? I think it's a beautiful city, but I can't find in on any of my maps."

"That's probably because in English you give it a different name. You call it Florence."

Her eyes widened. "No kidding? How stupid of me." She struck her forehead with her hand.

"Not at all. It's a natural mistake."

"Which city do you live in?"

"Padova. But it English you call it Padua. It's close to Venice."

"Venizia," she smiled with delight. "That one I figured out for myself."

We both laughed. Then she became serious.

"Was Firenz bombed?" Somehow I knew she would want to pronounce the city's name correctly, so I taught her to say it before explaining that it had been badly damaged, but that Padova had been less harmed, and Venezia fairly well protected.

"Why are you in Galesburg?" she asked.

"My wife lived here. We were married in your Hotel Custer."

"No kidding? Is she here, too?"

"No, I'm afraid she's dead."

"Oh, dear. I'm sorry. Was she killed in the war?"

"Yes. She died in a bombing raid in England."

"That's so awful. I am sorry."

"Thank you. This was one of her favorite places in Galesburg."

"The switch yard?"

"Yes."

She nodded. "It's just about my favorite place, too."

"Do you come here often?"

She nodded again. "Sometimes my friends and I ride our bikes here. They mostly want to ride back and forth over the bridge. But I like to watch the trains, so I come here sometimes by myself."

We watched the scene below.

"My wife said she felt like she was watching a ballet," I said.

"Wow! That's amazing. That's how I feel. I've never told anyone else, but do you want to know what I call it in my own head?"

"Of course."

"The Gravity Dance." She paused and gave me time to look down once more. "It's kind of like science and art come together. I know it's physics that makes the cars move and hook up, but it looks like a dance. I think your wife would have understood that."

"I think she would have understood it and would have loved to hear it described that way. Thank you for sharing that with me."

"You're welcome."

She sighed. "I'm afraid I have to go home now. I haven't done my chores yet." She walked back to her bicycle. "I have enjoyed our conversation," she said with the same self-conscious formality that had marked her greeting earlier.

"As have I. Very much."

"I hope you enjoy your visit to Galesburg---and that it doesn't make you too sad."

"Thank you. And I hope you continue to enjoy your postcards and that you get to visit Firenz someday."

"Yes. I plan to."

She pedaled back the way she had come.

I think, Marco, that I have never wished that I might have been a better person more than I did as I watched her ride away.

Nochie had met a Jamaican woman, Maggie, who was training to become a nurse in the Canadian hospital where he had been sent. She was several shades darker than he and beautiful in the elegant way his mother had been. She moved with the same unstudied grace and had the same welcoming ways. Two boisterous, but not misbehaved, children filled the Broad Street house with laugher—a laughter that I hoped echoed Aaron and Judith's.

"As you can see, Maggie has completely redecorated the place," Nochie said proudly as he gave me a tour. "I couldn't have lived here otherwise. She insisted we keep it, and now I'm glad we did."

In place of a Flemish interior, I now found myself in something more brightly French—a Renoir or even a Gauguin. The only thing familiar to me was the Murano glass decanter that still stood on the mantle over the living room fireplace.

"Everything else reminded me too much of Ruth," Nochie said when he saw me looking at it. "But somehow I think of that piece as belonging to you and Judith."

"I'm glad," I responded.

We settled in that room after the children had gone to bed.

"Who lives in your old house?" I asked.

"No one. We keep it as a guest house. Excessive for Galesburg, but then I have to do something to keep up with the Joneses and that's not easy for a colored man."

"But you must be one of the richest men in town."

Maggie half laughed, half snorted. "Doesn't make a lot of difference." She spoke with a lilting speech that suited her personality.

"It makes some. But Maggie's right. I'm only the second Negro teacher in the Galesburg system. We're still the only black family north of the tracks, and remember that club where my Mother worked? We still can't be members there. It was only after I became the basketball coach that one of the country clubs let us join."

"And our kids have to sit in the back rows or balcony when they go to the movies," Maggie added.

"It sounds like…." I hesitated.

Nochie read my mind. "Like the ways Jews were treated in Europe?" he finished my sentence. "A little, I know. But things will get better. One of our neighbors sued a drugstore when he heard they refused to wait on us. He and a lot of his friends refuse to go there. We're starting an NAACP Chapter in Knox County, and we've gotten a lot of support. Having a college with a strong abolitionist history helps."

Maggie looked at her husband with love deepened by respect. "He's doing good," she said simply.

"There's something else I want to tell you about." Nochie walked to one of the bookcases flanking the fireplace and removed a photo album. He opened it, handed it to me, and pointed to a picture. Fred and Violet stood in front of a tree covered with exotic blooms, their arms around each other.

"I never saw either of them smile that way," Nochie lamented. "The picture was sent to my grandmother in Peoria, with the last letter any of us ever got from her."

"She's certainly beautiful."

Nochie nodded. "I've done everything I can think of to find out what happened to them. I've written to the company he worked for. I've contacted the State Department. Even talked to our Senators and Congressman. No one has gotten anywhere."

"Does the company in Bali still exist?"

"The Belgian firm that owned it still exists, but the establishment in Bali was destroyed and they haven't tried to rebuild it. All of the records there were destroyed, too. The last they heard is that all the foreigners were rounded up and marched off. They don't know where. It's as if they all just disappeared."

"I'm very, very sorry."

"I've told him we have to move on, but he can't let it go," Maggie said.

"I've decided to go to Bali," Nochie said as he returned the photo album to its shelf.

"What?"

"I'd like to take the family, but Maggie thinks it's too dangerous. We're still discussing it, though."

"What do you think, Enrico?" Maggie asked me.

"I think you have a good life here, in spite of the problems. I think you probably won't be able to learn anything more in Bali. I think it's a long way to go. But if it's truly important for you, you may not be able to put it behind you. In any case, I'm confident that you'll know what you have to do and will make the right decision."

"Of course, you're right," Maggie said, nonetheless shaking her head.

"When would you go?"

"Next summer. I'll have three months, more if I need it, since I can easily afford to take a year off if I go."

Nochie had done considerable research on the logistics of getting from Galesburg to Jakarta and then on to Denpasar. He had found out about hiring a guide, finding some accommodations, and so on. He described these in detail, with obvious excitement, while Maggie looked on skeptically.

"If you decide to do this, and mind you, I'm not suggesting that I agree with you, I may be able to help," I said.

They both looked surprised.

"I don't know anyone in Bali, nothing like that. But I have made contacts in diplomatic circles around the world and one of those might be of some assistance. Just let me know."

"I'd appreciate that, my friend," Nochie said.

He drove me to the train station early the next morning. We stood on the platform watching for the Zephyr coming from California. I turned to him and put my hand on his arm.

"I think every day that if I had not taken Judith out of Galesburg I would have saved a great many people from a great deal of suffering."

Nochie grabbed my hand in both of his. "You must stop doing that."

Without saying anything more we watched a distant beam grow larger and brighter as the sleek train grew nearer.

"Plan to stay longer next time," he hugged me.

"Take good care of that lovely family."

335

He nodded. "Please give our blessings to your new family. I'll let you know what I decide."

We both knew that he would go to Bali, and that the chances were minimal that he would find the answers he wanted. The most he could hope for was some closure.

The tracks took my train along the perimeter of the switch yards as it headed out of town. I could see a freight car making its slow, gradual descent to connect with a noisy but controlled crash to the cars already attached to an engine.

A gravity dance, I thought to myself. That's exactly what it was, Marco.

Chapter 16

Minneapolis, Fall, 1990

I have friends outside of the University who tell me that they find the phrase "structured academic world" something of an oxymoron. No nine to five day, three months off each summer, long breaks throughout the year, only a few hours each week in the classroom, etc. But for those of us who live it, the structure can be oppressive; admittedly, most of us would not give it up for a "real" job, however. It is a life literally regulated by bells. We may not salivate, but like Pavlov's dogs we hear a bell and respond—either by warming up or winding down. One must be in the same room every MWF at ten or every TTH at 11:15. The department meets at 3:15 the first Monday of every month, the Budget Committee every other Tuesday at 3:30, and on every Wednesday from four to five-thirty, the Long Range Planning Committee works on its five-year plan (or ten-year plan, depending on the current president's vision). Office hours must be fitted in, and oral exams arranged weeks in advance. The tedium of this is most apparent after one has luxuriated in the autonomy of a sabbatical year. Psychological re-entry requires one to reset one's emotional as well as biological clock and adjust to finding the cherished periods for doing research in short spurts rather than in substantial segments. After having had long stretches for sustained reflection on the things that interest one most for several months, it is difficult not to feel some anxiety. There were things to catch up on at our offices, and when one has also spent those months away from home, as Roger and I had, there are also the inevitable domestic chores that demand attention.

Thus even though I was very curious, it was several days before I opened the thick envelope Howard Pletcher had sent to my home. It lay with a stack of mostly junk mail in my study until I picked it up the first Friday evening after our return. Pletcher would return himself in a few days, I thought to myself, and I should be ready to discuss it with him. Roger had gone for a run around the lake near our house, so it would be a while before we had dinner. I took the envelope and a generous portion of Scotch and settled myself on our patio, enjoying what I feared might be one of the last late afternoon days when it would still be warm enough to sit outside.

The manuscript consisted of over two hundred pages, arranged in sections, each of which was titled with a location and year. On the first page of each of these was a description of what seemed to be a post card of the sort one finds in museum gift shops. With one exception, each named a photograph of a painting by Carlo Crivelli and provided a message that might have been written on the back. There was no address.

How could I not be intrigued? I became more and more engrossed as I read and barely acknowledged Roger when he came back from his run and announced that he was going to shower. He startled me a bit later when he asked if I wanted another drink.

"This is amazing," I said. "You have to read it."

"Maybe tomorrow. I have too much paperwork to get at tonight."

Reluctantly I put down the chapter I was reading---one that actually took place in Minnesota, and helped him to make our dinner. As soon as we had cleared up, I took the pages to the living room and read as long as I could before lingering jet lag took over and I had to go to bed. I had to leave Enrico and Judith at end of 1935.

Roger was already up when I got went into the kitchen the next morning. He was sitting at the table and looked at me, strangely apprehensive.

"I almost woke you. I think you'd better look at this."

He pushed the front section of the Minneapolis Tribune across the table toward me. A headline on the right, above the fold read, "Art Expert Found Slain in London." Underneath a picture of Howard Pletcher smiled out at the reader.

The Tribune had a good relationship with the Minneapolis Institute of Arts and relied heavily on advertising revenues from Bo's, so the author had done what he could to be tasteful. However, the sordid details were difficult to prettify. Pletcher's body, naked, garroted, and "debased" had been found in an alley behind a bar of "questionable reputation" in Soho. An investigation was underway, but so far the police were releasing no information.

"Jesus Christ." I sat down and took several deep breaths.

"I think I'd better read that manuscript now," Roger said. "Did you finish it?"

"No."

We both finished it by late afternoon.

Neighbors had invited us for grilled steak that evening. Roger, uncharacteristically, chose the wine to take without much thought. Two other couples were there and talk was of little besides Pletcher's death. His long relationship with William Beauchamp, who had died two years earlier, was well-known. They had lived openly together in a mansion just a few doors from that of his deceased parents, where Theodore Beauchamp, Jr. now lived with his own family. Our friends politely inquired about our year abroad, but conversation kept returning to the incredible event.

"We ran into Howard in Amsterdam just ten days ago," Roger said.

"He was on his way back from a funeral in Italy." I did not tell them about my meeting Howard at the Rijksmuseum, nor, of course, about the manuscript he had sent.

"You knew him really well, didn't you," a neighbor asked us.

"Evelyn knew him better than I did, though we've both been to his and William's home often," Roger replied.

"William was Chairman of my department when I was hired," I said. "He and Howard had already been together for several years. They were the first gay couple we knew who'd essentially been living as a married couple."

Several others nodded.

"Howard was one of William's first doctoral students," I continued. "He came from Fargo."

"It said in the paper that his father still practices law there," someone added.

I nodded. "His mother has the finest sculpture collection in North Dakota---maybe the finest private collection in the Midwest. I went there once when I gave a talk in Brookings. Howard insisted that I rent a car and drive to Fargo to meet his parents. They have what amounts to a sculpture garden. They are incredibly nice people. I can't imagine how this must be affecting them."

"Did he go to gay bars here?" someone asked.

"I don't think so. He just didn't seem the type."

"People do lead secret lives, especially abroad."

"William has been dead over two years now. Maybe...."

Speculation continued and I felt increasingly uneasy. As early as we politely could, Roger and I played the jet lag card and said goodnight.

We had already had a fair amount to drink, but I did not stop Roger when he said he would fix us a brandy and soda.

"What are you going to do with that manuscript?" he asked as we settled in the living room.

"What do you think I should do with it?"

"Burn it."

"Seriously."

"I am serious."

"I don't think I can do that—at least not right away."

We sat quietly for a few minutes and then he said, "I assume you had no idea that William...."

"Was a spy? Of course not," I said a bit heatedly.

"Okay, okay. Settle down. I was only joking. But why did Howard give you the memoir?"

"I told you. He wanted to mail it to someone here and he happened to run into us."

"And he trusted you."

"Yes."

We were quiet again.

"Okay, we have to say it out loud," I ventured. "Do you think his, ah, what happened to him in London is connected to this?"

"If it is, I hope no one knows he sent you the manuscript."

"You think he might have gotten killed because of it? That's why you want me to get rid of it?"

"Yes. I mean, I don't know whether it has anything to do with his murder. But it's possible, and I don't want to take any chances."

"But no one could know about it. Our meeting at Le Drugstore was a complete coincidence. And when we met for coffee at the Rijksmuseum, who could have known about that?"

"And he gave you nothing there?"

"Nothing."

"And no one saw you?"

"Of course people saw us---it was the Rijksmuseum and we met in front of The Nightwatch. You know how mobbed that area always is."

"You know what I mean."

"I think we're being paranoid even to talk this way. Even if someone was watching him, our meeting would have appeared totally innocent. There's no way to connect me to this. I didn't even know anyone ever called William 'Billy'."

"The Beauchamp's must be going out of their minds. Howard and William's liaison was hardly a secret. But even though William is dead, everyone who knew Howard will still connect him to the family."

"Theodore still lives on Lake of the Isles near Howard----or near where Howard did live. The

343

parents are dead, of course. I don't know about the sister. I think she lives in Paris or Geneva or somewhere like that."

"Who's the Director of the MIA now?"

"He's new. His name is James Preston. He came from the Kimball in Fort Worth while we were gone."

"So you can't guess how he'll handle the scandal?"

"No, I've never met him."

"Maybe you could give him the manuscript."

"No, at least not until I have met him. If Howard had trusted him, wouldn't he have just sent the thing to him?"

"I don't know. Maybe the very idea of sending a copy to *anyone* didn't come to him until he happened to run into you."

"Well, just give me a while to mull this over. I want to re-read the memoir. I'll think of something."

Roger smiled and walked over to my chair. He took my chin in his hand and kissed me.

"I know you will. Let's go to bed."

We had rented our house to a couple from Norway who had been visitors in the Medical School. The house was actually cleaner than it had been when we left; but there was still the pile of junk mail to dispose of and yard chores to attend to. Thus it was late afternoon before I returned to the memoir. Even if I had been able to ignore the cloak and dagger aspects of what I read, the potential explosiveness of what I held was salient. The art world has become a hot house for the blossoming of scandals---charges and countercharges concerning authenticity, rightful ownership, and questionable curatorial ethics. Whatever I would ultimately decide to do, I knew I had to put the manuscript somewhere safe. On the way to my office Monday morning, I stopped at the library and left it at the reserve desk with some other materials I was going to use fall semester and had already deposited there.

When I arrived at the Art History Department office in the handsome but undeniably worn brick and stone building in which it was housed, all was in turmoil.

"We were robbed last night," the secretary told me breathlessly. "Files were ransacked, offices vandalized, typewriters and other equipment stolen. It's a disaster."

A strand of yellow police tape stretched across the doorway to my own office. A University police officer was busy at the file cabinet.

"May I come in?" I asked him across the tape.

"This is your office?"

"Yes. I'm Professor Evelyn Conger. When did this happen?"

"It had to be sometime after 10. That's when the last student left the library down the hall. Give me another few minutes. I want to finish getting some prints and pictures."

Break-ins are fairly common on university campuses. What was unusual about this one was its extent: seven faculty offices in addition to the departmental office, the slide room, and the library. The petty cash box was empty, a projector and several electric typewriters had been taken, and the offices of individuals disturbed to differing degrees. In my office the only disturbance apparently had been a large box of unopened mail---a year's worth---that was sitting on the floor next to my desk. A few drawers of my file cabinet stood opened, as did the drawers of my desk. But nothing seemed have been removed or even significantly messed up.

"Let me know if you discover that anything is missing," the young officer said as he closed his bag.

"Since I haven't had a chance to go through that mail," I said, pointing to the scattered pile on the floor, "it will be hard to say. I've just gotten back from a year's sabbatical abroad."

He shrugged. "Whatever. Do you think there might have been anything of value?"

I laughed. "Not to anyone but me, I should think."

He handed me his card. "Well, just in case, you can always give me a call."

I dialed Roger's office, but he was not there. As I was replacing the receiver a colleague rapped on my open door and greeted me from across the tape that the office had replaced when he left.

"Welcome back," he said ironically.

I walked over and awkwardly embraced him across the yellow tape.

"Did they get your office, too?" I asked.

"No, luckily. Though it's always such a mess that the police scarcely believed me. The gang of scoundrels only hit the offices on this side of the floor. Are you missing anything?"

"I don't think so."

"Good. You read about Howard Pletcher, I assume. Incredible."

We chatted for a few moments about the tragedy and then he hurried off to a curriculum committee meeting. I was just beginning to pick up the mail puddle at my feet when there was another knock on the still open door.

A man of medium height, medium complexion, and military haircut stood with a firm stance in the doorway.

"Professor Evelyn Conger?"

"Yes."

He opened his wallet and flashed a badge. "I'm Agent Sam Brown of the Twin Cities FBI."

Surprised, I sat up more straight. "The FBI is investigating this break-in?"

"No. I'm here on a different matter. May I come in?" He obviously was not really asking permission since he removed the yellow tape even as he was speaking.

"Certainly. Sit down." I pointed at the university issue green vinyl office chair next to my desk.

FBI agents do visit professors from time to time. Students applying for posts requiring clearance often give our names as references. But there was something unusual about this man. Perhaps his brown suit looked too expensive or his demeanor too assured. Or, I thought to myself, perhaps the events of the last fortnight have just infected me with a severe case of paranoia.

"I'm assisting in the investigation of the death of Howard Pletcher."

"Really? I wouldn't have expected that to be an FBI matter either."

"Well, naturally I'm not at liberty to discuss the details of the case. I understand you saw Mr. Pletcher in Amsterdam."

I was astonished. "My God, how do you know that?"

"Again, I'm not at liberty to say. Am I correct that you met him there?"

"Well, my husband and I did run into him at a restaurant."

"Was that the only time you saw him?"

"No. Howard and I met the next day at the Rijksmuseum. We looked at a few pictures, had coffee, and then he left to catch a flight to England."

He nodded. "Were you aware that he would be in Amsterdam when you were going to be there?"

"No. Our meeting was a coincidence."

"The meeting in the restaurant?"

"Yes."

"But the meeting at the Rijksmuseum was not an accident?"

"No. We arranged that when we met at the restaurant---a place called Le Drugstore."

He jotted something down in a small black notebook.

"You may have been one of the last of his acquaintances to see him before his death. Would you mind telling me what you talked about."

"Not at all, but I don't think it's very relevant. There was no time to talk about much at all at Le Drugstore. He said he was just leaving to go to a concert. He told us he was passing through Amsterdam and going to London the next day. And we arranged to meet for coffee the next morning. At the museum he told me had been to a funeral in Italy. We talked about some mutual friends, some art exhibits, that's really all."

Why did I not tell him the whole truth? I can't really explain my holding back; I just felt on edge.

"Oh," I added. "We talked about getting together once we were all back in Minnesota."

"But you made no specific arrangements?"

"No. It was all very casual."

"Did he say anything about his plans in England."

"Not really. He did mention that he wanted to see a Landseer retrospective at the Royal Academy. I actually teased him a bit about that--- Landseer, in my opinion, is a very dull painter."

Agent Brown's look expressed his impatience with this sidetrack.

"And," I hurried on. "He said he hoped to get tickets for an opera at Covent Garden. I'm sorry, I don't remember which one."

He wrote in his book and nodded and then looked closely at me.

"Did he give you anything?"

"Give me anything. No. Why?"

"Just a routine question."

It did not, of course, feel very routine.

He reached into a pocket of his suit coat and handed me a card.

"I'd appreciate it if you'd call me if you remember anything else." He stood up and began to leave and then slowly turned back around and looked down at me.

"You and your husband had been in Italy, too."

He said this so matter-of-factly that I didn't have time to be astonished that he knew this. "Yes, but that was two or three weeks before Mr. Pletcher was there, and again, purely a coincidence."

"I see. But did you know the young man whose funeral he attended?" He flipped to a page in his notebook. "A Marco Zollino?"

"No."

"Or his father, Enrico Zollino?"

"Only by reputation. He was prominent member of an important committee that works on returning artworks that have been stolen or confiscated or plundered. He was also a friend of our former chairman, William Beauchamp. But I never met him. My specialty is Flemish art, not Renaissance Italian."

Again a look of impatience passed over his face. "But did you go to the Crivelli Museum when you were in Padua?"

"Very briefly."

"And you did not meet Mr. Zollino?"

"No. The only person there was a young woman at the desk. Does the death in Padua have anything to do with Pletcher's death in London? I thought Zollino's death was an accident."

"Yes, so it seems. There is probably no connection. We are just checking all leads." He slipped the notebook into his pocket. "Well, thank you for your time, Dr. Conger."

"You're welcome. And by the way, please give my regards to your colleague, Agent Steen. He's been here several times making inquiries about students. I've always found him very pleasant."

"Yes, Agent Steen. Of course. I'll be sure to give him your regards. Thank you again."

I did not know any Agent Steen. The only Steen I knew was the one who had painted "The Merry Family"---a seventeenth century genre painting, a reproduction of which was hanging above my desk.

"Okay, now you *have* to get rid of the manuscript," Roger insisted that evening after I had told him about the day's events. "This is beginning to make me very, very nervous."

"Me, too. The number on the card he gave me is different from the one in the phone book for the Twin Cities FBI."

"That in itself doesn't prove anything."

"But when I called the number in the phone book, and asked for Agent Brown, they said there wasn't anyone by that name."

"It still doesn't prove anything. There may be agents whose identity is kept secret."

"I suppose."

"Do you think Zollino had anything to do with that other art historian who was a spy in England---the one that had some connection to the Queen?"

"Anthony Blount. His being a spy didn't become public until the late seventies or early eighties. And his connection was that he was in charge of the palace art collection. It was a huge scandal. It's funny—Howard mentioned an article about him when we met. Who knows whether Zollino or William had anything to do him and the others. I wouldn't be surprised---the art world is pretty small, everybody seems to know everybody, at least a little. And in Britain, the connections are so much tighter."

"There's something else I have to ask---- though you'll probably think I'm really paranoid. Do you think the guy who was killed in Padua---the one whose funeral Howard went to---do you think his death may not have been an accident."

"Oh, my God, I hadn't thought about that. But of course----if they wanted to kill Howard because they thought he had the memoir then surely they might have taken care of Marco, too."

"Where's the manuscript now?" Roger stood up. "I'm going to burn it."

"It's on reserve at Walter Library."

"What?"

"I put it there with my other course materials this morning. It's in a folder that identifies it as a paper on Vermeer. No one will ask for any of the stuff until classes begin. And you can't get it without a University ID card."

"Don't be silly. An FBI card will certainly work just as well."

"Right. Just give me a few more days."

He sighed. "This isn't a game. And it's not an academic puzzle like whether Rembrandt or one of his students painted something."

"I know. But the manuscript deals with issues I care about. Howard told me he thought the memoir explained how someone with deep aesthetic values could be lacking in moral integrity. Maybe it does. And that matters. But it's even more important for other reasons. What I really care about are the thefts, and the fact that there may be fakes and forgeries hanging about. Don't you think I have an intellectual and ethical obligation to help expose all of that? And there's the murder in Copenhagen, and God knows what else. Surely we have to make sure that someone who knows what they're doing investigates all of this."

"Not if it gets us into a world of shit."

"Just a few more days. If I don't come up with an idea, I promise I'll let you get rid of it. I'll even set a fire in the fireplace myself."

He shook his head, at once expressing disagreement and resignation.

"Thank you."

But I, too, questioned my own resolve. What I had not told Roger was that when I had come home that afternoon, I had had the distinct impression that someone had been in my upstairs study. Nothing was out of place; quite the contrary. Everything was precisely where I had left it. Too precisely.

I was waiting for Roger the following afternoon when he drove into the garage.

"Change your clothes. I'd like to walk around the lake."

A few minutes later we set off on the tree-lined path that led to a path along the shore of Lake of the Isles. The leaves had already begun to take on the brownish, yellowish hue that promised the brilliant colors that October would bring. A few geese flew overhead, the first of the flocks that would desert us during the next weeks. The day was still warm, but the lake already gave off a chilly breeze caused by nights with temperatures that hovered near the freezing point.

Roger took my hand. "You've decided what to do, haven't you."

"Better than that---I've done it. I retrieved the manuscript from the Reserve Desk this morning, and went directly to the Post Office in the Student Union. It's on its way to the editor of *Art Forum.* I didn't tell him who sent it. I just marked the envelope 'Personal' and attached a post-it note to the first page saying it should interest him.

Roger grinned. "Clever girl. What do you think he'll do with it?"

"I have no idea."

"What if he doesn't read it?"

"Don't be silly. Just the strange descriptions of post cards will be enough to make him drop everything else. Then I'll have done my best to save the art world," I said with self-protective irony. "And I'll bet you a hundred dollars that the next issue will be a doozey. Better yet, he'll undoubtedly get genuine authorities involved."

We walked along a gentle curve at one end of the lake and shortly found ourselves across the road from a large grey stone mansion. We both slowed our pace and turned to look at it.

"I thought the Beauchamps might have put up a black ribbon or something on their front door,' I said.

"No way. They'll do everything they can to avoid calling attention to any connection with Howard's death."

A few yards further down we stopped again, this time to look at the large red brick house where William and Howard had lived for years. There was no black ribbon, but someone had placed a large wreath of fall flowers on the front door.

"Good," I said.

We walked quietly and more slowly than we usually did around the lake. Across the water from the Beauchamp mansion I stopped again and pointed in the direction of several homes. "I think the Albrights must have lived in one of those houses---maybe they still do. Will we ever walk or drive around this lake without thinking of all of this?"

"No," Roger answered simply.

"Do you remember that night in Padua when we saw that couple in the restaurant?"

"Of course."

"I have a theory about what was happening."

"And?"

"I'm going to write it up and give it to you."

"You think you know what happened?" he looked at me incredulously.

"No, but I think I may have a possible explanation."

Roger smiled. "That's all we can ever get from a theory."

Chapter 18

Padua, August, 1990

Marco parked the Ferrari on Via Dante, got out, and walked around to the other door. He gave his hand to his mother as she stepped out with her usual grace. She took his arm and they walked around the corner to the restaurant.

"I still don't understand why you wanted to dine here---and so early."

"I'm bored with our usual places. We haven't been here for a while, and you've always thought the food is adequate----if not quite up to the Carravagio. We can talk more easily here. When we go to the Carravagio or Michelangelo we're always interrupted by someone we know. "

In her high-heeled taupe shoes, Antonia was nearly as tall as her son, and she carried herself as elegantly as a woman half her age. Strangers were always astonished that she was old enough to be his mother, though she always managed to hide the intense satisfaction this gave her. Marco hoped the waiters would fuss over her, and they did not disappoint him. They were attentively escorted across the room.

Only one other couple had already been seated---a middle aged pair dressed as only American tourists would be. Marco smugly compared his mother's costume to that of the seated woman who clearly put comfort before style. He noticed, with some surprise that at least they had had known how to order a fine bottle of the Friuli.

"It is a great pleasure to see you in The Crivelli again," the waiter bowed as he pulled out a high-backed chair for Antonia. "May I bring you an appertif?"

"We'll just start with a bottle of the Blanco Friuli, please, and a small tray of the vegetable antipasto. "

He smiled and left the table, while the other two waiters poured Pellegrino and set bread sticks before them.

"Thank you again for the scarf, darling boy. You did not need to bring me anything, you know."

"How could I go to Como and not bring back something silk? I must say it goes very well with your suit. And you've arranged it perfectly."

"Thank you, dear. It will be easy to check myself in all of these mirrors."

They both laughed heartily, sharing a inside joke they had about the way in which use of too many mirrors betrays a lack of imagination on the part of interior designers.

Antonia leaned her head subtly to in the direction of the other occupied table. "English or American, do you think?"

"Definitely American. I saw literally hundreds of those awful shoes on tourists in Venice last month."

"Poor thing," his Mother responded and they laughed gaily again.

The waiter came back with their wine and poured it carefully. "This is the second bottle I've served tonight. I have to say, I was surprised that our other diners knew about it."

"Perhaps they just ordered the most expensive white on the menu," Antonia said. "That's what they all do, you know."

"Mother, be careful, they might hear you," he laughed.

"Oh, they can't understand us," the waiter assured them and they laughed again.

"Can I bring you anything else now?"

"No, thank you, Giovanni. I'll let you know when we're ready to order."

The waiter bowed, backed away from the table, and signaled to his staff that they should commence serving the other table.

"Mother, I want to get right to the matter I told you I want to discuss." He leaned back and sat more erectly against the back of his chair.

"Yes, yes, darling. Please do, the suspense has been killing me all day. I hope everything is all right between you and Susanna. Please don't tell me that she's called the engagement off."

"Nothing like that, Mother. And she's handling all the wedding plans perfectly."

"Excellent. So what is it?"

"Well, it has to do with the museum. I want to do something to make it more prominent---put it on the map, as it were."

"But, my dear, we've never fooled ourselves about Crivelli. We love him, of course. How could we not, living with your father all those years? But he will never be able to compete with Giotto. Not even your father would have imagined that in his wildest dreams."

"All right, then, let me put it this way. I want to put myself on the map."

"What are you talking about?"

"I have a very realistic sense of my own talents. I didn't inherit any of Father's artistic skills. He was always so kind about praising my management skills, but let's face it, they are limited, too."

"But, Marco, you have done such a good job managing the family's estates and assets. Surely that keeps you busy enough. And you'll soon have your own family to care for."

"And I want to do as good a job as you and Father did. But I want more. I want some--some fame."

Antonia smiled and sat back, looking at her son with the patient affection that typically accompanies a mother's love.

"All right, tell me what you have in mind."

"I'm going to publish the memoir."

"No," Antonia's single word was whispered but still conveyed her horror.

"It will definitely put the museum on the map. It's exactly the sort of scandal that turns something ordinary into a tourist attraction."

Marco knew that his mother would find the prospect appalling, That is precisely why he had brought her to this restaurant---a public place where they would not be seen by friends, but where, at the same time, she would not be likely to cause a scene. She was far too refined a person to lose her dignity in so open a setting. If he made his announcement to her here, she would have time to let the idea soak in, and whatever private displays of anger or shouted objections came later might, he reasoned, be somewhat tempered. That they would come, he had no doubt. He rested his hands on the table and tilted his head to one side, ready for a reaction that might be more extreme than the one he hoped for.

Antonia's shoulders slumped forward, her elbows rested on the table, and her head fell into her hands. The beautiful scarf seem to wilt as her body seemed to melt.

One of the waiters quickly approached the table. "Is Madam all right?"

"Yes, yes," Marco motioned him away. "We're fine." He glanced at the table where the Americans were sitting to see if they were watching. The man seemed to be concentrating on his meal, but the woman self-consciously looked all around the room in an effort to appear not to have been staring in the direction of their table. The plethora of mirrors undoubtedly gave anyone who wanted ample opportunity for observation.

Another waiter approached. This time his Mother waved him away and her dismissal was almost a hiss. Marco drank his wine and offered to pour his Mother some when he refilled his glass. She refused with a similar contemptuous flick of her hand. But she was ready to talk. She pressed herself against the back of her chair and gripped the edge of the table, as if to steel herself before making her case.

"It is utterly out of the question. Your father would be horrified."

"I'm not so sure. Nowhere in the manuscript does he say that he wants me to keep it a secret."

"He didn't have to---it goes without saying that he would not put the family's honor at that kind of risk. Everyone thinks he's a hero---and he is. No matter what he did, he always acted in good faith. But some people wouldn't understand that. No, you simply can't do it. I won't allow it."

"Mother, I really want your agreement. But I've made my decision and the memoir is mine. I can do with it what I choose."

"Please, Marco. You have to listen to reason. So many people will be hurt----not just our family. Billy's family, The Sparry, who's knows who else might suffer."

"Billy's dead. Lady Sarah and Charles Richmond have been dead for years. They're the only ones that matter."

"Don't be ridiculous. Think of us----do you want to be known as the son of a spy?"

"I've thought about this a lot. I don't think I'll be hurt at all. People will talk, of course. But our real friends will understand. The gossip will die down after a while, and people will flock to the museum."

"That's absurd." Now Antonia downed her wine. Marco reached for the bottle but she slapped his hand away. "I'll do it myself, thank you," she said bitterly.

A waiter began to make his way toward them again, but again she waved him off. A large group of people entered the restaurants---- Scandanavians, Marco guessed, and the attention of the staff was diverted. The Americans prepared to leave. Marco saw that both of them cast a last curious look in their direction.

"Why don't you at least wait until I die?" Antonia snapped.

"Mother, you won't die for years. Think of it this way----it will be exciting."

"I don't need that sort of excitement. Have you discussed this with Susanna. What will her family say?"

"Susanna will love the attention. I don't really care what her family thinks. They're so happy that she's marrying into a wealthy family that they probably won't care one way or another."

"Don't be crass. Of course, they'll care."

"Then they'll get used to it. They'll have to."

"And you expect me to get used to it, too."

"I hope so."

"I won't. I won't allow it."

A waiter had somehow managed to arrive at our table before either of us could motion him away.

"Are you ready to order?"

"We won't be staying," Antonia stood and without a backward glance walked toward the restaurant door.

"I'm very sorry. My mother has developed a bad headache," Marco quickly placed some bills on the table.

"Well, I certainly hope we'll see you again soon," said the waiter.

What a lie, thought Marco.

Marco steered his car around the bends in the hill leading up to his Mother's home. When he pulled up in front of the front entry, he stopped the car and started to get out.

"Don't bother getting out. I can manage myself. I really would rather not see or talk to you any more this evening."

Marco sighed. "All right, Mother. I'll let you get used to the idea, and then I'll come up tomorrow and discuss the details of my plan with you."

Antonia frowned and shook her head but did not say anything more as she got out of the car and walked to the front door. Nor did she turn to wave or smile or blow a kiss as she usually did. Marco drove around the loop that enclosed a garden of roses and rosemary at the top of the driveway. He thought about driving to Venice to see his fiance that night, but decided against it. A light meal, a bit more wine, and an early night would be the best thing to prepare himself for what was certain to be an ordeal the next day. He drove halfway down the hill and parked in front of his own small, pink house. He took wine, bread, and cheese onto the patio and watched the sunset, thinking about the furor he was about the cause.

Looking up the drive to the villa, he had a vivid image of the afternoon eighteen months ago when his father had left his son's place and started to walk up to his own home. Halfway up the hill he had crumpled. By the time Marco reached him, he was dead from a massive heart attack. He had given Marco the manuscript at luncheon that very day, and had made it clear that after his death, his son was free to do as he chose with it. Marco was certain that he would approve of his decision to make it public.

Perhaps he would wait until after his wedding in November. Or, better yet, wait until the post-holiday lull in January so that he would garner the greatest amount of attention possible. Yes, between Christmas and the beginning of Lent---Crivelli would like that. And with these thoughts, he retired, and fell quickly into a deep sleep.

Antonia did not sleep. She sat next to a window in the library on the upper floor and watched her son on his patio until it became too dark to see him any longer. Her maid was in Venice that night visiting family, so her concentration was not disturbed.

Mothers know their children's sleeping patterns and Antonia knew that Marco would soon be fast asleep----and stay that way for two or three hours before beginning a more fitful night. Knowing that her time was limited, she quickly took a flashlight and a set of keys she kept in a small intaglio cabinet next to the front door and made her way carefully down the hill to her son's home. The keys were unnecessary; as usual, Marco had not locked the house. He had also left on a small light above his front door, dim but bright enough to illuminate the small Mezuzah that Enrico had refused to remove---an artifact that Antonia had always found slightly distasteful. Now it seemed to give her the courage she need to proceed with her task.

The lights inside had all been turned off. Antonia waited a few seconds to listen for any sounds that might cause her to abort her mission. The only sound was that of a small fan that Marco liked to turn on in his bedroom---a white noise that he insisted helped him sleep. She walked slowly and softly to Marco's study, just to the left of the front door. Carefully she closed the door behind her and swept the beam of her torch around the room. She was almost certain that the manuscript would either be in one of the drawers in his desk or file cabinet. She started with the desk. Nothing. She turned to the tall oaken cabinet, and breathed a great sigh of relief when she finally found it lying alone in the bottom drawer. The stupid post cards clipped to some of the pages caused the upper left hand corner of the manuscript to hang awkwardly downward. She had just closed the door and stood up when light flooded the room.

"For God's sake, Mother, what are you doing?"

Marco took a few steps into the room, clothed only in a pair of silk pajama bottoms.

"Don't try to stop me, Marco. I have decided to burn this."

"Excuse me, Mother. It does not belong to you and your decision simply does not carry any weight."

"Please, my darling. I'm begging you. Wait at least until I die, so I won't have to suffer the humiliation you seem intent to bring upon the family."

"Don't be absurd---you're going to live for years and I want to make the museum famous now."

"But your father and grandfather---and all the others. They are heroes. Your plan will destroy their reputations----not to mention ours."

"Nonsense. It will make Father even more famous---and he'll become even more of hero in the eyes of many people. Trust me."

"I can't do that. I'm sorry."

Marco crossed the room. "Give it to me, Mother."

"No."

Antonia moved to Marco's right, but he moved to block her way. As he stepped he went a bit off balance, just as Antonia reached out to push him away as she quickly tried to avoid his block. To her surprise, her son fell forward and hit the cabinet with a thud. She briefly considered taking advantage of the opportunity to escape, but turned to look back and make sure he was all right. He did not move. She put the memoir on the edge of the desk and knelt by him.

"Darling? Are you all right? Did you bump your head?"

Still no movement. The angle of his neck was hideous, she now saw, and he was completely motionless. She touched his bare, smooth shoulder. "Marco. Say something, please, my darling." There was no response of any kind.

She decided to wait a minute or two to give him time to regain consciousness. She sat back against the side of the desk. She was able to deny to herself what had happened, but not for long.

She knelt again next to him, this time placing two fingers of her right hand along the side of his neck. There was no sign of a pulse. Growing more and more frightened, she moved her fingers to the inside of his wrist, but once again felt nothing. She sat back against the desk and fought to control her own breathing.

Later she would wonder how she managed to do what she did. What wells of courage or cowardice enabled her to stand up, take hold of the manuscript, and return to her own house? Her memories of that night were shadowy, as if she had been in a dream or awful nightmare. She removed the paperclips that held the postcards to pages, and tore all of the papers into small pieces. These she carefully flushed them down the toilets in the upstairs and downstairs lavatories. She put the paperclips neatly in a desk in her own study, and then returned to the chair in the library where she had earlier waited for the lights to be extinguished in Marco's house. She waited exactly two hours and then took the flashlight and keys and walked down the hill again. After depositing the torch and keys on a table next to the front door, she walked into the kitchen and picked up the telephone on the wall next to the refrigerator.

"Please come at once. This is Antonia Zollino. There's been an accident."

She explained to the ambulance staff and the police that she had been unable to sleep and had gone into her library to fetch a book. From her window she had seen a light in her son's study. Thinking it strange, she tried to telephone him. When there was no answer she got her flashlight and the keys to his house and went down to investigate for herself. She managed to relate all of this coolly and calmly. Then she fainted.

The investigation was brief. It was obvious that Marco had risen in the middle of the night and gone to his study for some reason. He must have tripped, and his fall had been at such an angle that he broke two vertebrae in his neck. The spinal column had been instantly severed. He could not have suffered, but of course it was a terrible tragedy.

Friends from around the world attended the funeral. One, Howard Pletcher, the longtime companion of Enrico's best friend, stayed several days to help Antonia through the first days of her grief. He mentioned briefly that he had found some things that Enrico had left for William. Antonia didn't bother to ask what they were. She simply said that he should take them. She seemed, in fact, not really to hear much of what he said. She spent most of her time looking into the distance— as if pondering in her heart the years of grief that lay ahead of her. He tried to assure her that the passage of time would help. It didn't.

Within a few months, the Museo Crivelli did get put on the map.

25901758R00199

Made in the USA
Lexington, KY
09 September 2013